Pariah

Pariah

BOB FINGERMAN

TOR®

A TOM DOHERTY ASSOCIATES

NEW YORK

PARIAH

Copyright © 2010 by Bob Fingerman

A Tor Book
Published by Tom Doherty Associates, LLC
175 Fifth Avenue
New York, NY 10010

www.tor-forge.com

Tor® is a registered trademark of Tom Doherty Associates, LLC.

ISBN 978-0-7653-2817-5 (hardcover)
ISBN 978-0-7653-2627-0 (trade paperback)

First Edition: August 2010

Printed in the United States of America

0 9 8 7 6 5 4 3 2 1

For my wife, Michele, who I love so much it's hard to fathom

ACKNOWLEDGMENTS

First up, I'd express everlasting gratitude to John Schoenfelder. After having read my first novel, John approached me to see if I had anything else up my sleeve. I told him about *Pariah* and he invited me to submit it. He loved it, and though it didn't work out with him, rather than let it die, he did a truly rare and generous thing and passed it along to the next person I want to thank: my great editor, Eric Raab. Eric shared John's passion for *Pariah* and made it happen at Tor. Which brings me to Tom Doherty, without whom there'd be no Tor, nor this deal. Thanks, also, to Whitney Ross, Eric's able assistant. I'd also like to express gratitude to Irene Gallo and Jamie Stafford-Hill for making *Pariah* look so terrific. Thanks to Bob Mecoy, for brokering this deal. To Kirsten Wolf, for providing another pair of sharp eyes. To Helene and Saul, my magnificent parents, for (among many other things) fostering in me a love for the written word. I'd be remiss if I neglected to extend my thanks and undying admiration to George A. Romero, for minting the modern zombie; even when we add our own new wrinkles, we're all just playing with Mr. Romero's toys. And, once again, thanks, love, and all good stuff to my astonishingly wonderful, loving, supportive, beautiful wife, Michele. I think that was longer than my allotted forty-five seconds.

Man needs to suffer. When he does not have real griefs he creates them. Griefs purify and prepare him.

—José Martí

part one

1

February, *Then*

Larry Gabler lay there, gasping, bleeding. At seventy-two, he was Abe's junior by eleven years, but at the moment he could have given Methuselah a run for his money.

"You gotta get home to Ruthie," he wheezed as sweat glossed his waxy face.

"Yeah, yeah," Abe said, pouring himself a stiff one from the bottle in his desk. The radio droned the barely cogent reportage of nerve-wracked correspondents attempting to articulate what was happening throughout the five boroughs—not to mention *the entire globe*. Abe took a tentative sip of the whisky, then downed it as he sauntered over to the window to catch an eyeful of uncorked chaos below. As he peered down, three taxis collided, the driver of one bursting through his windshield like a meat torpedo. People were jostling, shoving, climbing all over each other, every man for himself, *the hell with the rest*. The sounds of screams and random gunfire echoed in the darkening canyon of office buildings, the sun ducked for cover beyond Jersey to the west. Mixed in with the usual filth in the gathered curbside snowdrifts was a new hue: deep red, and plenty of it, like big, bloody snow cones.

"Oh yeah, I can't wait to get down into all that," Abe said.

The stray who'd brought Larry limping in cowered, nearly catatonic, on the other end of the waiting room's lumpy sofa. She was a good-looking young Puerto Rican, maybe in her early to mid twenties. Maybe Dominican. Abe couldn't tell. Young was young, old was old, Hispanic was Hispanic. Larry let out a chalky groan, farted loudly, and slumped forward, chin on chest, blood oozing from his nostrils.

"I think your friend is dead," the Latin girl murmured.

"He was dead when he came in," Abe replied. "I could smell it all over him. You get to my age and death's one of the few things you can recognize easy."

Abe looked at the blood-soaked material around Larry's chewed up calf, the slacks shredded. He downed another shot of whisky and made for the door.

"Where you going?" asked the girl.

"I gotta pay Menachem Bender a visit."

"Who?"

Without explaining, Abe left the office of Cutie-Pie Infant Wear and hastened down the hall to Menachem Bender Men's Big & Tall to pay a visit. Abe tried the door. Locked.

"Bender, you in there?" He pounded a few times, rattling the pebbled glass with Bender's name and logo painted upon it. "Bender, c'mon! It's me, Abe Fogelhut! You in there?" No answer. Abe cased the hall, then elbowed the loose pane out of the frame, the glass crashing to the linoleum beneath. Taking care not to cut himself, he opened the door, experiencing the giddy thrill of breaking into his neighbor's business as well as a jolt of bowel-tightening fear. "Bender!"

Nothing.

Abe gave the unlit room a quick once over, then stepped in, flicking on the overhead fluorescents, which buzzed in protest. A cursory look at Bender's books made clear Cutie-Pie wasn't the only outfit in the garment trade to have a lousy last quarter. "Oy," Abe sighed. "My condolences." Abe stepped around the desk toward the storeroom, nearly tripping over Bender's body, a .38 clenched in his white-knuckled hand. Bits of skull and brain matter flecked the adjacent wall and floor. Abe raised a hand to his mouth and then lowered it, realizing he was going to neither scream nor throw up. He just shook his head and opened the stockroom, repeating his previous sympathies. Turning on the light, he allowed himself to smile.

"Perfect," he said, eyeing stacks of unsold winter wear for enormous outdoorsmen.

Moments later, he returned to Cutie-Pie to find Larry hunched over the Latina, violently munching on her entrails. The contents of Abe's stomach disgorged, searing his throat. Larry didn't even look away from his still-twitching repast as Abe, grateful he'd retrieved the revolver from Bender, emptied the cylinder into his undead partner. The fifth shot removed the top of Larry's skull and he collapsed onto the girl's remains. Abe spat bile onto the floor, took a gulp straight from the bottle of Cutty Sark, swished it around, then spat again.

"Okay," he said, affecting as much calm as possible. "Okay."

He wiped his mouth with his hankie, took a box cutter and sliced open one of the myriad boxes of his unsold stock of *Baby Sof' Suit*® infant winter onesies. "Okay," he said, "time to redeem yourselves."

Five-foot-five Abe, with his thirty-inch waist, stepped into an XXXL pair of *Bender's Breathable Sub-zero Shield*® *Sooper-System*™ *Weather Bibs*, a double-insulated hunting overall for fatties who like traipsing off into the wilderness to shoot helpless critters. Leaving the bib down, Abe began stuffing onesies down the pants, padding himself from the ankles up. When he'd reached maximum density he pulled up the bib, heaved on the matching camouflage parka, and stuffed in more onesies. With the hood cinched tight around his scarf and a pair of snow goggles, Abe resembled Santa Claus geared up for combat.

"Okay," he said again, this time muffled, "let's go home."

July, *Now*

Flat on his back, Dabney lay awake in the open, the sky above him a slab of starless slate. No clouds differentiated the opaque murk that hung above, but it wasn't a rich blackness, either. It was grayed out, lifeless. Stars would be nice. Maybe the moon. Something. Instead there was nothing, nada, zip. How could that be? Maybe his eyes were going. Beneath him the silver-painted tar paper was lumpy and hot, still retaining the heat of the day. He felt the texture with his thick fingers, creased and peeling, much like his own skin, which was sunburnt from spending all his time up here on the roof. Let the others rot in their apartments, he figured. *I'd rather rot in full sight of God.*

Dabney touched his forehead and plucked a strip of his peeling skin away and pressed it onto his tongue, tasting his own acrid saltiness on the paper-thin jerky substitute. He let the rind sit there for a while, building up sufficient saliva to swallow it. He knew this was disgusting behavior, but so what? He was doing a self test of what senses he could stimulate. Taste: check. Touch: check. Sight: negative. Hearing? All was quiet above and below so Dabney forced an acidic burp. Check. Smell?

Smell.

Smell had taken a beating in recent months, not that smell had ever been his favorite. The nullification of smell was sort of a blessing, given the circumstances. So, three out of five, for the time being. Morning would come and sight would soon return to the roster.

Four out of five.

Not bad.

"Jesus, even a little air movement would be an improvement. Movement. Improvement. A *breeze* through the *trees* would *please* as it rolled over my *knees* like a *disease* or honey from *bees* and it would *ease* my . . . my . . . Fuck. Lost it."

With the rhyming game over, Karl rolled over on his side; the mattress where he'd been lying was damp with perspiration. Moisture he could ill afford to lose. Karl stared at the wall, or at least in the direction of the wall. It was so dark he couldn't see it, but it was there, a thin layer of protection between him and them. And he wasn't even thinking about the *big* them. The capital T *them*. He was just thinking about the them that constituted the others in the building. His neighbors.

All the windows of apartment 5B were open but you'd never know it, the air was so still it felt like a vacuum. Karl inhaled deeply through his nose, some buildup within the nasal passage creating a high-pitched whistling noise. He breathed in, out, in, out, changing the tempo, attempting to negate his insomnia by nose whistling some half forgotten pop tune, the melody of which had come unbidden from the depths of his subconscious. What was that tune? Now he began to hum it, a ditty sans lyrics. But there were lyrics. He knew that much. This was killing him now. The more he hummed, stretching out the notes, the less the words came into focus. This was killing him. Well, not really. But it wasn't helping.

Weighing, like, a hundred or so pounds was killing him.

Being dehydrated was killing him.

Not sleeping was killing him.

The earworm was merely aggravating.

With internal creaks and pops belying his actual age of twenty-eight, Karl swung his legs over the side of the bed and touched his toes to the bare wooden floorboards, which were as warm as everything else. What kind of world was this where even the floor was tepid? Floors were supposed to be cool to the touch. Even in summer.

Before stepping from the bed, Karl groped at his night table for matches. Though he was loathe to strike one and add to the heat even a little, he was more averse to stubbing his toes or tripping over something. After living in this apartment for the last few years you'd think he'd know the lay of the land, even blind. But he didn't. His sweaty palm found the book of matches and Karl snapped one into life, the brightness singeing his eyes for a moment as they adjusted to this pinprick of light in the absolute dark. The small dancing light found the blackened wick of one of the candles, which sputtered to life, creating a pool of comforting incandescence.

Karl had lots of candles, gifts from his mother, aunts, grandma, and past girlfriends. Even female coworkers—Secret Santa crap. What was it with women and candles? He'd gotten them as gifts, pretended he'd appreciated them, then thrown them all in a box in his closet. Now he was grateful for them—except the scented ones. He'd learned that lesson the hard way. The fresh, fruity, cinnamony, flowery aromas reawakened his dormant sense of smell, unfamiliar odors rousing the olfactory receptors, which in turn refreshed the revulsion from the overwhelming tang of rot outside. It had only taken one Apples 'n' Spice candle to teach him his lesson. He'd lit the wick, basked for a moment in the delicious bouquet, and then puked from a crushing whiff of the ceaseless alfresco parade of putrescence.

So, unscented.

In the light Karl could make out the trappings of his bedroom. The posters on the wall—Kiss, Slipknot, Metallica, Judas Priest, Ozzy, Motörhead, Korn—reassured him, though none of those bands was responsible for the rogue melody assailing his brain at the moment. What was it? Familiar yet unfamiliar. It was sort of pretty in an annoying kind of way.

Karl's eyes roved to The Wall of Beauty, a veritable tapestry of pinups, centerfolds, magazine clippings, and most personally gratifying (and now, in retrospect, most painfully sentimental), Polaroids from the good old days when he was "getting some" and could occasionally convince his conquests to pose for him in the raw. When things had been different he'd been discreet and kept these pix salted away in a private place, but now? Now they were on permanent display.

Karl got up from the bed and shuffled over to the wall. The flickering candlelight made the images seem to writhe. Though there was some mild twitching south of his personal equator, it was insufficient for the purpose of autoeroticism. Eroticism! What a joke. Is there anything less erotic than jacking off before an altar of two-dimensional representations of nubile flesh? Of *any* flesh? In this case, *dead* flesh? All dead. At least Karl assumed they were all dead. So, did whacking to these beauties' images constitute virtual necrophilia? Back in the day, one of Karl's fave porn starlets offed herself. Consequently, his massive cache of videos in which she'd appeared became anathema to his libido. He gave the tapes away to a friend less burdened by . . . what would that be? Sentiment? Conscience? Ethics? Empathy? Plain old decency?

Decency seemed an antiquated concept. So when he could work up the energy these days, he spanked to dead ladies. Were there any other kind?

Karl ran his fingertips over some favorite images. Long of leg, wide of hip, narrow of waist, all with come-hither eyes. His prize was the Polaroid of Dawn-Anne McCarthy, his junior high crush. He'd run into her years after they'd graduated, on line at a store here in the city. Her disdain for him in junior high had vanished and for a few dazzling weeks they'd fulfilled every last one of his adolescent fantasies about her, and several his pubescent mind had been too inexperienced to even conjure.

Until he'd blown it, of course.

"You were the best, baby," Karl said, touching the tip of his index finger to the flossy hub of Dawn's sex. He exhaled with conspicuous melancholy, not that there was anyone to notice or lend comfort. "You were my Everest."

Karl flushed with embarrassment at his floridity, then looked up at the ceiling and considered going up to the roof. Maybe it was cooler up there. Maybe there was some air up there. Then he considered Dabney and reconsidered, slunk back to bed, blew out the candle, and curled up on his side on the edge, in an attempt to avoid the damp spot.

Which was warm.

"You asleep?"

Across the hall, in 5A, Ruth Fogelhut poked her husband of forty-six years in his xylophone ribs with her chicken claw of a hand, her hard, pointed fingers raking his translucent epidermis and leaving behind scarlet trails—not that either could see them in the dark.

"Who sleeps around here? Especially . . ." Pause for a brief dry-throated coughing fit. ". . . with you torturing me all through the night. Sleep? What is this thing you call sleep? I should be so lucky to sleep. Even a nightmare is preferable to your constant *mutchering*."

"You don't have to be so unpleasant, *Abraham*."

"Is that supposed to chasten me, '*Abraham*'? What, I'm a five-year-old and saying my whole name is a scold I'll abide? Abe, Abraham, call me whatever you like. Call me Ishmael, for all I care. Sleep. Sleep's a sweet memory."

"I'll call you a shit, how's about that?"

In the blackness, Abe smiled in triumph. In all her years, Ruth was never one for cursing. It was beneath her, such vulgarity. Swearing was for the common folk, the hoi polloi. But take away amenities like food, running water, electricity, hygiene, etc., and even Emily Post might call you a *cocksucker* at dinner.

"I'm sorry, Abe. *Abe*, is that better?" Ruth's voice was croaky and plaintive. It sounded like it was coming from something not quite human, something rattle boned and cotton mouthed. Something mummified and meager. Oh wait, it was. Ruth, once a breathtaking, slightly Rubenesque ringer for a young Ruby Keeler was now a crinkly sack of bones, nearly bald, with craters like eggcups holding her dulled, gummy, gray eyes.

"Abe's fine," Abe mouthed, almost silently. Why raise one's voice? Gone were competing noises, like traffic and planes roaring across the sky. Gone were the cries of children, or mugging victims, or brawlers from the bar catercornered from their apartment. Gone were the ghetto cruisers with their booming systems, the bass so deep you could feel it in your colon. Gone were the nightly aural assaults from the garbage trucks, the thunderous growl of the crusher mechanism, the clash and clang of the emptied cans being slammed back to the pavement, the inarticulate badinage of the sanitation workers. Who'd think you'd miss that crap? "Abe's fine," Abe repeated, as much to reassure himself as Ruth. It felt better to talk about himself in the third person, made him think of himself as not quite real. Reality sucked. *Abe's not fine*, he thought. *Who the hell is fine nowadays?*

"I can't sleep."

"Really?" Abe said, the sarcasm creeping back, edging out his miserable attempt at tenderness. "You could knock me over with a feather." The fact was, you could knock either of them over with a feather, and not a particularly large feather at that. Two skeletons with a soupçon of withered meat held together by decrepit membrane lying side by side in a dilapidated sarcophagus.

One flight down, on the fourth landing, ear pressed against the door of 4B, Ellen Swenson clasped a hand over her mouth, suppressing the urge to call out to her husband, Mike, who dozed sporadically in their apartment, behind their currently unlocked door. Ellen had left her left flip-flop wedged between the door and the jamb and tiptoed across the narrow hall to eavesdrop. Mike didn't believe her assertions about their neighbors, the jocks—the *former* jocks, at any rate. They were regular guys. Beer guzzlers. Hockey players. Bullies. Republicans. *Regular guys, for crying out loud.* Guy's guys. Because they were so surface, to Ellen they also were something of a mystery. Mike's argument, by way of Freud, was that sometimes a cigar is just a cigar, but Ellen didn't buy it. With empty apartments still available, why'd they choose to live together when they arrived here? She didn't just accept things at face value.

She had her theory, she needed proof and this gave her something to do when insomnia hit, which was almost invariably every night, especially since nights became interminable. No light, no entertainment, no conventional diversions. So Ellen made her own fun. As a girl she'd been a fan of Nancy Drew, Encyclopedia Brown, and even Scooby-Doo, so this meddling kid would tumble the jocks' game if it killed her. If it didn't, the boredom might.

The plus of a nearly silent world was that sound traveled. Sometimes that was a minus, but not right now. They must be in the living room, Ellen surmised. They sounded close. Really close.

Like, right by the door. But sound had a way of tricking you in the absolute dark. All she wanted was to hear something incriminating. Something to lord over Mike, to prove she was right.

"I don't even know why I listen to you, Mallon," came Eddie's voice. Eddie, Ellen figured, was the alpha dog. He barked louder, seemed scarier. He was the one Ellen feared. Pasty, ginger Dave just kind of annoyed her. "You're wrong about everything."

"Dude, you need to take it easy on the water."

"*Vaffanculo*, dude. Don't mother hen me." Eddie slammed the jug down on the counter to emphasize his dominance—*case closed*. "Fuckin' twerps across the hall," he spat. "Fuckin' Swensons!"

At the sound of her name, Ellen stiffened.

"We should just beat the shit out of Mike and take his woman. Make her our sex slave. Only two fuckin' women in here—"

"What about Gerri?"

"*Only two fuckin' women in here* and one's like ninety and the other's married and monogamous. Fuckin' monogamous! What kinda selfish outmoded shit is that, anyways? Don't the Jews share everything on those kibbutz things? This is like that now, yo. This here. I'm tellin' you, bro, *it ain't right*."

"Hey, chill out," Dave scolded in a hushed voice. "Sound carries, you know?"

"I don't give a shit," Eddie boomed. "Let her hear. Let 'em both hear. *Hey, Swenson, I'm gunnin' for your woman, bitch!*"

At that, Ellen's insides felt like they were imploding. It wasn't funny anymore. Though neither Dave nor Eddie were the strapping behemoths they once were, both still were formidable. Mike and she wouldn't stand a chance against them in a physical confrontation. *Sex slave.* As she began to tremble, Eddie let out a burst of loud, bellicose laughter.

"I'm just fucking around, Dave. Chill."

Chill, indeed. Even in the stultifying heat, Ellen's skin erupted in goose pimples, sweat turning cool on her forehead. Like a silent movie blind man she extended her arms and groped back toward her apartment door, slipped in and triple locked it in case Eddie wasn't "just fucking around."

Alan massaged his temples, removing his glasses, which were streaked and stained with sweat and skin oil. His "T-zone" was working overtime, his eyebrows smearing translucent patterns onto the lenses. Candles flickered, adding to the already oppressive temperature, but what was he supposed to do if he couldn't sleep, just lie there and stare into the tenebrous void? He wasn't in the mood to draw, so reading was the only thing left to do since television and the Internet became extinct. All his batteries were dead, so no more Walkman or iPod. Music was becoming but a sweet memory, along with regular meals, luxuriously long showers, movies . . . hell, everything.

Alan kept rubbing, feeling his pulse throbbing away just under the gauzy layer of dermis stretched over his skull. He contemplated dipping into his dwindling supply of store-brand ibuprofen, acetaminophen, or aspirin. Eyestrain. His mother always warned him about ruining his eyes by reading in inadequate light. She also warned him about sitting too close to the TV, but that advice was now moot. He wanted to keep reading. This was a good book, a real page-turner. His father used to lecture him about wasting his mind on junk. He'd urged Alan to read the classics, to broaden himself, to refine his mind. But Alan persisted in reading potboilers. Alan liked escapism when things were still good. Now escapism was his only luxury. His collection of sci-fi and crime paperbacks was worth its weight in gold. Scratch that; gold wasn't worth anything any more. It was better than gold. *Sorry, Dad. Maybe Chaucer or Dickens or Goethe or Balzac or Sartre or whomever would have made me a better person. Hard to say. But right now I'll take my fantasy, thank you very much.*

Horror, on the other hand, he left to molder on the shelf.

The pain in his temples encroached into the middle of his head, meeting at the bridge of his nose, the beat incessant, insistent, insufferable. He switched from massaging the sides of his head to working between the eyes. He was going to have to stop reading and sink into the insomnious darkness. He really didn't want to medicate himself. Alan licked his fingertips and pinched out the candles.

He slumped back onto his mattress. His face itched, still unused to being so thickly bearded; he had not mastered the art of the dry shave. Naked, sweaty, furry, blind until sunup, head pounding, and dry heaving from the fetor. Alan depressed the button on his digital watch. The red LED display announced it was 3:27 in the morning. Sunrise was about two hours away. An eternity. As Alan scratched and convulsed he drifted off, the only person in the building actually asleep.

One flight down, situated above the boarded-up abandoned Phnom Penh Laundromat, apartments 2A and 2B were vacant. No one wanted to live that close to the street, and 2B housed bad memories.

1

Blackness was ebbing. The room began to take on a dark, sickly bluish-lavender tint, like the walls were bruised, heralding the start of a new day. Ellen lay on her side, facing away from the twin windows beside the bed, watching the wall change color. The purple drained away, replaced by jaundiced ochre, which as brightness increased lost pigmentation. Finally the normal drab off-white hue solidified, the glaringly bright sunlight accentuating every imperfection in the wall's surface—each crack, each patch of Spackle under the substandard paint job. The wall was scarred beneath the paint, reminding Ellen of her former boss, a woman with an unfortunate complexion who'd applied way too much base in a sad effort to mask what imperfections lay beneath. Instead all she did was draw attention to each pit on her acne-ravaged face, a hopeless topography of dermatological strife. Too much makeup was the female equivalent of the shoddy toupee. Whenever Ellen had seen a man wearing an obvious rug—and most of them were pretty damned glaring—she always figured no one really liked or loved him, because no one would allow her husband or good friend go out in public looking that foolish.

The wall was pitted, a trifle buckled, somewhat bulgy in the middle. Their building was old, almost a hundred, but still settling. A couple years back she'd read in *New York* magazine that her block was right near a fault line. Maybe the earth would one day just start to shimmy and shake and swallow them all up. Better the earth than those *things*.

As hot as it was at night, it would be worse during the day, but at least she could see—not that seeing was much of a blessing. At night her field of vision was a wash of pitch black, unless she lit a candle. She could remember herself the way she was before. She could imagine some meat on her bones, some tone in her muscles. Hell, she could nostalgically remember some rolls of fat that she'd wished would go away. *At night.* During the day she could really absorb how awful she and everyone else looked. It had gotten so bad that your archetypal Auschwitz inmate would look at the residents of 1620 York Avenue and say, "Damn, those are some unhealthily skinny-looking motherfuckers."

Or sentiments to that effect.

Ellen poked Mike in a furrow between his ribs until, with effort, his eyelids separated, revealing red-rimmed, yellowed, mucilaginous eyeballs. His mouth, a thin, wide, desiccated trench while sleeping, clenched and unclenched, lines radiating in parched spokes from his dull gray lips, which back in the day were red and full and the most kissable in the world. His mouth, as it attempted to form his first words on the day, pursed like the shriveled sphincter it was, lost in curly beard growth. Ellen still kissed that puckered bunghole of a mouth, but now it was perfunctory, a sad nod to past romantic glory.

"What?" Mike's voice was Gobi hoarse.

"I think we need to bar the door better. Like, push some furniture up against it to make it impenetrable."

With considerable effort, Mike sat up and rubbed crumbs from his eyes and nose.

"Why?" he croaked. "You think the amblers are going to get up here? They haven't since that one time and I think it's pretty well—"

"Not the amblers. Dave and Eddie. I heard them talking last night and—"

Mike gave her a sour look.

"Oh, *what?*" she said, folding her arms across her slatted chest, her breasts drooping like withered cutlets. Not the supple breasts of a successful twenty-seven-year-old Upper East Side urban-professional mom. They were more like the breasts seen in a magazine spread on depredation in Ethiopia or Somalia or some other godawful place— the kind of breasts that play landing field to legions of flies and their owners don't even notice. These ruined teats had fed their child. They'd been large and full and life sustaining. They'd been ample and erotic. They'd been real ego boosters. Now they were depleted paps.

You're no longer a mom when your child is dead—your *former* child.

Everything was *former*.

"You're crazy," Mike managed. "If they'd heard you out there, who knows what they would have done to you?"

Ellen had a pretty good idea, based on Eddie's brief but memorable rant last night. She didn't think they were above rape; if those jock assholes were slightly less malnourished she'd live in serious fear of them. Especially Eddie. Her assumption they'd gone the way of Fudgy McPacker might not be as watertight as she'd thought, and losing the comfort she took from the notion they'd been focusing their brutish carnality on each other didn't improve her spirits.

"Anyway, promise me you'll never do anything stupid like that again."

"It wasn't *stupid*, Mike."

"Okay, not stupid. Uh, foolhardy. Ill-advised. Perilous."

"It's like you actually care."

"I . . ." Mike began to sputter like an Evinrude. "What the . . . I . . . Of course I . . . What kind of way is this to start the day?"

Ellen shrugged and stepped off the bed, drifting toward the kitchen. "You want some water?" she asked Mike, whose face twitched apoplectically. He blinked a few times, then nodded, and she left the bedroom. Let him stew, she thought. She had no reason to torment him, but it killed time. Besides, it would give her something to apologize for later. The hours had to be filled with something, so why not a little domestic turbulence? Sex took too much energy, and besides they were both so thin and kindlinglike it just wasn't fun any more. Bones ricocheting off bones, loose skin flapping around, bad smells. But it also passed some time and sometimes that was enough. They'd read all their books and magazines. Neither had any talent worth pursuing. Mike had been into photography, but that was no longer an option. She wrote bad poetry back in the day, but now why bother? What would she write about, the death of everything? Been done and done and done to death.

In the kitchen, Ellen poured half a glass from a 16.9-ounce bottle of Kirkland Signature Premium Water. But the water was far from premium. It was rain water. Ellen couldn't remember how old the bottle was. They filled a whole case of them last rain. Ellen traipsed back into the bedroom where Mike now stood by the window staring straight across the alley at the neighboring building, not ten feet away. The windows there were stripped of any coverings and all were dark, bereft of life. There used to be noisy neighbors. Directly across from them there was this Latin couple who'd blast salsa music at all hours of the day and night. They'd openly do drugs by their windows, smoking pot, doing lines. Once, the man spotted Mike peeping at them and made a finger gun and mouthed, "Pop, pop, pop," then winked and flashed a gold-accented toothy grin.

Mike leaned out the window and peered down into the alley. Stragglers who'd broken off from the herd shuffled back and forth, having breached the gate that someone in a panic must have left unlocked. Mike cleared his throat and a couple looked up, their dulled eyes twitching in recognition of something delicious. One let out a faint but audible gasp and began to limp in Mike's direction.

"Be careful," Ellen said as Mike leaned out further, bent at the midriff.

"It's like you actually care," Mike threw back at her, but when he did so, he smiled.

Ellen sidled up to her husband and put her hand on his back, feeling guilty about pushing his buttons, especially so early in the day. She could have at least waited until after their scant breakfast.

"I brought your water," Ellen said, holding up the small juice glass, an old jelly jar with Huckleberry Hound on it.

Mike lifted his hands off the window ledge and straightened at the waist, eager to drink, unmindful of the window frame. His head slammed into the sash and his feet lost purchase on the smooth floorboards, thrusting his upper portion forward. Ellen dropped the glass and grabbed for Mike, her hands moist with perspiration, muscles neutered by malnutrition. She made contact with his left bicep but it slipped away. He pitched forward, his bony, naked ass slamming against the sash as his legs pinwheeled by her astonished face. An inarticulate screech was the only sound she could manage as her husband fell out the window.

Swallowing hard, she rushed to the other window, the one with the fire escape. It was possible he'd survived, that they could rescue him. She pushed the curtains aside to reveal the folding security gate and stared at the padlock like she'd never seen it before. The gate had been there from the previous tenant, a model not approved by the fire department. The combination. She couldn't remember it. Mike had it somewhere.

His laptop.

His dead, useless, worthless laptop.

Now the blood in her veins seemed to slow. She dragged her feet across the floor toward the open window Mike fell through. She didn't want to look, but desire was not a factor. She poked her head out, her posture exactly aping that of Mike's mere moments ago. In the alley below, Mike lay splayed on his back, his spindly arms and legs arranged almost comically about him. From her vantage point he looked like a human swastika, legs bent in a cartoonish running position. His face stared straight up and they made eye contact. He wasn't dead. Ellen's mouth opened and closed but no sounds came out. She wanted to shout something comforting; some final thought Mike could take with him. "I brought your water," seemed entirely deficient.

The zombies advanced on Mike, shambling forward. Ellen's teeth began to chatter and Mike's eyes implored her to say something. Anything. With effort she managed to mouth, "I love you," but mute. *Please let him die before they reach him. Please.*

A small pool of blood was forming beneath Mike's head, and Ellen noticed his neck was at an odd angle. A four-story fall. His neck was broken. He was paralyzed. *Please let him be numb all over. Please at least spare him the pain.* Mike's eyes began to swim and lose focus. *Let him lose consciousness.* The first of his defilers stooped over and dropped to its knees, baring its teeth. At least Ellen couldn't see its face, but she knew what it looked like. Cadaverous, leathery skin, yellow as a dead plucked chicken, translucent enough to display dull plum-tinted veins, blackened gums receded all the way, teeth huge, eyes glazed—if it even had any.

A shriek echoed through the alley as they tore into Mike, picking the meager flesh off his bones with those horrible teeth, digging their jagged nails in, peeling him. Ellen was locked in position—sympathy paralysis. She wanted to close her eyes but was unable. She watched at they dismembered Mike. With ingenerate knack, one scored perforations around Mike's left shoulder with its teeth then jerked the arm clean off and began to devour it, ripping the meat off the bones. Another disemboweled Mike, unintentionally inviting several others to mooch off the uncoiling spoils. Bestial growls accompanied the feeding frenzy, the things poking at each other, scrabbling, circling like hyenas. More stumbled into the alley from the side street, attracted by the noise, the scent of fresh blood. Soon all she could see were their backs hunched over the spot on which Mike lay. Her nails dug into the brick beneath the ledge, grinding them down, a rudimentary no-frills manicure. Tears blurred her vision.

"I brought your water," she said again, her voice thinner than she was.

"Ellen," a voice cried out from below. "Don't look at this! Pull your head inside!"

Was Mike trying to spare her? That was so Mike of him, always trying to protect her feelings, even now. She was sorry she couldn't oblige, though. She was vapor locked. *Sorry, Mike. Sorry about everything.*

By the time her temporary immobilization eased, all that was left of dear, sweet Mike was a dark crimson stain on the pavement and some picked-clean bones. Ellen wrested her fingers from the mortar, contemplated jumping, reconsidered, and slumped to the floor, hugging herself, taking no solace from her bony limbs and digits.

Former mother.

Now former wife.

Next door she heard Eddie bellow something unintelligible. But his tone, as always, was ugly and portended trouble.

And now she was alone.

3

"Open the door, Ellen!" Alan implored.

He'd raced up the stairs and now pounded on the door of 4A. This was excitement no one needed or wanted, least of all him, but he couldn't just sit in his apartment and pretend it hadn't happened. He'd heard the howl from the alley and had looked down in time to see Mike's head come off, a sight he hoped Ellen had been spared from her vantage point, but probably not. He'd looked up from the alley's floor and seen Ellen perched at her windowsill, eyes like saucers swimming in roomy sockets. Ellen didn't seem to hear him. He'd pled for her to look away. Instead she'd watched her husband transform from significant other to outdoor buffet. And it wasn't even eight in the morning.

"Ellen, come on!" Alan cried. "Open the door! Please, Ellen!"

Across the narrow hall the door to 4B opened and Eddie appeared, standing in the doorway in his boxers, which hung too low beneath his diminished waist. "What's the fuckin' ruckus?" he said, just oozing compassion.

"Mike . . . ," Alan began, then stopped himself. Eddie'd find out soon enough, but why tip the hand? If he and Dave were un-aware of Mike's demise, why let them know? They'd just up the harassment ante on Ellen.

"What *about* Mike?" Eddie said, raising an eyebrow.

"Nothing. I just need to talk to Ellen."

"What for?"

"Jesus, Eddie, whyn't you mind your business? You're like a hausfrau looking for gossip. I swear; if we still had power you'd be sitting on the couch watching your *stories*."

"I've got no problem busting your fuckin' lip open, wiseass," Eddie growled, wagging a finger. "Just you remember that. Seri-ously."

"Uh-huh. That's great," yawned Alan, indifferent.

"You just better hope I never bulk up again, faggot."

Alan smirked. "I count on it."

And with that, Eddie slammed the door shut. Once upon a time Eddie had spooked Alan, but that was fifty or so pounds ago. Now they were both in the same weight class. Fact was Alan had a little *more* meat on him than Eddie because he'd been better at squirrel-ing away, much better. Not that Eddie needed to be privy to that info. Alan tried the doorknob again, rattling it. Locked, of course. Who'd keep an unlocked door, especially with those goons next door? After several minutes, the clack of multiple dead bolts un-locking came from the other side of the door and it opened a crack, revealing Ellen's gaunt shell-shocked face.

"I don't know what to say," Alan said, feeling stupid for having said it.

"Come in, Al." Ellen opened the door wider and stepped aside, which seemed a formality considering she was too attenuated to block his entrance. She wore a pale-pink tank top that accentuated her lankness, her neck cords so pronounced Alan fought the in-sane temptation to strum them.

"I saw what happened. When you didn't answer the door I was afraid you'd done something to yourself."

Ellen just stared at Alan, eyes glassy with grief. She plopped herself down on a wooden dining chair and Alan could hear the bones in her ass knock against the hard surface. The sound made him wince, but she didn't notice. After a few hushed seconds passed, Alan pulled out a chair at the table and joined her, seating himself slowly, carefully, mindful of the hard-on-hard dynamic. No one had padding any more. "The bigger the cushion, the sweeter the pushin'" days were over.

Ellen's arms hung limp at her sides, her wrists grazing the lower rim of the seat of the chair. So many hard angles. Alan had lusted after Ellen when she and Mike moved in six years ago. That was before she'd been a mother—not that women who'd had kids weren't still sexy, but motherhood was a sacred institution. Wasn't it? Was anything sacred anymore? Anyway, this wasn't a booty call. Ellen had no booty. Her ass had been so perfect, a flared, ripe pear. What was Alan thinking?

That was crazy.

Now more than ever each life was precious. Mike had been precious to Ellen, even though they bickered. Alan heard them. Alan's thoughts were jumbled. He'd liked Mike well enough. Mike was a good neighbor. They'd even hung out together a few times, back in the days before. Hanging out after didn't count, because choice was no longer a factor. Alan slapped himself across the face, snapping himself out of this unproductive internal loop, the sound stirring Ellen from her torpor.

"What did you do that for?" she asked, somewhat horrified.

"Sorry, my mind was kind of malfunctioning. Nothing to be concerned about. I'm here for you, Ellen. Sorry. Won't happen again."

"No, it's okay. It was just kind of weird is all. But it kind of helped, in a way. Seeing you slap yourself was odd enough to wake me back up." She paused for a few long beats, then added, "Mike's dead, you know."

"Yeah, I know. I saw. I was calling up to you, trying to get you not to look. I don't know if you heard me."

"*Ohhhhh,*" Ellen said, a faint smile playing on her drained lips. "That was *you.* I thought it was Mike. I wasn't thinking too straight. That was really considerate of you. Thank you."

Ellen looked and sounded far away, which might be for the best. Though Alan knew they were dead, he'd been spared having to witness any of his loved ones being devoured. Strangers, sure. By the dozens. But family? Mercifully no. As Ellen evinced the thousand-yard stare, Alan's eyes roved about the kitchen. Pretty bare, like everyone's. His eyes drifted over each surface, eventually finding their way back to his vacant hostess. He tried to envision her fleshy past self. He'd done her portrait a few times in pastel, pencil, even ink, so her face was pretty well ingrained in his psyche, but it was hard to conjure and superimpose on this bloodless husk. He'd wanted her to pose nude, but Ellen thought that would make Mike jealous, even if it was strictly business, no hanky-panky. *What the hell was the point of being an artist if you couldn't get chicks to pose in the buff?* Alan had wondered. There are no other career-specific perks. Alan had suggested that he document her pregnancy with some tasteful nudes, but again the answer was no, even though she'd thought it a good idea at first. That was a real pity. Her breasts had gone from admirable to astounding during those months, and then stayed that way for quite a while. He'd never seen her nude back when that would have been a thrilling experience. Now he routinely saw her in various states of undress and it was tragic.

With the merciful exception of the Fogelhuts, most of the residents had adopted a slightly more "progressive" version of permanent casual Friday. Their building, 1620 York Avenue, was a "clothing optional" residence. Maybe it was hypocrisy or maybe it was modesty—which seemed so passé—but Alan kept his clothes on when dealing with his neighbors. It's not like he strutted around like Dapper Dan, wearing a suit and tie, but he kept his shorts and T-shirt on. *Let the others sashay around in the raw.*

"Can I get you anything?" he asked, attempting to stay grounded in the now.

"Huh? Oh, no, no. Just stay with me."

"Okay, as long as you need."

"No, I mean *stay* with me. Stay in the apartment. Move in with me."

Alan looked at her face, trying to glean how serious she was. *Serious as a heart attack,* as the old axiom went. Once upon a time that would have been the answer to his prayers, but now?

"Move in?"

"Move in. I don't want to be alone, especially with those two Neanderthals next door. Listen, I loved Mike, Mike loved me, but these, I dunno, these are savage times. I can't think about what's prim and proper and what will the neighbors say? '*Look, that whore's shacking up with someone new already.*' Who would think that, except those creeps across the hall? Can you imagine what my life will be like if they think I'm—Christ, I can't even *say* it. *Available*? Oh, Jesus. *Fuck that.* Mourning and starving are all most of us do, anyway. It's not like you have to move your shit up here, but stay with me. Sleep in the same room. We don't have to even sleep in the same bed if you're not comfortable with that. There's a foldout couch in the living room, but . . ."

Ellen rambled on, the stream of words blurring. Alan became aware that she was gripping his wrist, hard, her thin fingers clenched together like a vice. They went all the way around his wrist now. That was disturbing. *Alan Zotz and Ellen Swenson*, he mused. Once upon a time he might have wanted to carve that on a tree, with a big "4E" under it. But what could he say? This was a cocktail of unmitigated grief and panic and adrenaline. When she calmed down she'd probably want him to move back out. This was temporary. Life was temporary. They'd all starve to death pretty soon, anyway.

Might as well go out one of the good guys.

4

Karl knocked on the door to the roof, not wanting to intrude on Dabney—at least not without Dabney's concrete approval. After a few more tentative taps, Dabney called out a brusque, "Whattaya want?"

"It's me, Karl. Permission to come above?"

Dabney half scowled and half chuckled at Karl's unfailing dorkiness. He appreciated Karl's respect for his personal space, but this was the roof for Christ's sake. He didn't own it. If Karl wanted to come up—if *anyone* wanted to—who was Dabney to say no? Though he seldom used it for shelter, Dabney had set up a shabby lean-to of corrugated aluminum and loose brick. When it rained he'd sleep under it, allowing the buckshot-on-metal clatter to lull him to sleep. It had been weeks since it rained last. Nonetheless, strewn about the roof were various containers for collecting water: garbage cans, buckets, plastic drawers, and file boxes. And a few planters with failed attempts at vegetable farming, all dead before they yielded anything edible.

Karl stepped out onto the blindingly bright tar paper; the sun was blazing full tilt to the east. He wished he'd brought sunglasses and sandals but didn't want to go back down just to come back up. Instead he squinted and winced, scorching his eyes and toasting his feet. Karl nodded at Dabney, who returned the acknowledgment before resuming his post on the lip on the roof, belly down on a mottled canvas tarp, head hung over the edge. Beside him was a pile of chunks of brick culled from the neighboring buildings, the roofs of which were all adjoined, separated by low walls which Dabney periodically demolished and raided for recreational target practice. The only constructive use the residents of 1620 had found for masonry—part of a renovation project that never got past the supply stage—was walling up the interior front entrance with cinder blocks, fortifying what the harried contingent of National Guardsmen had hastily thrown up to bar entry to their building. Up and down the block, doorways both residential and commercial were boarded up with rusting slabs of corrugated sheet metal. FEMA had done a bang-up job of sealing everyone in and abandoning them. Now many of the fortifications were shearing away, the elements having corroded the substandard no-bid bolts.

Karl walked over to where Dabney lay and squatted next to him, looking over the edge from a safe distance. Heights and Karl didn't cozy up. Besides, the view was torment. Directly across the avenue from them was the linchpin of their collective woe, a tantalizing siren that beckoned, but one they could never answer: the Food City Supermarket. Behind its boarded-up façade, they imagined, lay a cornucopia of uneaten, unspoiled canned goods, bottled water, batteries that still had juice in them, you name it. Sure, the produce and meat had gone bad, but there was likely an embarrassment of provisions in there, all hopelessly out of reach. Sandwiched between the east and west sides of York Avenue, as far as the eye could see in both directions, north and south, was a sea of doddering bodies, all with but a single purpose: eat anyone stupid enough to venture from the safety of his or her home. Karl had witnessed it many a time.

Food City was situated in a big steel-and-glass apartment building, the only truly modern high-rise for blocks. Next door to the supermarket, its entrance raised and bordered by a small enclave of benches and shrubs, was a bank. Above the supermarket was a shallow inset area—maybe five feet deep, eight feet high, the full width of the market—that allowed the air-conditioning units to vent. Right above that were the windows of the first tier of dwellings, permanently sealed, like newfangled hotels and office buildings.

All up and down the avenue, as the status quo grew worse and worse, either lots were drawn or people went nuts or whatever, but folks made countless attempts from the neighboring buildings to gain entrance to Food City. Karl had observed what in other circumstances might have been comical stabs at it all go awry—real life Wile E. Coyote-style maneuvers. Several jokers driven mad with desperation tried the Tarzan thing, throwing a line out from a high window, lassoing a streetlamp, swinging, falling. Unlike Tarzan, though, they'd all ended up being torn to shreds, their final resting place the guts of those undead things down there.

Some had attempted a different approach, still from above, casting a line from their windows or roofs down to the streetlamp right in front of the market. They'd anchored the ropes like a clothesline, then shimmied across the street, only to find themselves stranded above the sidewalk, still with ten feet between them and the air-conditioning alcove. Even then, what would they have done? There was no way in from there unless you knew how to dismantle an industrial air-conditioning unit. These were regular citizens, not special ops personnel trained in breeching bulwarks. So they either shimmied back into their shelters, or dropped to the pavement and were devoured.

Some aspirant swashbucklers slapped together homemade armor. Egged on by their hungry neighbors, they'd either lowered themselves to the sidewalk from windows or fire escapes, or even more imprudently breached from within their blockaded front doors, which inevitably led to an unstoppable tsunami of zombies surging into their dwellings, costing all within their lives. The ones with enough foresight to reseal the entranceway usually didn't make it ten feet from their homes before the horde picked them clean. One did get as far as the entrance to the supermarket, and even managed to detach the moldering sheet metal, but the doors had been automatic. No power; no way in. He'd pounded on them as much in exasperated fury and disbelief as in attempt to actually infiltrate the emporium. His makeshift armor just made the zombies work a little harder for their meal, but like a boiled lobster, the shell came off and they enjoyed the tender bounty within.

Now, because of one of Dabney's brick tosses, the supermarket doors gaped open, the pavement glittering with fragments of safety glass, taunting everyone.

And the avenue might as well be a thousand miles wide.

"Watch this," Dabney said, selecting a chunk of brick from the pile. He hefted it once or twice in his palm, getting the feel for it, then lobbed it down into the crowd. It disappeared amid the shoulder-to-shoulder multitude of shuffling cadavers.

"Fuck," Dabney spat in annoyance. He picked another nugget from the stack and this time took aim. "That one," he said, not specifying which one, which would have been difficult to do anyway. Which one, the rotting one? The ugly one? The one with the bad skin? The one with its skin peeling off? With the exception of their clothing and hair, to Karl they all looked the same. It was a good thing there were no rules of political correctness regarding the undead. "They all look alike, huh?" Karl imagined someone saying, in that shrill, strident, bygone PC tone. Just what the world would need: zombie special interest groups. People for the Ethical Treatment of Zombies—PETZ.

Karl smirked at the notion.

Dabney launched the missile and this time it slammed down on the skull of a bald zombie. Even from the roof they could hear the crunch as it penetrated bone and punctured what lay beneath. Brain? Only in name. The thing collapsed amidst its fellows, one less head bobbing aimlessly in the ocean of bodies. Dabney and Karl high-fived. This was one of those enjoyable, rare male-bonding moments.

"Wanna have a go?" Dabney said, jerking a thumb at the brick pile.

"Yeah? Why not," Karl said. He chose a slab of jagged slate and stood up. Dabney maintained his horizontal position on the tarpaulin.

"Flat ones don't throw as good," Dabney said, but Karl didn't intend to pitch it like a ball. He cocked his arm, pressed the slab against his chest, then swung out his arm, a light flick of the wrist sending the wedge spiraling like a Frisbee into the crowd, where it sliced off the side of a female zombie's face with a juicy thwack. She didn't hit the dust like the one Dabney clobbered, but she let out an satisfying yowl and thrust both her hands up to the gaping wound.

"Damn," Dabney said, his tone reverential. "I never would've thunk to throw like that. I always go for the solids, but that was pretty sweet. Nice goin', kid."

Karl basked in the praise. As the runt of the building he always felt nothing was expected of him but failure. This was a defining moment, scoring approbation from John Dabney, resident loner. In a city full of vacant apartments, Dabney chose to live on the roof. The others barely acknowledged his presence, but Karl found him fascinating. Dabney held onto his role as iconoclast. Dabney was . . . cool.

"It's only a matter of time, you know," Dabney said, eyes hooded.

"What?"

"This. This here's a waiting game. Look at those misbegotten things." He pointed down at the street dwellers. "They're same as us, only different. Maybe they're reanimated flesh, I dunno, whatever it is. But they're not from Mars and they ain't made of plastic. Look at 'em. I mean really look."

"It's hard from up here."

Dabney shot Karl a scowl. "Don't be so damn literal. They're fallin' apart, same as us. They don't eat each other. How long can they keep truckin' around on empty? We know we're gonna die if we don't eat, but I figure so will they, eventually. I'd like to live to see it happen. I'd like to set my feet down on pavement again, even if ain't exactly gonna be tiptoeing through tulips."

"Me too."

"It's a waiting game and nobody knows how it's gonna play out, but play out it will. It has to. Things rot. They're rotten as hell. Their hides might be tanned as shoe leather, but mark my words, they'll fall. It's nature."

"I suppose."

Dabney frowned.

"All this talk's makin' me hungry. You want something to eat?" Dabney said. Karl's stomach growled in anticipation of food. He had stuff stashed in his crib, but an offer of food from Dabney augured something mysterious and tantalizing. What did Dabney keep in his private stash? "Yeah, you do," Dabney answered, lifting himself from the tarp. He strode across the roof to a sooty, bunged-up metal contraption fashioned from salvaged commercial exhaust ducting. He bent down and opened a crudely hinged door he'd cut out of the cylindrical appliance. "It's a smoker I made," he said, by way of explanation.

"A smoker?" Karl repeated.

"Like a smokehouse. For smoking meat. Last I checked, refrigeration went the way of the dodo, right? So, smoked meat."

"Meat?" Karl gasped. He was salivating.

"Meat. Jerky. You got a beef with vermin jerky? I got rodent jerky and pigeon jerky. Doesn't sound so appealing when you know what it is, but it's not so bad. Wanna try it?"

Dabney reached into the box and pulled out a thin, fluted strip of dusky matter and offered it to Karl. He smiled. Jerky. Karl thought of the old Jerky Boys pranks. Was this a prank? It didn't seem like Dabney was the type. Karl accepted the barklike sliver and tentatively raised it to his nose, taking a sniff. Instantly his mouth began to water and with no further hesitation he took a bite— manna from heaven. Karl almost began to cry but stopped himself. That would be unmanly and he didn't want to seem so in front of Dabney. Not today. Not after impressing him. The meat was salty and dense and tough, but the flavor sent him back to his college days when he'd subsisted on mac 'n' sleaze and bags of teriyaki jerky from the 7-Eleven.

"Enjoy that," Dabney said. "Won't be much more, I don't think."

Karl's heart almost broke at the thought. "What? Why? Why not?"

"Haven't seen any critters around in the last week or so. None airborne, none skulking around on the ground. No squirrels, no rats, no mice. Sure as hell no cats. Anyway, I think what I've got in there is the last of it. The bottomless empty is right around the corner. After that, we are all well and truly screwed."

That was a helluva pronouncement. Karl studied the older man's leathery puss—peeling, brown, raw, not unlike the jerky he was consuming. If they started dying in the building would they mimic the behavior of those things on the street? Would this turn into some Manhattan version of the Donner party? Of the Andean soccer team incident? Karl flashed on the movie *Cannibal! The Musical*, the comedy about the Alferd Packer, which didn't seem so funny anymore. He thought about Jeffrey Dahmer and Andrei Chikatilo and Ed Gein. Wasn't Idi Amin a cannibal? *Oh fuck that*, Karl thought. *I'd rather die. I'd rather feed myself to those things than eat a human being. You have to hold onto who you are. Life isn't that precious. At least not any more it isn't. Maybe those sons of bitches ate each other because there were still things to live for. Their circumstances had been way different. Packer and the Donners and those soccer players had a world ahead of them.*

Dabney eyeballed Karl's twitching face, sensing his thought process.

"You know what one of those Uruguayan footballers had to say when they picked him up?" Dabney asked, his voice neutral. "It's a quote I remember because it seemed so fucked-up at the time. Now, I don't know how I feel about it. The kid was talking about how they'd cooked their teammates. He described the meat as, 'softer than beef but with much the same taste.' It's animal nature to survive. Man's an animal. To survive, folks adapt. Whattaya think of that?"

Karl doubled over and puked up the jerky. When he finished retching he remained bent over, hands gripping his knees to keep from toppling over, thick ropes of bilious saliva drooping from his twitching lower lip.

"Last time I offer you any chow," Dabney said.

Eyes stinging, Karl glared at the lumpy puddle between his legs, his face broiling with shame. Whatever cred he'd established he'd just pissed down his leg. He'd reverted to Karl the Puss—no more, impossible to be less. He felt anger coursing through his wracked body. Anger at himself, anger at Dabney, anger at everything.

"If you had food this whole time," he bleated, revolted by his wheedling tone, "why didn't you share with us?"

Dabney sighed, not angry. Seemingly bored with the question. "Because I sing hard for my supper. No one ever stopped you from hunting and gathering. I don't own the roof. You want food, show some damn initiative. Don't come whining at me because you're a bunch of spoiled Upper East Side ninnies. Grow some hair."

Karl straightened up and made to leave.

"Clean your mess up before you go, kid. I might not own the roof, but it's still my turf. Don't be leaving your mess here."

Karl opened and closed his mouth a couple of times, but he couldn't access any words that might redeem the moment. Dabney cocked his head like a wary dog and closed one eye in warning, shaking his head in silent rebuke. The gesture said, DON'T SAY A WORD. Karl looked around for a towel, saw none, then looked back at Dabney, who offered nothing but the stern authoritarian glower of someone about to lose his cool.

"What do I clean it with?"

Dabney pulled a rag out of his back pocket and tossed it to Karl, the motion reminiscent of that old Coke commercial with Mean Joe Green tossing the kid his sweaty game jersey. Karl thought a joke might help, and when he caught it he said, "Thanks, Mean Joe," instantly regretting it.

Dabney turned away and resumed his vigil at the edge of the roof.

"Stupid, stupid, stupid," Karl chanted as he mopped up his puke.

5

"That Zotz better watch his mouth is all I'm sayin'," Eddie said, stomping around the kitchen.

"Let it go, dude," Dave said. "It's no biggie."

"It *is* a biggie. It is. It's fuckin' *huge*. First he gets lippy like, what, he wants a piece of me? He thinks he can handle The Comet all of a sudden? Like suddenly he's a big man? He's a little pussy, that little bitch. I'd stuff his fuckin' crayons and paintbrushes up his ass if I didn't think he'd fuckin' love it."

"Just chill, Eddie. Come on, seriously, you're gonna give yourself an embolism or something. Park it and chill."

Eddie paced a couple more times, then grudgingly heeded Dave's counsel, taking a seat on an ottoman. He clenched and unclenched his fists, kneading his thighs, swallowing his lower lip. He threw his head back, the veins bulging on the sides of his neck, his Adam's apple jutting out like a walnut. His nostrils flared like a horse's as he exhaled over and over, sweat pouring off him. Dave watched Eddie attempting to decompress, to defuse. Ever since they'd met in high school they'd been inseparable buds, Dave the calm one, Eddie the hothead.

"The Comet" had been Eddie's hockey handle—hokey, but apt. He'd been an awesome center whose speed and ferocity earned him an athletic scholarship to Rutgers. Dave had been goalie but he'd often kept his eye more on Eddie than the puck. Eddie tossed bodies around like they were nothing, which to him they were. It was magnificent to behold. Unfortunately he spent as much time in the penalty box as on the ice. Too much high-sticking. Too much hooking. Too much fighting in general. Too much blood on the ice.

Dave came over and ran his fingers through Eddie's hair, petting him, trying to soothe him.

"Don't do that," Eddie snapped. "What're you doing? I don't need that shit, man." He stood up, vibrating with barely contained rage. "You can't do shit like that to me!"

Dave looked at his roomie, incredulous.

"I'm a little confused, Ed," Dave said.

"What? What? What's to be confused about? I don't want you fuckin' touching me all girly like that."

"But we . . ."

"That's not about . . . fuck, what's the word?"

"Tenderness?"

"Exactly!" Eddie said, his face split in both triumph and disgust. "That's *exactly* it! *Tenderness.* Tenderness is for women and fags. We're not fags, Dave. We just have to let off some steam once in a while. Nothing wrong with that. Sex and tenderness have *nothing* to do with each other. You think all those guys in prison are fags? Hell, no, dude. They just do what they gotta do. Adaptation isn't conversion, okay? You think they trawl for dick once they get sprung? Bull-*shit*! They head straight for the *punani*! You need to remember that shit, bro."

Yeah, but we're not getting sprung, Dave thought. *This is all there is.*

"Whatever," Dave said, and left the room.

"What's the matter, is it your time of the month?" Eddie said. With that he erupted in laughter.

Dave stepped into the foyer and paced a few times, then opened the front door and stepped into the unlit common hall. This was the world now. A staircase leading up from the walled-up street entrance, the larger square landing of the second floor, the flights of stairs connecting each level, the narrow landings, the roofs, period. The entire rest of the planet was off limits. *Why does Eddie have to be so nasty*, Dave wondered. *We're all under pressure. We're all in the same boat around here, not like he's the only one who's suffering, the only one who's hungry, the only one who's afraid.*

Dave trudged downstairs to the sealed-up foyer. In the pitch dark he pressed his back against the almost-cool cinder blocks, girding himself for physical punishment. Better to not dwell on Eddie and his foul moods and fouler humor. That kind of shit had been funny in the locker room before and after a game, but now it cut deeper, seemed uglier. In the dark, Dave calmed down and collected himself. "Work it off," he said, then inhaled and exhaled deeply several times. Midway through a half-assed stretch his elbow touched something clammy and fleshy and he let out a very womanish screech.

"Work what off?" came the drab, croaky response.

"Jesus," Dave barked, "don't *do* that. Hey, who *is* that? Who the hell hangs out in the dark? You trying to give someone a freakin' heart attack?"

"Work what off?" The croaky voice was neither masculine nor feminine. It reminded Dave of the possessed girl's in *The Exorcist*. The question was posed without any urgency or even curiosity. It sounded mechanical. That's what made it so disturbing.

"Jesus Christ. *Gerri.*"

With his heart audibly thudding in his chest Dave began jogging up the stairs, taking each landing, then the next flight, and so on, up to the roof door. When he got there he hesitated for a moment, then gave it a loud rap with his knuckles and threw it open. Dabney was there, sitting in the shade of the stairwell, reading a battered paperback.

"Yo, John, mind if I do some laps?"

"Knock yourself out, kid," Dabney said, returning his attention to the book he'd borrowed from Alan. As Dave began to jog north, Dabney added, "But not literally. I don't wanna have to haul your carcass downstairs." Then he chuckled. Same joke, different day. Different day that might as well be the same, for all intents and purposes.

Goddamn Gerri Leibowitz, Dave thought. Eddie had dubbed their old neighbor The Wandering Jewess, a haggish woman with an explosion of ratty grayish brown hair radiating from her seemingly vacant head. Sometimes she was stark naked, sometimes she wore a thin housecoat, and always she toted around the withered carcass of her dead Yorkshire terrier, cradling it like a baby. She had no fixed abode, sometimes sleeping in the neighboring building from whence she'd originated, sometimes in the halls, sometimes the roof—though not Dabney's. He didn't cotton to her at all. Gerri would occasionally spend a night or two in one of 1620's vacant apartments.

Though comprised of all the fleshly ingredients, in essence she was a ghost.

Dave and Eddie had come over from three buildings north, when that building was breached. The zombies had flooded in and made short work of the residents on the lower floors. Dave and Eddie escaped, just barely. Since then, the rooftop door to the stairwell of that building was solidly blocked. No one could forecast which building Gerri would materialize in from day to day. Didn't much care, either, but she was a perpetually unnerving presence.

Dave built up enough speed to use the short walls dividing the roofs as hurdles. The sun lashed his bare back and sweat poured off him like a race horse. This was stupid. He knew this was stupid. Who was he trying to keep in shape for? Himself? The end was nigh, as the Bible thumpers put it. Why even attempt to stay fit? He was a rail, each muscle, each tendon, each ligament, each vein and artery stood out in sharp relief. He was a walking—jogging to be more precise—anatomical chart. This wasn't definition. This was depletion. Everyone in the building had a six-pack.

Six-pack.

Just the phrase made Dave want to bawl. How sweet would a six-pack be right about now? Some tasty ice-cold beer? As perspiration beaded and ran down his hairless chest, Dave imagined himself a tall, amber bottle of Bud, his sweat sexy commercial-style condensation on a flagon of his favorite brew. And began to cry.

6

February, *Then*

"This'll pass. You watch."

"I dunno," Dave said, then took a swig off his Stella Artois. Eddie and he sat side by side at the bar, both watching the muted television suspended over the liquor shelf. Since both sets were tuned to FOX there was no need for sound, the text tickers scrawling across the screen covering the major points in bullet form. Dave's stomach was double knotted and the beer wasn't helping. He drank it anyway.

"You dunno," Eddie sneered. "Have a little faith. The government'll take care of it."

"That's funny, coming from you, Mr. Libertarian."

"Hey, I'm what you call a *social* libertarian. I just don't want no one tellin' me who I can and can't screw, what I can and can't drink, or if I wanna smoke a doob or do a bump I gotta go to jail for that shit. The government should keep its nose outta my private fuckin' business, know what I'm sayin'?"

"But they can bail us out when bad shit happens, huh?"

"Catastrophic disaster shit? That's right. That's their fuckin' *jobs*, bro'. Our tax dollars at work. Send in the fuckin' Marines."

Dave was about to point out that they didn't have any Marines left to send in any more, but bit his tongue and took another mouthful of beer. Most of our troops were still abroad, the National Guard was spread thinner than an Olsen twin and chaos was erupting everywhere. Footage of cities on fire—entire *American* cities—filled the wide screen monitors. Dave was accustomed—indifferent, even—to seeing foreign cities ablaze, but American ones? It was bad enough when the towers came down, but this was epic. Presently, footage of St. Louis in flames was splashed across the screen, the visibly shaken anchorwoman—he'd heard they were called "sprayheads" in the news biz—mouthing silently. He could lip-read enough to catch the gist, and the worry was creasing her copious makeup. It had been the same all day: an epidemic of violence and cannibalism. Ridiculous sounding, but there it was.

"This is your WMDs," Eddie said. "Right there, in HD. This is some chemical shit the sand niggers cooked up in some fuckin' cave. Our guys'll come up with the antidote and then we'll get payback."

"Where'd you get that from?" Dave asked.

Eddie pointed at the ticker. Dave wasn't so sanguine about the source of this mayhem, nor about getting revenge. According to the news—and on this point there seemed to be no dissenting views—the state of affairs was global. What was happening here in New York was happening in Paris and Tehran and Madrid and Hong Kong and so forth. Still, the cause was up for conjecture and debate and people needed to assign blame. What good was a crisis if you couldn't say, "It's so-and-so's fault"?

From outside the bar the assortment of unsettling noises grew louder. A concussion rocked the small building, spilling Eddie's beer in his lap.

"Fuck this shit."

"I think we should head home," Dave suggested, not wanting his mounting terror to show too much. Eddie looked at his emptied mug and wet lap and rose from his stool without a word.

The twosome hesitated at the door. An SUV plowed down some pedestrians in a mad attempt to beat the light, sending bodies flying through the air, one thudding against the plate glass window, adding a red smear to the pink neon glow.

"Jesus!" Dave shrieked.

The bartender, an old school drink slinger with a permanent scowl, grabbed his keys and a sawed-off shotgun from under the bar. "I let you out you're out for good," he said. "I ain't lettin' ya back in, no matter what I see happenin' out there. You're on your own."

"Uh-huh," Eddie said.

"I'm serious." He turned to face the others at the bar. "Anyone else wanna leave, now's the time. After these two, you stay until they says otherwise an' that's it. Lockdown time at Casey's."

A couple of other patrons polished off their drinks and plodded over to the door, reluctant to put the barkeep's edict to the test. The rest stayed put, watching the televisions, gorging on chicken wings. Eddie and Dave locked eyes and like they'd done before matches, punched each other on the shoulders.

"You ready for this shit?" Eddie said, uncertainty tingeing his voice.

"No," Dave said, opting for honesty.

"You'll be all right." Eddie smiled. "You're with me."

"Awright," the bartender said. He undid the lock and pushed open the door a hair. "Get out, quick." As an afterthought he added, "An' good luck." Then he pulled the door shut and locked it behind them. Eddie and Dave lived across the avenue and halfway up the block, but that short distance looked like an uphill battle, even though it was downhill. Dave looked south and saw black smoke rising from various unseen fires. The body that had hit the window lay dead a few feet away, its head collapsed from the double impact. A military troop transport rumbled up York Avenue with little regard for the foot traffic that surged around it in blind panic.

"See?" Eddie beamed, "Here comes the fuckin' cavalry!"

The vehicle roared by and Dave and Eddie saw bloodied bodies affixed to the sides, scratching at the armored plating. The bodies looked broken but agitated. A man clung to the side, his head facing away from the truck, twisted one hundred and eighty degrees the wrong way. Drool and blood hung in long swaying loops from his shattered jaw. As the truck passed, Dave and Eddie gaped as they saw the troops inside being attacked and consumed by similar assailants. With another, "Fuck this shit," Eddie took off in the wake of the truck, which momentarily cleared a path. Dave followed, slipping once or twice on fresh blood that leaked from the vehicle. They were more like Custer's cavalry, with York Avenue as Little Bighorn and the infected as the Sioux and Cheyenne.

As Eddie fished for his keys at the front door to their building a freshly reanimated little girl, no more than five or six, sprang up and attempted to bite his forearm through his thick leather coat. Eddie knew this kid. Not by name, but he'd seen her and her mom in Carl Schurz Park. Her mom was a bona fide MILF and he'd always slowed his jog to get an eyeful of her cleavage. The kid had been cute, too, though more than once he'd seen her pitching a fit for ice cream or cookies. Now the kid's blood-streaked face was contorted into a parody of childish greed, and human meat was all she craved. One eye bulged from its socket, the white showing all the way around the iris.

Without a moment's hesitation Eddie punched her square in the face, shattering the small skull within. She dropped to the pavement, disoriented but not motionless. Twitching, she rocked herself side to side, like an upside-down turtle.

"Fuckin' cuntlet!" Eddie bellowed, examining the bite marks. Assured he was uninjured, he raised his foot and stomped on her head, splattering bone and brain onto the sidewalk. Dave froze a few feet shy of the episode, raising his hands to his mouth. Eddie unlocked the vestibule door and with great impatience shouted, "You in or out, Dave?"

Dave sidestepped the stain that used to be a little girl and, once safely inside the entrance hall, puked. He then looked helplessly at Eddie, who was examining his bare forearm. A little discoloration from the bite was evident, but that was all.

"If that little cunt didn't still have her milk teeth I might be in trouble," Eddie said, brow creased as he mulled this over. "Seriously. That was close."

"Yeah," Dave said, wiping his mouth.

Their neighbor, Gerri, stood at the top of the steps, looking bedazzled. As they stepped past her onto the second floor landing she pointed at the vomit.

"You can't leave that there. It's unsanitary."

"Yeah, yeah," Eddie grumbled.

Gerri's Yorkie, Cuppy, skittered down the stairs and began lapping up Dave's sick.

"Sorry," Dave murmured. "I'll get it later."

7

July, *Now*

"Do something, you piles of pus."

Even before things got as bad as they'd gotten, Abe Fogelhut knew the drill. He was eighty-three years old, the TV and radio were shot, he'd never been much of a reader—except for the occasional paper, and even there it was strictly the *Post* or the *News*, never the hoity-toity bleeding-heart *Times*—so he did what old people do: he sat by the window and watched the world putrefy, counting off the minutes until the final letdown. If he had any balls he'd have hurried the process up. Why forestall the inevitable?

Because as lousy as this life was, this was all you got.

The final reward was finality, period. Except these days it wasn't, so death had lost some of its appeal.

So Abe did what he did. Today, much like the day before, and the day before, and the day before that. He'd arranged his frail, emaciated body into a semblance of comfort in the threadbare up-holstered chair, parted the dingy chintz curtains, opened the dusty venetian blinds and took his position as eyewitness to nothing. The throng milled about—same old, same old. Nothing ever changed.

Even the ache in Abe's empty belly had quieted to a dull numbness. He'd actually welcome the sharpness of the hunger pangs, but you can get used to anything. And that was the problem. He was used to the way things were.

With some effort, Abe opened the window, leaned his head out a little, worked up some glutinous saliva and spat into the mindless crowd directly beneath his fifth-floor dwelling. The thick, pasty blob plopped onto one thing's noggin and the schmuck didn't even have the decency to notice, to become outraged or even annoyed. They never reacted. Abe sighed with resignation and eased back from the window, repositioning himself in his seat. "This is what it comes down to," he muttered. "This is what passes for entertainment in this hollow semblance of a world. *Feh.*" He mashed his head back into the cushion and clamped his eyes shut, grinding his already nubbin teeth, taking shallow breaths. "What's the point?" he moaned. "What's the goddamn point?"

"What's the point of what?"

"Exactly."

Ruth shuffled into the room, her slippers shushing against the worn carpeting. He kept his eyes shut. She was unbearable to look at. The skin under her sharp jaw was a loose curtain, whatever nasty business lurked beneath barely hidden by her translucent epidermis. Abe could avoid looking at himself. He didn't bother with mirrors any more, not since he stopped shaving. His whiskers had itched at first, but they concealed the sins of his lank flesh so they earned their keep. Plus, why waste water these days? For the sake of vanity? Vanity was outmoded folly, even in light of the facial hair. Abe smelled like the old parchment he resembled, his skin felt like membranous cheap leather. He'd stopped changing clothes on a daily basis weeks ago. Why bother? He'd stopped bathing before that, except to wipe a damp sponge in a desultory manner under his pits and over his balls and ass.

But to see Ruth in the same situation was intolerable. She'd always taken such pride in her appearance. She had been vain, back when vanity wasn't such a futile pursuit. Now she looked like a wizened mummy sheathed loosely in drab Kmart dressing. If Abe had anything in his belly to vomit up upon seeing her, he would, as a eulogy to her former beauty.

"What's the point of what?" Ruth repeated.

"Of anything. Of everything. Of answering that question."

"Then what's the point of asking it every day?"

"Exactly. Exactly so."

"I hate talking to you when your eyes are closed," Ruth complained.

"I hate talking to you when my eyes are open."

Weeks ago that rejoinder might have brought tears to Ruth's eyes, but she knew what Abe meant, and if she had any more tears to cry she still might shed a few, but she was dry as the Sahara. Abe listened to Ruth hobble back out of the living room and gradually opened his eyes again to stare out the window. Though Jewish in name, he'd always been an atheist, and nothing he'd ever seen or experienced dissuaded him from that. This was it. This was all you got. So, he'd live as long as possible, and when the time came that he keeled over in his chair from starvation and dehydration, at least he'd be able to say to himself that he'd ridden it out.

Whatever that's worth.

It wasn't like he didn't envy the dumb bastards who had faith. They were the lucky ones. They just assumed, even in light of the nonstop reality show outside, that when you died your soul departed for a better place. Those ambling piles of rot out there were just empty husks.

In the kitchen, Ruth foraged in the cupboard. They still had a few tiny provisions, most provided by the generosity of their neighbors, but those would soon be depleted. There was a box of melba toast, some peanut butter, a can of lima beans, a can of SpaghettiOs and an individual stick of Slim Jim beef whatever-it-is. There were also three plastic gallon jugs of water. The pipes were as arid as she was, so they no longer bothered to test the faucet. All it did was groan, and if she wanted to hear that noise she'd stay in the living room and listen to Abe.

Unlike her husband, Ruth's faith had come back to her, and that was before things had turned to shit. Around the time of her mother's death, Ruth had renewed her bond to Judaism, which had caused much consternation in her husband, who thought she was cured of that foolishness.

When Ruth turned sixty-six, her mother, Ida, ninety-two and more vegetable than animal, finally gave up the ghost. At the time of her death, Ida's age and weight were the same; she was bedridden, had virtually no brain function and, if this was possible, looked worse than Ruth looked currently. Prior to her actual demise, bits of Ida had predeceased her in the form of amputated limbs gone sour from gangrene due to poor circulation.

At the time it had put Abe in the mind of an old World War II joke about a captive American in a German POW camp who is on work duty fixing the roof in the rain. He slips while mending a hole and catches his leg on a rusty nail. He ends up losing the leg and re-quests that the guard send it back to the States to be buried. The guard is sympathetic and honors the request. The same POW is back on work detail and fixing another roof hole when the same thing happens. He loses the other leg and makes the same request, which is also honored. The POW, now legless, is on work detail in the lumber mill. He is feeding planks through a table saw and loses an arm. He makes the same request to have the limb sent back to the States for burial. This time the guard denies the appeal. "But why?"

the POW asks. "Because," the guard says, "the commandant thinks you are attempting to escape, piece by piece."

That joke lost its appeal as old lady Ida escaped piece by piece from the Golden Acres Assisted Living Facility of Maspeth four times—plus she'd gone blind from diabetes, was incontinent, lost the power of speech, didn't know who the hell she was, where she was, if she was. And as one terrible thing after another befell Ida, Ruth began going to the local temple to make her peace with God. By the time Ida mercifully kicked the bucket—no mean feat considering she *had* no feet—Ruth was very active in the temple and Abe was very alienated from his wife. They lived together, but apart. It would have bothered him more if he was still sexually attracted to her, but that part of their relationship had "escaped" long ago. He'd watched Ida's nightmarish living putrefaction and thought to himself many times, *There is no God.* Ida had never been his favorite person, but no one should have to go through what she did before snuffing it. He wouldn't wish that on Hitler.

Well, maybe Hitler.

And Stalin.

But that's about it.

From outside, a guttural yawp burst the bubble of silence and Abe heaved himself to the window in time to watch the spectacle blossom below. This was new: one of the pus bags had sunk his teeth into another, much to his victim's consternation. As the aggressor tore out a chunk of the other's rotting flesh, both uttered unutterably foul noises, setting off a wave of restlessness through the normally torpid crowd. The antagonist choked down the chunk of fetid flesh, quaked a little, then vomited it back up. A spastic skirmish ensued.

"You gotta see this!" Abe shouted. "Hey, honey . . . ," *old habits die hard*, ". . . these sons of bitches have finally started in on each other!" Abe clapped his hands in delight. "They're evolving! Soon the miserable bastards will be at each other's throats, just like regular people!" Abe began laughing and coughing simultaneously.

"What's so great about that?" Ruth said.

Abe caught his breath, sighed, and squinted at Ruth. "You really know how to suck the joy out of the moment."

"How is that joyful? What is joyful about those things attacking each other? It's horrible. They're horrible."

"Irony is lost on you, Ruth. You never could handle it. It's funny to me, see, because in spite of all the terrible things you could say about those sacks of waste out there, they always seem to get along, even if it's completely mindless. But now they're pushing and shoving. Even dead and reanimated we're hardwired for odium. Even those brain-dead heaps of flesh eventually manifest hostility toward each other. It's the human way to be inhuman."

"And that's a good thing?"

"Just go away, Ruth. Let me enjoy this. Forget I said anything. Please."

Abe poked his head back out the window.

Things were back to normal. No pushing. No shoving. No turbulence. Just the usual vegetable parade. He mashed his head into the upholstery and, eyes shut, pondered the quiet. Once upon a time he'd have cherished such silence but not now. He missed the sound of traffic. The buses that used to run along York, even their whining hydraulics.

Sitting there, eyes closed, a faint sound wafting past the discolored chintz oozed into Abe's ears; one in addition to the brainless lowing of the shamblers. One that he couldn't place, dull and echoey. With effort Abe disengaged from the chair and craned his head out, looking north—*nada*—then south—*bingo*! Something was plowing uptown through the crowd, weaving past abandoned vehicles left at jagged angles. As it approached the sound amplified. Thumping. "The hell?" Abe said to himself. It was moving at a decent clip. A car. No, *taller.* One of those mini-SUVs, only he couldn't hear the roar of an engine over the wet thud of rickety bodies jouncing off its hard surfaces. Maybe a hybrid; they ran silent.

Abe wanted to shout to its pilot but there was no point; that machine wasn't stopping for anything. But unless those things had learned how to drive, at least there was evidence of life beyond this sapped bunch. As it neared the building Abe got a good, albeit fleeting, look at the vehicle. The front end was a dark mass of blood-drenched concavities. Though he was pretty certain those things didn't feel panic, it was clear they weren't thrilled with becoming temporary hood ornaments as they were bounced up off the pavement, or ground up below.

As the small sport ute plowed northwards it hit the shell of a dead car masked by the crowd. The savage impact echoed through the canyon of buildings and again Abe witnessed a driver explode through his windshield. "Poor bastard," Abe sighed, anticipating the crowd swarming on the mangled driver, ripping him to shreds as the entrée du jour. But they didn't. An aperture opened in the crowd before the now-smoking wreck of his ride.

"What the hell?" Abe said, confounded.

The zombies were spreading out, away from the area where the driver's body lay. Abe couldn't see him, he was out of range and masked by the multitude, but there was no doubt they weren't all swarming him. A bestial moaning came from that direction, making the hairs on Abe's neck rise. "That's new," he gasped.

With reluctance, he tore himself away from the window as Ruth entered the room.

"What was that?" she cried.

"A crash," he said. "A car. It crashed. I gotta see if anyone else is seeing this."

As he left the apartment Ruth shuffled over to where he'd been for her own look. In the hall there was a commotion of voices. Abe heard Karl shout something about the roof and in spite of his protesting legs, he hied upstairs. As he neared the top few steps an explosion rocked the building and he gripped the handrail to avoid tumbling back down.

"My heart," he sputtered.

When he stepped onto the tar paper he saw black smoke churning up from below. Energy spent, he shuffle-jogged the rest of the way, joining some of the other men at the edge of the roof.

"I didn't think hybrids blew like that," he panted.

"The car he hit did," Karl clarified. "Anyway, why do you think it was a hybrid?"

"I didn't hear the engine."

"Engine was makin' plenty of noise," Dabney said. "You're just a bit deaf, old-timer."

Abe was about to protest, but Alan shouted, "Are you guys nuts? Who cares what kind of car that was? A person's dead!"

"Yeah, and they weren't eating him," Karl added.

"Maybe," Dabney said.

"I saw it, too," Abe confirmed. "They were spreading out. It was weird."

"Maybe they smelled some leaky gasoline," Dabney countered. "Backed off 'cause they knew it was gonna blow."

"That's giving them an awful lot of credit," Karl said.

"Animals know when trouble's afoot," Dabney said. "Thunderstorms and earthquakes. We don't know dick about those things except they like eating us. They could have all kinds of animal cunning. Some heightened senses. They can smell blood."

Hearing that, Alan thought about Mike and turned to go downstairs to check on Ellen, who'd popped an Ambien or two earlier and was out like a light. Just as well. Two fresh kills in rapid succession would be too much. As he passed back into the building the others continued to debate what they'd just witnessed.

"Too much excitement for one day," he said to himself.

As he let himself back into Ellen's apartment, Eddie and Dave tore out of theirs and Alan was grateful, at least, to have avoided them.

8

Alan stared across the queen-size mattress at Ellen, who slept peacefully. He didn't know how to feel. When he'd come back in, through her Ambien-induced haze she'd burbled something dreamily at him, and before he knew it they'd been a tangle of naked limbs. Mike had died a scant few hours earlier. Died was the least of it. That made it seem peaceful—in their current predicament almost enviable. He'd been *devoured*, and here Alan lay, in Mike's bed, perhaps even on Mike's side—chances were that Ellen snoozed in her normal spot, so Alan was occupying a dead man's very personal real estate. Talk about fate tossing him a live grenade.

Ellen's body, even dissipated, still held attraction for Alan. Okay, it was a sort of hot emaciated-supermodel Buchenwald kind of sexiness, but she still had that certain indefinable something that put lead in Alan's pencil. Thinking of pencils, Alan grabbed one and a scratch pad and began to sketch her.

Gone were the pleasing soft curves, but if he could get into an Egon Schiele state of mind he could do some good work. Some people found Schiele's work erotic. Alan didn't happen to be one of them, but one must adapt to the here and now. Ellen's areolas and nipples were dusky, almost burgundy, in sharp contrast to her pale skin. Her wasted breasts pooled on her chest, flattened empty sacs, yet he'd sucked on them like they dispensed the antidote. Unlike the others, Ellen steered clear of the roof and had gotten paler and paler in the weeks past. The triangular patch of black pubic hair stood out in sharp relief against her ashy skin, thick and matted with sweat and the commingled fluids of their lovemaking.

It didn't feel like love. It had felt desperate, rapacious, panic stricken, violent. It had also been the first pleasurable expenditure of energy Alan could remember since everything turned rotten. Even with their bones grinding together it was the fulfillment of a bygone wet dream. *Fee! Fi! Fo! Fum! I smell the blood of an Englishman. Be he 'live, or be he dead, I'll grind his bones to make my bread,* Alan remembered from childhood. *What the hell kind of fucked-up thing is that to teach a kid? Grind his* bones *to make my* bread? What kind of bread is that? And now the things out there wanted to do the same basic thing, only skip the carbs. We'll just eat you alive, thanks all the same.

Alan's drawing was not turning out the way he wanted. Ellen looked twisted and knotty, her contours convex where they oughtn't be, concave likewise. Her tangle of brunette curls a greasy amorphous blob, obscuring her face save for one closed eyelid tinted dark as a shiner. She looked as if she'd been elongated on the rack like some accused heretic during the Inquisition. His pencil said Ticonderoga but it might as well have read Torquemada by the way it rendered Alan's fluky new girlfriend. The First Grand Inquisitor of Spain would have been proud to reduce a human being to Ellen's pitiful status—all in a day's work in the name of the Lord. The problem with the drawing was that it was perfect. It looked just like her.

Ellen didn't need to see this. Alan crumpled the drawing and tossed it out the window, where it landed right on the blood-smeared spot on which Mike had met his fate. *What would Goya do?* Alan wondered. The phrase reminded Alan of those WWJD bumper stickers and T-shirts and friendship bracelets and whatever else they emblazoned that catchphrase on. *What Would Jesus Do?* Well, from the looks of things, he'd abandon his precious flock and let them rot. Good thing Alan didn't believe in that nonsense or he'd be pretty disenchanted with the Almighty.

Back to Goya and an artist's duty. Though he did plenty of pretty canvases, ol' Francisco didn't shy away from capturing ugliness. Alan thought of Goya's painting, *Saturn Devouring One of his Sons.* In it, the mythological giant grips the partially dismembered naked body of one of his sons, the giant's eyes insane with paranoia and perhaps a tinge of grief as he gnaws off his progeny's head. Alan had plenty of firsthand experience seeing bodies being dismembered—and documenting them. In his apartment he had several walls covered top to bottom with drawings and paintings he'd done of the mob outside, both individual and group studies. He was the Audubon of the undead—keeper of the visual record of humanity's demise.

But for whom?

Who would look at these renderings? The likelihood of future generations was pretty much nil. Time travelers? Space aliens? No, this was art for art's sake. Like the need to breathe and eat, Alan had discovered he was predisposed to do art. He'd always wondered how pure his drive was. Did he merely create in order to impress others? He'd mostly done work for print. Now there was no audience. For a while he thought he'd only do art if there were remuneration upon completion. What a price to pay to confirm one's dedication. His apartment was a gallery devoted to but a single theme: *THE END.* Pencil drawings, pastels, pen and ink, a few watercolors, which strictly speaking weren't done with water. Not with their water shortage. He used urine, which worked out fine. The yellow pigment added authenticity to the subject matter. At least he could work in oils. Plus, the thinner got him a bit high.

So art still had its little dividends.

And he'd bagged the model of his dreams.

Who now stirred.

"*Mmmmm*," she purred. "Hello."

Speaking of high, Ellen looked a trifle baked. He wondered how many Ambiens had she'd taken, then choked back the notion that she'd maybe tried to join Mike. Her eyes swam in their hollows, unfocused. As she blinked herself back to cognizance she looked confused, rabbity.

"You're not Mike. What are *you* doing here?" Her query was accusatory. She shook her head, attempting to reengage her brain. "I'm sorry. I'm sorry. Mike's dead. Mike's dead now. Alan. I'm sorry." She attempted a smile, but her mouth made the wrong shape. "What a day, huh?" A failed attempt at mirth employing the frowsy cadence of a secretary at the water cooler.

"Yeah," Alan mumbled.

"What's that smell?" she said, wrinkling her nose.

"Uh, a fire outside. I'll tell you about it later."

"A fire?" she repeated, eyes still glassy.

"Yeah. It'll keep."

Ellen eased closer to Alan on the rumpled bedclothes and pressed her head against his bare chest. She draped her arms around him. He yearned for his monastic apartment.

"So," she whispered, "are you moving in or not?"

An entreaty.

An invitation.

A trap.

With the pretext of needing some things from his pad, Alan disengaged from Ellen and fled her constricting lair. With nimble assurances he edged out into the common hall and left her standing in her kitchen. At the cessation of the multiple clicks of her dead bolts engaging, the door across the hall swung open and there stood Eddie, looking wry and malevolent with a fishing rod in his hand.

"You don't waste any time, do you?" he leered. "Y'know, I always figured you for queer, but I doff my lid to you, Zotz. You got right in there like a champ and got the booty. Hats off, bud."

"What are you . . . ?"

"Don't play dumb, champ." Waggling the fishing rod to make his point, Eddie held up Alan's smoothed-out crumpled drawing of Ellen. "I did a little fishing in Lake Swenson." He turned the drawing over, its back flecked with bloodstains.

Alan stared at his handiwork in disbelief. "With everything going on outside you rescued that drawing from the alley? Are you fucking insane?"

"Car crashes are a dime a dozen," Eddie said, grinning, "but art is forever."

"*Car crashes are a dime a*—" Alan shook his head like a wet dog trying to make sense of that statement. "What? Name the last time you saw a car driving by."

"Been ages. But it didn't do us any good, did it? Anyway, other sounds were of more interest. Ellen never moaned like that with Mikey boy, I can tell you. Even back in the day."

Alan shoved Eddie into his apartment and closed the door behind them.

"Jesus Christ, Eddie. She might hear you," Alan said, jabbing his finger into Eddie's ditchlike sternum.

"Everyone hears everyone, Casanova. Sound travels. Especially when you're bangin' a screamer. She was making so much noise

I thought she was gettin' eaten alive. I guess maybe she was, actually." Eddie smirked. With a plastic magnetic banana he affixed the drawing to his refrigerator door, admiring it. "Not like the old days, though, huh? Back in the day Ellen had some boasty titties. Well, you make do with what you've got, right? Don't let the perfect get in the way of the good enough."

"Look, don't make a big thing of this, okay?" Alan said, hating the vaguely inveigling tone in his voice. "Ellen has enough on her plate. . . ."

"None of us have enough on our plates," Eddie interrupted.

"I meant figuratively. Jesus. Anyway, this is just a temporary thing. I'm just trying to . . ."

"Get your dick wet. I understand. Dude, if there's anyone in the building who's on your wavelength it's yours truly. That sensitive artist shit worked its hoodoo. I get it. Some chicks dig jocks, some dig nerds. I should've known Ellen was a nerd whore. Just look no further than the late Mikey Swenson. What was his racket? Computers?"

Mike had worked in the IT department at an investment brokerage down on Wall Street, so point to the observant jock.

"Look, just keep it on the DL, all right? Let the woman grieve in peace."

Eddie sniggered. "Okay. On one condition."

Alan sagged. "Name it."

"Keep the nudie art comin'. I want you to keep me supplied with fresh whacking material. I don't know why I didn't think to tap you sooner, what with all other resources being nonexistent. Not like I can log onto Bang Bus any more."

"You want me to do porno art of Ellen for you?" Alan gaped.

"Not just Ellen. And not the way she looks now. I'll come up with some scenarios for you to do up for me. Okay? Okay. Now get the fuck outta my apartment."

Alan traipsed downstairs and fell onto his bed in a daze. This was what prison must be like. Alan had always wondered if he could endure incarceration—especially long term. He figured his only survival skill would be doing pervy fantasy art for the other inmates. The rapists would want rape fantasies. The murderers would want murder fantasies. The hyphenates would want hybridized fantasies, one from column A, three from column B, and so on. And now a blackmailing ex-jock was leaning on Alan for post-apocalyptic pinups.

What would Vargas do?

9

April, *Then*

"She's turning blue, Mike. She's turning fucking blue! You have to do something!"

"What am I supposed to do, Ellie? What? Go to the Duane Reade? Call a doctor?"

Ellen held Emily, barely a year old, and watched her tiny mouth open and close like a fish out of water. She'd wrung every drop of nutrition from her mother and the coffers were nearly bare. Ellen hated rationing, but what else was there to do? Mike was right, what could he do? Go out there? Sure, only ·to never return. Baby in tow, she tromped over to the front windows and radiated hatred at the undead things in the street below, milling about as ever, even in the freezing rain. She threw open the sash and leaned out, sleet stinging her face. She shielded Emily, pressing the small head against her depleted bosom.

"Fuck you all!" Ellen shrieked. "Fuck each and every one of you goddamned parasitic motherfuckers!"

Emily started to cry.

"What are you doing?" Mike bleated as he hastened to the window, grabbing his wife's arm. "You could drop her."

"And what, Mike? *What?* She'd be taken days before her time? Maybe I'd be doing her a favor. Look at this fucking world we've got here. And look at this family. A *balls-less* dad and a *worthless* mom with *sand* in her tits. She's gonna fucking *starve*, Mike. *Starve.* So will we, ultimately, but Emily's got no reserves. She's wasting away. And *blue.*"

" 'Balls-less'?" her husband peeped.

"*That's* what you got from all that? Brilliant."

Over the prickly clatter of sleet the zombies heard the commotion above and stared up at the scene of domestic turmoil, hunger being the only urge left to animate their lifeless eyes. Ellen looked away from Mike back at the throng. She could win this bunch over in a second if she'd just fling herself and the petite hors d'oeuvre in the organic-cotton sling down to them. The lunch crowd would go wild, then move on. She remembered how the world had gaped in stupefaction and revulsion as Michael Jackson dangled his infant son out a hotel window. The multitude below, with their caved-in faces and bleached skin, reminded her of Wacko Jacko, but *she* was the one dangling the baby.

She slumped against the wall beneath the window and joined Emily in tears. Mike closed the sash and crouched down to comfort his girls, but his touch and gentle tone brought none. They were disconsolate and he was, truth be told, *balls-less.* But who wouldn't be? Was it balls-less or just common sense to not leave the building? How could he? Ellen and Emily's wailing grew louder, amplified by Mike's sense of worthlessness. He rose and left the room to get some water for Ellen, but by the time he reached the kitchen, forgot his reason for being there, opened the front door and stepped into the common hall, his own expression as absent as those normally worn by the zombies.

"Quite a racket they're raising," Abe said, gesturing into the door, which hung ajar.

"Huh?" Mike said, his thoughts muddled. He blinked and focused on his neighbors, Abe and Paolo, the good-looking South American from 2B. "Oh, yes. Rough day."

"Aren't they all?" Abe said, earning earnest nods from both younger men.

"Indeed," Paolo added. "These are dark days."

Feeling the need to talk to people who presumably wouldn't scream at him, Mike joined in, though he wasn't feeling very conversational. "They're hungry, Ellen and the baby. Hungry and tired. And frustrated. Ellen wanted me to go out and get supplies, but that's not going to happen."

"And that, my friend, is the difference between your generation and mine," Abe scoffed. "If *I* had a starving child you can bet your last goddamn cent I'd be out the door trying to provide for her, damn the consequences."

"Easy for you to say—," Mike started, but Abe cut him off.

"Damn right it's easy for me to say. As I recall you were home when this all began. Me, I hadda schlep all the way from the garment district to get home. I braved all kinds of madness to get home to my frightened little wifey. Granted, if I'd had some foresight I'd have stopped at the grocers before coming in, but hindsight's twenty-twenty."

"It was different then," Mike stammered. He'd really thought other men would commiserate with him over female troubles; bad to worse.

"Different! Feh. There were those lousy zombies all over then and they're all over now. What, you think they weren't chowing down on everyone in sight that day? Eighty-three years of age, *I* managed to get myself home intact. If any of you young *men*—," the word curdled in Abe's mouth, "—had any *cojones* you'd go out and do what I did. Show the same resourcefulness and—"

Mike was tiring of having his gonads impugned and was about to protest—albeit weakly—when Paolo chimed in, his machismo also under attack.

"*I* have the *cojones,* Abraham," Paolo spat, pique scoring his rugged features.

"Yeah, yeah."

"You challenge me? You saying I don't have the *cojones* of an old man?"

Abe chuckled. "I sure as hell hope you *don't* have a pair like mine."

Paolo's expression softened as Abe winked at him.

"These are dark days," Paolo repeated, a bitter smile sneaking past his anger onto his lips.

"Amen," Abe agreed. The sound of the crying, which hadn't abated, brought the three men back to the matter at hand. "Regardless—and I don't want to get into a shouting match—but the fact remains that there is a woman and a *child* who need sustenance and it's a *man's* job to provide."

Mike's face flushed. Sitting at computer consoles for the last decade hadn't exactly toughened him up or primed him for hunter-gatherer mode. Men of Abe's generation were built differently. They were shaped and hardened by war. Abe was a vet of World War II. Mike's only combat experience involved button mashing on a game controller. Countless hours spent on *World of Warcraft* and *Call of Duty* didn't count. He nudged the door open an inch to look in on Ellie and Em. Though the volume had decreased, both were in a bad way. And Ellie had said Em was blue and meant it literally. The apartment could be warmer and even though they were all wearing layers, they were cold in the damp chill.

"That baby needs to eat," Paolo said, voice steely.

"I know, I know," Mike replied, eyeing his shoes.

"If you are not enough a man to go, I will."

"Now wait a minute—"

"Abraham is right," Paolo said, in his formal, mild accent. "He is an old man and he made it here. He's told us many, many, *many* times of his perilous journey. We were lucky, you and I and some of the others, to be here already, but he and John came late. And they suffered."

Mike was about to assert that they'd all suffered, but point taken. Abe had walked the walk. As an old man was wont to do, he'd recounted his trek often—maybe even embellished a little— but scrawny old Abe Fogelhut had bested all the "young bucks."

"My gear is down in the locker," Abe said, but Paolo waved him off.

"I do not need hand-me-downs, *señor*."

Paolo about-faced and trundled down to his apartment.

"*What?* I insulted him?" Abe scoffed.

"You insulted both of us."

"Shaming isn't the same thing. A little shame is a good thing."

"If you say so."

From their respective windows the residents of 1620 watched Paolo make it halfway across the avenue before being overwhelmed and consumed in his insufficient version of Abe's improvised survival gear.

Abe retired his heroic saga.

A week later, Emily died.

Mike manned up enough to dispose of the petite corpse, sparing Ellen the details. He hoped the wrappings were sufficient to keep the creatures from eating her. But then again, they only seemed to go for live flesh.

Did that count as a blessing?

10

July, *Now*

Karl stood by his open window, looking out across York Avenue. Between the zombies and the abandoned cars, including today's fresh one, the street was so packed you couldn't see the pavement, but Karl knew it was sticky as a movie theater floor in the glory days of Times Square. The street below, however, was shellacked with immeasurable quantities of blood. With the fire having burned itself out, the only noise was the hum of flies and the occasional grunt or moan.

Karl often wished he'd been old enough to enjoy the myriad adult entertainment palaces that had operated freely in the days before "America's Mayor," Rudy Giuliani, had cleaned up the city. It was getting harder and harder to remember "important" figures from the days before the pandemic. Giuliani had been on a mission: to make the city safer and more antiseptic for its citizenry, but mainly for the tourists. New York had endured decades' worth of bad image, fostered by both fact and distortions in the media. America overall had a skewed conception of the Big Apple: graffiti-streaked, litter-strewn, oozing with degenerates of every ilk who were ready to ply their vile talents on wholesome, unsuspecting visitors.

Karl had relocated to New York from Ohio for the express purpose of being plied vilely, but it never happened. Like a nomad in the desert he'd followed a dreamy ignis fatuus of chimerical pendulous bosoms swaying to throbbing disco beats. By the time Karl got to Fun City, however, Times Square no longer resembled the one captured by filmmakers like Martin Scorsese, Paul Morrissey, or even Frank Henenlotter. This Ohio boy had wanted *Taxi Driver*, *Forty Deuce*, and *Basket Case*.

Instead he got *The Lion King*.

Karl got a job, an apartment, and an education in reality versus illusion. And shortly thereafter it all went south. People started dying and coming back and eating each other and the rest was history. Who was to blame? No one knew, or at least no one was saying.

"*Thanks, Mean Joe*," Karl spat, a vicious parrot tormenting himself. "*Thanks, Mean Joe. Thanks, Mean Joe.* Oh yeah, Dabney's really going to welcome me up there again. Beyond thinking that I'm the biggest douche in the world, now he probably thinks I'm a racist. *Thanks, Mean Joe.* What else is he going to think? Stupid dumb stupid-head! Of course some hick from the hinterlands is going to be a cracker redneck racist. I'm just fulfilling my genetic-slash-socioeconomic obligation."

Karl continued to glare at the graceless meat puppets stumbling around beneath his window, more vegetable than animal. Meat. Vegetables. Karl's stomach growled. He wished he had more of Dabney's vermin jerky. Rat. Pigeon. Squirrel. Whatever it was, it was good. The way they meandered down there, individual forms swallowed by the massiveness of the crowd, Karl could cross his eyes slightly and blur the overlapping double image. Meat. Vegetables. The surface pulsated like stew burbling in a boundless Crock-

Pot. Meat. Vegetables. His life had been reduced to a sad homage to those cartoons where starving castaways on a desert island pictured each other as anthropomorphized hot dogs and steaks and hamburgers. Karl's stomach lurched and he cursed himself for having purged Dabney's vittles.

The shadows were beginning to deepen as the sun started setting. Soon the oppressive darkness would spread, drowning everything in pitch black, and another seemingly endless night would begin. Another reason Karl had been seduced by the city was that like heights, the dark was not one of his favorite things. When Karl had first moved here, he loved the fact that the streetlights kept the city bright all night long. Now it was country dark.

Back in Rushsylvania, Ohio—a tiny blip in the already bliplike Logan County—it got so dark at night you couldn't see your hand in front of your face after a certain hour. There had been streetlamps outside, but they didn't saturate everything with that pervasive sodium-vapor lambency that city lights did. For most of his childhood Karl slept with a night-light, much to his father's chagrin. A night-light was a crutch, and Manfred Stempler wasn't raising any cripples, emotional or otherwise. Manfred got the bright idea to go camping in Hocking Hills State Park. Nine-year-old Karl had been dead set against it, preferring to stay home and watch late movies under his blanket on his eleven-inch black-and-white TV.

"Manfred Stempler is not raising a sissy," had been his dear papa's response.

So off they went. Could his father spring for one of the cottages in the park? No way. That wouldn't be "roughing it." A tent was pitched, a campfire was made, and with as much detachment as a spooked nine-year-old could muster, Karl observed his older brother, Gunter, and their father enjoy themselves in the great outdoors. "Is this so bad?" his father kept asking, and though Karl's shaking head said, "No, no, no," his eyes held a different answer. When the last traces of daylight ebbed away, swallowed by the earth and foliage, the campfire's light seemed pitiful and inadequate. The woods made noises. Karl wasn't a superstitious kid, so he didn't believe in monsters—which in light of the current state of affairs was kind of funny—but there were things creeping about, rustling the leaves, crunching the soil, which unsettled Karl.

Small oases of light had dotted the periphery from nearby RVs, accompanied by the purr of generators and the occasional drunken whoop, but it felt like the surface of Mars to Karl. Just because someone is born in the country doesn't mean he's not a city boy by nature. At home he'd secreted away a prized single from destructive Gunter and evangelical "all contemporary music is the devil" Manfred: David Lee Roth's "Yankee Rose." Roth was Manfred's worst nightmare: a sex-charged metropolitan hedonistic Jew in showbiz, put on this Earth to lead impressionable youths—like his sonny boy—down the primrose path to Hell. Karl would listen in secret to Diamond Dave rhapsodize, "*Show me your bright lights, and your city lights, all right!*"

That had been 1986.

And Karl started planning his run from Logan from then on.

New York City was to be his Yankee Rose, resplendent in bright lights, city lights.

Even with its Lugosily ghoulish name, Rushsylvania—population just shy of six hundred—boasted a nearly 100 percent white populace, all good Christian folk. Everyone was pink and fair-haired. His father—Big Manfred—was very active at Rushsylvania Church of Christ on East Mill, epicenter of nowhere. Every Sunday Manfred escorted Karl, Gunter, and their mom, Josephine, into the bland house of worship. White faces upraised praising their lily-white version of Jesus, all soft, mousy brown hair and blue eyes, very European, very not Middle Eastern—very, extremely, super *not* Semitic.

If Christ had been portrayed in art as he actually looked in life,

Christianity never would have caught on. All those generations of European artists westernized the Christ to conform to standards suited to their parishioners' predilections—early market research. A Yasir Arafat-looking spokesmodel wouldn't have put asses on the pews. Pushing the Christ was all about marketing and demographics. But tell that to Big Manny.

And then count on the beating of your life.

For all the times his father whipped out the Bible—and occasionally whipped him *with* it—Karl couldn't remember a single time Big Manfred cracked it open. He wasn't even sure his father could read. But it had made a compelling prop, thick of girth and bound in chipped oxblood leather.

Karl remembered the Lord's Supper service on Sunday mornings—an odd time for supper, but why quibble over details when illogic reigns supreme? The bread, representing Christ's body, cups of juice, representing Christ's blood, passed out to all. Those who believed in Christ as their personal savior were invited to eat the bread and drink the juice that was dispensed. What a ghoulish practice. Though Karl didn't miss that old-time religion, he could go for some of that body and blood right about now. A big heaping helping of Nabisco *Body of Christ*. Yum. *Blessedly bland bites in every box.* He looked at the zombies on York. Mindless, conformist, primed to eat bodies and drink blood.

The sun was almost gone for the day. Five stories below, the seething stew turned a deep burnt umber. Accompanied by a chorus of growls from his abdomen, Karl stalked over to his bed and willed himself to sleep, intoning a sacred hymn.

"She's a vision from coast to coast, sea to shining sea . . ."

11

The deeper Ellen slept the harder she pressed herself into Alan's hollows, her spine folded against his sunken abdomen, the top of her head resting on the manubrium of his sternum. They were "His" and "Hers" anatomical dolls, spooned for easy storage. Or burial. Both were so skeletal they could easily fit together in a standard coffin, with room to spare. And yet her presence was comforting. Alan hadn't expected that. Now back in her apartment, he found the sound of her breathing, though a touch raspy, soothing. At night, beyond the depth of the darkness, the city was chillingly quiet. Even the buzz of the flies abated at nightfall. It was the kind of thought Alan only entertained at night, but he wondered if flies slept.

Somewhere out there, almost imperceptibly, a wind chime occasionally tinkled, a New Age death knell. It meant that somewhere there was a breeze, but that somewhere wasn't here. After a few moments the tinkling abated. To suffer insomnia, as Alan often did, was like a wakeful coma, sensory deprivation with no restorative benefits. At least summer nights were relatively short. If anyone were still alive once winter arrived—a very unlikely prospect—the nights would be unendurable.

Slick with her perspiration, Alan's fingertips traced Ellen's chest, down along her lower abdomen, into her thicket of pubes. He let his hand rest there, cupping her bony mons veneris. Where there should be a rise of fatty flesh there was just taut skin on bone. Alan had liked his women waxed or clean shaven, but now pubic hair was a desirable trait. With no padding, anything to reduce potentially hazardous friction was a good thing. Knocking boots was now knocking bones. He remembered those psychedelic posters of skeletons in various sexual positions, cheesy stoner *Kama Sutra* astrological home décor.

Back in Forest Hills, where Alan had grown up, he had a downstairs neighbor who was the quintessential Deadhead. This guy, Lazlo, traveled all over to hear the Dead warble the same tunes over and over. He had what seemed like thousands of bootleg concert cassettes salted away in chronological order in file cabinets. He grew his own weed. He had a big Jew-fro and wispy teenage mustache. He made his own batik T-shirts. Alan wondered if Lazlo was still alive, and if so, what were his feelings on current affairs? Were the dead outside grateful?

That seemed like such a stoner musing.

Lazlo had the zodiacal humping skeletons poster. And R. Crumb's "Stoned Agin!" The rest were Dead posters by various artists of varying quality.

It was strange not sleeping in his own bed. He was used to lying awake all night downstairs in his place. If he got out of bed he could navigate in the dark. Though the layout of Ellen's apartment was identical to his, the furniture placement was different. He couldn't get up and just instinctively move from point A to point B without lighting a candle, not that there was anyplace to go.

But what if he needed to relieve himself?

That did it. Just the thought made his urethra tingle. Pissing seemed like such a waste of fluid, but was still necessary. The more he thought about it, the hotter Ellen's bony backside burned against his groin, trapping heat, preventing fleeting succor. The less he drank the more it stung to urinate, but it had to be done, even if it felt like passing acid. His insides rumbled with discomfort, the sensation of pins and needles inside his penis magnifying with each passing moment. He had to uncouple from Ellen and take a leak. It was that or piss on her ass, which was not an option—he didn't know her *that* well.

Easing away, Alan's crotch slowly broke free of Ellen's rear end with a moist *shluck*. She made some sleepy mouth noises, smacking her lips, then rolled onto her stomach. Free of contact, Alan maneuvered off the bed, stumbling slightly, as this mattress was farther from the ground than his, then patted the air in front of him, blindly making for the nearest window, not lifting his feet off the ground, shuffle-walking.

Several muted toe stubs later he reached the wall and felt along it. The moon was out and the faintest amount of bluish light outlined the window frame. As he edged to the right he remembered that this was the window Mike had fallen from. *Why tempt fate?* he thought, edging along to the window with the fire escape. As in most New York apartments, a sturdy window gate barricaded this portal, but beyond the gate the window was open and Alan positioned his penis between bars and let fly. The spattering ricocheted off the cast iron stairs, amplified by the all-consuming silence.

Ellen awoke, excited. "Is it raining? Mike? I mean, Alan?"

"No, no. Sorry I woke you. It's only . . . I was taking a leak. Sorry."

"Oh. Oh. It's okay. I just thought . . . Rain would be wonderful, though, wouldn't it? It's been so long. What, like a month, maybe?"

"Almost. It's been dry, that's for sure." Mundane chat about the weather. The more things change . . .

"Yeah. Remember how they used to have water shortages," Ellen continued, "and they'd tell you not to shower for more than five minutes or to not water your lawn in the suburbs. 'Don't wash your cars,' they'd say. Or, 'kids, don't run the fire hydrants! Not during a water shortage!' Those assholes didn't know what a water shortage is." Though the words were sharp there was no bitterness in Ellen's tone. She sounded wistful. "You coming back to bed?"

"I can't sleep."

"Come back to bed and I'll suck your cock."

How could those words, cribbed from every hackneyed porno movie ever made, sound so melancholic and uninviting? Alan's penis, still scorched on the insides from the caustic urine, twitched in expectation. Even now it wanted to do the thinking. No amount of *this is wrong* from the brain could dissuade the little head from wishing to be ministered to. The corpora cavernosa began to fill with blood. *Maybe it will help you sleep*, his penis signaled. *Come on, we're all on the same team. You can't fool me with this self-righteous "gotta do the right thing" hooey. Get me into that mouth and we'll finally get some much-needed rest. Do it.*

"Come back to bed, Alan." And he did.

Ellen lay next to Alan, the sour taste of his ejaculate lingering in her dry mouth. It had been a while since she'd fellated Mike, so she couldn't compare offhand, but it had never been about taste or texture or any criteria she'd applied to other comestibles. But maybe that would change with Alan. Even rawboned, Alan's cock was thicker and firmer than Mike's. And wasn't spooge a source of protein? Protein was hard to come by.

These are the thoughts of a lunatic, Ellen chided internally. *My husband is dead. The father of my dead child, Mike, with his bad posture and small, thin penis is dead. Chunks of him are resting in the alimentary canals of walking corpses that still linger beneath my window. His bones are still in full view from the window. I did nothing. I could have gone up to the roof and gotten bricks from John to drop on the heads of the guilty. I did nothing. My baby died. I did nothing. I'm not a wife. I'm not a mother. I have no career by which to define myself.*

"I *am* nothing," she said aloud.

Alan slept soundly. Good. She'd done some small amount of good. Now it was Ellen's turn to leave the bed, only she knew the lay of the land and made a beeline for the front door, unlocking it. She stepped onto the landing. She could hear Eddie berating Dave behind their front door, but only his tone registered, the dull roar of an underdeveloped mind purging. In the unbroken darkness she plotted the course upward toward the roof without incident. It was only as she stepped onto the tar paper and felt a soft, wonderful breeze across her clammy skin that she remembered she was completely naked. Whatever. She closed her eyes and basked in the gentle caress of the faint airflow.

Though the sky was cloudy there was sufficient moonlight to see their roof, the tarnished reflective silver paint creating an eerie network of geometric outlines to follow. The other roofs, topped in traditional black tar paper, were invisible. It was like she was marooned on a trapezoidal island floating six stories above the ground.

Ellen padded across the rooftop and stood at the lip of the slight incline that led to the roof's west-facing edge. The pitch of the acclivity was maybe thirty degrees or less, wheelchair accessible should someone confined to such a chair wish to roll themselves off the roof to their doom. She was sure that was not the intent of the slope. And besides, the only way up to the roof was the stairs.

There was no wall on the York-side end of the roof, just a faint rise of decorative cornice, then a straight drop. A fall from here might do the trick.

No, she didn't want to join Mike.

Ellen lay on her back, staring up at the moon's pitted face, almost full, but not quite. The air movement felt both invigorating and soothing. It was the middle of July and she wondered if any of them would live to see the fall. And those things on the street, how long would they continue to shamble around? How many survivors were there in Manhattan, or the outer boroughs? Were there other naked women lying on rooftops in the vicinity, staring up at the moon? Or clothed ones? Or men? Or children? If so, was that a comforting thought? What was comforting? That Alan was sleeping in her bed? She wanted Alan there so she wouldn't have to be alone, yet here she was on the roof. Dabney didn't count.

She used to define herself, like zillions of other people, by what she did for a living. Her career. Now her career was living to see the next day, for no discernable reason other than just to do it. Now she was defined by her sex. She and ancient Ruth were the only two females in the building—*maybe the world*. Gerri, the floating wild card, didn't count. She came and went by and large unnoticed.

"Gettin' a moon tan?" came a deep voice from the dark. Dabney.

Whether modesty was démodé or not Ellen felt the flush of embarrassment. It wasn't like Dabney could see much, but her nudity made her feel vulnerable. Ellen shook her head. Like *she* was anything to look at—a flimsy rack of bones held together by a pallid veneer of skin, her slack abdominal skin lightly puckered by a petite frowning cesarean scar. What a fox. She didn't see much of John, not being a habitué of the roof, but he still seemed formidable. At least that was her mental picture.

"S'okay," Dabney said, his voice a baritone purr. "Moon rays don't do any harm. Sun'll just give you cancer, not that it much matters. What's cancer gonna do? Shave a few precious days, maybe hours, off your life?"

"I think I should be going," Ellen said.

"Not on my account, I hope. Only visitors I get up here are the fellas. Nice to hear a sweet voice. One lacking testosterone."

"Oh." Ellen didn't know what else to say.

"How's your lesser half?" Dabney asked.

"Huh?"

"Your lesser half. I'm just joshing. Mike. How's Mike? He hasn't paid me a visit in a while."

"Mike's dead."

A faint breeze filled the awkward silence. Dry leaves rustled in the corners of the roof.

"When did this happen?"

"This morning."

"I didn't know. I'm sorry. With everything on the avenue, nobody said anything. How did it . . . I'm sorry. I don't mean to pry."

"It's okay. Mike fell out the window. I think he broke his neck. He just lay there as they ate him. He was still alive. But not anymore. Just like my baby."

Dabney leaned against the stairwell housing, where he'd been all along, wondering if it was possible to suck all the air out of a room outdoors.

Answer: YES.

12

"You're wasting candles," Ruth scolded.

"I want to read."

"In this light? You'll ruin your eyes. Besides, since when are you a reader all of a sudden?"

"Since there's nothing on television last I checked. Since I can't sleep and I'm tired of inspecting the insides of my eyelids. It's never too late to better yourself, right? So consider me bettering by the second."

"*Ucch*. All right, but do you really need four candles burning?"

"You want I should get eyestrain? You've got me talking like a peasant."

"That's my fault?"

"You used to say I didn't read enough, that reading would better me. So here I am, reading, and now it's 'don't read, you'll ruin your eyes.' You're talking out both sides of your mouth, and with your teeth out it's particularly repulsive."

"Why are you so cruel?"

"It's all I have left. *Feh*. You need your beauty sleep, fine. I'll adjourn to the sitting room, your majesty."

A clap of rainless thunder taunted them as Abe grabbed the platter on which the candles were arranged and left the room. *Tsuris* he did not need. He'd borrowed a couple of books from the kid in 3A, some cockamamie science-fiction *chozzerai*, but it was diverting enough. The writer, a fellow named Philip K. Dick, seemed bent on doling out as much torture as possible to his characters. Abe enjoyed others suffering even worse than he. At least Abe knew where the hell he was—he was situated in his misery. The poor schmuck in Dick's book didn't know whether he was coming or going; his reality kept shifting on him. What a lousy predicament. It was a riot.

Another sequence of rolling thunder followed him down the hall. "So rain already," he griped. "Enough with the foreplay."

Mixed in with the thunder were other sounds. A crash followed by the peppering of ruptured safety glass on pavement. That accompanied by the plaint of countless zombies.

"The natives are restless," Abe said with a smirk. "It's a regular hootenanny out there."

In the bedroom, Ruth stared into the void. Abe wasn't always easy to deal with, but at least he wasn't always such a bastard, either. She'd been spoiled, she realized, by all his years away at work. She'd kept a few jobs here and there in her younger days, but they were usually part-time and often for relatives. Sure it was nepotism, but for such lousy pay, who'd make a fuss? She worked a little at a travel agency (Uncle Judah); a printing plant (cousin Sol); a catering hall (cousin Moshe); a small-time talent agency (cousin Tobias). When Abe came along she became a full-time housewife, then an overtime mother. Three children she'd raised, almost single-handedly.

That wasn't a job?

Abe made her feel like she was living the pampered life of a queen because she didn't have to schlep to an official place of work. Sure, Abe brought home the bacon—all right, not bacon; they kept kosher, give or take—but Ruth slaved, too. And for the meager allowance Abe doled out? It was indentured servitude. Even when they got along she'd prayed for liberation. Where was her own personal Moses to lead her to the Promised Land? Three children, and God only knows where they were or what their fates were. Was it too much to ask of God to at least know? Were Miriam, Hannah, and David even among the living? In her head she thought it possible, but in her heart, and more persuasively in her gut, she doubted it. So that meant the grandchildren were gone, too.

When God doled out the punishment he really laid it on thick, but she *believed*.

Ruth believed because of the absoluteness of the fate of mankind. The scientists had their theories, back in the first few weeks, before the television and the radio were kaput, but the theories didn't hold much water. Biotoxins. Germ warfare. Terrorism. Advanced mutated Creutzfeldt-Jakob disease. Anthropoid spongiform encephalopathy.

No.

This was the work of a vengeful god. This was the work of a god who'd had enough, and who could blame Him? People had been doing terrible things ever since they arrived on the scene, but in just the span of her lifetime it went from not so good to bad to worse to unimaginable. Politicians got slimier and greedier and less trustworthy. Wars weren't waged for noble causes, they were pecuniary agendas. The younger generations kept getting stupider and more selfish and less humane. Popular culture was all in the toilet. Bad language was rampant. Overt pornographic imagery had infiltrated regular television—Ruth didn't know from cable firsthand, but from what she'd heard it had been the telecast version of Sodom and Gomorrah.

Craziness.

Gone were any kind of values one could hold dear. The people of her generation were shunned by society. The only ones who cared at all about them were the politicians, and that was only because the older generation still got out and voted. So, politicians and the pharmaceutical companies. Everyone else just was biding their time waiting for all the seniors to drop dead and vacate apartments like this one. Geriatrics and gentrification didn't often cozy up. But that was just a personal beef. Donald Trump and his ilk didn't erect the real estate that mattered. The Tower of Babel had been built again, at least metaphorically, and this time God was playing for keeps.

God had had enough of his naughty children.

Death was near, Ruth felt. Abe would be in for a rude surprise when he found out his soul would continue to exist even after his mortal form didn't. In the next world—*Olam HaEmet*: "the World of Truth"—he'd have to answer for all his bile when they played back his life for him. Abe wasn't a bad person—mean, maybe, but not evil—but his lack of faith would surely not be looked on with favor. *Gehenom* awaited Abe. It wasn't hell, and he could move on, but he'd have to do some serious soul-searching—literally—to purify his untidy soul.

The depiction of the afterlife wasn't explicit in the Torah. That's where the goyim had it made. It was so black and white. They got scary fire and brimstone if they were bad or the Pearly Gates and Paradise if they were good. The Torah was more enigmatic. As a good Jew you were supposed to focus on your role in this, the material world. An eternal reward was a vague but effective motivator to stay on the correct path. All Ruth knew was that the soul went on for eternity and that was good enough for her. She just hoped that

Abe would get his act together and make peace with God so they could link up in this nebulous afterlife.

And the children and grandkids.

And maybe Cary Grant.

Sure he was *treyf*, but *oof*.

Abe held the book close to the candle, straining to read the small print. Though he enjoyed Dick kicking the crap out of his poor deluded bozos in their subterranean Martian hovels, drugged to the gills with their little Perky Pat doll setups, the pain in his eyeballs negated the pleasure. Besides, he was actually envious of these fictional characters. Sure they'd been forcibly evicted to live on Mars—which was a complete crudhole—but at least they could get bombed out of their gourds and have these collective fantasy trips courtesy of some kooky hallucinogenic drug called Can-D. Or was it Chew-Z? It was both. Whatever. It was a crazy book, but Abe found himself embroiled in its labyrinthine plot. Dick was a nut, but an imaginative nut.

He put the book down and closed his eyes and rubbed them—hard. With spots and tiny patterns of organic hieroglyphs swimming on his orbits, Abe sat back in the chair by the window and enjoyed the fireworks. Abe rubbed some more, even though it was supposedly bad for you. When he pulled his hands away and opened his eyes again, flashes of light joined the spots and indecipherable microscopic pictographs. A distant clap of thunder echoed throughout the dead city, followed by a chorus of idiot groans from the undead. Abe blinked and pretended he was crocked on Dick's wonderdrugs.

"I'm on Mars," he whispered. "I'm in my hovel. Where's my dolly?"

As the spots and runes melted away Abe realized the light

wasn't self-induced. Lightning? No, this flash of light cut right across his ceiling. From below. *What the hell?* Abe manually un-crossed his sleeping legs, flung himself out of his chair and hobbled on limbs of pins and needles toward the window. Just as he hung his head out a swath of light was cutting across the tops of all the cabbage-heads, forging south—*a flashlight beam!*

"Jesus H. Christ! Jesus H. Christ!" Abe gasped. He ducked his head back in and shouted, "Ruth! Hey! Ruth!" Another small thun-derclap swallowed his thin voice. "God damn it! *Ruuuuuth!*"

"What? What is it already?" Ruth screeched from the bedroom. "You'll wake everyone!"

"Good! Come in here! Quick!"

"What is it?"

"Come in here!"

Abe was trembling all over. He leaned back out the window and shouted at the departing beam of light. As it receded down York the horde seemed to spread out before it, creating a path.

"Hey, wait!" he shouted, his frail voice swallowed by another burst of thunder. In his ferment he launched into a convulsive coughing fit, his watery eyes following the light until it disappeared from sight. Now his coughing tears mixed with tears of despair.

"What's the commotion?" Ruth whined. Though she was shrouded in darkness Abe could picture her bitter, disbelieving face. "What're you dragging me out of bed for?" Her mental image of Cary Grant faded into nothingness.

"There was a light out there!" Abe said, gesturing at the street below, wiping his eyes.

"A light."

"A light, for Christ's sake. A light! A light!"

"Abe, it's thundering out there. Ever hear of a little thing called lightning?"

"It wasn't lightning. It came from down there! *Down* there! Not *up* there! *Down!*"

Ruth sighed the sigh of a long-suffering martyr and waddled back to the bedroom, leaving Abe wondering if he'd dreamt the whole episode, his mind suggestible to the transcendental literary powers of Can-D.

Or Chew-Z.

13

"They're beautiful in a hideous kind of way," Ellen said, admiring Alan's studies of the undead. A week had passed since their coupling and Alan had invited her to his studio to see his work. No one else in the building had been permitted into his sanctum sanctorum. "My God, there are so many of them."

"And no two alike," Alan said. "Just like snowflakes."

"Not quite," Ellen frowned.

"Fingerprints?"

"That's a bit closer. It's like you're cataloguing them."

"I guess I am. Passes the time. Cave paintings of the future."

Ellen's eyes roved over the dizzying cavalcade of renderings. Beyond their technical excellence, Alan had captured something she hadn't stopped to consider about the things outside: their innate humanness. Those things weren't always *things*. They had been Homo sapiens. Alan's meticulous artwork, while unsentimental, betrayed an element of latent humanity in the subject matter. The tilt of a head, the softness of a brow, the turn of a mouth, all reminded her that these empty vessels once had inner lives. They'd been friends and neighbors.

"I'm amazed at how unbiased these are," Ellen marveled.

"They don't hate us. They didn't ask to be what they are."

Ellen fingered the edge of a pastel of an armless male zombie with half its face missing. It had no pants and its penis was gone, but not its scrotum and testicles. She scanned the other images. Males, females, all dismembered in various ways. Not a single one was intact. How had she never noticed that before? She hastened to the window. Resting on the sill was a pair of binoculars, which she snatched up. Though they were packed together down there, she confirmed what Alan's drawings portrayed; not a single one of them was complete. On some the damage was more evident than others—whole missing limbs were easy to spot—but all were mutilated beyond the general rot. It made sense. Most had been savaged when they were still people. They'd died and been resurrected.

Missing ears, noses, jaws, chunks of shoulder, gaping gashes, hollowed out cavities where their bellies should be. She noticed that many were nude, their clothes having either fallen off or been forcibly torn away. Some trailed lengths of dehydrated intestine, which others stepped on. Several had cutaways through which their withered internal organs could be seen, just like those "Visible Man" model kits her kid brother made, only less pristine. The legless pulled themselves along with their arms, almost lost in the crowd, trod on by the others, but they kept on. Ellen looked back at the wall of Alan's portraits, trying to match ones there with the crowd below.

"It's like a Bosch painting out there," she said, sounding dazed.

"Bosch was an amateur. The Black Death was a stroll in the park. Those pussies had it cushy." Alan smiled at Ellen.

"Don't talk like that."

"Too dark?"

"No, too vulgar. You sound like a more cultured version of Eddie."

"Gotcha. *Ecch*. Okay, I'll refrain from the cussing. But seriously, the ninnies—is that okay?" Ellen nodded. "The ninnies of the fourteenth century had it good compared to us. But what we've got going on is a logical extension. Rats and fleas spread the bubonic plague. See, rats infected with the disease were brought to Europe through trade with the east. At least that's the theory I remember. Fleas on the rats transmitted the disease to people. I mean those weren't exactly hygienic times. Open sewers, people shitting out their windows—excuse me, *relieving* themselves. Just like us, right? The plague spread like wildfire. The symptoms were obvious to anyone with eyes. You'd get these buboes, which were swollen lymph nodes. Along with your high fever you got delirium. The lungs became infected and an airborne version spread from person to person through coughing, sneezing, or just talking. Maybe this whole mess started with fleas or rats. Who knows? I'm sorry, this isn't history class."

"No, it's interesting."

It wasn't really, but it passed the time. Ellen had never been much of a history buff, but Alan was smart and men liked to hear themselves talk, so why not indulge him? Alan plucked a thick volume off his bookshelf and gestured with it, the book a prop to lend credence to his thesis. Subconsciously, he'd pat the book after each sentence, punctuating his thoughts, drumming them in. He might have made a fine teacher, Ellen thought, but school had never been her favorite place.

"Is the test gonna be essay or multiple choice?" she said, smiling.

"I'm sorry, should I stop?"

"No, I'm just kidding." Not.

"Nature's been trying to wipe humans off the face of the Earth for centuries," Alan continued. "The influenza pandemic at the end of World War I? Once it got going it knocked off about twenty-five to thirty million around the world. Maybe more. And quick, too. It came and went in a single year. Remember that SARS nonsense? All those little gauze masks people were running around with? Everyone looked like Michael Jackson for a couple of months? Same thing during the influenza epidemic. You could get fined for ignoring flu ordinances. So many folks were croaking there was a shortage of coffins, morticians, and gravediggers. Over time I think AIDS would have surpassed influenza, but it was all a rehearsal for this. This is the one that humanity doesn't make a comeback from."

Ellen just stared out the window. "No, I don't suppose so. But maybe."

Alan smiled and shook his head. That there was even the slightest room for optimism boggled his mind. He felt a small pang of envy. And then a larger pang of hunger. He stepped out of the room and into the kitchen, his departure unnoticed by Ellen, who seemed in a sort of trance. Maybe his little death diatribe was ill advised. Ellen didn't come down for a dissertation. Whatever. What was done was done. Alan couldn't unsay it. He opened a cabinet and took down a can of pork and beans and fished the can opener out of his cutlery drawer. After licking every atom of sustenance off the lid he scooped out two equal portions onto plates, then used the can opener again to remove the can's bottom, which he also licked clean. He then got out his metal clippers and cut the can from top to bottom and carefully unfurled the cylinder, making sure not to cut himself. He tongued the exposed insides of the can, leaving them gleaming.

"Waste not, want not" went the old saw.

When he returned to the living room, which he used as his studio, Ellen was lying on the floor, eyes closed. At first Alan thought all that death talk finished her off, but he saw her rib cage rise with each soundless breath. Had she fainted?

"Ellen?"

"*Mmmm?*"

"Want something to eat?"

Ellen propped herself up and nodded, looking dreamy. Looking spaced out. She remained seated on the floor as she accepted the dish of beans and they ate in silence, slowly. No one wolfed down food but the zombies anymore. When they'd finished cleaning their plates, Alan took them back into the kitchen. Washing up was a thing of the past. He wiped the plates with the hem of his shorts. That was as good as it got, cleanliness-wise. Take *that*, Board of Health.

When he returned, Ellen was on his couch with her back to him, nude, her body arranged in an undernourished homage to the classic Ingres canvas, "Grande Odalisque." She'd even wrapped a towel around her head and held a flyswatter where Ingres's model held a feathered fan.

"Want to immortalize something alive?" she asked. "Barely, but still."

Alan thought about the drawing of her he'd inadequately disposed of and his malignant arrangement with Eddie. If only he'd burned it. This wasn't about the drawing, anyway. It was about protecting Ellen from Eddie's vicious gossip. And was Ellen ready to see a truthful depiction of herself? That was the bigger issue. Alan had tossed away that drawing because he thought it would hurt her. How should he proceed? Whenever he'd done portraits of, let's say, *aesthetically challenged* people he knew, he always embellished a little, flattered where possible while maintaining sufficient fealty to the model. He'd hand over the art and the subject always seemed pleased. But Ellen, damaged as she was, would likely see through such a chivalrous ruse. Better just to portray what was.

"Okay," Alan said, picking a pad and terra-cotta Conté crayon off the floor.

"Don't you want to paint me?" Ellen asked.

"Uh. A drawing would be quicker."

"You have someplace else you need to be?"

"Good point."

Alan opened his paint box, a sturdy wooden one that had belonged to his grandfather. He kept his brushes bristle up in a mason jar nearby and selected a hogs hair filbert and a hogs hair round to lay in the basic structure in thinned burnt sienna. He already had a primed canvas stapled to a lapboard. Proper stretchers were a sweet memory. The canvas, with its dry bluish-gray layer of wash, was on the smallish side but would have to do, like everything else in short supply. Alan never wanted to be a miniaturist, but so be it.

As Alan sketched Ellen's basic form in small but confident strokes, he really studied her body. It was about 10:30 in the morning; the light in the room was somewhat diffuse as the sun was still at the east end of the apartment. By the time the sun hung over York, casting direct light into the room, he had the basic form blocked in. The light would be strong for a couple of hours. As the illumination grew stronger, so did the highlights on Ellen's body, sweat glinting on each raised vertebra, each dorsal rib, her raised hipbone. Though emaciated, the essence of her former loveliness was still evident. Lighting made such a difference. Maybe this painting could be both flattering and honest.

"Can I have a glass of water?" Ellen asked, breaking what Alan realized had been several hours of total silence.

14

"*Ooh! Ooh!* There, across the street. Something's happening over there at the Food City! I saw somebody go into the market. Someone's stealing our food. Well, not *our* food, but you know what I mean!"

"It was bound to happen," Ruth said.

"What? A food thief? You bet your sweet bippy! I keep vigil, nothing gets past me!"

"No, no, *no*, not the alleged food thief."

"Alleged? Then what? What? What was bound to happen?" Abe turned away from his post at the window and glared at his wife.

"Losing your marbles. Senility. Dementia. Whatever you want to call it. You spend all day staring out the window and you're bound to start seeing things."

"I'm not seeing things," Abe sputtered.

"Exactly. You're *not* seeing things because there's *nothing* to see. Like the lights in the sky the other night."

"Not the sky, the ground."

"Uh-huh."

"There was some kind of fracas."

"Fracas," Ruth repeated.

"A brouhaha."

Ruth just stared, her mouth pursed. Abe dabbed his sweaty forehead, wiping a trickle of stinging saltiness from the corner of his eye. He blinked a few times and looked back out the window. Nothing was any different than usual. The host of rotting cabbages was muddling en masse in perfect, unbroken harmony.

"I just thought I saw . . . Ah, nuts."

Abe looked again, his eye drifting to Food City.

"Aha!" he shouted. "Aha! There!" He pointed at the doors, the glass of one was broken. "There! The door's busted. I heard that. I heard a crash. So there!"

"So?" Ruth said, unmoved. "They broke a window. Wonderful. In addition to eating us they're vandals now. I'm thrilled. And now the supermarket's full of them. I can see why you're cheering."

"They just mill around," Abe said. "They don't break windows."

"They did," Ruth said.

"I don't think so," Abe said.

But didn't know if he believed it.

"I wish I had me a gun," Dabney said as he lobbed a half brick from his perch. "And bullets," he added. "Lots of bullets. I don't want this to be one of them tricky 'Monkey's Paw' wishes where you get a little of this but none of that and it works out bad. A gun and lotsa bullets and maybe a scope for aiming. This brick throwing shit's all well and good if you're a fucking caveman, but damn."

Karl, who had risked Dabney's scorn and come up to the roof, sat nearby, handing chunks to Dabney, like an old-time cannoneer supplying his gunner. He'd mind his p's and q's today. No repetitions of the "Mean Joe Green" incident, as he'd come to think of it.

"Another thing would be nice about having a scope would be I could really see the damage I inflicted," Dabney continued. "From up here it's too small. I wanna see the heads pop. I wanna see the chunks spatter up, the bits of bone and brain. I wanna know that I've put 'em down for good. Sometimes I think I see 'em get up again and there's no way I can hit the same ones twice. I don't have that kind of aim, least not freehand. But with a nice rifle? Shit, heads would be poppin', son."

"Yeah, that'd be cool."

"You humoring me?"

"No. I think it would be totally cool."

Karl didn't think it was *that* cool, but why make waves? Rifles and scopes reminded him too much of Big Manfred, who'd been as devout a hunter as he'd been a Christian. "Hey, Bambi, have a little of this," had been his oft-repeated jibe when "thinning the herd." "Hunting whitetail" sounded like one of the triple-X titles Karl had yearned to see on the marquees of the Deuce, but he'd kept that to himself. Big Manfred wouldn't have seen the humor. The same went for "buck fever," which sounded like gay porn. Big Manfred definitely wouldn't have found that the least bit amusing. Guns. Bullets. A scope. The truth is, Karl thought if you're going to make a wish, why not just wish none of this had ever happened in the first place?

Dabney lofted another hunk into the crowd and it dropped between bodies. He clucked in disapproval, then turned away from the cornice, massaging his bicep, sweat spilling off him. Above, the sky was clear and bright and in other circumstances would be lovely to behold. Dabney lay on his back on the tarp and closed his eyes, shielding them with a large hand, wishing for rain. The clouds that roved the sky from time to time were a sadistic tease. Karl studied the older—but not old—man. He was still, in relative terms, beefy. When Dabney had shown up he'd weighed in at close to three hundred pounds so even now he looked formidable.

Karl's attention drifted over to Dabney's smokehouse. Was there still meat inside? Karl wondered if he should ask. Didn't he deserve a second chance? Could he risk sneaking up when Dabney was asleep? No, that would be a bad idea. Lined up along the low wall on the southern side of the roof were Ruth's flowerboxes. With seeds she'd collected from the last fresh vegetables—cucumbers, green peppers, peas, and tomatoes—she'd attempted to grow food for the building; a noble effort that never made it. Small spindly tendrils had poked out of the soil, but the lack of rain and the oppressive heat baked them before they'd blossomed.

Dabney rolled back onto his belly, then hoisted himself to his knees, crawled to the edge of the roof and looked straight down.

"You know how frustrating it is looking down there every day and seeing the top of my truck taunting me?" Dabney said. "Every day. Least those motherfuckers could do is turn it over, but they got no strength it seems. Just numbers. Turn it all the way over, onto its back like a turtle. Then I wouldn't see it no more."

Jutting out into the street at a forty-five degree angle languished the van Dabney had plowed into the building seven months earlier. Painted on the pale blue roof in black was the legend, **DABNEY LOCKSMITH & ALARM**, then smaller, **SERVING ALL FIVE BOROUGHS SINCE 1979**, followed by his phone number in really big purple numerals. The front end was crumpled, the small hood popped open, revealing a blackened engine block. The back doors hung open, jostled every few moments by figures that passed by or through them. No doubt sun-shy zombies squatted within.

"It mocks me. Reminds me I didn't make it home."

"Home is where the heart is," Karl ventured.

"You say some stupid-ass nonsense, son," Dabney said, but he was smiling.

"I know."

"My van and that goddamn supermarket. Ain't that a bitch?"

"Yup."

Eddie and Dave, back when they'd been brawny, had hoisted Dabney from the roof of his van as the zombies groped for him. It was the first and last altruistic act either of them had committed, and even then, Eddie had needed lots of persuasion. "That nigger'll just eat all our food," he'd complained. "I mean look at him. He's a fuckin' house. He'll probably rape all the women, even the old bitch. Niggers don't care, man. Pussy is pussy to their kind." The old "project your sin onto others and disparage them for it" routine. Talk about calling the kettle black. Ever since the rescue, Dabney was merely "that nigger on the roof," as far as Eddie was concerned, though he'd never have the temerity to utter those words within earshot of Dabney, lest he end up pitched down to the congregation as a tasty morsel. Not that Karl would object. Eddie was every jock asshole that'd terrorized Karl over the years, all rolled into one.

He reminded Karl of his dear old papa.

Big Manfred was a sportsman.

Big Manfred was a bigot.

Big Manfred hated almost everything Karl held dear.

"I miss my music," Karl squawked.

"Where'd *that* come from?" Dabney turned from his perch and looked at the slight young man. This normally placid little white boy was shivering with agitation, eyes popped wide and despairing. The right corner of his mouth was twitching.

"What kind of life is this? What are we doing with ourselves? We're biding our time until we just shrivel up and die!" Karl's voice was stretched almost as thin as his small body, but there was vitality in his anguish. He sprang up and, fists clenched at his sides, glared up at the sky. "What is this? What the fuck *is* this?" He waved his arms around, gesticulating at nothing and everything. "What? What? What is this? What is the point? What's the fucking point?"

He began to hyperventilate.

Dabney rose and stepped toward him, unsure of what to do. Talk to him? Tackle him? Give him a hug? Karl's face was pulled taut, like his skull was trying to escape its fragile prison of skin and muscle. Dabney reached out and Karl slapped away his hand, then punched Dabney in the mouth.

The force of the blow surprised them both.

Karl sidestepped Dabney and walked in measured, deliberate steps up the rise toward the edge. Dabney massaged his jaw and watched. He wasn't mad at Karl. If anything, he was a bit spooked by the sudden change in his visitor. Karl stood right on the lip of the drop and stared straight ahead.

"Are you happy?" he asked the air in front of him. If the question was meant for Dabney, it didn't sound that way. "I'm not."

"No one's happy, son. Listen, Karl, step away from there. I mean toward me. Back away from there. Not forward. Don't jump."

"Don't jump."

"Right. Don't jump."

"You ever see that old cop show, *Dragnet*? Or any old cop show, for that matter? There always was an episode where some kid would try LSD, or sometimes even just pot, and he'd be up on the roof of the local high school or church or wherever. He'd be some square from Central Casting's notion of a hippie or beatnik. Or sometimes he or she would be 'the good kid who's fallen in with the bad crowd.' And there this twenty-five-year-old high school student would be, saying things like, 'I can fly, man. I can fly. I just know I can,' and Joe Friday or some other stiff in a fedora and skinny tie would be trying to talk the kid down, but not off the roof. 'Don't do it, son, you're having a bad trip.' Yeah.

"I don't want to jump. I don't want to fall. My balance is fine. I used to play games like this as a kid. I'd pretend that I was way up high, only I'd be down on the sidewalk, walking along the thin edge of the curb. If a breeze came and unsettled my balance, if my footing got away from me and I dropped to the asphalt, in my mind I'd fallen into a bottomless chasm. There's no breeze. I'm challenging God to knock me off this roof. Bring a wind. Sweep me away. I'm not worried. My dad always said 'God is in the details,' and I believe that. Because look at this world of ours. Seems like God's missing the big picture, don't you think?"

"I thought it was 'The devil is in the details.' "

"No. That's wrong. That's a variation. What's funny is that we're not quite sure who to attribute the quote to. The consensus goes with Flaubert, but some say Michelangelo. Others go with the architect Ludwig Mies van der Rohe, or Aby Warburg."

"How come you know this shit?"

"It's called retaining trivia. Maybe someone would be kind and call it knowledge, but it's not. It's trivia. It's why I would have made a great 'Lifeline' on *Millionaire*. It's why I kicked ass at Trivial Pursuit. I can throw facts at you and quotes and all kinds of shit. But it's all meaningless."

"It's not meaningless."

"Yeah, right. Keep telling yourself that. Every Sunday my dad dragged us all to church, but you know what? In spite of that, I *still* believe in God. They taught us that God made man in His image, and that makes perfect sense. Man is a petty, awful creature. So, from that I deduce God is the pettiest and most awful creature in the universe. We're God Lite. Are we being punished or did God just get bored and come up with a way to wipe us all out and have some fun watching the carnage in the bargain? Who watches NASCAR for the racing? People watch for the chance to see someone blown to smithereens—several someones if they're lucky. I know that's not an original observation, but it's true. God's watching this sick show and laughing His ass off.

"I'm rambling."

Karl stepped back from the ledge and headed for the stairwell. As he opened the door he turned to Dabney.

"Sorry about the jaw."

The door closed behind him and Dabney just stood and looked into the empty space Karl had just occupied at the ledge. He felt tired all over. Two roofs away he saw Gerri staring off into space like one of the things.

Maybe it all was meaningless in the end.

15

"Is that what I look like to you or is this what I actually look like?"

Ellen stood at the easel admiring Alan's immortalization of her in oils. With tiny orangey highlights on her back from the interior candles and her extremities rim lit from the light spilling from outdoors, she actually looked radiant. All but she was softly de-emphasized, warmly enveloped in rich shadow. The pose was Ingres but the painting was pure Rembrandt, its understanding of chiaroscuro complete and accomplished.

"Alan, it's remarkable."

Ellen recalled ads in her ladies' supermarket magazines for a syrupy hack named Thomas Kinkade, so-called "*Painter of Light*™," that self-appointed appellation rendered in precious curlicues. With his squinty little eyes and fey mustache, Kinkade embodied American kitsch at its worst: cloying, banal, and tacky. Alan was a genuine painter of light—and dark. Though the figure on the small canvas was gaunt, it radiated eroticism. The sweaty pinpricks of light drew attention to the sharp contours, but somehow didn't detract from the innate femininity of the subject. The subject. Ellen. Herself.

In all her years she'd never been captured so vividly. There were probably thousands of photographs of her, maybe even some good ones, but they all fell short. They were surpassingly two-dimensional. This representation didn't just lie there, and even though it was a portrait of her present condition, it had life.

"May I have this?"

Alan hadn't considered his attachment to this painting. While he painted he sort of zoned out, focused on technique and execution, but now that it was done he could stand back and judge the work. It was good. The best he'd done in . . .

Ever.

He knew it was good because even with things the way they were he was reticent to give it away. In his gallery of death he'd managed to create a single image that was, of all things, both tragic and optimistic. Ellen could see Alan was debating inside his head. For the first time in months she felt like she wanted something that wasn't just a staple. But maybe this *was* a staple; one she'd forgotten a woman needs. This fed her sense of self. This fed her vanity. How long had it been since she'd applied makeup or thought about her body as anything other than a rundown, withering collection of deprived tissue? Alan had painted a twiggy but eminently fuckable woman, and that woman was her. Twiggy. Ellen's mind raced back to the waifish '60s icon. Small tits perched on a rack of bone—Keane-eyed and shaggable.

"Yeah, of course," Alan said. It seemed like an eternity of deliberation, but only a few moments passed.

"I'll cherish this," Ellen said. "I didn't think I was capable of cherishing anymore. Or coveting. But I couldn't bear to not have this painting. And besides, you'll get to be with it every remaining day we have. *Mi casa es su casa,* remember?"

"Uh-huh."

As Ellen reached for the artwork Alan stepped between her and the canvas.

"Wait a little while. Oils take forever to dry. I can't just pluck it off the board without wrecking it."

"I'll take the board."

"I need the board to paint on."

"Are you reneging?" Ellen's expression was puzzlement with a hint of dander.

"No, not at all. Just let it dry a while longer. I'll bring it up later. Or tomorrow."

"You're sure you're not reneging, because . . ." There was an edge to her voice.

"No, no. I swear," Alan said. "I don't want to mess it up or tear it. Later. Scout's honor."

As Ellen went up the stairs, touching the wall to guide her, she felt a curious combo of up-till-now dormant emotions. She felt flattered, acquisitive, manipulative, feminine. She'd already manipulated Alan into cohabitating with her. Isn't that what she'd done? Fresh on the heels of Mike's demise she'd played on Alan's compassion and hoodwinked him into her tender, needy trap. And it felt good. At first she'd felt she'd been pathetic, but now, in light of Alan's painting, she retroactively amended that take. She'd used her feminine wiles. She beamed. She still *had* feminine wiles. She'd *seduced* him. Maybe it was with shock, grief, and tears, but he'd taken the bait.

She still had *it*.

And there were hoops for Alan to jump through before they all collapsed into nothingness.

"Here," Alan said, handing Eddie a dashed off, slightly altered pastel copy of the painting. In it Ellen was more robust, her buttocks rounder, her spine less protruding.

"*Pfff,*" Eddie sniffed, his disdain slap-in-the-face obvious.

"What's wrong with it?" Alan sighed.

"It's too nice."

"Nice?"

"What's the word? *Tasteful.* How's The Comet supposed to get his jerk on with something like this? I want you to draw me humping the shit out of her."

"No. Nuh-uh. No can do."

"Why not?"

"Because it's totally disgusting. Listen, this is too high school for me, okay? I used to con my way out of schoolyard beatings by drawing naked girlies for jackasses like you, but forget it. What're you gonna do, take my lunch money?"

"I'll beat the shit . . ."

Alan arched an eyebrow.

"I'll spread the word that that whore is spreading for you like Velveeta. You think she wants to hear that shit, the widow lady in her hour of grief?"

As Eddie smirked in triumph, Alan's indignance slackened to indifference.

"You know what?" Alan said. "Whatever. Do whatever you want. I did you a nice piece of work and you didn't like it. I used to get paid good money for art like that. The one aspect of the apocalypse I kind of dig is assuming all those unappreciative art directors are dead. I'd hand in a beautiful piece of art and they'd either grunt approval or pick it apart. I don't need bad reviews from a scrawny ape. You know what else? You can tell whoever you want that Ellen guzzles my cock morning, noon, and night. Tell them whatever you want. Make up any kind of deranged shit your feeble mind can come up with. Who cares? Be a gossipy little bitch. Everyone knows your 'secret,' so why should I protect Ellen's? She's a big girl. It's the *end of the world*, Eddie. No one cares who's diddling who. No one even cares that you fuck Dave, or vice versa, or whatever."

"That's a fuckin' lie!" Eddie growled. "The Comet don't play that!"

Laughing, Alan snatched the drawing from Eddie's table and walked out the door.

"The Comet. What a retard."

"*Oy*, my sciatica," Abe muttered, rubbing his thighs at the top of the stairs to the roof. He unlatched and pushed open the door and stepped onto the puckered surface. The bubbles in the tar paper reminded him of pizza, with its enticing puffed-up, reddish orange surface, peaks and valleys of sauce and cheese. Up the block from his office in the Shtemlo Building was a hole-in-the-wall pizzeria that made the best sauce—not too sweet, not too bitter. Perfect. The Punchinellos who worked there were torn straight from the pages of an Italian joke book, stereotypes all—bushy eyebrows and mustaches, arms hairy as apes', speaking in *Dese'a*, *dems'a*, and *dose'a* spumoni-Inglese. For twenty-two years Abe had gotten pizza there and never knew their names. That was New York for you. Intimate anonymity. You could see the same people day in and day out and never know a damned thing about them.

"You know the latch was closed."

"Yeah," Dabney said. "I forget who was up here last, but sometimes I get locked out. S'alright. Not like I come down anyway. Knees bugging you, Abe?"

"Knees, back, everything. Bursitis, arthritis, a little bronchitis, you name it. I'm an old Jew. Everything hurts. What doesn't hurt doesn't work."

Dabney laughed. "Don't have to be Jewish for that shit."

"Oh yeah? So what hurts you, Mr. Non-Jew?"

"No, I don't want to have that conversation. I'd rather keep this on the upbeat tip, if it's all the same. Whyn'tchoo come on over and park your narrow behind?"

"Suits me." Abe, clutching Alan's Phil Dick paperback, stepped over to the shady spot where Dabney sat, his back against a low wall. With some difficulty Abe took a seat on that wall, the top of which was capped with curved tile. "I can't sit on the floor like that. I'd never get up again." He propped open the book and slipped on his smudgy reading glasses. Dabney took the cue and fished out his own book and was about to read when Abe slapped the paperback closed and said, "How can it never rain and be so goddamned humid? It's getting maybe a little gray on the horizon, do you think? Or am I crazy?"

"No, there's some gray. Could just be haze."

"Haze. Yes. Yes. No cars and we still got smog." He trailed off. "What are you reading?"

Dabney held up a copy of *Time Out of Joint,* by Philip K. Dick. Abe showed Dabney his borrowed copy of *The Three Stigmata of Palmer Eldritch.* They both smiled.

"Courtesy of that Zotz kid, am I right?" asked Abe.

"You are correct."

"I think maybe that's all that kid has is Dick."

"No, that would be those meatheads in 4B and C. They got all the dick they can handle."

The two men laughed.

"I don't know who those schmucks think they're fooling keeping separate apartments. You can hear their *mishegoss* whenever they get up to it. When I was in the service we had some fellas like them: straight laced and hard as nails on the outside. Guys with the pictures of femmes fatale of the big screen and so on. But they didn't fool anyone. Once they were safely away from home, they were off to the races. You know that's why New York and San Francisco are, um, *were* knee deep in *faygelehs*, right? All these fellas come home and they've got a choice: go home to Podunk and step back in the closet, or stay in the port town and make a new life. They chose wisely, I think."

"So you think it's okay to be homosexual?"

"I don't care one way or the other. Never did, so long as their attentions weren't on me. I had a few make goo-goo eyes at me; that I didn't care for. But live and let live, I say. And now, what difference does any of it make? People are going to expend energy on carnality come what may, and use the available outlets—or in-lets. Whichever. I'll tell you, the best thing about getting old was that my libido, which controlled me all my post-adolescent life, finally died. Too bad it came right along with all this mess. I never got to enjoy my belated Age of Reason. And the hell with Viagra. Viagra's only good if you've got a young honey waiting in your bed. No pill in the world could make me want to *shtup* the pill I'm married to." Dabney snickered. "Yeah, easy for you to laugh. That woman is no picnic." After a reflective pause, Abe looked up and, rubbing his knees, said, "I need to take my constitutional. Want to join me?"

Dabney helped Abe up off the wall and the two men strolled the roof. After two circuits of their building, Abe suggested they walk to the end of the row, assuring his companion he could make it over the walls. Dabney was in no mood to carry Abe back home. He liked the old geezer but would just as soon spare himself the piggyback routine. When they reached the north end of the line, Abe needed to sit down again. There was a rusty folding chair near the two oxidized bicycles permanently bonded to a metal guardrail. With their tires rotted away and everything glazed in a multihued orange patina, they looked more like modern art than defunct transportation. Abe was huffing and puffing like he'd run the marathon. Twice.

Dabney looked at Abe, who sat there panting, hands gripping his quaking knees. Though the geezer's face looked all right—partly because it was enshrouded in beard—his hands were cadaverous, the skin like yellowed tracing paper speckled with liver spots. His fingertips came to disturbing points, the skin so close to the bone it barely masked it. A drop hit Dabney's nose and he wiped it away with annoyance.

A drop?

A drop!

Annoyance transformed to rapture, his eyes shooting up from the old man to the sky above, which was thick with dark gray clouds. Another drop plopped right in his eye and Dabney's grin was so broad he feared his face might halve itself. More drops began to pelt the two men. Abe stopped rubbing and looked up in disbelief. Within the minute a downpour was dousing the two men, who clasped each other around the biceps and jigged. After a few waltzing rotations Abe broke free and began to unbutton his shirt. "Modesty be damned," he cried.

"Damn straight," agreed Dabney.

Both men peeled off their clinging duds and basked in the refreshing deluge.

"We have to tell the others!" Abe said, eyes wide.

"I'll do it. I can get to the building faster than you, old timer."

Dabney raced across the rooftops doing the low hurdles in record time, the water streaming down his naked body. When he reached the stairwell he threw open the door only to be greeted by a scream. He stepped back and there stood Ellen and Alan, both clutching stacked containers to collect water.

"I'm sorry," Ellen said. "I didn't mean to scream. You just surprised me. I'm not used to having a naked man greet me on the roof."

"S'alright," Dabney said, stepping out of the way.

They quickly arranged the assortment of pots and cans, which joined the garbage cans, buckets, plastic drawers, and file boxes already there, then stripped nude and joined Dabney in the aqueous bacchanal. Alan handed Dabney a bar of soap.

"You don't miss a trick," he said, accepting it gladly.

Dave appeared at the door, followed by Karl, who had escorted Ruth upstairs. Straightaway everyone was naked, except Ruth, who looked away in embarrassment.

"Where's Abe?" she moaned.

"Oh shit," Dabney snorted, midlather. "I'll go get him." Trailing suds, Dabney tore ass across the roofs. When he got there, Abe was sitting in a concavity full of water, like a shallow tub, kicking his feet like a toddler in a wading pool. Dabney tossed the soap into the basin and soon Abe was lathering up, his eyes closed in euphoria.

"You forget the simplest of pleasures when you're denied everything," Abe said. "Bathing. Being wet. It's marvelous."

"Ruth was wondering where you were. She's up on our roof."

"Is she naked?" Abe gasped, his beatitude shaken.

"No."

"Oh thank God. No one needs to see that, least of all me."

"It would be kind of a buzzkill."

Four rooftops over, the tempest orgy continued. For the first time in months laughter was the dominant sound—that and the roar of torrential rainfall. Karl and Dave had erections, but neither thought of sex. They were just pleasure boners from the sheer joy of being wet. The cloudburst was luscious. Karl and Dave were splashing each other with bucketsful of water. Their bodies, virtually hairless except for rain-matted pubes and armpit patches, glistened in the diffuse light. Ellen looked at Alan's hairy body, his thin chest carpeted in wet black fur. Even dissipated, his was a man's body. The others were boys', not that that was a bad thing.

Even Dave looked enticing. Eddie was the one who really frightened and offended her.

She was delighted he wasn't present, but his absence was peculiar. Still, her answer for now: who cares? His loss.

Safely on the other side of the stairwell housing, Ruth tilted her head up and let the cataract wash over her cataracts. She'd been scheduled to have phacoemulsification the week after martial law was declared. Now she was stuck with cloudy vision of a cloudy sky. She pulled some matted strands of hair away from her eyes, her fingers straying up her forehead, which seemed to go all the way to the back of her head. Maybe it was better she couldn't see that well. In her mind she could still picture herself as she was. Abe, too.

"Hey," Abe said, making Ruth flinch.

"Oh, you scared me." Even with muzzy vision she could see he was starkers. "*Ucch*, Abraham. Even you?"

"Even me what?"

"With the nakedness. Isn't it bad enough those youngsters are doing it? And the colored? From them I expect it, but you? Oy, there's no fool like an old fool."

"Even in the rain you manage to rain on a parade. Uncanny. Suit yourself."

Abe joined the others as they clasped hands and gamboled around.

"This feels so . . . *pagan*," Karl cried with glee.

The others agreed and Karl basked in the moment. Big Manfred would vomit if he ever saw his son cavorting like this: naked, turgid, wanton. After a while the rain subsided to a light drizzle and various moans of disappointment rose from the group. The air actually smelled fresh. Dabney trotted over to his customary perch, lay on his belly in a deep puddle, and peered down. The horde hemming in his wrecked van was soggier than usual, but otherwise unaffected by the rain. They stumbled and jostled same as ever. Seeing his van always made his stomach ache. Dabney looked away, not wanting to dampen his spirits. A rainbow spread over the buildings to the west.

It was so corny he couldn't believe it.

February, *Then*

"Come on, man, move that shit!"

Dabney leaned on his horn again, knowing full well it was an act of futility. Traffic was snarled in every direction. He'd decided to take the FDR, but what a mistake that had been. After a few hours he managed to exit onto York Avenue. His home, a two-bedroom apartment on the twelfth floor of the Martin Luther King, Jr. Houses on 110th Street and Lenox Avenue, awaited, his terrified wife, Bernice, holed up therein with three guns—all of which were legal—and sufficient ammo, if not skill, to protect herself. Already, within hours of the crisis's advent, looting and street violence were rampant. Road rage was devolving into something worse, every face of every driver and passenger in every vehicle transformed by primordial fear. This wasn't merely anxiety. Even panic would be a step toward calm.

The sidewalk traffic wasn't any better. Dabney looked out the side windows and saw donnybrooks everywhere. Store windows were being smashed both accidentally and on purpose. Some just gave when too many bodies pressed up against them, causing explosions of cubed glass, like geysers of diamonds. Mixed in with the hysterical humans were these new bloodthirsty monstrosities. Across the hood of a car jutting diagonally half in and half out of its space a woman was being disemboweled and devoured by a trio of dead-eyed freaks, her fluids splashing onto the asphalt. Dabney fought the urge to open his door and try to help. Help what? She was dead. And if what they were saying was true—and he believed his own eyes, so yes, it was—whatever was left of her when the threesome were done eating would get up and join them. A quartet. Now multiply that over and over, ad infinitum. All up and down the avenue similar scenes were happening.

And no one stopped to help.

The few cops that remained were looking out for their own welfare, and Dabney couldn't blame them. Pop-pops erupted from all over, some of the bullets downing the cannibals, others ricocheting off hard surfaces. A slug pinged off a lamppost and put a dime-size crater into Dabney's windshield, small fissures radiating from it. Dabney took a hand off the steering wheel and pressed a finger to the spot, feeling cool air passing through a tiny hole. He hoped the integrity of the windscreen would maintain. Just long enough. He had to get home. He fished out his cell phone again and tried to call, but nothing doing. All circuits were tied up. *Please try again.* There was nothing to do but keep pushing northwest.

Something heavy slammed onto his roof and Dabney felt as if his blood stopped circulating for a moment and a vacuum formed in his lungs. A body rolled down his windshield and under all the noise of chaos he heard that twinkly crackle of the glass straining under the body's weight. If the windshield broke, those crazies would get in and get him. With mere inches between his and the next vehicle, Dabney accelerated, then reversed, bumping both cars to his front and rear. The body rolled off his hood, its smashed face casting a dead glare his way as it dropped out of sight under the van. The door of the car to his front flew open and the incensed driver starting walking back toward Dabney, slapping a five-cell Maglite flashlight against his open palm. Dabney couldn't believe it. In the eye of the shitstorm this moron was going to give him grief about a tiny bumper thump.

"What the fuck, dude?" the guy said, glaring at Dabney. No one was in his right mind. No one. Dabney checked his door locks.

As the guy neared, another blood-drenched cannibal scrambled over a motionless car and sank his teeth into the Maglite guy's throat. Dabney's mind raced even as all around him remained stationary. His thoughts came rapid fire: *Okay, now that asshole's definitely not moving. His car is stuck in my way. Can't reverse. Can't move forward. He was gonna kill me. In all this, he was gonna kill me. I gotta get home. Look at this shit. On the sidewalk it's more spread out. I'm near a hydrant. There's a gap. I'm near a hydrant. That guy was gonna kill me. But now he's dead. I gotta get home.*

Dabney bit his lip hard, then yanked the steering wheel hard to the right and bulled his van past the hydrant onto the sidewalk. *Fuck it*, he thought. *Everyone out here is gonna die, anyway.* There was little to contradict that thought, but even as he rationalized his decision to mount the sidewalk and plow through the pedestrian pandemonium he couldn't help but vacillate between *I'm committing vehicular manslaughter big time*, and *I'm performing euthanasia on an epic scale.* There really was a fine line between mercy killing and mass murder. And did it count as murder if they came back to life? Dabney could lose sleep over that ethical conundrum later, if he lived that long.

Bumps, thumps, screams, and percussive squelchy crunching sounds were the soundtrack to his trek north, his shallow hood being battered and spattered. As his windshield wipers strained against the profusion of blood and viscera, a stream began to leak through the small aperture. Bodies bounced off the front grille. After fifteen protracted minutes he ran out of wiper fluid and the blood began to congeal, even as it was slicked back and forth. Visibility was nearly nil.

"God dammit," Dabney keened. "God dammit."

Tears flowed down his round cheeks. This was wrong. Every-thing about this was wrong and fucked-up. What was he thinking? He'd left the house to install locks and window gates. Panic was good for sales and of late sales had been slow. He needed the year-end business. He shook his head. How had he let this happen? All kinds of folks—mostly white and willing to pay extra for rapid emergency service—had phoned. He smelled cash. But for what? Greed was a sin, sure, but stupidity should be the eighth deadly sin, because it was going to get him killed.

Traffic ahead actually eased a bit. He could see patches of gray-black asphalt through the havoc. He hit the accelerator and surged forward for a few glorious, optimistic seconds and then *WHAM!* A westbound Volvo sprang forth from the side street and spun Dab-ney's van. His blood-caked windshield imploded, covering him in wet fragments of safety glass. Unseeing and startled, his foot slammed down on the gas and his truck plowed into the front of a building, the engine sputtering and then silent.

With both ears ringing, Dabney wiped the blood, sweat, and tears from his eyes and saw a large confederacy of cannibals com-ing at his vehicle. The accident had smeared several all over the pavement, but there were so many. More than he'd seen anywhere else. These weren't cannibals. These things weren't human. They looked human, but they weren't. Not any more. Some had been gutted and dismembered but here they came nonetheless, dripping gore and spilled innards. People didn't do that. The news was right.

These things were dead but still moving around.

And hungry.

He tried starting the engine again. No use. He looked at his crumpled hood and saw steam jetting out. He had moments be-fore the ravenous mass outside reached his van. He clambered out onto the hood and climbed onto his roof.

Over the tinny roar in his ears he heard voices. Though the front of the building he'd crashed into was boarded up, there were people calling out from the windows above.

Hands reached down.

He was saved.

And getting home was no longer an option.

16

July, *Now*

"Hey, where's Eddie?" Dave asked.

Ellen was flabbergasted. "*You* don't know where he is?"

"No. I haven't seen him today. I can't believe he missed the rain."

"That is pretty odd," Alan said, glad the ape hadn't been there to ruin it.

"Now I'm worried," Dave said, looking it. "I knocked on his door on the way up. I just assumed he'd follow and once I got up here I got all jazzed and forgot about him."

Without dressing, Dave went back into the building and ran down to Eddie's door, which was unlocked. He stepped into the apartment and called out a couple of times, going from room to room, leaving puddles. Eddie wasn't there. He then tried his place with the same result. On each landing he pounded doors and called Eddie's name to no avail. He wasn't around. The elation from the rain dance burned off quickly as worry set in.

"He's not in the building," Dave said as he stepped back onto the roof. The others were all there, except Ruth who'd hobbled back to her apartment in disgust. Abe still sat naked on a low wall, basking in the waning precipitation. After being distracted for a moment by how long and low the old man's testicles hung, Dave stalked off in search of his comrade, unsurprised that no one offered to help.

Working his way north, the first building Dave tried was the one directly next door. Dave gave the stairwell door a few yanks but it remained locked tight, the norm since they'd thrown together this tattered kibbutz. The next building the stairwell door was unlocked and blackness waited within. Dave poked his head in, reticent to venture into the strange building. Maybe it wasn't as secure as theirs. Who knew? It all depended on how well the slapdash exterior fortifications had held up and if the former occupants of the building had bolstered them from within. No, if the zombies had gotten in they'd have made their way to the roof by now. In the back of his mind Dave remembered the front door was secure, but that gloom yawned like a hungry mouth. Maybe just Gerri lurked down in the dark. The Wandering Jewess's absence at the rain party didn't disturb Dave at all. She was a ghost; what did ghosts need with rain?

"Hello?" Dave called. "Eddie? You there?"

No answer.

"Eddie?" Dave shouted. The sound reverberated off the walls. Dave was in no mood to go spelunking in an unfamiliar building. Not naked. He wondered if he should go back for his clothes. It had stopped raining and like the moisture on his body, his jollity was evaporating. Any dampness now was fresh perspiration. After a few more tries, Dave gave up and moved on to the next building, which was the one he and Eddie had resided in previously. Maybe Eddie had gotten homesick or something. Maybe he needed something they'd left behind. Eddie did periodically make trips over there to mine their old digs for abandoned artifacts. The stairwell door was blocked, as ever, but he pounded on it a few times anyway, to no avail.

Holding the handrail because of the wetness, Dave stepped onto the fire escape and carefully walked down to the top floor. Both windows were closed and locked, gated inside. He went down to the next landing and tried the left window. It had no gate but was locked. The right one was locked and gated. According to Eddie, gates were for pussies. "I'm not paying to live in a cage," he'd declared. "Faggots wanna live like zoo animals, that's their problem. I'd like to see some nigger come through our window and try to steal our stuff. I'd Luima the shit out of him. *Literally!*" Then he'd laugh and glare at their unprotected window as if willing someone to breach it. That was then, of course. With the zombies, everyone kept their gates locked, even though the likelihood of one getting up a fire escape was pretty negligible.

On the next landing the right window was gated, but the left—theirs—slid open, vulnerable as ever. About a year earlier he and Eddie had crouched in silence out here, stifling giggles as Eddie videoed the couple next door doing it. It wasn't that they were that great looking, but it was still exciting. Eddie would play that tape often; he called it his "hunting trophy." Dave stepped into the dark apartment. The sky had turned colorless but was bright, so his eyes adjusted quickly.

"Eddie?" Dave called again.

"Don't come in here," a husky voice responded.

"Eddie?" Dave ignored the admonition and raced into the apartment, tripping over a pile on the floor. His knees hit the bare floorboards hard and he yelped in pain, then rolled onto his side to massage the injured joints. Both were abraded and wet with blood. He clenched his eyes shut as he rubbed them, stars swimming inside his closed lids. "Ouch, Jesus."

"I told you not to come in here." It was Eddie's voice, but he sounded different.

When Dave opened his eyes he looked directly into another pair, only these looked glassy with indifference. He blinked a few times, then jerked bolt upright and scooted backward away from the unblinking visage.

"Gerri!" he yawped.

Though dim, there was sufficient light to see that Gerri was dead, yet still she clutched the husk of her late Yorkie.

"What happened to Gerri?" Dave whispered.

"I did."

"Whattaya mean, Eddie? What happened here?" Dave stood up and looked down at Gerri's body. It was folded in half at the waist and pearly gelatinous spume speckled her rangy bare buttocks. One of her flaplike teats spilled out of her torn housecoat. Her neck was twisted at an unnatural angle and blood leaked from both nostrils and the corner of her mouth. Purple hand-shaped bruises clasped her shoulders. Dave looked up from the cadaver at Eddie, who from the waist down was bare, blood smeared on his hands and across his groin.

"Why don't you have your pants on, Eddie?"

"You're one to talk." Eddie said.

"What did you do, Eddie?" Dave asked. It was a formality. It was obvious what he'd done.

"I was wandering around, y'know, burnin' off some rage. I decided to visit the old crib, grab some copies of *Sports Illustrated*— like that one with the chick with the seashells on her boobs—and anyhow, who's sittin' on our old couch but the Wandering Jewess. Some rat was bitin' on her ankle and she's just sittin' there, so I stomped the little fucker. See?" He pointed at its furry remains. "So I ask her if she's okay, right? I tried a little, what was your *special* word? *Tenderness*. Anyway, one thing led to another. Listen, with a harpoon of cum built up you don't think so straight, bro. Pussy is pussy. I needed to get it in there and this bitch was all there was. Zotz is bonin' the merry widow, D. Doesn't leave much for the rest of us swingin' dicks."

"Was it consensual?"

"Guy does one year prelaw and he thinks he's Alan Dershowitz."

"Jesus Christ, Eddie."

"Hey, least she died with a smile on her face."

On Gerri's dead face was a rictus grin nobody in his or her right mind would describe as a smile.

"Oh, *Eddie.*"

"Hey, hey, hey. Don't take that tone with me. The Comet needed to get his freak on with some genuine *la fica*, okay? You jealous? That what this is? You know, fuck this bitch, all right? I put it to her good and she didn't make a peep. No struggle, nothing. So, yeah, I guess it was consensual. She didn't complain a bit. Least she could've done was moan or something. Shown some appreciation. Like anyone ever paid her any mind. She should be fuckin' flattered The Comet paid her withered snatch a visit."

Dave was about to say something when Gerri sat up and let out a noise that shrank his balls—something between a hiss, a growl, and the toilet backing up. Her head jerked on its shattered neck, the jaw opening and closing, tongue lolling. A small amount of blood and bile spurted out and she was up on her feet.

"Fuck, that was quick!" Eddie shouted. "Oh fuck man, *fuck!*"

Nude or not, Dave knew something had to be done before she got her bearings—fresh ones moved *fast.* He grabbed an elephant-foot umbrella stand near the doorway and smashed Gerri in the face, snapping her head backwards. The sickening sound of her top vertebrae shattering lurched the meager contents of Dave's stomach into his mouth, but he tamped it down and swallowed, hammering her back. Even with her head resting against her upper back and hanging upside down she kept uttering foul bestial grunts, blood-thickened saliva oozing down into her flaring nostrils. With her head on the wrong way Gerri groped blindly and Dave pummeled her with the stand, which spilled umbrellas with each blow. How many umbrellas were in the damned thing? Big ones and small ones fell to the floor, which was also now drenched in Gerri's various leaking fluids.

Finally he drew back the elephant foot and rammed her in the chest, sending her toppling back toward the rear windows. Steering her spastic body wasn't easy, but after several more strategically aimed blows she crashed through the window and plummeted to the ground in the alley that had claimed Mike Swenson. Dave looked out the window and saw Gerri twitch a few times, then stand and limp off to merge with the other brainless things shuffling around down there. Satisfied she wouldn't be joining them again, Dave dropped the battering ram and slumped to the floor.

"Wish you'd been that hardcore on the ice, bro," Eddie said.

"Yeah, thanks for all your help."

"Hey, The Comet's impressed, buddy. I'm giving you props. That was awesome."

"Yeah. Just leave me alone, okay?"

"Fine. What*ever*. Just tryin' to give a compliment is all, bro. No need to get all menstrual and shit. The Comet's outta here."

Eddie pulled on his shorts and left through the front door as Dave retched onto the floor, his spew mixing with Gerri's congealing blood.

The Comet.

The Rapist.

The Murderer.

Dave felt like one of those battered wives on *Cops*. The ones who kept telling the arresting officers—often through split lips and sporting impressive shiners—how their men were really *good* men. "He's a *good* man, officer! He's a *good* father, officer! I *love* him, officer!" On went the cuffs and these scumbag deadbeat drunken pieces of white trash would get thrown in the backs of the cruisers looking glad for the vacation away from the wife and kids. The patrol car would drift away from the double-wide and poor beaten wifey, with her missing front teeth and eye swollen shut, would bawl at the absence of her man.

Dave knew just how those dopey broads felt.

17

"God *dammit*, stop bitin' on me."

Two days after the rain the mosquitoes came, spawned in pools of still water. The tenacity of some life-forms was incredible. Dabney refused to leave his spot, but the bites were a stiff price to pay for the hour or so of jubilation. He sat in his lean-to and swatted at the pesky bloodsuckers, swearing under his breath. After a while he couldn't bear to sit still any more and got up and walked to his perch. Though the sun hadn't fully set—and when it had the skeeters would really get to their deviltry—it was too dark to see whether the undead were being fed upon, too. The thought made Dabney's mind race. If fleas and such could spread plague, if bugs bit on the zombies, then bit on a human, could that spread the contagion or whatever it was? Dabney thought about the West Nile virus and how the city had trucks drive around spraying poison through areas beset with mosquitoes. The only result he could recall was lowered birth weights in the areas the insecticide had been deployed.

West Nile was another so-called medical emergency that the local media had blown all out of proportion. Fear was always a powerful ally to keep people tuned in. *Look out, West Nile will get you*, like it was some kind of microscopic boogeyman. A few old folks got ushered into the afterlife minutes before their time by West Nile, but that was about all. Still it panicked the city and suburbs several seasons in a row.

Malaria.

That was another story. Dabney had done some time working freighters in his youth and had traveled through some places rife with malaria—Haiti, Panama, and bits of Southeast Asia. He'd seen locals, but more frighteningly shipmates come down with it. One by one the crew of his last ship was afflicted. Fever, the shakes, head and muscle aches, tiredness. Nausea, vomiting, and diarrhea. Anemia and jaundice. In the most extreme cases kidney failure, seizures, mental confusion, coma, and death. The skeeters spread malaria around like a whore spreads ass—amongst other things.

Maybe, unlike yellow fever and malaria, zombification wasn't transmitted through mosquito saliva. Studies had disproved that AIDS could be spread through mosquitoes, so that was of some comfort. It was bad enough to get turned into one of those shambling sacks of meat from getting attacked by one, but to have it happen through a bug bite seemed so wrong. *Here's hoping zombie fever is more like AIDS*, Dabney thought.

"Jesus God," he sighed. "This is what passes for optimism these days."

Dabney stepped over to his smoker and retrieved a small sliver of whatever-it-was jerky. There wasn't much left. Dabney hadn't eaten anything but his homemade charqui and the occasional can of okra or peas in weeks. Wasn't this that Atkins diet? It was funny how the white folks in the building had donated their okra and black-eyed peas to him, kind of like a canned goods drive consisting purely of donated Purina Nigger Chow—well intentioned, but racist all the same. Why'd they have this stuff in the first place?

Martha Stewart or someone on the cooking channel must've inspired them to buy these "exotic" ingredients, but then they chickened out when it came to actually eating them. *Give 'em to the darkie; they eat anything.* Dabney smirked because there was some truth to that. He recalled holiday trips to rural Tennessee, eating his Aunt Zena's chitlins and bear-liver loaf. That was some crazy shit. Or chitlins with hog maws. Shit, anything with chitlins was pretty fierce, especially drowned in hot sauce. Neck bones, backbones. Black folks had to be resourceful in their cooking; recipes formulated by dirt-poor bastards making do with what the white folks considered garbage.

And now, at the end of the road for humanity, Dabney was chewing on vermin jerky.

The more things change . . .

18

"I don't even know why the fuck you're worried. Who's gonna care? And if they did, what would they do, call the cops? Stop sweatin' it, bro."

Dave had been freaking ever since the Wandering Jewess met her fate and it was getting on The Comet's nerves, big time. Granted, her lickety-split resurrection was a tad harrowing, but shit happens, you deal. That was Eddie's personal philosophy. If pussy wasn't available, you made do. But if it presented itself, detours were made to be taken, even if they were skanky and gross.

"Seriously, bro, you're wearing me out with all your pacing around. Relax."

"I can't. You killed her, dude. Then I *re*-killed her. How fucked up is that?"

"No, no, no. That was fuckin' *awesome*. You were just like, *bam-bam-bam*, workin' her over with that fuckin' elephant hoof." Eddie laughed as he conjured the image. "That was *awesome*!"

"It wasn't awesome, it was disgusting. It was fuckin' horrific."

"Dude, *whatever*. You wanna be a wet blanket, go ahead on, but don't harsh my mellow. I thought it was the bomb, bro. For the umpty-millionth time, Dave: *no one cares.* No one even knows she's missing. She was a ghost even before I ghosted her. Look, she was barely there, anyway. She was just a creepy shadow lurking in the dark."

Dave stopped pacing and considered Eddie's words.

"Listen," Eddie continued, slapping away a mosquito, "I don't want you to waste any more time on this. Think of it this way, she died in the service of makin' your bro feel better, like a skeezed-out dehydrated Laura Nightingale."

"Florence Nightingale."

"Whatever. She saved a life. *Two* lives."

"How do you figure?"

"I was ready to kill Zotz, so she saved his life, not that that's that good of a thing, but fuck it, man, she helped me get the lead out and fuck it, it was an accident, anyway. It's not like I *meant* to perish her scrawny ass. She just kinda broke is all. Dem bones, dem bones, dem *dry* bones . . ."

"I'm made of tougher stuff," Dave said.

Eddie smiled and slapped Dave on the back. "That's the boy. It was a *'tragic'* mishap," Eddie smirked, framing his face in air-quotes. "Simple as that."

"Well, that's the last of it," Karl said, staring into his empty cupboard. Not a morsel of food was left. In the last week he'd nursed each scrap in his coffers; now all he had to chew on was air. His stomach growled and he punched it hard. "Shut up," he growled back. The kitchenette swam as his eyes teared up, hard edges wavering in lachrymosity. His knees felt flaccid but he willed himself to stay on his feet for fear if he hit the linoleum he'd never rise again. "This is so weak," he moaned. Was there anyone he could hit up for nourishment? Even the experts at rationing were down to fumes. The end was closing in, all righty.

He stepped out into the hall and at the top of his lungs shouted, *"Tenants meeting! Tenants meeting! All convene in the hall, please! Tenants meeting!"*

What could it hurt?

The first to answer the call was Eddie with a curt, "The fuck do you want, runt?" Dave followed Eddie into the hall, hopping as he cinched up a pair of sweatpants. It made Karl think of couples he'd known who'd pick up the phone during sex, then sound annoyed. Why'd they pick up in the first place?

Ruth stepped onto the landing across the hall and blinked at Karl. Though he stood only five foot five-and-a-half, he still towered over Mrs. Fogelhut, the only person in the building significantly smaller than he. It was her only endearing quality. "What's the hubbub?" she asked in her grating way.

Joining Eddie and Dave on the fourth floor landing were Alan and Ellen, both of whom emerged from her apartment. Eddie had mentioned Ellen had shacked up with the artist. Karl's mouth drew into a thin jealous slit. *Artists always get the chicks,* he thought bitterly. Then he mentally kicked himself for such a puerile thought.

"What's going on?" Ellen asked, looking up at Karl, who clung to the banister for balance. He felt woozy from nerves and hunger, but though he wasn't a fan of public speaking he was even less an admirer of starvation. "Yeah, what's up, Karl?" Alan added. The range of expressions varied from concern (Ellen), to puzzlement (Alan), to annoyance (Eddie), to indifference (Dave), and finally incomprehension (Ruth). Abe and Dabney weren't present, but Karl felt satisfied with the brisk turnout. At least he still had his pipes. He hadn't planned out his spiel, but he knew he should choose his words carefully. Eloquence might be the only armament in his arsenal. Feeling all the eyes burning into his fragile form he looked down, took a deep breath, and cleared his throat.

"Get the fuck on with it," Eddie snarled.

"I'm hungry," Karl peeped.

"Oh for Christ's sake," Eddie spat. "Like you're the only one jonesing for chow. Don't be pullin' that shit," he said wagging a threatening finger at Karl. "Next time you call a meeting make it your funeral, you whiny little bitch."

"Except for the miserable mosquitoes, we're *all* hungry, Mr. Stempler," Ruth echoed, stepping back into her apartment.

Karl hung his head, braced for the final rejections.

"You all out?" Alan said, his face evincing the pained look of a man about to do the decent thing even though he didn't want to. Karl nodded, shame coloring his bleached-out features. Like an ashen Rod Roddy, Alan waved the little guy over with a half-hearted, "Come on down."

"Not much left," Alan said, gesturing at Ellen and his combined provisions. "But what's ours is yours, right?" Ellen nodded. Karl's shoulders began to heave up and down as he tried to stifle tears, but failed. He began to keen like a baby, collapsing to the hard kitchen floor with a rickety kerplop. Once a mother, always a mother, Ellen's maternal instinct kicked in and soon she was cradling Karl's oversize noggin in her lap, absorbing his plentiful tears with her thin cotton summer dress. Though the touch of another human being, especially a female one, was of some comfort, Karl tasted every flavor of humiliation a person could as he sobbed into Ellen's flat stomach. Ellen joined Karl, and soon both were wailing. Alan stood there not knowing what to do, flapping his arms at his sides.

"I, uh. I'll make us something to eat," he said. "Yeah, uh. That's what I'll do."

As the two entwined figures on the floor filled the air with grief,

Alan arranged three small plates of melba toast, turkey jerky, and dried fruit of undetermined classification. All that remained was some uncooked pasta, a few cans of chicken broth, tomato paste, artichoke hearts, a half jar of olives with pimentos, and some stale zwieback from when Ellen's baby had begun to teethe. That and the water jugs was all there was. Maybe they could stretch it for a week or two, but after that, hello starvation. August was just a couple of days away. Alan wasn't about to blub like his two companions, but one tear escaped as the absolute hopelessness of their situation sank in. Autumn was his favorite season. Too bad he'd miss it.

19

Abe finished yet another Dick book, *Time Out of Joint,* and stuffed it between his scrawny thigh and the armrest of his chair. This one was less tripped-out than *Three Stigmata,* but still pretty wacky. In it, the main character discovers things aren't quite as they seem. A soft drink stand replaced by a slip of paper that reads: SOFT DRINK STAND. The mundane tilted on its ear. Things spiral off in a Dickian direction from that moment on. Illusion or whatever, Abe could use a soft drink right about now. Although it was the second day of August and a faltering breeze actually paid intermittent visits, it was still hot as hell and a frosty grape Nehi would sure hit the spot. Did they even make Nehi anymore? The quick answer was that no one made anything any more, but recently. Did they make it as of days, weeks, or months before Armageddon arrived? Just the thought of a sweating twelve-ounce longneck of that carbonated purple nectar put a nostalgic smile on his face.

Abe inched his chair a bit closer to the open window and leaned out, watching the throng.

"I'm sick of this show," he grumbled. "Don't they ever show anything but reruns? How's about another NASCAR smash-up? Do something new, you cabbage-heads! Anything!"

As Abe's shouting grew louder a handful of the undead lackadaisically raised their heads and looked up. A noseless one moaned as it made eye contact with Abe, but there was no further reaction. Abe snatched the paperback from where it was nestled and hurled it out the window, beaning the one missing its schnoz.

"How ya like them apples?" Abe bellowed, then winced as he realized he'd pitched Zotz's book. "Ah, shit." End times or not, Abe figured it was a crappy thing to not return something he'd borrowed. "Ah, fuggit," Abe mumbled, chuckling at the word. "Here's to you, Norman," he said, standing up and unzipping his fly. A deep amber stream of piss scorched its way out as Abe grimaced and pivoted his creaky hips side to side, raining on as many of those undead piles of pus as possible. "Fug all you fugging sons of bitches!" As the last stinging droplet leaked from his urethra, Abe's eyes went wide, and not from the stinging. Something very odd was unfolding below, and this time it wasn't some murky nighttime phantasm. This was happening in broad daylight.

From the south a tiny figure cut north through the multitude, parting it as Moses had the Red Sea. As the lone figure moved forward the undead closed ranks behind it, sealing the temporary divide. Was this some machete-wielding maniac on a death trip? If so, how'd he last this long? Body armor? What? Abe squinted and fished his smudgy glasses out of his breast pocket. The figure was a block south, still too small to make out, but even from here it was obvious that no violence was occurring. This individual brandished no weapon. He just seemed to be strolling through the crowd, unmolested. Maybe this *was* some mirage. It was broiling hot, as per. Abe took off his glasses and wiped them as clean as possible.

The figure made slow progress, but this was happening. This was no delusion.

"Hey! Hey! Hey!" Abe shouted. "Hey, up here!"

No reaction.

Abe kept shouting, loud as he could. Still the figure forged ahead, but never looked up. With all his shouting, where was Ruth? Ignoring him, most likely, convinced he was the old man who cried wolf. *Fug her.* Abe tried hollering a few more times without luck. He tried to move but was petrified by the sheer anomalousness of what was happening. The figure was now half a block south and Abe still couldn't make out its gender or age. The zombies pulled back from it, some letting out foul noises of displeasure. The figure seemed completely unperturbed, walking placid as a Zen monk.

"Hey! Hey! Hey!" Abe shouted again. "Hey, up here! Please!"

As the figure neared their building, Abe could see it was a woman. No. Not a woman, a *girl*, maybe in her teens. From the fifth floor it was hard to tell, but she was young, that much he could see, and dressed in black even in this heat—a black tank top, at any rate. He could only see her from the waist up, the cabbage-heads blocking his view somewhat. He had to tell the others but as she came fully into focus, Abe's mouth dried up and stopped working. With Herculean effort, Abe uprooted himself to leave the room. He staggered into the kitchen and took a swig from the water bottle. Mouth lubricated, he ventured into the hall and after a few inaudible croaks managed to yell, "*Help! Help! Help!* Everyone come quick! Help!"

Once again Eddie was the first to answer the call. Since he'd not been interrupted midthrust, he was only slightly hostile. "What the fuck's all the noise, old man?"

"There's a person outside!"

"Another maniac pullin' a Dale Earnhardt? I woulda heard that."

"You missed it *last* time. Anyway, no! A *girl*. Just a person! No car!"

"Yeah, right."

Karl stepped onto the landing as Abe repeated his last thought. "What?" Karl stammered. "What person? What're you talking about?"

Ellen and Alan joined the others, as did Dave. Ruth was a no-show.

"For the love of Mike, come to my apartment, quick! She's out there! *Quick!*"

"It's a woman?" Karl asked, dazed.

"Whattaya mean 'Mike'? Mike is dead, old man," Eddie said. "He's out there walkin' around? Hey, Matlock, Mike was a heap of bones and gristle last I heard." Looking over at Ellen, Eddie added an insincere, "No offense."

"It's a figure of speech," Abe shouted. "Anyway, just look out the windows!"

"This is bullshit. Grandpa Munster's popped his cork."

"Listen, you pea-brained gorilla, I *saw* what I *saw* and if you don't believe me, fine! Go chase yourself! But everyone else please, please, *please* come see!"

"If you weren't so old . . . ," Eddie began, but all ignored his half uttered half threat and followed Abe into his apartment. When they crowded around the two front windows all was normal, just the usual Undead Sea. Abe poked his head out and looked up and down the avenue. Nothing. Ruth shuffled in and groaned in exasperation.

"It's bad enough you drag me into your lunacy," she lamented, "but the others? Leave them alone, Abraham."

"Did I imagine that car? Was that just some phantom hallucination? No, it wasn't, was it?" Abe twitched with emotion. He'd seen her! She was there moments ago. "You were all too slow," he grumbled. "She was there, I swear it! *She was there.* She must've gone inside someplace."

The others stayed by the windows for a few more minutes, then began to file out of the Fogelhut's apartment. Alan gave Abe's shoulder a squeeze and said, "It's okay, Abe. No harm, no foul."

"Fuck you, 'no harm, no foul.' Don't you condescend to me. I saw what I saw and if you had any brains you'd help me draw her attention. Maybe she was deaf, because I raised a ruckus and she didn't even notice. She was cutting through that crowd down there like a shark. It was like a zipper opening and closing, the way they got out of her way then closed ranks after she passed. I'm telling you, *it happened.*"

"Okay, I believe you." Alan turned to Ellen, who hovered by the door near a mortified Ruth, and said, "I'll be down in a few. I just want to give Abe the benefit of the doubt."

"Again with the patronizing," Abe groused. "Fine, whatever. Let those *putzes* do as they will. Show some sense and give your *benefit of the doubt.*" The last sentiment came out curdled, but Alan didn't mind. Each manned a window and watched the street. Ruth shuffled back into the bedroom and closed the door, fed up with Abe's figments. After about fifteen minutes Abe himself began to doubt what he'd seen. He mopped his sweaty brow with a heinously discolored hankie, his features collapsing in sorrow and embarrassment.

"Maybe I am losing my marbles," he said in a hushed tone.

"Who isn't?" Alan allowed, hoping it didn't sound condescending.

Alan stepped away from the window and as if on cue the girl emerged from Food City, a shopping bag in each hand, which she placed on the ground to adjust something in her ears. Headphones! She was wearing headphones!

"There! There!" Abe shrieked, spinning Alan around. Alan's

jaw nearly hit the floor. As the girl stood before the supermarket, the undead backed away, moaning and hissing. They gave a wide berth and she stepped into the street, aimed south. Abe sputtered, "She can't hear 'cause she's got one of those Walkman thingies!"

Alan tore out of the apartment and into the hall. He ran down to four and pounded each door, all the while shouting, "Abe's right! Get down to the second floor, Abe's right!"

Others rapidly joined Alan in vacant 2A, Abe kvetching, "Sure, *him* they believe."

Everyone crowded by the windows screaming at the tops of their lungs as the figure, now patently obviously a young woman, began to head south.

"We can't let her get away," Ellen squeaked.

Redoubling their efforts they shrieked raw-throated, over and over, *"Help us! Help us! Help us!"*

With her back turned away from 1620, the girl stopped and plucked an earbud out, head cocked like a dog hearing an unfamiliar noise. Seizing the moment they upped their clamor, shrieking, *"We're here! We're here! We're here!"* like a nightmare version of the wee folk in *Horton Hears a Who.* The girl looked this way and that, but didn't turn around. As she was about to replace the earbud she turned and saw them. *She saw them!* With their hearts almost escaping their chests, everyone let out a collective gasp, then began waving their arms in a frenzy. As the girl walked toward the building the zombies all recoiled from her, their noises of reproof stomach turning. The girl moved leisurely, like she didn't have a care in the world. Now that they'd gotten her attention they watched her approach in silent awe. Without a doubt this was the most extraordinary thing any of them had ever seen. Ever.

When she was right below them, the zombies spread out around her, she the pupil, the exposed street the sclera of the eye she'd opened in the crowd. She looked straight at them and plucked both buds out of her ears. Even through the low din of zombie protestations they could hear the tinny ratta-tat-tat of loud percussive music piping from the tiny speakers of her headphones.

"What's up?" she asked in the tone of someone just running into an old acquaintance. Her nonchalance turned every person by the windows into one big goose bump, hairs rising on necks and arms, Adam's apples bobbing in quandary. Maybe Abe's derangement had affected them all, because no one in this world or the next had ever displayed such placidity, least of all in a circumstance like this.

Not even Jesus.

"We need your help," Ellen managed, forcing out each word like a fist-sized chunk.

"Uh-huh. Okay." Big pause. The girl stuck a finger in her ear and jiggled it. "Whattaya want?"

"For starters, we're starving."

"Uh-huh."

And with that she turned around and headed back into Food City, the zombies after a few beats closing the zipper. Everyone stood by the windows, immobilized and mute. On York the scene coalesced into its usual monotonous norm, no breaks in the rotting mob, no sign anything different had ever occurred. Ellen blinked herself out of her stupor and whispered a faint, "Did we just see what we just saw?"

10

As they hoisted the fifth load of canned and dry goods into the windows of 2B, the girl looked up at them, indifferent as when she'd arrived. Everyone was sweatier than usual, but there was a feeling of giddiness and camaraderie that hadn't been evident in the group since ever. One bag toppled over in the excitement and several mouths involuntarily began to drool at the sight of such delicacies as Hormel Chili, Dinty Moore Beef Stew, Del Monte Lite Fruit Cocktail, and more. Even good old SPAM. Several eyes were also leaking, but with anticipated pleasure for a change.

"Okay, then," the girl announced, her voice wholly monotone. With that she picked up her own shopping bags, turned around and began to head south in no particular hurry. On her back was a bulging button- and badge-festooned Hello Kitty backpack, its beady black eyes as blank as hers.

"Wait! Wait!" Ellen screeched, hating the desperation in her voice.

The girl stopped and looked back. "What?"

What?

"Can't you stay?" Ellen shouted, regaining composure.

"Why?"

Why? Was this chick for real? Was she so shattered by the world she couldn't even be horrified by it any more? It was possible. It was certainly possible. Around her, for the first time in months, the zombies' barely functioning brains were engaged, and they didn't like it. The bounty in the building above tantalized them, out of reach. For a moment Ellen wondered if the zombies were as hungry as she was. The girl was clearly abhorrent to them. Inarticulate confusion and chagrin reigned, displayed in a chorus of guttural grunts and thick, phlegmy hissing. In direct contrast, the girl stood there, calm as a mink at a PETA rally.

"Why?" Ellen repeated, dumbfounded. "Because we *need* you to stay. Won't you *please* stay and help us?"

The others all nodded encouragement at Ellen, mutely acknowledging their acceptance of her as their advocate. As they fought the urge to tear into the groceries they watched the back and forth between the two females, their heads looking up, then down in unison, like spectators at a lopsided tennis match.

"You want me to stay," the girl said, sounding it out for her own benefit.

"Yes. Yes we do. Very much. Please stay. We'd be very grateful if you did."

Ellen was trembling, trying to keep it together. The girl stood there and looked at her feet, which were encased in black combat boots. She wore longish black cargo shorts, low on her hips, exposing a generous helping of her very healthy-looking belly. She had no boobs to speak of, but possessed wide, womanly hips. Her hair, also black, was short, choppy, and boyish. She wound and unwound the cord of her earbuds around her hand, pondering, occasionally fanning away a pesky fly. Epochal seconds passed.

"Yeah, okay," she finally responded, voice flat as the world before Columbus.

Ellen and Alan set up her expandable dining table on the roof and Dabney fired up the slightly rusty hibachi he'd found two roofs over, preparing to share their first communal meal since they'd been forced into these straits. Paper and plastic plates and utensils were distributed, freshly liberated from Food City along with all the comestibles. Everyone greedily eyed the various cans and boxes as they were freed from the plastic shopping bags, their colorful labels beacons of the feast yet to come.

"Fuckin' awesome," Eddie declared, holding aloft a bag of Doritos.

At first the meal had been hard to enjoy, everyone's reawakened sense of smell welcome as the scent of grilling meats and veggies seduced them, then not so welcome as they choked on the stench of their rotting neighbors down in the street. But good smells triumphed over rotten and soon dishes brimming with steaming hot meat products and vegetables were devoured with relish. Real relish. Jars of it. Condiments had reverted to seasoning status, to enhance but not *be* the main course.

The mood was high and the behavior almost courtly, each course consumed amidst choruses of "please" and "thank you." Even Eddie was caught up in the graciousness. His mama would've been proud. The SPAM family of products—Hot & Spicy, Lite, Oven Roasted Turkey, Hickory Smoked, and Classic, of course—had never tasted so good.

"This is like filet mignon," Abe said, savoring a chunk of the briny potted meat.

"Better," Karl said, shoveling a heap of baked beans onto his plate. "Oh my God, I can't believe how great this is."

Innumerable permutations of the same sentiment were repeated throughout the repast, punctuated by grateful belches and the occasional fart. When everyone was too stuffed to budge, Abe, being the resident old man of Jewish persuasion, uttered the customary cornball joke that follows big meals: "Waiter, check please." But rather than the groans of embarrassment he'd gotten in the past from his family, laughter erupted, even from Ruth. Abe blinked in astonishment and said, "No one ever laughs at that line. We should starve to death more often."

"*Ucch*, Abraham. Quit while you're ahead." Even Ruth got a laugh.

It had been a long while since anyone's stomach ached from overeating, but that was the case, and the pain was delectable. A symphony of *blurps* and *blorps*, gastric juices breaking down adult-size portions, serenaded the residents of 1620 as they rubbed full bellies and had seconds and thirds. When no one could cram down any more, Alan and Karl brought the soiled disposable dishes and so forth to the edge of the roof and rained the debris down on the zombies below, feeling smug in their well-fed state. Ellen's smile faded and her brow furrowed as it hit her the girl was not among them. She hadn't even partaken of the feast.

"What kind of ingrates and assholes are we?" she gasped, slapping her forehead.

"Huh?" Alan said, turning to face her.

"The girl. The girl! Our good Samaritan! We didn't even invite her to join us. Are we insane?"

"Crazed by hunger, yeah," Eddie said.

"It was an oversight," Abe said. "No disrespect intended."

"No disrespect? We're idiots," Ellen said.

"Don't ruin the mo—"

Ellen raced downstairs and into 2A, where the girl sat by the window, feet up on the sill, nodding her head to the rapid beats assailing her ears. Ellen smoothed her features, then stepped over to the girl and gently tapped her shoulder. The girl looked up and again plucked out an earbud. "What's up?" she asked.

"I, uh. We just ate, and I feel like a real idiot that we got so caught up in our celebration and all that we, uh . . . Christ, this is mortifying, that we, uh, forgot to invite you. It's unconscionable and . . ."

"I ate earlier." She was about to replace the earbud, but Ellen grasped the girl's wrist and prevented it. The girl wasn't miffed at all. She was indifference incarnate. Her sangfroid ruffled Ellen.

"Still," Ellen said, "it was wrong of us and I'm really so, so, so very sorry."

"No sweat." Again the girl made to replace her headphone.

"I, uh," Ellen half laughed and managed a fretful smile. "I, that is, we don't even know your name. We should have been having this dinner to celebrate your arrival. The food just made us forget the whole raison d'être for our party, which is pretty stupid."

"No big. Can I, uh?" She gestured with the rappity-tapping earbud.

"Your name. Could you at least tell me your name?" Ellen hoped she didn't sound hysterical, but this girl's demeanor was rattling her, big time.

"Mona."

"Mona, I'm Ellen," she said, offering her right hand, which Mona shook. Her handshake was unexpectedly firm, though it might just seem so to Ellen, her hand being so frangible.

"Okay then." And with that Mona slipped the earbud back in and resumed nodding her head.

Ellen stood there, uncertain what to do. Though there was no belligerence from Mona whatsoever, she felt as if royalty had dismissed her, which was irrational. Maybe Mona was just getting her bearings, a stranger in new surroundings. Up close and personal, Ellen admired Mona's complexion, which was smooth and perfect, the bridge of her nose and cheeks lightly freckled. Mona's eyes, though listless, were blue as the Caribbean. Her lips were bee-stung, and pointed up slightly in the corners, as if caught in a permanent smirk. Ellen's eyes traveled down Mona's neck, which was solid and round, not a course of concavities and sinew like her own. Maybe now that food was back on the menu Ellen could look forward to being curvy again. What a thought.

Freckles speckled Mona's shoulders, which flared out in a strong V, and while her arms weren't exactly muscular, they were solid. All of her was solid. Ellen cast her eyes toward Mona's legs, which rested on the sill, one ankle cocked atop the other, the toe of the boot tapping out the tattoo of her private tunes. Tattoos. *That's* what Mona was missing. Though she looked the type her skin was bare of decoration. Her calves looked formidable. This girl did a lot of walking. Maybe in no hurry, but she'd been out there on foot, somehow surviving.

"Okay then," Ellen echoed, certain Mona wasn't listening, and turned and walked back toward the door. As she reached for the doorknob Mona said, "Hey," causing Ellen's chest to seize.

"Yes?" Ellen answered, heart thudding.

"This my space or do I hafta share?"

"N-no. This is yours, if you want it. The apartment across the hall is vacant, too, if you'd like that one better. Or there's one on the fifth floor if you . . ."

"This is fine."

Ellen was about to say something, but Mona poked the buds back in and that was that, which was probably for the best. Ellen stepped into the common hall, closed the door to 2A, and stood there, still feeling that sense of unreality. She could hear sounds of reverie from the roof, the jubilant mood persisting. Ellen felt none of it now, but didn't want to be a killjoy. Let the others luxuriate in the moment. *Eat, drink and be merry,* she thought, *for tomorrow we suss out our benefactress.*

"Maybe she's just antisocial," Alan said, wanting to fall asleep while still enjoying the sensation of fullness. How long had it been since anyone in the building had gone to bed not hungry?

"It's more than that," Ellen said, her tone firm. "It's like she's not quite there."

"That's kind of a snap judgment, isn't it? How long has she been here, five hours? She's been out there on her own for who knows how long, probably lost everyone she ever knew. Yeah, she seems a little out of it, from what little I saw, but she'll come around. We're like a bunch of needy kids she's been saddled with out of nowhere. Give her a little time to adjust. You should be grateful she showed up."

"I am. Don't put words in my mouth, or thoughts in my head, or whatever. I'm deliriously happy that she's here. Hopefully we can get her to stay and go out and get more. If she's immune to those things, hell yes I'm grateful. I didn't hear any of the rest of you calling out to her to get her to help, so cut me some slack, Alan."

"Jeez, relax a little. Just get some sleep, please. Tomorrow's another day." And with that he rolled over and blew out the candle, illustrating that the conversation was over.

Ellen lay on her back absentmindedly rubbing her full stomach. *Her full stomach.* What the hell was she so worked up about? Alan was right. This girl was a godsend, simple as that. Was she jealous? Oh Jesus, if that was it she needed help. A young nubile girl arrives and what, she's afraid she'll lose her man? Oh that's insane. But maybe that was what was troubling her. Mona was a pretty young thing with a pretty young body. On the one hand maybe Alan would cast an impure eye her way, but on the other, so might the apes across the hall. That would take some pressure off.

If Mona stuck around, Ellen could maybe fill out her skin again, put the curves back. Her breasts had once been brimming with milk, sustainers of life. She'd once had the tiny mouth of her infant daughter suckling her large, distended nipples. Her nipples had been in a perpetual state of stimulation. They'd felt raw, but vital. Mike had grown jealous, even resentful of the baby. "That's my turf," he'd said, insisting it was a joke, but Ellen and he knew full well that many truths were said in jest. "She gets one year grazing privileges, tops," Mike had said, "then all rights revert to yours truly." They'd laughed, but Mike would watch the baby nursing and raise an eyebrow, tap the crystal of his watch. "One year," he'd repeat. "Not a day longer."

Ellen's hand drifted up from her belly and felt the hollowed lobes of flesh. She'd have them back. Maybe they wouldn't produce sustenance any more, but they could make Alan happy. She traced orbits around her areola with her fingertip, the nipple responding, straining up to greet her digit.

Her baby.

Her dead baby.

She almost had to struggle to remember her name.

Fully hydrated for the first time in ages, Ellen lay there and shed nary a tear. She was all cried out. The world was a dead place full of dead things too stupid and stubborn to realize it. She remembered the boys in her old neighborhood that ran around playing cops and robbers or cowboys and Indians. They'd shoot cap guns or finger guns at each other shouting, "Pow! Pow!" even if they were firing caps. Then the recipient of imaginary lead was supposed to fall down. "You're dead!" the boys would shout. "Fall down!" If the victim defied them with an impudent, "Uh-uh, you missed," or "Make me," arguments ensued and sometimes fists would fly.

Those things outside were poor sports that refused to fall down. She could feel them, still restless from their encounter with Mona. There was *some* cognizance there. Maybe it was rudimentary, but those things knew something was up. Some groaned in their clabbered subhuman manner, sounds so thick and ugly they prodded Ellen's bowels. *Think happy thoughts*, Ellen commanded herself. *You will be beautiful again. You will be desirable again. Alan already desires you. You will be vital again.*

Mona isn't a threat.

Dabney lay on his tarp, staring up at the cosmos. The haze had cleared and for the first time in weeks the sky was pinpricked with countless stars. He ran his tongue around the inside of his mouth, sucking small deposits of food from between his teeth. His belly churned happily. There were leftovers on the table, which remained on the roof. Leftovers. How decadent. The only thing lacking in this equation was a cigarette. Oh sweet Lord above, a cigarette would be glorious. The thought sent a shiver of pleasure through his body. Dabney eased up off the ground, trod over to the table, and scooped out the remnants of a can of peas, then drank the pea water, swishing it around like a funky mouthwash. He thought about dental hygiene. Maybe that girl could get some toothpaste and Scope and whatnot. Listerine, but not the nasty medicinal kind. That minty stuff. Or the citrus kind! If it tasted like orange soda he'd gargle all day and keep the gingivitis at bay.

And cigarettes. Definitely cigarettes.

He was sorry he hadn't spotted her. All his time up here playing lookout when there was nothing to see and the one time something was brewing he'd been napping on the job. Abe got that glory.

"Thank you, God," he said aloud, just in case he seemed unappreciative.

With his lantern burning, Dabney polished off every morsel that remained.

"I wouldn't mind breaking off a piece of that," Eddie said, the only one in the building rubbing south of his belly. "Oh yeah. I didn't get that good of a look, but she looked fuckin' young, bronus. A little light in the tit-tay department, but I don't care."

"Sure, whatever," Dave replied.

"Whatever? *Pfff.* Okay, bro, fine. More for me."

Dave sighed expansively and shook his head.

"What? What, dude, *what?* You're actin' like her showin' up isn't the greatest thing since *Girls Gone Wild.*"

"Of course it is, but Jesus, Eddie, you're already thinking about nailing her and she just got here. Plus which, unless rape is your new thing, maybe you oughta test those waters before you go assuming she'll have anything to do with you."

"Y'know, I never noticed what a sad sack o' shit you can be sometimes. And you better stow that shit about the rape. That's *our* business and no one else's, *capisce?* I get wind of you spreadin' that around and . . ."

"And what? Oh that's right. Murder's on your résumé, too."

Eddie got up off the futon and stomped over to Dave, who sat on the carpet, back to the wall. Eddie stood with his legs spread wide, a posture of unquestionable dominance. He kept making and unmaking fists as he stared down at Dave, who looked up with defiance.

"What? You gonna hit me?" he asked. "You gonna *kill* me?"

Eddie glared at Dave, looked away, looked around the room. After a minute his posture relaxed, the expression on his face uncertain. "Why you gotta push my buttons, bro?" he asked, his voice a soft whine. "This was a good night and you had to go bringing up that old business."

"*Old business?* It was what, a week or so ago? If that?" Who kept a calendar any more?

"You know what I mean. Look, whatever, okay? The Wandering Jewess was a mistake, bro. I told you I didn't mean to . . . The Comet just got a little out of . . . Anyway, truce. Okay, bro? I don't wanna end the day on a note like this."

"How about a note like this, then?" Dave pulled Eddie's shorts down.

With his eyes closed, Eddie conjured what's-her-name's face in place of Dave's.

"So who's the boy who cried wolf now, huh, Mrs. Bigshot? Who's the *gantser macher* around here?"

"It isn't nice to gloat, Abe," Ruth said, but she smiled in spite of herself. Abe had done well. Very well. She curled around him and in the dark allowed herself to imagine Abe as he'd been when they met. To her complete surprise, Abe put his arm around her shoulders instead of shrugging her away. "Okay, maybe you can gloat a little. Our hero." She kissed his cheek and restrained herself from smacking her lips to ease the tickle from his beard. Let the goyim have visions of sugarplums dancing in their heads. As Ruth drifted off she dreamt of shaving cream and fresh razors for Abe.

And soap and paper towels and deodorant.

She seldom cleaned the house any more—just the occasional cursory run with the broom—but now a radiant vision of Lysol and Comet and Soft Scrub and refills for her Swiffer, both wet and dry, floated through her brain. Suddenly she was young again, dancing like Fred Astaire—to heck with Ginger; Ruth wanted to lead! Her partner was a mop and the setting a palatial kitchen. As she danced every surface she passed gleamed, shaming every commercial for every domestic cleaning product ever made. White surfaces shone bright as a thousand suns. Was that a speck of grease on the stove top? With the grace of a dozen Baryshnikovs, Ruth leapt through the air and obliterated the offending stain with a balletic stroke of her sponge. And not some off-brand sponge, but a good one! An O-Cel-O!

Joined by a spectacular rainbow, sunbeams flooded the immense chamber. Disney-esque forest animals capered about—small cartoon birds chirping, tiny white bunnies hoppity-hopping, deer sweet and charming as Bambi—and Ruth shooed them all away with her magical mop. "No filthy dirty animals in my spotless kitchen," she scolded in tones dulcet as Beverly Sills's.

As the last critter fled the room the kitchen began to shake and shimmy, cabinets opening, dishes spilling to the floor, smashing to bits, creating fissures in the immaculate ceramic tile. Shards of shattered glass and china littered her utopia and her ears were assailed by the cacophony of raining utensils. The sun faded and the sky turned an ominous gray. The booming stentorian voice of God rang out.

"Get off of me. Ruth, *please*. Get off."

"What did I do?" Ruth said, voice quaking.

"You're crushing my arm. My arm's gone numb."

Ruth awoke to Abe jostling her head and shoulders in an attempt to free his sleeping arm.

"Oh for heaven's sake," Ruth sneered. "For this you wake me?"

"I got pins and needles. You want me to get gangrene like your mother?"

"You have to bring my mother into this, may her soul rest in peace? *Ucch*, Abraham."

Ruth turned away from Abe as he rubbed his arm. *Please God,* she thought. *I don't ask much. Just send me back to my happy kitchen. And while you're at it, send Abe some more pins and needles.*

Karl pressed his lips to the Polaroid of Dawn-Anne McCarthy spread-eagle, then with a gentle flick of his wrist sent it spiraling down into the crowd below. *"Au revoir, mon amour,"* he whispered. He'd spent the last fifteen minutes removing all the pinups and centerfolds from his wall, balling them up, tossing the crumpled wads of paper out the window, watching them bounce off the empty noggins of the horde. The repetitive motion reminded him of feeding the animals at the Cleveland Metroparks Zoo—one of the few enjoyable memories he could conjure from his childhood that involved the presence of his old man—and equally rare for its involving animals *not* being killed by Big Manny. Each wadded-up piece of pornography stood in for a bygone peanut or piece of bread, and for a change thinking of those edibles didn't make his empty stomach lurch because it wasn't empty. Praise be.

The cleansing had nothing to do with faith, though. Not faith in the Almighty, at any rate—faith in maybe making time with the new arrival. Though he'd only glimpsed her as he'd hoisted up bag after bag of groceries, she looked incredible. And the way she was all dressed up in black with that funky knapsack, oh baby. She was a hip chick. She'd probably be into the same tunes. She looked like a Korn fan. Metal. Maybe Goth, which wasn't really Karl's thing, but he could fake being conversant in matters Gothy. He knew from The Cure and Bauhaus. Wasn't that enough?

This cleansing was an act of optimism, his first since everything hit the shitter running. Her arrival was miraculous. No, this was no time to be thinking about God. If he thought about God he'd inevitably think about Big Manfred and that was the mental equivalent of saltpeter. Why ruin the moment? He was still young enough to pursue a girl like that without feeling like a dirty old man. She looked to be "of age," not that a thing like that matters when all the lawmakers and law upholders are dead, dead, dead. *What's the age of consent in New York?* But he'd have to be shrewd and charming. As sure as he was that he wanted her, he was equally certain that Eddie would make a play for her, too. Not that a hip chick like her would ever fall for a knuckle-dragging throwback like him. Dave, on the other hand, seemed perfectly content in his "se-cret" love for Eddie. He reminded Karl of all those Republicans who'd hoisted themselves on their own petards, preaching intoler-ance while pursuing clandestine same-sex relations. In public toilets. With male prostitutes. With underage senate pages. Real guardians of virtue, they were. Big Manny had voted for them all, the hyp-ocrites. Oh irony. And all it had taken to nudge Dave out of the closet—mostly—was the apocalypse.

Karl plucked the final Playmate off the wall, a sloe-eyed Hawai-ian hottie, Lourdes Ann Kananimanu Estores—Miss June 1982. This was tough. He'd "gone steady" with this gatefold since finding her in a thrift shop back in Akron that didn't care how old you were as long as you had cash. He'd secreted her into his childhood bed-room and made sweet imaginary love to her countless times, his eyes tracing every velvet inch of her soft tan body. He'd overlooked her taste in music—The Rolling Stones, Bette Midler, The Cars, Bob Seger, Jimmy Buffett, The Eagles—in light of her overwhelm-ing beauty. And he knew if they ever met he could swing her around to the real deal. Bette Midler? *Jimmy Buffett?* Well, she *was* from Hawaii.

Was she dead, too? Most likely.

She was probably one of those shambling piles of flesh-hungry rot. Maybe she'd been torn apart. The thought was too awful to contemplate. He held her in his quaking hands, unable to cast her into the abyss.

"There's such a thing as too much optimism," he said, folding her up with care and stowing her in a drawer. "Always have a back-up plan," he added, patting the closed dresser.

Just in case.

Dabney was in his usual spot, selecting a suitable chunk to lob. When he found one that felt right, conformed to the hollow of his palm, he inched closer to the edge and scoped out the scene below, looking for a target. In his day he'd been a fair hand at amateur pitching and darts, so even though nine times out of ten he'd pick a recipient and miss, he at least liked to make the effort. He spotted a likely candidate down below, a slightly rotund one, seemingly stuck in one spot. From Dabney's vantage point he couldn't see why, but the corpulent corpse's spilt entrails had tethered it to the base of a nearby streetlamp, and it was further anchored by the feet of its companions. It stood perfectly still as its cohorts shambled aimlessly around it.

Dabney rotated his wrist a couple of times to loosen up, then chucked the brick, admiring its graceful arc as it plummeted down across the avenue, then delighting in the unexpected as it collapsed the head of its intended target. The fat zombie disappeared as it sank into the crowd, creating a lumpy speed bump for its confederates. Dabney chuckled as he opened a can of mandarin orange slices and took a swig of the tangy syrup, the small, soft wedges of citrus brushing against his lips. He swished the liquid around in his mouth, savoring the sweetness. He remembered when he'd been laid low with chicken pox and then later mumps as a boy and how his mother had given him dishes of mandarin orange slices as a treat. They'd perked him up then just as they perked him up now, but thinking of his momma added a touch of melancholy and he put down the can and let out a mournful noise. "Oh, momma," he sighed, then took in a big mouthful of pre-served fruit. "Oh momma."

"Why'd you do that?"

Dabney nearly shat himself, unaware he had company. He spun around and saw the girl. He was the only one in the building who hadn't met her yet.

"You startled me," he said, smoothing his features.

"Sorry." She didn't sound or look sorry, but she didn't seem sarcastic either. "Why'd you do that?"

"Do what?"

"Throw the brick."

"The brick? Oh, it's something to do. Gives 'em something to chew on besides us."

The girl contemplated his answer, then stepped over to the ledge and peered down, the toes of her boots resting right on the lip. Dabney began to sweat. "You ain't planning on doing anything rash, are you, miss?" he asked. "Uh, miss? What's your name, again?" He said *again*, but he didn't know in the first place. For the first time since he'd arrived he felt out of the loop and rude, to boot. He should have come down and introduced himself. Thanked her. These tasty citrus slivers had come courtesy of this spooky little white girl and he hadn't the manners to let her know he felt much obliged. He was too taken with his self-appointed role as The Roof Man, like some powerless superhero, or enigmatic loner, or plain old antisocial oddball.

"Mona," she replied.

"Mona," he repeated. "Well, Mona, you're not thinking of doing anything foolish are you?"

"Like what?" she asked.

The feeling of déjà vu struck Dabney, this scene less heightened than Karl's would-be jumper scenario, but weirder. Karl had been in an agitated snit. This girl was quiescent as a newborn at her momma's teat.

Stop thinking about momma, Dabney thought.

"Your standing right on the edge has me a little nervous is all," he said. "Maybe you oughta come away from there and let's get introduced. My name's John Dabney. Most visitors to my roof just address me as Dabney, but either will do. And I guess technically it's not *my* roof, per se, but I sort of think of it that way." He felt foolish running his mouth but didn't stop. "I guess I owe you an apology, Mona." He paused, hoping he'd engaged her, waiting for the stock response that didn't come. The buzzing of flies filled the pregnant pause with white noise. *Why was it called* white *noise?* Dabney wondered. White neighbors. White noise. He blinked back to the moment, looking at the girl who hadn't moved an inch. She was stolid as a figurehead on the prow of a ship, expression serene, skin unblemished. "I owe you an apology," he repeated, trying to anchor himself in the present.

Thoughts of his seafaring days assailed him. That fat zombie sank like a ship in the ocean of ambulatory corpses. Thoughts of his momma ricocheted around his upper story, too. Maybe those orange slices were spoiled. No. They tasted just fine. Delicious. He'd smoked hashish many moons ago, while in Tangiers. He'd sampled peyote and psilocybin mushrooms while out west. This was the way of the mind and Dabney didn't pretend to know what he was all about, least of all on a neuron-by-neuron basis. It was the girl, maybe. Dabney was used to dilapidated specimens like Ellen and Ruth, even though they barely ever manifested in his domain. To see a healthy female so impalpable was putting the whim-whams on him. She turned to face him and sat down, crossing her ankles. Relief flooded Dabney. Even if it weren't his fault, had the girl tumbled off his roof he'd have felt responsible—at least partially. Worse yet, the others might tar him with a grief-stricken guilty brush. The only thing worse than having no luck is to get some then lose it in a trice.

"What for?" she asked.

"Huh?"

"The apology?" Asked with unblinking eyes.

"Oh, *oh*. Oh, for not introducing myself earlier. For not showing my appreciation for the wonderful food you've brought us. I should've come down and said thank you. I would have. I don't want to make excuses, it's just . . ." Dabney trailed off and considered his next words with care. "I hope you don't take this the wrong way, 'cause I mean no disrespect, but, uh, how come those things don't attack you like everyone else?"

"I guess they don't like me." Dabney looked at her, waiting for the rest, but that's all there was. No further embellishment. The statement lay there like roadkill. "I need sunglasses," she said, then got up and walked back into the stairwell.

Dabney stared into the half empty can of orange slices.

Or was it half full?

"We need to send Mona out for more supplies," Alan said. "Specifically *toilet paper*. I don't mean to be disgusting or anything, but just as with great power comes great responsibility, so too does food come with an unfortunate byproduct. Not that responsibility is unfortunate but . . . All I'm saying is . . ." Alan moaned from behind the closed door, tossing the crap-smeared wad of newsprint out the bedroom window—there was no window in the bathroom. Only a couple of broadsheets remained of his last copy of the *New York Press*. "Who'd ever think you could be sentimental about something like toilet paper? Or those moist butt wipes? Oh, those were heavenly."

"Agreed," Ellen replied. She knew just how he felt. Unlike the rabbit pellets she was used to producing, all those victuals had gotten her innards producing waste again, and it wasn't pretty.

"I mean, it's bad enough hanging your ass out the window to relieve yourself, but to then sandpaper yourself is the icing on the cake," Alan continued with an audible wince. "So to speak. It's all so medieval."

"Enough already," Ellen said, marching away from the closed portal. "We need to have a building meeting and compile a list of necessities, provided of course that Mona's zombie repelling wasn't some fluke and that she's even willing to go out there and do it again. So I'll get some paper, and top of the list will be moistened butt wipes."

"*Huzzah,*" Alan shouted. "Thank you!"

Alan vacated the window and looked around for anything else to tidy with. Maybe Mona would come through with the goods, but until then he needed to do something. As bad as the *Press* was to read, it was twice as bad to wipe with.

A year or two ago Alan had undergone a minor surgical procedure and had been given an overnight basket by the staff, mostly dull items like a cheapo toothbrush, no-name toothpaste, a packet of generic facial tissues. But the highlight was a pump-spray bottle of *Personal Cleanser*. Friends would come by and he'd amuse them with its label, which bluntly proclaimed it to be "No-rinse, one-

step cleansing for the perineum or body" containing "Gentle surfactants [to] aid in the removal of urine and feces." He'd brought it
home for a goof, but it had made his life far more bearable over the
last several weeks. When he'd moved in with Ellen, he gallantly
shared the last few spritzes with her, and now he wished he hadn't.

Oh, for those gentle surfactants.

Alan's butt stung from the newspaper and felt distinctly unclean. He felt like some tormented Bible character, which was already easy to do given the state of the world. But this was more
personal. A civilized adult man should not have to walk around
with a poo-crusted tush. He rummaged through a nearby drawer
and filched a pinkish baby-T and finished his hygiene ritual. The
soft cotton-poly blend did a better job and was much kinder to his
hinder. Why hadn't he thought of this before? Satisfied he'd done
the best he could, he lobbed it out the window to join the *Press* in
the alley below. Hopefully Ellen wouldn't mind or even notice
that he'd used a garment of hers. Then it hit him.

Oh fuck me.

Oh double fuck me twice.

Not hers. This wasn't some hipster baby-T, it was an *actual*
T-shirt that had belonged to her baby, no doubt imbued with all
manner of sentimental value. Perspiration began to pour off his
forehead.

Oh Jesus.

As a child, Alan and his mother had been invited by a coworker
of hers to spend a weekend at the workmate's summer cabin in
Upstate New York. The work chum was a charming man, but Alan
disliked him because he figured the guy wanted to put the make
on his divorcee mother. Little had unsophisticated seven-year-old
Alan realized the guy was gay. After dinner Alan excused himself,
then raced into the guest bathroom and spent a fitful several minutes
vomiting through his ass, only to be confronted with an absence

of toilet paper. Panicked, sweaty, ass raw from the torrential out-
burst and too humiliated to cry out for toilet paper, he searched
the tiny rustic chamber in vain for anything to wipe with. He
ended up using a flowery lavender hand towel, which he balled up
and tossed out the window. In a private after-dinner moment Alan
scooted outside and buried it in the adjacent woods. Weeks later
the coworker asked his mother if she had accidentally packed the
towel with her things.

Hopefully Ellen wouldn't notice.

"I want batteries," Karl said, clutching his exanimate boombox.
"Lots of batteries."

"Maybe some of those emergency lights, like for when there's a
blackout. It would be awesome to have light after dark again. To
read without eyestrain? That would be amazing," Alan chimed in,
Ellen playing secretary and jotting down all the suggestions. All but
Mona had gathered in Ellen's apartment and were seated in the
sweltering living room, made all the hotter by the group's body
heat.

"Hey, what about one of those camping generators?" Dave said.

"Good one," Eddie said, slapping Dave's back.

"I'd like some fresh razors. Oh, since we're talking batteries,
how's about a couple of those electric razors?" Abe suggested, earning him appreciative *oohs* and *ahhs* from the hairy-faced men in the
room.

"And a fuckin' hair clipper," Dave said, ruffling his scraggy
hair. "'Scuse the language," he added, looking at Ruth's reproach-
ful expression.

"Eventually, and I know it's not a necessity, but maybe some art
supplies," Alan said.

"Yeah, like you said, '*not a necessity*,'" Eddie sneered. "So chill on that shit, Picasso." Since Alan stopped furnishing him with custom whacking matter, Eddie had ceased to be an art lover.

"Slow down," Ellen said, her pen skating across the sheet of notepaper. The list was pretty long. The basic necessities were more nonperishable foodstuffs, fresh water, Alan's precious—although she must admit they were superior, especially in the absence of bathing—moist butt wipes as well as traditional toilet paper, soap, toothpaste, dental floss and dental rinses, more candles and flashlights, and deodorant. "I don't know how many trips Mona is going to want to make."

"Hey, if she's immune to those things, what else has she got on her schedule?" Eddie snapped. "We makin' her miss her soaps? *Pfff.*"

"Yes, the exercise will do her good," agreed Ruth, earning her a rare smirk of approbation from Eddie.

"And who's to say she wants to be our little errand girl?" Ellen countered. "Who's to say she won't look at this, go '*the hell with these a-holes*' and hightail it out of here, list in hand, gone, gone, gone?"

"Why so pessimistic?" Alan asked.

"I just don't want to overwhelm the girl by being too greedy," Ellen said. "We have a potentially very good thing with Mona and I don't want us to turn into a bunch of jackals who drive her off with our yard-long shopping list."

"Girlies love to shop," Eddie said.

Ellen ignored him and reviewed the list. "Okay, in terms of needs versus wants, this is a pretty reasonable list. But how's she supposed to carry all this?"

"She could take my shopping cart," Ruth suggested.

"Old ladies and their shopping carts," Eddie scoffed.

"I don't see you making any useful contributions to this discussion," Ruth sniped.

"Maybe she could boost a car," Eddie said. "I could tell her how." No one was surprised that Eddie possessed this know-how.

"You think if she knew how to drive she'd be hoofing it?" Karl said. "How's she supposed to get through all the forsaken cars down there?"

"Maybe she could just take the shopping cart from the market. It's not like anyone will mind," Alan threw in. Nods all around.

"One more thing," Eddie ventured. "*Guns.*"

Karl looked askance at Eddie.

"*Ooh,* I don't know," said Ellen, with a slight frown.

"What don't you know? Guns would come in mighty useful against those fuckers out there."

"How? We'd be like hunters in a blind shooting at ducks. You can't shoot them all. We'd still be stuck here."

"We should have guns," Eddie reiterated.

"It would be sport shooting, nothing more," Ellen added.

"So?"

"So what's the point? I don't like the thought of guns in the building. You think if you shoot a bunch you're going to win a prize? This isn't Coney Island, Eddie."

Typical patronizing Upper East Side Jewy liberal, Eddie thought. What Ellen thought was, *I don't like the thought of you having guns, Eddie Tommasi. Too dangerous for the rest of us chickens.*

"Just ask her, okay?" Eddie said, smoothing his features. "Let her be the judge. She brings 'em back, great. She doesn't, so be it."

Having omitted Eddie's request for firearms, Ellen handed over the list and asked, "Is that too much, Mona?" She'd decided to always address the girl by name when speaking to her. Her theory was that maybe she'd had her sense of identity eroded by walking amongst the undead for however long she'd been out there on her own. Ellen was as determined to reclaim this girl as she and the others were to having her run errands for them.

"Maybe more'n one trip," Mona mumbled, folding the slip of paper and tucking it in her pocket.

"And you're cool with going back out there? We don't want to pressure you."

"No big."

And with that she wedged the earbuds in—her signature gesture, like Carson's golf swing—and rappelled out the window via the ratty rope they'd used to haul her in. When she touched down on the roof of Dabney's ruined van she looked up at Ellen and the others, all of whom wore the expectant look of latchkey kids afraid mommy would never return.

"I'm getting new rope, too," she said, dangling the frayed end.

The others nodded yes and Mona climbed off the vehicle, the zombies spreading out with a sibilant anthem of reproach. As she headed north toward Eighty-sixth Street, her Hello Kitty knapsack looking back at them with its vapid beady black eyes, the throng opened and closed, a long, wide mouth that couldn't devour this one small girl. When she turned the corner everyone but Abe, the self-appointed lookout, left 2B to resume the daily grind. Abe sat and watched as the zombies settled down, some still hissing and spitting like rabid bipedal cats. He pawed his scruffy chin, images of cranky and crotchety cowboy sidekicks floating in his mind. All he needed was to be stirring a pot o' beans on an open fire to complete the picture, and now, with this Mona girl, the pot o' beans was attainable.

That's who I look like, Abe mused. *A Jewish Gabby Hayes. Well, not after I shave off this soup strainer. Oh, I can't wait.* He leaned on the windowsill and his smile faded, his stomach soured. From this same vantage point he'd watched this apartment's previous tenant, Paolo, get devoured down below.

Abe hoped Mona could remove that stigma from this empty dwelling.

The sun was setting and although there was plenty of food in the building, Ellen couldn't stop herself from looking out the window every few minutes. This wasn't about food, anyway. If anything, at this moment having a full stomach just stoked her agita.

"You're gonna wear a groove into the floor," Alan said, in a poor attempt to break the tension.

"I'm just worried, okay? Am I allowed to be worried? She left hours ago and it's almost dark. Maybe something happened to her. Maybe she isn't immune and it was some fluke and we sent her out there and now she's dead. And if that's the case then it's all our fault and we're responsible for sending a young girl to her death."

Alan opened his mouth to say something and then shut it. He'd already paid lip service to Ellen's anxiety and it had done no good. It was troubling that Mona had been gone for the better part of the day. He'd posited several plausible scenarios. It was possible that several items on the list had proven more difficult to procure than others and that Mona was traipsing all around town in an attempt to accommodate every request. It was also possible that she had forgotten how to find her way back, even though she had neatly printed the address of the building in big block letters on the list. Maybe she lost the list. It was imaginable that she had gotten to one of her destinations and gotten jammed up by the zombies— *but that she was all right.* She was just temporarily waylaid and would be back soon. For Ellen's sake he had to keep the propositions upbeat.

But it was also quite reasonable to assume that Mona had been devoured.

Ellen's eyes darted back and forth from the street below to the sky above, both growing darker and more ominous. She wound her hair around her fingers and chewed the ends. Alan again attempted levity by suggesting she'd get split ends doing that but Ellen just looked at him like he was an idiot. Alan sat there internally reciting the names of hair products and quoting lines from TV commercials. *"If you don't look good, we don't look good." Vidal Sassoon. Pantene Pro-V. Paul Mitchell. L'Oreal. What the hell was the one with those stupid commercials where girls would rub it into their scalps in public and semipublic places? And for all intents and purposes they'd be having noisy orgasms? Then they'd emerge, from like the toilet on an airplane, tousling their shimmering manes and everyone would look at them with lust and envy? What was that stuff? Some herbal something? Maybe Mona should pick up some of that. Ellen could do with some shiny locks. What kind of thinking is this? Yesterday there's no food. All that matters is some clean, drinkable water and food that will sustain the organism for another twenty-four hours. Now it's "Ellen could use a nice shampoo." I must be out of my friggin' gourd.*

"Seriously, Ellen, I'm sure she's fine."

"Oh really? You can say that authoritatively? You know that for a fact do you? How interesting. Because, see, the way I see it, none of us knows a damned thing right now and for all we know chunks of her are being digested—if those things even digest. I mean, do they? Do they eat and shit and breathe? What do they do besides stumble around and eat us when they can? They sure made short work of Mike. They gobbled him down like no tomorrow. But are there piles of zombie scat out there composed of my husband? Are there? We don't know. I don't know. None of us knows anything!"

Should I get up and hug her? Alan wondered. When he'd gotten into fights in the past with women—various girlfriends and one ex-wife—after all the sour words and recriminations and accusations and *you did this* and *you did that* it always came down to something simple like she just needed a hug and a kiss. Then the situation would calm down and laughter would come and then maybe, in the best of times, they'd make love or at least have sex. Was this one of those occasions where a hug was the answer? Alan got up and gently placed his arms around Ellen's shoulders.

"What? *What?* You want sex now? What the hell is *wrong* with you?"

"I don't. I don't want sex," Alan stammered. "I just thought maybe a hug would . . ." Why bother finishing the thought? He withdrew his arms and turned to resume his place on the couch.

"Where are you going? I didn't say I didn't want to be hugged. I just . . . I'm just freaking out." She shot another glance out the window. "Maybe you should fuck me right about now."

"What?"

"Do I stutter? Maybe you should fuck me. Now."

"But this wasn't about sex, honest. I swear. I wasn't being . . ." Was she toying with him?

"*Just fuck me.* I need to be penetrated. I need to have something tearing my mind from Mona. But don't think about Mona while we're doing it. I know she's healthy and young and I'm not. Well, I'm young, but you know what I mean. Her body versus mine. Don't fantasize about her. Or don't think about her being torn limb from limb like chicken. You won't get an erection from a thought like that. Maybe Eddie would, but Christ, I don't want to think about what gets Eddie off."

Ellen marched into the kitchen, shucked off her baggy army-surplus shorts and cotton undies, grabbed the counter and pushed her ass out at him. "Do it," she commanded. Normally a take-charge woman was a turn-on, but this was a lot of pressure combined with deeply troubling extenuating circumstances. Alan dropped his pants and massaged into being a serviceable if slightly spongy erection. "Don't be gentle. Don't be slow," Ellen ordered. Such hard words. Such hard angles. Though he didn't want to think about Mona, he did think about the food. Food would soon inflate everything back to normal.

Alan followed Ellen's edicts and pounded away. She gritted her teeth and bucked against his pelvis, meeting each thrust with equal force. Alan thought about stacking china and how delicate porcelain was. He thought about building model kits as a boy, then dropping rocks on them or blowing them up with firecrackers. He hoped their bones were up to this punishment. It had been a while since he'd run out of vitamins. How was his calcium? How was Ellen's? They should have added a good multivitamin to the shopping list. And Jesus, lots of items from the pharmacy. What were they thinking? Just food and batteries? They'd been discussing keeping it to necessities. What could be more necessary than vitamins and headache remedies? Some pink bismuth. And not store-brand. Pepto Bismol. Or Pepcid AC! Some antidiarrheal. Oh yeah, that's hot stuff. That's the stuff of a *Penthouse* letter. Why not just start contemplating osteoporosis? Or scoliosis? Or any other bone-wrecking -osis?

"I want you to come inside me," Ellen snarled, thrashing her head back and forth. This was very odd. This wasn't a hate fuck. Alan had only experienced that phenomenon once or twice in his past, especially with his ex-wife. She'd stare up at him, eyes squinted in concentration, slowly and with great deliberation intoning, "*Fuck my cunt,*" over and over. This wasn't like that exactly, but it was certainly angsty. And very aggressive. Ellen snapped her head back and her hair whipped across his face.

"Clairol," he said, slapping his forehead. "Clairol Herbal Essence!"

"What?"

"Nothing," he said, feeling lava pump into his face. He smacked her ass and pumped harder to throw her off the scent of his wandering mind. After several more minutes of violent hammering he obliged her request. His knees and thighs immediately turned to jelly and he sank to the floor. Ellen slumped beside him. She pressed her head against his chest and murmured, "Hold me."

It always came down to a hug.

And as he ran his fingers through her oily hair he silently mouthed, *Clairol Herbal Essence.*

FEBRUARY, *THEN*

It had been two weeks earlier that Ellen had teased Alan as he trudged up the stairs, Bataan Death March-style, with case after case of Kirkland bottled water. Nothing had really happened yet—certainly not on the level into which it would blossom—but Alan's girlfriend, Tammy, had convinced him that preparedness wasn't anything to scoff at. So there he'd been, doing the lion's share of lugging, wishing for an elevator.

"All you need are some camouflage fatigues and a headband," Ellen said with a smirk as he approached her on the landing. Her infant daughter, Emily, was suckling a full, barely veiled breast. Though Alan found nothing sexy about nursing—lactation was not a kink he found appealing—he was enamored of Ellen Swenson's boobs and any peek was welcome. Tammy, tart-tongued and efficient, was all nipple and no tit, her chest a smooth plane of milky white skin dotted with two pencil eraser-size pink protrusions. Though not in love with Tammy, Alan was fond of her, but he craved suppleness and Ellen had it. He blinked away his unchaste thoughts and refocused on Ellen's eyes.

"Huh?" Despite the temperature outside, his face was awash in perspiration.

"You and the gal pal are really kicking into survivalist mode."

Alan eased the case to the ground with a thud, panting. "Better safe than sorry. That's Tammy's philosophy."

"It's just some infected rats," Ellen countered. "They'll be dead in no time. You've seen all the open manholes everywhere."

"Yeah, I know. Between the rats and the noxious fumes, driving back with the supplies was a bitch."

"You keep a car in the city?" With all that was going on, *that* was what Ellen marveled at. It made Alan smile. These were the real concerns of full-blooded New Yorkers. Not rats biting and infecting commuters down in the subway and pedestrians on the street. Not crews in hazmat suits spelunking the city's subterranean infrastructure for the last two weeks, pumping who knows what kind of toxic gas down there in hopes of obliterating the ferocious rodents. Not people either stumbling around hacking in each other's faces looking like death warmed over or sporting surgical masks. Where you parked: *that* was a thing at which to marvel.

"Tammy keeps it in Brooklyn. It's her car."

"Ah," Ellen said. "*Brooklyn.* Remember when Manhattan was the place to be? Now it's Brooklyn."

"Now it's Brooklyn," Alan agreed.

That exchange had been two weeks ago. Now, Alan was side by side with Mike, Ellen's husband, hammering nails into planks of plywood to further buttress the closed-off entranceway to their building. Over the clatter of their work Mike shouted, "This doesn't bode well!"

"What?" Alan stopped hammering, as did Mike.

"This. This doesn't bode well. Us sealing ourselves in, FEMA barricading the only exit . . . this doesn't look like it's gonna be resolved anytime soon."

"Soon?" Alan replied, taking a breath.

"Yeah, soon. I've got faith. This'll blow over. Everything does. A monsoon hits, people die. Still, life goes on, normalcy resumes. Tsunamis. Collapsed levees. Earthquakes. This'll blow over. New York's a tough town."

Alan nodded at Mike's hopeful platitudes but wasn't buying. And anyway, according to the news, New York wasn't alone in this predicament. This was global.

"I tried to load up on reserves," Mike continued, "but it was pretty picked over at D'ag's and Food Emporium. I don't get why Food City closed up so soon. What's that all about?"

"Maybe 'cause it's not a chain," Alan posited. "The owners probably just took what they needed and booked."

"Maybe," Mike allowed. "Still, I think we're pretty well stocked. I think if we pushed it we could go a month, but *that's* not gonna happen." Mike smiled without conviction and looked to Alan for reassurance. "We'll be fine. London during the Blitz and so on. We'll be okay," Mike nattered.

Alan closed his eyes and drifted inward, Tammy's face imprinted in the darkness behind his eyelids. Phone service had been spotty at best and it wounded him that she and he had parted badly. Right after the Costco trip they'd had a nasty public fight and after he'd finished hiking his half of the supplies up to his apartment she'd screeched, "Don't thank me all at once you fuckin' prick! *Aw*, your arms hurt, your poor, delicate, artist's arms! *Aw*, you got a fuckin' callous on your precious digits?! You'll be fuckin' glad I'm 'an alarmist,' you asshole! Mark my fuckin' words!" She'd slammed into her Honda CR-V and sped off, and though they'd since made up via Instant Messenger, that was the last he'd heard from her. Land lines were tied up or nonoperational. Cell service? History. And now the Internet was iffy, too.

Even though Tammy had stocked up equally, Alan wished she'd stayed, not because of that but because she was on the ground floor of a private house in Bay Ridge. He thought of the Three Little Pigs, he residing in the brick house, she in the wood. At least it wasn't straw. He suspected he'd never hear her voice again.

Tammy's face rippled away, replaced by Ellen's. Alan wasn't sure why but he always went for tart women (as opposed to women who were tarts). Ellen, whose serial hallway flirtatiousness—especially since she'd had the baby—always seemed seasoned with a smidgen of sarcasm, was close to Alan's ideal, at least physically. At the moment, convinced he'd never know the touch of a woman again, Alan resented Mike. He resumed hammering, then stopped, sighed, and gave Mike's arm a gentle squeeze.

"I'm taking you into my confidence, Mike. I'm serious, no fucking around."

"Okay."

"Seriously, Mike. This is life or death stuff here."

"I know, I know. This is super serious."

"This isn't just fortification, Mike. We're sealing ourselves into our crypt. The cavalry isn't coming for us."

"Sure they are."

Alan looked deep into Mike's worried, wearied, eyes. People with kids had to think positive. "No, Mike, they're *not*. This is it."

"You artistic types are so gloom and doom," Mike said without judgment. "I don't roll like that. It's a disaster, granted, but people rally. Maybe we batten down the hatches and wait, but—"

"Fine, Mike, cling to your illusion, but," and here Alan lowered the volume to a barely audible whisper, "I've got plenty of supplies. Tammy and I bought a buttload."

"Yeah, Ellen mentioned you were stocked up."

"*Not so loud,*" Alan hissed. "I don't want to become the Sally Struthers to 1620's starving children. I'm offering—*so long as we keep it on the QT*—you and Ellen some of my stuff. Water, canned goods, whatever. You've got a kid to feed. But it's between us. I don't want the others to know. I can't feed everyone."

Conspiratorial, Mike nodded and then threw his arms around Alan, his voice cracking. "We're fucked, aren't we?" He began to sob and Alan, ensnared by the other man's limbs, mourned the death of Mike's optimism. He thought about his last exchange with his mother—and it was a *last* exchange, with her Luddite tendencies and shunning computers and the Internet even when Alan had offered both so she could be more connected. She of the landline and rotary kitchen phone. There's one sound no child ever wants to hear and that's the sound of a frightened parent. His mother's final words to him, choked and perforated by little intakes of air, trying so hard not to cry, to be strong for her boy, were, "I'm all out of turkey. I'm almost out of food and I'm afraid."

I'm afraid.

Those two words made it all real for Alan. Not the news. Not the panic on the street. Alan wanted to comfort her but it was impossible. He couldn't get to her. A lifelong mama's boy and he was trapped, travel between boroughs prohibited. In that moment his insides turned to liquid.

"Mom," he'd begun.

The line went wild, wailed electronically, died.

He'd held the receiver like it was a totem imbued with the essence of his mother. It had held her voice, a voice he'd never hear again. Why hadn't he gone to her at the onset? Or brought her here?

Because he'd been dumb enough to think this would pass, too. He didn't recradle the handset. He just held it and stared at it.

The thought of his mom, alone and terrified.

His mom, the rock. The tough lady.

Yeah, Alan thought now, eyes stinging and wet, *we are so fucked.*

AUGUST, *NOW*

Karl and Dabney lay on the tarp, the rock pile untouched. Both were admiring the crowd below, awaiting the return of Mona, both psyched to see her do her Moses thang. Between them were a couple of empty cans, one from cling peach slices in light syrup, and the other string beans. Both men were happy and felt a sort of father-and-son companionability. Dabney rolled onto his side and belched, the gassy reflux sweetened by the aftertaste of peaches. In direct response, Karl let out a melodious fart and both men laughed. Their spirits were fine and low comedy wasn't beneath them.

"Did you like *Blazing Saddles*?" Karl asked.

"Why, 'cause it had a black sheriff?"

"No, because it had farting. That scene by the campfire, all those cowboys eating beans and letting off."

"Oh, yeah. That." Dabney chuckled, feeling foolish for having thought this was some well-intentioned attempt at ebony and ivory racial bonding. But this was nothing to do with the late, great, Cleavon Little. It just had to do with passing gas, something everyone could enjoy, race immaterial. Why was he feeling so stuck on race? The only races that mattered now were humans versus zombies. Skin color was passé.

But he still wondered how it would be if his van had made it home.

He lived in a project, a honeycomb of ten thirteen and fourteen story buildings. All manner of mayhem likely went down there. Even when things were normal it was no great pleasure. Project rats—the human kind, not the rodent kind—whose idea of fun was pissing and setting small fires in the elevators and stairwells. Graffiti. Litter. Noise on top of noise. Every time his wife went out after hours he was nervous that she might not come home or would get molested or what have you—no matter how many times she assured him that other men didn't lust for her the way he did.

Dabney reached over and ruffled Karl's hair.

"What'd you do that for?" Karl asked, his face suddenly confused.

"Never ruffled a white boy's hair before."

"You're not getting all funny on me now, are you, Dabney?"

Dabney laughed. "Not if you and I were the last two folks on Earth, son. I'm just missing my own boys and they didn't exactly have the kind of hair you could ruffle. I figured I'd see what a white daddy might feel. Greasy, but not so bad."

"You had sons?"

"Two, plus a girl. Both boys grown, left home. I like to think maybe Johnny, my eldest, might be alive—he left the city. A while before my van crashed I spoke to my youngest, my girl, on my cell phone one last time before the signal went dead. Like everything else." Silence hung between the two men, neither articulating the thought that Dabney's offspring were likely dead, too. "Yeah, well. At any rate, I hope that Mona comes back soon."

"Yeah, me too."

"Is she back yet?"

At Ruth's grating query Abe shuddered to wakefulness, slapping a fly off his nose. He'd dozed off, the constant ache of hunger no longer there to keep him vigilant. Just like the good old days, after a thick pastrami and tongue sandwich from Second Avenue Deli, he'd grown slumberous on a full belly.

"You were sleeping?" Ruth's voice rose, her tone accusatory. "*Ucch*, Abraham, you're given one simple task, to keep an eye out for our fairy goddaughter, and you botch it."

"It's not like I fell asleep on purpose!" He lifted himself off the chair, glissandi of pins and needles strafing his quaking legs, and hobbled off to pee in the bucket in defiance of his prostate. "If she came back she'd have said something. I would have heard. What, I'm the only one around here who can keep a lookout? If she came back she'd call up, wouldn't she? Hah?"

"Who knows? She's an odd girl. And don't go putting the blame on everyone else. You volunteered to keep an eye out for her."

"Yeah, yeah, yeah, whatever." Abe shook off the last few burning droplets and zipped up, wishing he'd asked Mona to pick up some Flomax; maybe next time, if there was one. He maintained his ornery posture but he knew he'd screwed up. He'd admit it to almost anyone but Ruth; she took too much pleasure in seeing him fail. How long had she been watching him slumber? It would be just like her to watch him rather than the street below, just to needle him for having blown his responsibility.

"No, not 'whatever.' You had an important task. Maybe a *younger person* should do it. I thought you were at *least* capable of doing a job that involved basically *sitting around* doing *almost nothing*, but apparently *nothing* is the only part of that you're actually *qualified* for any more." Her voice lanced through his ears, sharp, pointy, shrill.

Abe exited the bathroom with the sloshing bucket and fought the urge to empty its contents on his fishwife's head. With all the dignity he could muster he padded by across the moth-eaten Oriental rug and tossed his amber-colored, slightly acid discharge out the front window. In his heart he hoped this act would elicit the stock slapstick cliché: that Mona would be down there, full shopping cart before her, wiping Abe's piddle from her face. It's not like he wanted to douse the poor girl, but his tossing the piss seemed the perfect setup for her return. But no *mwah-wah-wah* comedy trumpet trill moment was in the offing. The liquid splashed the mindless shufflers and that was that. The last vestiges of light faded, darkness returned, Mona didn't.

"This is not good," Abe muttered as he lit a candle. "This is not good at all."

"So where is she?" Ruth said, her voice small.

"Like I know. Like suddenly I'm the Amazing Kreskin." Abe looked at Ruth's face. Even in the shadows it was obvious she was more than upset. She wasn't hollering and screeching and fussing and nagging. She was silent. Abe shuffled over to her and held her, pressing her balding noggin against himself. It would be too cruel if Mona didn't come back, but life was nothing if not immeasurably cruel. He patted his wife's back gently and tried to make his assurances sound heartfelt. Even if Mona didn't come back, the coffers were well stocked. They'd last a few more weeks. He kept petting Ruth, hoping the tears leaking out of his eyes wouldn't drip on her. Then the jig would be up.

"I can't believe that spooky little bitch ditched," Eddie said to the top of Dave's head. Dave was busy, so he didn't reply one way or the other. But Eddie didn't need confirmation. He could *totally* believe it. Why the fuck would *anyone* voluntarily stay with a bunch of losers like the ones in this building? Eddie yearned for being someplace else. There had to be other survivors, somewhere. Pockets of tough motherfuckers holed up, giving the zombies what for—*real* men with guns and weapons. That totally sucked about this bunch. No weapons. Sure, some kitchen knives, even a couple of professional-grade meat cleavers, but no guns. If Eddie'd stayed in Bensonhurst he'd have access to plenty of guns, but here on the Upper East Side? Please.

What had he been thinking moving up here?

Okay, so he'd enjoyed the bar scene on York Avenue. He'd nailed a lot of slim high-maintenance Jewesses on his innumerable pub crawls and contrary to stereotype, those women sure knew how to give head. Eddie had thought Italian chicks like the ones in his old neighborhood were proficient, but they were rank amateurs compared to the JAPs he'd scored with 'round these parts.

In Brooklyn, fellatio was merely a Catholic stalling act to keep the cherry intact until the wedding day. How many girls had kept Eddie out of their cootchies by offering up auxiliary inputs? That was a laugh. Eddie thought about all those girls lined up trying to get into Heaven now. Saint Peter would be all like, "What? You safeguarded the 'gina but let 'em do what in your what? Sin is sin, Sweetcakes. Scram!" In cars, attics and basements, in stairwells and on rooftops, in all the clandestine locales available to him in his youth he'd done everything *but* get in the front bottom. He'd lost his own cherry, so to speak, at fifteen to a twelve-year-old she-devil named Roxanne who sat in her bedroom window and smoked menthols and taunted and teased all the neighborhood boys. Eddie thought she'd singled him out for her affections, but it turned out she'd blown every kid on the block, and some from not on the block, and some from Borough Park, and some from Bath Beach, and some from as far as Bay Ridge. And some who weren't even so young, like her uncles and cousins.

And so Eddie formed the opinion that maybe the fairer sex were all whores, like his pops implied in a not-so-subtle fashion when addressing Eddie's mother as such. Eddie's mother was such a flirt it was easy to see why his pops drank and on occasion showed her the back of his hand. She didn't fight back much, maybe a little harsh language, but she knew she was guilty of whatever and besides, why screw up a good thing? She had a nice house and a nice car. Eddie's sister Patty, though. She was a tramp, no doubt.

So anyway, here he was, in a faggy neighborhood, bereft of cunt, getting a blowjob from his former Ice Knights teammate. *Go Rutgers*. Eddie rolled his eyes impatiently. Dave was getting all fancy, licking it like a lollypop and fiddling with the balls. Eddie just wanted to bust a nut and go to sleep, but whatever. Dave had gone full-bore homo and there was nothing to do about it. The facts were the facts. Look at Dave's lack of interest in the spooky little shorty who'd shown up and brought home the groceries. And Dave harshing on him for wanting to tap that ass? You'd think Dave would want to give his a break. Whatever. The little chick was probably never coming back anyway, so Eddie would make do.

But he wished Dave would just hurry the fuck up.

Three in the morning, give or take. Moans of brain-dead protest accompanied by regular knifelike squeaks of a trolley wheel in need of a spritz of WD-40. The squeaks increasing in pitch and loudness, and then silenced. The inhuman groaning continues, growing in fervor. The strike of a match, the smell of sulfur followed by paraffin, and then barely audible bare-footfalls creeping across bare floorboards.

Alan slid the front window open the whole way and looked down at York. Standing in the center of the aperture of the crowd of spread-out zombies stood Mona, looking up at the building, nodding her head in time with whatever tune she was mainlining. Alan just looked down at her for a moment, waiting for her to call out and announce her return. But she didn't. She just stood there leaning her forearms on the push bar of the extra-large shopping cart she'd liberated from wherever, the cart overstuffed with swag.

The crowd was well illuminated, Mona having affixed a high intensity dual-beam LED flashlight to the front of her cart. In the shockingly bright, cool white light, the faces of the undead looked especially ghastly. Every deformity, every laceration, every cluster of rot underscored by deep dramatic shadows, like the ultimate campfire ghost-story teller. During the day the zombies kind of blended into an undifferentiated mass, but now, lit up in the dark, deep black shadows separating them like bold outlines in a wood-cut, each one boasted a uniquely disturbing visage.

Alan fought the urge to grab a pencil and begin sketching, but he studied these specimens, making mental notes. One in particular caught his eye, a female with its head dangling backwards from some hideous past injury. Its deadened eyes stared up at him—or at least in his general direction—and Alan found himself craning his head upside down to make out the face.

Gerri!

"Holy shit," Alan gasped. He'd wondered where she'd gotten off to and here was his answer. *When did this happen?* Before he could get dizzy he righted the angle of his head and looked again at Mona. Finally she glanced up and saw him in the window and gave a minimal wave. Alan gestured for her to stay put, then scampered into the bedroom and roused Ellen with an urgent whisper-hissed, "Mona's back!"

Ellen lay there for a second or two, then sprang up like a jack-in-the-box.

"What?"

"Mona. She's downstairs. We gotta help her unload the cart and get her back inside."

Ellen bolted off the bed, stark naked, and made to get down to 2B.

"Uh, Ellen, honey?" Alan said, gesturing at his own nude body. Ellen took in her nakedness, then nodded and bolted back into the bedroom. Within seconds both had thrown on shorts and shirts and made for Mona's dwelling. When they reached the front windows, Mona had changed position from last Alan saw her. She now sat Indian-style on the roof of Dabney's van, another flash-light in her lap, the beam fanning across SERVING ALL FIVE BOR-OUGHS SINCE 1979. She also held a brand-new length of Day-Glo pink mountaineering rope, which she tossed up to Alan, who tied it securely to the nearby standpipe.

Later Mona, Ellen, and Alan shared a round of warm Pepsi around the dining table, Mona sitting on the edge of her chair, her Hello Kitty backpack mashed against the backrest.

"This used to be the super's apartment," Alan said as a conversational gambit.

Mona nodded.

"That's how come there was a rope here in the first place. Although I'm not quite sure what Mr. Spiteri used rope for."

Mona shrugged, indifferent.

"Shouldn't we tell the others that Mona's back, safe and sound?" Ellen asked.

"If no one came to help, clearly they're all still asleep. Let 'em rest," Alan said. "They can enjoy a nice start to the day tomorrow." Alan surveyed the piles of stuff Mona had brought back. "You really did an amazing job out there, Mona. Just great. Thank you."

"Uh-huh."

"No, seriously. You shouldn't be so modest."

"I'm not."

"We were getting pretty worried, I don't mind telling you, since you were gone so long," Ellen added, gently grasping Mona's hand. "Not that I mean to imply that we thought you should have been quicker," she added. "Far from. We just were concerned."

"Uh-huh," Mona said.

Uh-huh.

Alan got up from the table to inspect the loot.

Is it just me? Ellen wondered. She looked at Mona's blank, pretty face and tried not to stare, not that Mona would notice anyway. Mona, as per, had the headphones blasting away. From the tiny speakers Mona's music always sounded fast and metallic, like angry insects devouring her brains via the ear canals. Maybe that was it. Maybe all the conservative pundits had been right. Maybe heavy metal, or whatever Mona was listening to, *did* cause brain damage. Maybe Mona had numbed herself with aggressive music as a way to cope with the harsh reality of the world. Maybe, maybe, maybe. But she was among friends now. Needy friends, admittedly, but friends nonetheless. Maybe she could wean Mona off the tunes—not cold turkey, no need for anything that dramatic, but some nice music to set the tone. *Oh my God*, Ellen thought. *I'm turning into my mother. What, some nice Barry Manilow? Some Ray Conniff? Some Yanni? Get a grip.*

"Check this out!" Alan cried as he held up a cardboard box. In the murk Ellen couldn't make it out, so he elaborated. "It's a solar camping lantern. How cool is that? She brought back one, two, three, four, holy smokes, *five* of the suckers."

Clutching the box, Alan hastened back to the table and planted a big kiss on top of Mona's head. Mona sort of half smiled and Ellen felt a pang of jealousy. *What the fuck?* she admonished herself. *Just stow that stupid shit, Ellen.* Taking his seat, Alan fished the slim, silvery rectangular lamp out of the box and squinted as he read the instructions by candlelight. " 'Recharging the battery from a completely discharged state takes about sixteen to eighteen hours in full sun.' This baby gives up to seven hours on high on a full charge. I can read at night. I can work at night! How awesome is that? Tomorrow this baby goes up on the roof."

"What makes you think they're for you?" Ellen asked.

"Wha' . . . Well, I, uh . . ."

"I'm just teasing, Al. Relax."

"Oh. Oh, okay then."

Ellen threw Alan a smile that was supposed to be reassuring but came off kind of askew. She was suddenly feeling a little mean. *Please tell me this isn't jealousy*, she thought. *Please. I can't be that stupid. That insecure. That stereotypically weak and womany.*

Alan was about to lavish more thanks on Mona, but he could see her eyes were closed and she was nodding in time to the music. It sounded like tuneful nu metal, and either the singer was female or male with a helluva falsetto. Alan looked over at Ellen whose own expression was cryptic at best. Before he blurted something he'd end up regretting, he sized up the situation as best he could. Two females, one hale and hearty, the other weak and wan. Ellen's eyes were adrift and she was fidgeting, picking at her cuticles.

"Ellen?" Alan whispered. She looked over at him, her head turning in slow mo. "Ellen, you okay? What's up? Aren't you happy Mona's back? And the haul? She rocked out. I mean, solar-powered lanterns? We didn't even *think* of that. And check this out: walkie-talkies." Alan tapped his temple with an index finger. "Smart cookie," he said, bulging his eyes Eddie Cantor-style for comic effect. Mona opened her eyes and looked at Alan as he was making the gesture. She eased out an earbud. He felt his cheeks flush as he stammered out, "I was just remarking how savvy you were to get those solar lamps. Very cool, indeed. And I saw some freeze-dried grub, too. Outstanding."

"Had 'em at the sporting goods place I got the rope from."

Eyes heavy lidded and glassy with disinterest, Mona popped the buds back in and turned up the volume.

"Wow," Alan said with a smirk, "I thought she'd never shut up."

14

Eddie liked what he saw as he stood before the full-length mirror on the bedroom closet door. He liked it a lot. Nude, he turned to his left and assumed a bodybuilder's pose, flexing his muscles, which were oiled with sweat, then turned to the right and did likewise. He'd taken the liberty of shaving his chest and stomach and he'd tweezed any stray hairs on his shoulders. He'd even shaved his pits and pubes. The sad excuses for men in the building had shaved their faces and Alan had gone so far as to have Ellen give him a haircut, but none of them, with the exception of Princess Dave, had physiques worthy of a full-body depilatory. Eddie knew he wasn't quite there yet, but soon. In the last few weeks the surfeit of food the spooky chick had furnished filled him in nicely. He'd resumed a workout regimen and Zotz had resumed a respectful distance, his smart remarks all but disappeared. Sweet.

"Oh yeah," Eddie grinned, rippling his abs. "Look at those pecs. Look at those delts." He did a half pirouette and clenched and un-clenched his buttocks. "And for the chef d'oeuvre, look at those glutes. *Marone*, what a sight to behold." He gave them an appreciative slap and then, with great reluctance, closed the closet door and stepped away.

His hair, deep black and long enough to wear in a ponytail, he now wore loose about his shoulders, Tarzan-like. He slipped on a pair of tight black Calvin Klein boxer briefs and espadrilles, and then stepped into the common hall. Sunlight directly overhead poured down through the skylight in the stairwell housing and he gleamed. He liked the others to see his return as resident Adonis, even though he didn't know who the fuck Adonis was—just that he was buff and handsome as shit. Well fed and in fine fettle, the only thing lacking was *una bella fica*. Ellen was beginning to look totally doable again, but she was glued to that douche, Zotz. It was real fuckin' adorable the way she latched onto that pencil-pushin' pencil neck. Made him wonder if maybe she and Zotz had been canoodling while she was still married to good ol' what's-hisname.

Wouldn't that be fuckin' perfect?

Oh, it *totally* made sense, too. Artsy-fartsy Alan worked at home, made his own hours. Who better to have a fling with? She was on maternity leave—what a con. Have a baby, get paid to stay home and watch soaps. What a racket. Then, when it gets boring, snag a nanny and back to the grind. You get to be a professional woman and an amateur mom. Having the cake and eating it, too. Fuckin' women. Eddie's mom, whore though she was, knew her place was in the home. Maybe she took some extra deliveries of protein paste from the odd mailman or milkman, but she was a housewife. That's what a woman should do once she decides to drop a litter. Tell that to these Upper East Side broads. *Well, now they're all fuckin' dead, so fuck 'em.*

Oh, how Eddie wished he could.

The spooky little chick made him uncomfortable, though. He'd tried to engage her in some friendly chitchat, but she seemed bored. How rude was that? With those earbuds stuck in her jug ears. And yeah, her ears *were* fuckin' big, too.

Eddie was beyond frustrated. That spooky little chick was always either nodding her head in tune with godawful noise—maybe he'd slip her a little Gino Vannelli—or out on errands. She was accommodating, he had to give her that. Any request and *voom*, off she went in search of. Yesterday Eddie had asked for one of those little travel DVD players and she'd brought back enough for everyone, which maybe made it seem a little less special to him, but so be it. *How fuckin' fun must that be?* he wondered. *Going into any store and boosting any shit you want? Shoplifting heaven!* With the DVD player he now had a reason to return to his old digs to retrieve his impressive porno stash. If he couldn't have the real thing he'd make do with some hot viddies.

He wanted to tap that ass, but you don't shit where you eat.

Or fuck where you eat.

Something like that. The time would come. She was a weirdo but she wasn't blind. Eddie remembered a TV special about this special kind of chimps called bonobos and how they had a pecking order. The top males had priority mating rights. The bonobos preferred fucking to fighting, but the males spent a lot of time intimidating their rivals for female affection. Eddie was an alpha all the way. She'd see that. Females always came around to the alpha. Soon enough he'd have the spooky chick and Ellen Swenson. He just had to play it smart.

As he mounted the steps, the old bitch in 5A stepped into the hall and let out a grizzled gasp as she took in his buffness. Though it creeped him out a little, he liked the thought that she'd have his physique scorched into her psyche. Imagine the horror she'd feel looking at herself by comparison. Or her shriveled, impotent husband. Hilarious.

"Can't you have the decency to put on some clothes?" she scolded.

As he passed by he stooped over, jutting his noggin like he was going to give the old bag a head butt. She flinched in terror and he sniggered. "Just messin' with ya, *ma'am*," he said. "Chill. Why do I gotta put clothes on, anyway? It's hot as hell and so am I."

She clucked and retreated into her dwelling, locking the door behind her. It was so unfair that the females in this building were all so lame. Old and wrinkled. Brain-dead and spooky. Kinda hot but taken. *Taken.* Now that Ellen was looking kind of nice again it just ate away at Eddie that a little weasel like Zotz was keeping all that lovin' to himself. Wasn't it just like a Jew to hoard the precious? Zotz. That was Jewish, right? Of course it was. And in the meantime, here was Eddie, fitter than them all, plodding upstairs to cut across the roofs to get his porn. No justice.

Eddie pounded open the door to the roof with the flats of his palms, earning a startled yelp from Dabney. Good. Eddie liked spooking the spook. Reminded him of past glories. Eddie remembered one night in particular that gave him pleasure but also chafed his balls. Pleasure was the fact that he and some buddies had beaten the holy hell out of a couple of wayward niggers who'd strayed into Bensonhurst and were trying to make time with a couple of the local girls—nice *Italian* girls. Well, not *nice,* exactly, but Italian. Annoyance was because it never made the news. No use crying over spilled blood, especially when there wasn't enough of it. At least he'd gotten away clean. Going to jail would have sucked, big time.

"The hell is wrong with you, son?" Dabney hollered. "Slamming up here like that. You wanna give me a heart attack?"

As a matter of fact, Eddie thought as he stalked by, ignoring Dabney's upbraiding. *And I'm not your son.*

Eddie reached his old building and headed down the fire escape to his window, still open like Dave had left it. Eddie hadn't returned since the Wandering Jewess incident. That was intense. Eddie thought about the way Dave had handled her and he felt pride swell in his chest. Dave was a *finocchio*, but still a man. That was some hardcore shit. The way he knocked her block off—or almost off. With an elephant's foot? Just thinking about it made him chuckle. Reminded him of his childhood *Rock 'Em Sock 'Em Robots*. Two robots pounding the bolts out of each other, one red, one blue. Eddie was always blue because his dad said red was a commie color. Papa knew best. That was a cool toy.

Eddie recalled his time with Gerri. Sure she was a vegetable—at least until she became the meat course—and nothing to look at, but he'd almost forgotten how nice pussy felt.

"Gotta get the porn," Eddie said. "Stay on point. Focus."

He vaulted through the apartment to his old room and threw open the door. At the foot of his bed, under a pile of clothes, was his dad's old army footlocker. He knelt down and undid the combination lock, which opened with a sturdy pop. Inside was his treasure trove. He felt like Indiana Jones scoring that shiny bauble at the beginning of *Raiders*. He'd forgotten to bring something to carry home the boodle, but nearby was his old gym bag, still overstuffed with dirty laundry. He unzipped it and dumped its contents on the floor.

"So *that's* where these were. Duh," he said, shaking his head as he put his Nike Air Mowabb cross trainers back in the bag. He then started loading DVDs into the sack.

As he struggled with the zipper, the bag now stuffed to bursting, he heard a sound from the living room. He ceased his activities and froze. There it was again, a soft shuffling. The Wandering Jewess had been evicted so what was this shit? Eddie gingerly placed the overstuffed bag on the bed and tiptoed into the hall. He held his breath and eyeballed the exit window. He was curious, but how curious? Wasn't the cat killed by curiosity? Eddie hated cats, with their rough tongues, bad breath, and haughty attitude. Who was the first to call vagina *pussy*? Why insult such a sweet thing by naming it after a cat? Whatever. The sound happened again. There was somebody in the other room. That spooky chick? Nah. Why would she come here? Cursing himself for pursuing it, Eddie stepped into the hall and slunk toward the living room.

A plastic cup from 7-Eleven rolled toward him, settling at his right foot.

"Hey," Eddie said, voice steely. "Who the fuck is there?"

Eddie poked his head into the room and several zombies stood there. The front door wide was open. As he turned to flee, two more stumbled from the bathroom, which was between him and the exit window.

"Fuck me," Eddie growled, cursing himself for the *stunod* that he was.

From the living room, one loped toward him, then tripped and fell as its legs became entangled in its own leathery intestines, which dangled from a gaping cavity in its lower abdomen. Its jaw hit the linoleum floor and came loose, leaving it cocked to one side and toothless. Eddie would have enjoyed the zombie's clumsiness were there not several others who shuffled his way, their paths free of stray innards. Eddie cursed the narrowness of the hall, a mere three feet wide, but long. *Goddamn railroad apartments.* The ones emerging from the john effectively blocked his exit, but he'd have to bull through. Hockey penalty time. Still, he wished he were less exposed. *Maybe the Tarzan wardrobe isn't the best idea.*

Eddie gulped a few deep breaths, then ran forward. He caught a female zombie in the face with his fist, sending her careening backward, ass over tit. Her head hit the doorsill and split open, spilling coagulated gunk, dark and thick as molasses. Her bathroom buddy, a rangy male with graveyard halitosis, lunged for him and from behind, slung his gangly arms around Eddie's waist. Eddie couldn't turn around, so he did a backward head butt, ramming the back of his skull into the zombie's face, praying all the while that the zombie wouldn't bite him. *Fuck that shit.* The zombie's grasp loosened and Eddie shrugged him off, spinning on his heel. Even though he knew he should flee, he was now pissed. He blundered back into his bedroom and slid open his closet door, the action so violent the door came off its tracks and fell against the inside wall. Eddie grappled with the door and flung it off to the side, groping for his hockey stick.

"*High-sticking,* huh? The Comet'll show you motherfuckers some high-fuckin'-sticking!"

Like some po-mo Spartan warrior, Eddie turned back into the hall, stick in hand, helmet his only other garment besides his briefs and espadrilles. With a vicious upward slash he took the head off the one that bear hugged him in the hall. From his bedroom in the middle, Eddie still needed to get to the fire escape at the rear of the apartment. The headless body convulsed as Eddie stepped over it and a palsied, rotten hand shot up and grabbed the back of his briefs, tearing them.

"The fuck?" Eddie cried. "Oh, you wanna play fuckin' games?"

He stomped on the thing's solar plexus, its withered organs emitted muffled popping noises. The arm went limp but the rigor mortis grip on Eddie's Calvins intensified, pulling them down like a macabre pastiche of the Coppertone pooch yanking down that little pigtailed girl's bathing suit. Eddie tore free, now wearing just the waistband and pouch in the front, like some poorly constructed jockstrap.

Only one adversary left, an eyeless one-armed creep of indeterminate gender, face composed—or decomposed—solely of strands of muscle tissue barely masked by shredded, papery epidermis. Eddie jerked back the stick, then rammed it as hard as he could through the thing's chest, impaling it. "Vlad don't have shit on me!" Eddie wailed. He raked the stick back and forth, the zombie clawing at it, trying to free itself. Eddie jerked it upward, lifting his foe off the ground. The rib cage split open like a zipper, bits of desiccated bone and sinew raining down as Eddie worked the stick up and down until the thing split in half. As it twitched pitiably on the floor, Eddie swung down the stick and delivered the killing blow, shattering its skull.

Eddie grabbed the bag of porn and stepped onto the fire escape, slamming the window shut after him, hoping against hope that those zombie *gavones* were the only ones to breach the building. Still, he wouldn't be coming back to the old roost. On the roof he checked the stairwell door to confirm its security status. It was sealed shut. Relieved, he slumped back against the warty black tar paper and caught his breath, quaking. So, they got in. That meant the half-assed fortification the Guardsmen had installed was wrecked. Great. He gulped air and punched his chest. Now that he was safe, the fear sluiced over him. Though it had to be ninety degrees he was shivering. *Calm the fuck down*, he admonished himself. *Don't be a fuckin' girl. Calm the fuck down.*

Even alone he won no prize for compassion.

15

"I'd forgotten how comforting banality can be," Alan said as he shut off the little DVD player. He'd been watching back-to-back episodes of *Three's Company.* "What a stupid show. Why did you have this in your library?"

"It was Mike's. He loved John Ritter."

Alan sat back, feeling a little bad about maligning the show. It *was* bad, though. Seriously bad. Maybe it had been nostalgic for Mike. A lot of boys watched it, along with *Wonder Woman* and of course *Charlie's Angels,* all because of the jiggle factor. Alan never found women who seemed stupid sexy, though, and Suzanne Somers embodied that to a preternatural degree. Watching her and getting aroused would have carried the psychic baggage of getting a boner from a hot retarded girl.

Alan looked over at Ellen. She was doing a crossword puzzle. The scene seemed oddly peaceful. Comforting. It was hard to reconcile this image of domestic tranquility with the sea of undead meat puppets outside. Ellen had filled in a bit and looked more like her old self, which was to say she looked very attractive. But to what end? Mona's arrival on the scene was a stay of execution, not a repeal. Okay, there were creature comforts. They had food again, and light at night. Alan was clean shaven and well groomed, so when the time came he'd now leave a good-looking corpse, or at least make an attractive main course. Moments ago he'd felt comforted by a moronic sitcom and now he felt like everything was utterly pointless. Seeing the predictable pandemonium that was the bygone world of Jack Tripper, Chrissy Snow, and Janet Wood just amplified the horror of reality. Alan pressed the eject button and replaced the disk in its case, vowing not to revisit their sunny vale of canned mirth. Enervated, he schlepped to the window to soak up a solid dose of actuality.

"That show was kind of funny," Ellen said, looking up from the puzzle book.

"It was horrendous," Alan said.

"I thought you just said it was comforting."

"Yeah, well I misspoke. Sue me."

"It's funny." When Alan didn't ask what was, Ellen continued, "There's a clue in this puzzle, 'ThighMaster mistress from *Three's Company.*' Isn't that a funny coincidence?"

"Hilarious."

"Bad moods can be very contagious, especially in close quarters."

"You saying you want me to leave?"

"No. Don't put words in my mouth. I'm saying is there anything I can do to alleviate your funk?" Ellen rose from the table and began to undo her blouse, but Alan turned away.

"Not everything can be solved with sex," he muttered.

"It used to be."

"There are a lot of *used-to-be*'s. Used to be Manhattan wasn't a massive graveyard full of corpses too stupid to stay still. Used to be we could go outside and walk around and not worry about being eaten. Used to be . . ."

"Okay, fine. I get the picture," Ellen snapped, refastening her buttons. "Look, I *really* don't want to get into a *thing*, okay? Why don't you go to your apartment and do some drawing or something? Maybe take a walk." Alan raised an eyebrow, but before he could say something snide Ellen added, "*On the roof.* Or the hall. Just go out for a while."

"I thought *this* was my apartment now."

"It doesn't have to be," Ellen said, and instantly Alan regretted his snippiness.

"I'm sorry," he said, but Ellen fanned him off, gesturing toward the front door. "Really, I didn't mean it. I'm sorry."

On the landing Alan stared at the outside of the closed door. *A domestic squabble,* he thought. *How banal. But not in the least bit comforting.* Could Jack maintain his pretense as a preening homosexual, keeping Mr. Roper ever at bay? Could Chrissy wear a top that was even lower cut, but not so low cut the network censors wouldn't let it air? Could Janet utter some pithy platitude that neatly wrapped up their dilemma with a trite little bow? Could he and Ellen pretend to be a happy couple while all else was unimaginably bleak?

Stay tuned.

Karl sat on his bed in his bare-walled apartment.

Along with all the pinups, gone were the posters of heavy metal demigods. *Thou shalt have no other gods before me.* Since the arrival of Mona he'd reevaluated his secular values and desires and felt nothing but shame. That he'd intended to attempt to bed her was something he'd have to live with in private. Thank God he hadn't articulated his impure desires to anyone, least of all her. In the passing weeks he'd born witness to her selflessness. And the way she moved unscathed by the ravenous masses outside.

Karl didn't believe in the Rapture, but he didn't *not* believe in it, either. The husks shuffling around outside weren't "left behind." At least that wasn't how it was supposed to go. But maybe they were. The Bible and Bible prophecy were so open to interpretation. He thought if you didn't get sucked up to Heaven you were to remain on the hellscape that was Earth and live out the remainder of your days, biding time until you went to hell. Where did those things outside fit into God's plan? Karl remembered some lines from Corinthians. "Death has been swallowed up in victory." And "Where, O death, is your victory? Where, O death, is your sting?" Death's sting and victory were pretty evident to Karl's eyes.

If Karl remembered right, at the Battle of Armageddon everyone who wasn't a believer would be slaughtered. Were those the zombies? That's a whole lot of unbelievers. Maybe those things outside were the husks of the righteous who'd ascended to Heaven, sort of the ultimate in recycling. Their earthly bodies no longer needed, they now were used to punish the remaining infidels—like him and his neighbors. Supposedly, after the Battle of Armageddon, Satan would be defeated and Jesus would set up the Millennial Kingdom in Jerusalem. Karl's posture slumped. It sounded so gaga, but then again, look out the window. People eating people—or at least things that used to be people eating people.

People. People who eat people,
Are the yuckiest people in the world. . . .

People used to whine about their bad luck or what a cruddy day they'd had. Sometimes people would try to equate a lousy day at work with the calamities of Job. A mean boss was hardly comparable. Your job sucked, but *being* Job sucked worse, *yet he still loved God.* So maybe this was the Tribulation. In which case, Karl hadn't seen the light until it was too late. He wondered if it was too late. It definitely was for those brainless pods outside, but Karl could still fill his heart with love for God. God was supposed to be merciful, though the physical evidence seemed contradictory to that thesis.

Karl's feelings about Big Manfred had altered, too.

Honor thy father and thy mother. Though Manfred Stempler had been a stern and brutish presence, perhaps Karl hadn't understood that he'd been so to fashion his sons into better adults. Karl wished he had a Bible, but he didn't and was too embarrassed to ask around. Besides, the others were likely heathens. Alan kept only escapist fiction and was an avowed atheist. Ellen, who could tell? Probably agnostic at best. The Fogelhuts, Jews, which was perfectly all right. Jews, Big Manfred had said, were merely unperfected Christians. Eddie and Dave? Sodomites. Maybe Dabney was different, but surely not the others. Perhaps he could ask Mona to obtain a Bible for him on one of her sojourns among the unclean. If it wouldn't be too much of an imposition.

Karl was mighty confused. Mona could walk among the undead. Wasn't that a Bible-style miracle? Was she an emissary of God? Her perpetual serenity seemed to denote some sublime characteristic. Was she imbued with the Holy Spirit? Karl heard her tunes, though. She listened to Evanescence; he heard it with his own ears. They were a Christian band, right? Or were they kind of wishy-washy about it? Maybe they were just spiritual. At any rate, he'd heard her listening to Black Sabbath, too, so what did that mean? What did any of it mean?

"Are you there, God? It's me, Karl." He made a face. Was it blasphemous to paraphrase Judy Blume in a time of spiritual crisis? "Anyway, forgive me for this inferior supplication, but I'm a little out of practice. Scratch that. I'm a *lot* out of practice. I'm so confused and everything. I've never stopped believing in You, but there's so much I don't understand, nor do I think I'll ever understand it. Forsooth. I'm sorry. I'm trying to be fancy. That's false.

But my entreaty is for real. Sorry, I won't try to talk all grandiose and whatnot. Ugh, this isn't coming out right at all. Listen, I know I've thought many impure thoughts, but I cleansed my chambers, okay?" His mind flashed to Lourdes Ann Kananimanu Estores—Miss June 1982—secreted in his dresser drawer. His emergency stash. "I don't want to cast out Lourdes Ann. Please. There has to be some beauty in my existence. I haven't masturbated in weeks. Doesn't chastity count for something? I don't mean to wheedle. You wouldn't have created perfection such as Lourdes Ann if it wasn't to be admired, right?"

Karl stared up at his ceiling, noting a long crack that ran diagonally from one corner to the other, bisecting the expanse of whitewashed plaster. Just the mention of Miss June 1982 flooded impure thoughts into his head. *No, no. Fight them. Fight the urge. But why bother? I'm doomed anyway, aren't I?*

Karl thought about those *Left Behind* books and the righteous so-and-sos who'd created them, particularly the really creepy older one, Tim LaHaye, which sounded like LaVey, as in Anton LaVey—two sides of the same coin. When Karl had first come to New York he thought Anton LaVey seemed cool. He had the perfect look, that cue ball head and pointy beard. High Priest of the Church of Satan and the author of the *Satanic Bible*. Cool. But maybe not. But still, cooler than Tim LaHaye. That guy had helped Reagan into his governorship, then the presidency. He even looked like Reagan. Was that some kind of extroverted narcissism? Wasn't that a sin? One reason Karl had turned his back on the church was that its loudest and most passionate proponents all seemed so corrupt, bullying, and insane. The clergy, the evangelists, the propagandists; none seemed all that holy.

Karl fingered his one tangible souvenir from Big Manfred, the one his old man had insisted he take before heading off to New Sodom: a Smith & Wesson Model 910S 9mm pistol. Karl had left it tucked away in its case since he'd arrived in New York, but now he held it in his hands. It felt alien, but it was the one thing he owned that his father had touched. Not a cross, a gun. Ellen was right. It would be pointless against those things outside. Karl ran his finger around the muzzle, sighed, then replaced the gun in its foam-lined case. Guns were not his bag.

If Eddie ever found out I had this . . . Karl let that thought die.

He got off the bed and returned the carry case to his underwear drawer, then stepped into the hall just as Mona was walking down the stairs from the roof, head bobbing as ever. Sunlight poured down the stairs through the open door and skylight, enshrouding her in a blinding white glow. He flushed and cast his head down.

"Need anything?" she asked, popping out an earbud.

"Uh, well jeez, I'm kinda embarrassed to say."

"'Rhoid cream?"

"Huh?"

"Roof dude wants 'rhoid cream."

Karl forced a laugh. "No, no. I want a Bible. Either the *King James* or the *New Revised Standard Bible*. Or anything, really, as long as it's officially a Bible. I don't want to put you out." Mona jotted it down in her notepad but showed no reaction. "I want to brush up a little and see if I can make any sense of what's going on out there."

"Uh-huh."

"I mean, maybe these are the End Times?" Karl inflected the statement as a question, hoping to engage Mona. "You know, like in the Bible? Like in the Book of Revelation?"

"Uh-huh."

"Okay then," Karl said, shrugging and smiling. "I guess that's all for now."

As Mona retreated down the steps Karl tried to make out Mona's thumping music of the moment.

"Uh, Mona?" he shouted, to be heard over her tunes. She stopped at the foot of the stairs and looked up, removing the earpiece again. "Uh, Mona, I was just wondering what you're listening to?"

"Ministry."

"Oh. Uh, what song?"

" 'Jesus Built My Hotrod.' "

"Oh. Okay, thanks."

She nodded and headed downstairs.

Karl was so confused.

"Are you still moping?" Ruth asked, incredulity marring any attempt on her part at a sympathetic tone. "My God, Abe, get over it."

" 'Get over it,' she says. Unbelievable. She accuses me of being derelict in my duty. She accuses me of being obsolete. *Get over it.* Maybe a younger man should take the crow's nest. Maybe I'm not the one to watch for the lights in the tower window."

"What tower window?"

" 'One, if by land, and two, if by sea; And I on the opposite shore will be . . . ,' " Abe muttered.

"He's rambling. I don't know why I bother."

Ruth shuffled out of the room, back to the bedroom. *Good,* Abe thought. *Like I need a stoop-shouldered harridan eroding the last vestiges of my manhood.* He sat by his post, a cup of coffee—neither hot nor iced, but room temperature—in his hand, staring out the window, awaiting Mona's return, walkie-talkie tucked in his breast pocket. He'd be damned if he'd allow Ruth the satisfaction of catching him slacking off twice.

" 'Beneath, in the churchyard, lay the dead," Abe recited, in schoolboy cadence, "In their night-encampment on the hill, Wrapped in silence so deep and still, That he could hear, like a sentinel's tread, The watchful night-wind, as it went, Creeping along from tent to tent, And seeming to whisper, 'All is well!' Yeah, right. *All is well*, my ass. *Gottenyu*, what the hell kind of poetry would Longfellow have wrought from this *paskudne* situation?" Abe settled back and wondered if anyone anywhere was writing poetry about the current condition. If they were it was probably awful, like everything else in the last quarter century.

Beneath, in the churchyard, lay the dead.

Abe leaned forward and looked at the dead, or rather the *un*-dead. How long could they keep going? They ate when they could, but that was infrequent at best—happily. Were their reserves of energy infinite? That seemed so unlikely. Those things kept going and going, like that stupid battery bunny, none keeling over from depletion. *You'd think,* Abe thought, *that eventually they'd just all collapse and the worst would be over. Sure there'd be a lot to clean up, but what a small price to pay.* Then again, as Abe often mused, you'd think a lot of things in this life. You'd think death was the worst that could happen. You'd think the dead would stay dead. You'd think getting terribly ill or the cessation of your Social Security checks would be the worst that could happen in your dotage. You'd be wrong. But being wrong was the biggest part of life. Wrong choices and regrets; Abe was up to his tits in both.

"You cabbage heads have got it good, you know that?" Abe hollered out the window at the crowd below. "Not a care in the world, eh? You think anything any more? Probably not! How lucky is that, you lucky sons of bitches? You don't even need TV any more! Look at this. It just hit me! This is the end of the evolutionary ladder, the perfect twenty-first century man! Not a thought in its head! Not a care in the world! Idle yet active, going no place, doing nothing, taking his sweet time, and vicious as hell if given the opportunity! Hey, Darwin, you cocksucker, congratulations!" Abe laughed, pounding his fist against the splintering slate windowsill, doing his old bones no favors at all.

At the other end of the apartment Ruth eased the bedroom door shut, muffling the splenetic ravings of her husband.

16

"You're crazy," Alan said, his voice rising in disbelief. "*SNL* was crap compared to *SCTV*."

"It's a matter of taste, not sanity, for God's sake," Ellen countered. This was stupid. How could Alan get so worked up over a TV show? A long-gone obscure sketch comedy show, at that.

"Or the *lack* thereof. Just because something's more popular doesn't mean it's better. Often it's just the opposite. Everyone says they like *SNL* better, but trust me, it wasn't."

"It was funnier to me, okay? Me. In my opinion. Opinion, Alan. O-P-I-N-I-O-N."

"I just can't see how an intelligent woman such as yourself could choose *Saturday Night Live*. Okay, it had some funny stuff, granted. I'm not saying it didn't. But it was nowhere near the quality of *SCTV*. That show was inspired and brilliant. It never pandered. Because they were outside the mainstream they got to be so much more inventive and as a result of being unfettered by having to please sponsors and, worse yet, the lowest common denominator, they created some of the best sketch comedy ever to originate in North America."

"Can't we agree to disagree?"

Alan was about to opine his distaste for that expression but let it pass. Let Ellen keep her clichés, both conversational and comedic. He slipped the silvery disk back onto its spindle and put his prized *SCTV* box set back on the shelf. He was tearing through pack after pack of batteries, watching them over and over again, but the laughter justified the waste. Too bad Ellen couldn't enjoy them. Sure, she thought they were sort of amusing, but that kind of faint praise just irritated him. He'd never met a woman who recognized that *SCTV* was infinitely superior to *SNL*. He'd never even met one that liked it all that much. Was this a gender thing, like The Three Stooges? Alan thought that kind of stereotypical men-versus-women stuff was bunk. He didn't like The Three Stooges, either. Ellen wasn't stupid, but she was a tad conventional. Maybe more than conventional. Pedestrian. More people liked *SNL,* it was as simple as that. It didn't matter. He could enjoy the *Second City* episodes with headphones on.

"I said *can't we agree to disagree?*" Ellen repeated, impatience straining her lovely features.

"Of course." They hugged and retreated to their corners, he to watch another episode, she to do another crossword puzzle. As he plucked another disk from the case Ellen cleared her throat theatrically and gave him a hard stare. "*What?*" he asked, hoping to avoid further turpitude.

"You haven't painted lately. Or done any drawing."

"I'm taking a breather, okay? Maybe I haven't been touched by the muse. Maybe I just want to chill and catch up with a little video. Am I allowed?"

"Of course you're allowed," Ellen said, attempting to keep her voice neutral. "It's just you were such a dynamo before you got that DVD thingy. I'm not saying you're not entitled to a little downtime, but . . ." Alan raised an eyebrow. "Never mind. Watch your shows. Enjoy."

"*Thank you.*"

Ellen watched Alan slip on the headphones, the gesture eerily evocative of Mona and her ever-present earbuds. As he lapsed into a state of televisual bliss, Ellen felt a virulent wave of disconsolation. Alan's posture seemed to mimic Mike's, the way he slouched on the sofa, legs up on the ottoman, ankles crossed. The way his toes flexed when he laughed. Alan's face relaxed as the vintage comedy soothed him, but Ellen's expression began to collapse. This couldn't be over an argument about their preferences in comedy. The wave of disconsolation turned into a wave of nausea. She got up from the dining table and bolted into the bedroom, reaching the window just as the rise in her gorge crested. A torrent of partially digested food spewed out, dousing the zombies below, none of whom seemed to mind.

How long had it been since she'd vomited? It almost seemed decadent. But maybe some of the food was tainted—lack of refrigeration and all. Ellen gagged up a few more blasts, then slumped down and let her head drop between her knees. For a few long unhappy months in high school Ellen had had a flirtation with bulimia. Alan reliving happier times in the living room; Ellen reliving unhappier times in the bedroom. Her puke splattered all over where Mike had been slaughtered, consumed, possibly digested by those filthy, hateful, unnatural things.

Mike.

Her husband.

Former.

Father of her child.

Former.

Former husband. Former child.

Former everything.

Her sobs drowned out by Alan's headphones, Ellen's body drew in on itself, convulsed in sorrow.

Eddie wiped spooge off his hand with a paper napkin, his right bicep burning from exertion. Ever since he'd liberated his cache of DVDs from his old boudoir he'd been Stroker Ace squared. Dave sat on the couch and thumbed through an old issue of *Time*, the cover story of which was rampant obesity in America. Ah, for the good old days. Dave wasn't really reading, though. He feigned indifference to Eddie's incessant onanism but inside he was seething. And hurting. How Eddie could prefer servicing himself over having actual sex with an actual human being was beyond Dave. It was like what they'd developed together was an accident, a phase. Dave kept offering to facilitate Eddie's pleasure, even if it meant Eddie's eyes being glued to the seven-inch monitor. But Eddie wasn't having it. Now that he'd scored his porn, Dave was out of the loop.

"How many times can you watch the same scene?" Dave asked.

"You know what you sound like? You sound like a fuckin' woman," Eddie scowled. "Anyone ever tell you that?"

"Just you."

"So maybe you should let it penetrate that thick skull of yours."

Dave chose not to take the opportunity to return an obvious smutty riposte. Instead he slid off the futon and left the apartment, garnering nary a peep of protest from Mr. Tommasi. Fine. Let him indulge in his pathetic backslide. Then he'd come crawling back to Dave and maybe, just maybe Dave would have him back. Who was he kidding? Of course he'd allow him back in.

Out in the hall Dave pressed his face against the cool stucco and sighed. When had his life devolved into a same-sex soap opera?

Were all the girls he'd banged throughout high school and college just a smoke screen? His attraction to them had felt real at the time, but then again, he never bonded emotionally with any of them. Real bonds had only been forged with male companions, especially Eddie. He let out a deep breath and walked up the flight of stairs to the roof. Dabney would be up there. Could he fake conviviality? It didn't matter. Dabney wasn't the type to natter on unless you expressly sought that kind of interaction. Let him sit with his pile of bricks and play "stone the zombie." Dave took another deep breath and pushed open the door.

Though the sun was lost in a gauzy white haze, the light was intense to Dave, especially after having been indoors. He shielded his eyes and fished his Giants baseball cap out of his back pocket. Instead of lying belly down on his tarp, Dabney was seated at an aluminum folding card table doing something Dave couldn't quite discern. A conversational opener presented itself—something to distract from his current romantic woe—so Dave, attempting to affect insouciance, strolled over and took it.

"Whatcha doing?" he asked as he approached. Dabney was hunched over and wearing thick magnifying glasses, something Dave had never witnessed before on the older man. He neared the table and saw many small parts, some loose, some still connected to plastic sprues. Dabney was building a model kit. *How adorable.* Wait a minute. Did Dave really think that? Was he being ironic or facetious or patronizing? No, it *was* adorable, this middle-aged man using a pair of eyebrow tweezers to delicately assemble parts from this, what was it, model airplane, maybe?

"Makin' a North American P-51D Mustang. Good way to pass time, plus the glue gets you a little high." Dabney looked up and smiled. "Just kidding. Takes more than a little glue for me. Speaking of which, you want a beer? You look like you could use one."

"Uh, sure. Thanks." Dave hadn't even thought to ask Mona for suds. Stupid. Dabney handed him a bottle of Heineken and Dave held back the urge to weep with gratitude.

"All these little parts and pieces. Been a while since I put one of these together. My boys used to be wild for these things. They liked doing the hot rods and whatnot, but I prefer planes." Dabney looked up at the sky, scanning for nothing. "I used to complain about the roar of jet planes, 'specially during TV shows. Used to have to turn the volume up to compete with them. Now I'd give my left nut for a plane to go zipping by up there. Even if it wasn't meant for me, least it would be a sign of something going on out there. Some sign that maybe there were others. Before Mona showed, last sign we had of life was that crash, and that was snuffed out before it even made an impression. I asked Mona if she's encountered any others on her errands and she said no. There's gotta be others. Just maybe not around here."

"How does she do it, is what I wonder."

"Yeah, well that's the sixty-four-thousand-dollar question, ain't it? How come those godless motherfuckers don't eat her up like the rest of us mere mortals? Yeah." Dabney finished off his beer, then tossed it over the edge of the roof, not even watching its trajectory. Out of sight it crashed, hopefully against the skull of one of the undead. Dabney snapped a tiny piece off the sprue and filed it smooth with a small wedge of sandpaper, his eyes on the instructions held in place by a small monophonic cassette player that warbled a well-worn tape of Ben Webster. "I'd like to see several squadrons of these strafing the bejeezus out of those assholes down there," he said, holding the box art up for Dave to admire. "Imagine that? A bunch of these babies blasting the holy living hell out of those cannibal bastards? That'd be sweet."

Dave nodded, sipping his beer. It was warm, so Dave pretended he was in Europe. He'd read somewhere that Europeans drank their beer warm. Sounded weird, if given the choice, but he'd never know firsthand. Dave looked out at the horizon to the north and wished he'd traveled, seen the world, broadened his vistas. Too late now. He then looked south and gasped.

"Look over there," he said, pointing.

In the distance a thick, black cloud churned skyward from below, its origin blocked by buildings. But somewhere, looked like maybe in the east forties, a fire blazed. Was that a sign of life elsewhere? Or maybe a gas line blew all by itself.

"Hold on a sec," Dabney said, reaching over to switch the dial on his radio-cassette player. He then stopped, midgesture, and let out a derisive snort. "Idiot. I was going to say, let's turn on the news. Pavlovian response, I suppose. You'd think after several months of this shit I'd know not to try. Then again, I got some sweet notes serenading. I'm building a model kit. I'm drinking a beer. It feels almost normal, 'cept for me living up on a roof. But even that feels kind of normal. It is normal, now. Amazing how the definition of what passes for normal is always changing. If normal means what's most common, those zombies are normal and we're not."

Dave nodded, taking another swig of Heineken. Normal didn't used to entail a physical relationship with Eddie—or at least not a sexual one. It had always been pretty physical. The only time in their past that had been sexual was when they'd fucked a couple of coeds in their dorm room. Dave shook his head, trying to dislodge the memory. He didn't want to think about Eddie now.

Both men's attention drifted southwards again as a loud thud, dulled by distance, was heard, followed by a ball of fire which shot into the sky, only to be absorbed by the black smoke. A succession of muffled explosions followed, each punctuated by thick clouds of melanoid brume. Easterly winds bent the plumes of smoke into choky question marks in the sky.

"What do you suppose it is?" Dave asked.

"I dunno. Looks to be pretty far east. Could be the old Con Ed steam plant, near the UN. Or did they tear that down? I can't remember now. Could be a lot of things, though. And unless we send our girl Friday down there to check it out, we'll never know. And frankly I don't think that would be a very good use of her time."

"No, I suppose not. Jesus, you think it will get up to us?"

"Don't be simpleminded, son. I wouldn't want to be in that vicinity, but we got us a few miles between here and there. Don't sweat it. And think on the bright side, maybe it's frying up a mess of zombies. Wouldn't that be something?" Dabney held up the half-finished Mustang and mimed a few swoops, adding appropriate *rat-a-tat-tat* sound effects. "Not quite as cathartic as a good strafing, but it'll have to do."

Whatever was going on downtown it was dramatic. Volleys of muted concussions recurred with some regularity and a significant portion of the southern sky was smudged, the undersides of the dark clouds tinged orange from the blaze that raged out of sight below. The cloud of smoke and soot blew north and soon the sky directly above began to sicken. The charcoal gray began to leech pigment away, the already anemic sky turning greenish gray. The air smelled bad, a combination of charred solid matter and burning petrol.

"Something always gotta come along and rain on your parade," Dabney muttered. He eyeballed the symmetrical rows of the new Brita Ultramax water purifiers arranged by the low dividing wall. If it did begin to rain, as it now threatened to, even those filters might not be sufficient to fully cleanse the tainted water. A heavy drop fell on his nose and he frowned, adding, "literally," as he restored the remaining parts of his model kit to the box. As more drops began to pelt the roof Dave bid him a quick adieu, and then fled into the stairwell. After a few moments Dabney took off his clothes and stowed them in his lean-to.

The water was cool and good enough for an impromptu shower. He stood in the center of the roof, head tilted back, letting the rain pummel his face, saturating his salt-and-pepper beard. He squeezed his facial hair, wringing out the excess wetness, letting the overflow cascade down his chest. Unlike the previous downpour, which had been so mirthful, such a communal affair, this time he stood alone. Maybe Dave had warned the others about the black cloud. Fine. Dabney didn't mind a solitary soaking. Let them be afraid. Rain was nature's way of purging poison from the clouds, putting out the fires below. Who was Dabney to question that? The rain seemed all right. It didn't burn or even prickle his skin in any way that raised a red flag. He opened his eyes as a very unscientific litmus test. No, the water didn't sting. *Good enough for my eyes*, he reasoned, *good enough to drink*. He removed the lids of the Brita dispensers.

What the hell, he figured. *Put those filters to the test.*

Karl had forgotten how reader unfriendly the Bible was, no matter which version—although he vaguely remembered the *Good News Bible* being dumbed down quite a bit. Awkward and often impenetrable phrasing. Contradictory accounts of the same events. Clearly it was the message and not the messenger. No wonder his mind had often wandered during church and Manfred's sermonizing. The language was nearly impermeable. After browsing through the earlier sections, he skipped to Revelation, figuring this most germane.

Karl had forgotten—or maybe blocked—the particulars, but the imagery came flooding back: God and His four demon monsters covered with eyes sitting by His throne, the monsters incessantly repeating, "*Holy, holy, holy, holy, holy, holy, holy, holy, holy* is the Lord God, the Almighty, who was and who is and who is to come!" The first creature like a lion, the second like a calf, the third had a face like a man, and the fourth was like an eagle—four creatures, each of them with six wings and loads of watchful eyes. Surrounding God's throne were twenty-four other thrones, occupied by twenty-four elders dressed in white garments, with crowns of gold on their heads. God's throne emitted constant lightning and thunder. Like the ultimate booming system.

It sounded more like a rave than Heaven.

And God, evidently, had the appearance of jasper and sardius, a forgotten detail that sent Karl scurrying to his dictionary, which explained that jasper was, "an opaque form of quartz; red or yellow or brown or dark green in color; used for ornamentation or as a gemstone," and that sardius was, "a deep orange-red variety of chalcedony," which he also needed to look up, only to discover that chalcedony was, "a translucent to transparent milky or grayish quartz with distinctive microscopic crystals arranged in slender fibers in parallel bands," which frankly didn't help at all. It wasn't very comforting to picture the Almighty made of stone, perched on His throne, with catchphrase-spewing monster lapdogs for company. How Jim Henson hadn't adapted this was a mystery; it would have made a perfect vehicle for the Muppets.

Some of Revelation rang true, or at least true-ish. The things outside *had* been raised from the dead. But Karl couldn't recall witnessing any procession before a large, white throne, nor did he see those not written in the Book of Life being cast down into a flaming lake of sulfur. And while the zombies were horrible— indeed *biblical* in their horror—Revelation was so specific about the plagues to befall mankind that omitting them didn't jibe.

Angels with giant sickles killing thousands.

Marks on everyone's foreheads, some put there by an angel, others put there by the beast.

Locusts flying out of Hell, each with a human face and wearing a miniature crown and breastplate, bearing the hair of women, the teeth of lions, and the stingers of scorpions.

Millions of angels riding horses with the heads of lions.

Hailstones and plagues.

Okay, so maybe there'd been a plague.

Reading this stuff was giving Karl the sweats. He felt like he'd submitted himself to regression therapy to recall repressed memories. When he got to the part about dogs not being allowed into Heaven he remembered Chessie, their retriever, and frowned that she wouldn't be there. Dogs got lumped in with sorcerers, the sexually immoral, murderers, idolaters, and everyone "who loves and practices falsehood." Was God afraid those doggies would pee on him because he looked like a statue? What good were those multi-eyed monstrosities if not to keep God's throne free of visiting pooches? Karl didn't like that.

Karl did like that the devil's new army was called Gog and Magog. That was kind of cool, but a bit beside the point—although Karl considered referring to the things outside as Gog and Magog from now on, to spruce up conversation. It seemed better than "those fuckin' zombies." In Karl's opinion, the apostle John, who'd penned this book, might not have been the most reliable witness. He might, in fact, have been a raving lunatic. This was just one man's account, which by current standards seemed like fairly sloppy reportage. How about corroboration? How about three sources? But then again, who knew? What was supposed to be metaphor and what was literal? What was parable and what was prophecy? Karl's head throbbed. As he popped a couple of Tylenols he noticed faint concussions in the distance.

Karl's apartment was in the rear of the building so he didn't bother looking out the window—his "view" solely that of the building across the alley. He hurried upstairs to find Dabney on the roof, nude in the rain, the sky above a miserable hue. Dabney didn't seem to notice Karl's presence; his head was thrown back, his eyes clenched shut. Was he humming or just mumbling to himself? Another dull thud erupted and Karl looked south, divining the direction of the noise. The sky there was blackened, flame licking up from below. As if in a trance, Karl made his way to the southernmost building. On the corner he stood on its fascia and stared at the distant conflagration, his stomach churning. He steadied himself, gripping a metal pipe.

"Oh my God," he said in a hushed tone, remembering a passage from Chapter 9:

The fifth angel sounded, and I saw a star from the sky which had fallen to the earth. The key to the pit of the abyss was given to him. He opened the pit of the abyss, and smoke went up out of the pit, like the smoke from a burning furnace. The sun and the air were darkened because of the smoke from the pit.

Maybe the mutant locusts would be coming after all.

17

This is unusual, Alan thought, paintbrush in hand, midstroke on the full-size canvas. Across the room reclined Mona—fully dressed—on a vintage velvet chaise; yet here he was painting while being tormented by a very insistent erection.

Mona's pose wasn't particularly sexy and her expression was vapid and mildly sullen as usual, her eyes lightly closed. In her lap was the Hello Kitty backpack, which she held like a real kitty. She remained perfectly still, which was a great plus for a model, except for her head, which almost imperceptibly nodded in time with her bromidic tunes.

So why was he hard?

She wore her usual longish black cargo shorts, Doc Martens, tank top. Nothing racy. Was it her expanse of exposed belly flesh? Her stomach was a smooth, unblemished plane of slightly convex skin, her navel a delicate vertical pit. It was pleasing to the eye, no doubt.

Mona's right leg dangled off the edge of the chaise and the left was bent at the knee, the foot resting on the cushion. And there it was: betwixt the top of her boots and the hem of her shorts. It was her calves. What a bizarre time to pick up a fetish, but there they were, round and firm and strong. Calves. Alan had noticed calves in the past, but usually in conjunction with high heels and the way calves really looked full and lush above a pair of pumps, but other than that they'd held no fascination for him before. Breasts, yes. Ass, definitely. But calves? And Mona wasn't wearing pumps. But now that he'd noticed them—especially the left one, which bulged from the bend of her knee and the pressure from her foot resting on the cushion—he couldn't take his eyes off them.

Alan took a swig from a can of lukewarm Fresca, burped, and got back to work. He'd blocked in the figure and was tightening up the areas of flesh, the clothing indicated as black negative space. He considered whether or not to add detail like the creases and folds in the material, but opted to keep the treatment more graphic. He focused on her face, drawing his eyes away from that luscious drumstick. Instead he studied her lips, always pursed in a slight moue. Highlights of early-afternoon sunlight coruscated on them and periodically her tongue would poke out to keep them moist. *Focus on the work.* Alan swirled his brush against the palette, mixing a pink subtle and sensuous enough for those lips.

As he daubed on small touches of roseate-hued pigment he felt a light touch on his shoulder and flinched, causing the brush to skate across the surface of the canvas, marring the work he'd done.

"Jesus!" he barked, spinning on his heel to see who'd caused this accident.

Ellen was there, looking guilty, her eyes cast down. She bit her lower lip, her expression conciliatory—until she noticed the bulge in Alan's pants. Then her expression hardened almost as much as the business in Alan's drawers.

"You asshole," she hissed.

"What?" he asked. "What? *I'm* the one who should be mad. You just made me . . ." Once again his words trailed off as Ellen looked up and locked eyes with him. He feebly gestured at the canvas, a Francis Bacon-like diagonal streak across the painted Mona's face. "I mean," he sputtered, and then his face assumed Ellen's previous expression of guilty conciliation.

"I should have known," Ellen spat.

"I'm just painting her portrait," Alan said, defensive.

"Yeah, with a fucking hard-on."

"It happens," Alan stammered. "It's sometimes an involuntary action, like breathing and the beat of one's heart. Autonomic. I wasn't even *thinking* about sex. It just happened, honest."

Mona, eyes shut and oblivious to this exchange, kept time with her tunes.

"Yeah, a pretty young thing comes to model for you."

"With all her clothes on," Alan added. "*With. All. Her. Clothes. On.*"

"Yeah, for now. This time."

"Don't be crazy. I'm just painting."

"You get wood when you paint the zombies outside? If you do, then all is forgiven. But look me in the eye and tell me you get hard when you paint them. Go on, tell me that."

"I can't. I don't. But that's different."

"Yeah. You don't want to *fuck* them. Well, that's fine. This is fine. Go ahead and *fuck* that little girl on the couch. Get *her* pregnant, too. See if I care."

"*You're* the one who wanted me to paint again," Alan whined, his words chasing her out the door. "*What,* I'm only supposed to paint zombies and *you*?" Ellen stormed out of the room, slamming the door behind her. The room shuddered and Mona's eyes opened.

"What?" she asked, looking at Alan.

"Nothing. Don't worry about it."

"Oh. Okay." Mona closed her eyes and Alan began to correct the pink streak.

Wait a minute.

Get her pregnant, too?

"It just bugs me is all," Eddie said. "She gets to go out and we're cooped up in this dump forever. And I'm sick of her stock answer: '*I guess they don't like me.*'" Eddie affected a nasally effeminate voice. "The fuck is *that* shit? No, she's onto something and she's too selfish to share the secret with us. This is some kinda bullshit power trip."

"That's crazy," Dave said. "What could possibly motivate something like that? She doesn't seem the type. That's too, I dunno, devious."

"Bitches are all devious, bro. *All of 'em.* I don't buy the whole brain-damaged thing she's putting over on us. The whole veggie thing. She knows what she's doing and *I don't like it.* Everyone in this lame building should be pumping her for how the fuck she does it."

"She's our savior, dude," Dave said.

"Yeah. She's our *savior,* dude. We're her fuckin' *pets.* She goes out and walks around and what? She's touched by an angel or something? Yeah, right. She's a *person,* same as us. She's got some kinda secret and I wanna know what the fuck it is and I aim to find out."

"And how do you propose doing that?"

"You know, sometimes you talk all fancy and I just wanna flatten you, Mallon. You pull that lawyery shit on me one more time— *one more fuckin' time*—and I'll lay you out. Count on it."

"Jesus Christ, Eddie. What's gotten up your ass?"

"Not you. Not ever. Look, just get the fuck outta here, okay? I wanna be alone for a while and sort some shit out."

"*Fine.*"

"Fine."

"And thus endeth the nagging," Abe said, sitting on the edge of the bed, holding Ruth's wrist. No pulse. No breath. Dead. Abe sighed and moved his grip from wrist to hand, his fingers meshing with hers, his posture defeated. He didn't look at her face, just stared ahead at the floor between his feet, nudging ruts into the pile of the carpet with the toe of his slippers, then smoothing them with the flats of his soles. "Ai, *yaaaaaaah,*" he sighed again, stretching it out. He tightened his grip on her hand. It had been years since he last held her hand, just held it. They used to walk hand in hand all the time. They even had correct and incorrect sides. It never felt right when he held her left hand; something seemed unbalanced. With his free hand he stroked his freshly shaven chin, a small scrap of toilet paper stuck there by a dot of blood. He plucked it free and neatly placed it on the bedside table.

"Oy, Ruthie," he said, then sighed again. In place of tears a lot of sighing was in the offing, Abe not being given to displays of emotion, even when there was no audience. No living audience, at any rate. With reluctance he turned to look at Ruth's visage; her eyes were still open. He hesitantly placed his fingertips on her eyelids and attempted to press them closed, but unlike the movies they wouldn't stay shut. Even in death Ruth was contrary. He pulled the sheet over her, debating what to do next. Tell the others? He supposed he'd have to. It seemed unlikely that Ruth would be springing back to life—or *unlife*, take your pick. She died the old-fashioned way, free of zombie molestation. She was clean. Well, sort of. Abe wrinkled his nose. Ruth had, as it was euphemized, "voided herself," filling the air with yet another bad smell and the sheets with something worse. How very un-Ruthlike. "Oy, Ruthie, Ruthie, Ruthie."

So much for the family plot, he mused. Ruth had made such a to-do over her desire to be buried alongside her parents and sister. She also figured he'd predecease her—so much for woman's intuition, too. What was he supposed to do now? She'd want a eulogy, a service of some kind. She'd expect the Mourner's Kaddish, in Hebrew, no less, and since his bar mitzvah he'd forgotten pretty much everything. Did she have a prayer book tucked away somewhere? Probably. He seemed to recall her filching one from her sister's funeral. Hopefully it was phonetic. He'd look later. But if he was to respect her wishes, which seemed the right thing to do, silly though it may be—pointless, even—so be it. She wouldn't be getting the whole *megillah*, but he'd do his best to accommodate her superstitions as best he could. He stared across the room at his reflection in the mirror of Ruthie's dressing table.

"*Avel*, vhat can you do?" Abe said in comic Yinglish inflection. In Judaism the mourner was called an *avel*. It was a self-admittedly bad pun. It brought him no comfort. "There goes that second Social Security check." Again the joke didn't help. He was bombing to an audience of none. Miriam, Hannah, and David had never laughed at his jokes, nor did their kids. Ruth had seldom laughed at them. It had been ages since he'd even attempted mirth, except for the lame waiter joke at the celebratory dinner on the roof. Everyone else in the building was listening to music again, and watching TV. Those little screens hurt his eyes. Most of Abe's music was on vinyl. And what he wouldn't do to be able to listen to some of his comedy records right now. The best medicine there is.

On shaky legs, Abe trudged into the living room and dropped into his threadbare upholstered chair, parted the dingy chintz curtains, opened the dusty venetian blinds. Déjà vu on top of déjà vu on top of feeling beaten down and laden with wearied grief.

More déjà vu.

A little Myron Cohen would be nice.

The door to 2B remained open at all times, that apartment being Mona's point of entrance and egress from the building. Since taking up residence in 2A, she'd taken to keeping the door locked, especially when she was out on errands. Everyone agreed she was entitled to her privacy and security; after all everyone else kept their doors locked, so why shouldn't she?

Karl's knuckles barely grazed the surface of Mona's door, his rapping so feeble even he could barely hear it. His chin mashed into the pit of his collarbone, his lower lip twitched in self-disgust. He was having such a hard time getting up the nerve to approach her. *Well, duh, you think maybe it's because you see her as some kind of heavenly force? Like some kind of earthly angel or at the very least some kind of saint or whatnot?* It was absurd. Not that Mona was possibly imbued with some holy powers, but that he was petrified. She was mellow, Karl told himself. Fact was, Mona was mellowness incarnate. Nothing seemed to bother her. Not even the things outside.

Karl's hair stood up all over.

Not even the things outside.

There was an angle he'd never considered. Maybe the things outside stepped out of her way not because she was imbued with the Holy Spirit, but rather was an emissary of Lucifer and her minions knew better than to obstruct her path, let alone devour her. *It made sense.* Everyone in the building was on death's door, starving, dehydrated, vulnerable, then along comes this pristine, beautiful young girl—temptation made flesh—offering every secular comfort.

Maybe in their final moments the denizens of 1620 would have found their way back to God, and here was this serpentine interloper, sent to obscure their potential moment of spiritual clarity.

She dressed in black.

She even wore black nail polish. She listened mainly to heavy metal. *Oh Jesus*, he thought. *Oh Jesus Christ.* How could he have missed this? Everyone was so blinded by her gifts that they couldn't see her for what and who she was: Lilith! Or if not capital L Lilith, then lowercase lilith, which was still not good. Even her last name was suspect: Luft. Luft was German for "air," a tricky name. Mona's personality seemed lighter than air. Air was a sustainer of life. She was keeping them all here, alive physically, but spiritually dead.

He was at last seeing through her deception. He'd seen The Light!

And now it was his job to let the others know.

18

Ruth's naked body lay on their bed wrapped in a clean white sheet, as dictated by Jewish tradition—it was the least he could muster since she'd have to forgo the plain pine box. In the back of Abe's mind he seemed to recall something about no coffin and the body being laid to rest, face up, and then concrete blocks being put on it, but the memory was sketchy. Sweltering in his mourning suit, tie cinched tight at his collar, Abe petted Ruth's "earthly remains" and chewed his lower lip.

He'd disposed of the sheets and mattress pad she'd soiled and tidied as best he could, masking any residual odor with copious amounts of Glade air freshener. It was not a pleasant task and his estimation of those in the funeral trade became more sympathetic as he'd toiled to prepare the body. It wasn't Ruth any more. Odd how once the life force had departed the body it ceased to resemble its former occupant. Sure, the face was the same, but the slackness removed the humanity. Her eyes were still open, damn them, and had caked over. Her jaw hung slack and cocked at an odd angle. Disturbing. Abe didn't believe in the spirit, but Ruth's death had transformed her, in spite of the homely details. It was the peacefulness. The body had relinquished her driving, vital force. In repose she didn't look like the bitchy yenta she'd become over the years. It was simple as that.

He'd told the others. Ellen and Alan said they'd attend Abe's ad hoc service, as did Dabney and Karl. It came as no surprise that the guinea bastard had shown nary a jot of sympathy or respect. At least his *faygeleh* friend had paid his respects, even if it was just lip service. What did come as a surprise was that the first to arrive was Mona, who'd made no sign of comprehension when Abe had mentioned news of his wife's passing to the girl. On this occasion her customary black wardrobe seemed apt, as did the unheard-of absence of headphones.

"Mona," Abe said, ushering her into his parlor. "Thank you for coming."

"Uh-huh," she said, but it didn't sound unsympathetic. It was just her way.

"Can I, um, do you want a drink of something? Water? Juice? Seltzer?" Abe felt funny offering her provisions she'd furnished, but what else could he do?

"No, thanks." Mona scratched an ear, no doubt feeling naked without her earphones. A few moments of silence passed, Abe standing there at a double loss, Mona looking at her feet.

"You know," Abe said, "I was the only one in the building who had to fight his way home through the first—what would you call it—outbreak of the zombies? It's true. The rest were home or nearby, but I was at work when it really began to hit the fan. Like you know, it spread like wildfire, but I managed to get home, all the way from the garment district to here. That's three miles, give or take. I couldn't leave Ruthie to deal with this alone. Oy, did she sound scared. Well, of course she did. She wasn't an easy woman, but I loved her. Maybe I didn't show it enough, especially lately, but I did."

"Uh-huh."

Mona sniffed loudly, and for a moment Abe thought this moment of human-scale tragedy had reached her, that she was moved. But no. It was just plain old congestion. She removed her backpack and opened a side pocket. "Uh, can I get that water?"

"Certainly, dear." *Dear?* Abe blinked a few times as he walked into the kitchen to pour her a glass of water. *Dear?* Though she looked nothing like his daughters, save for the color of her hair, Mona put him in mind of them. Miriam and Hannah, his brunette beauties, having gotten his coloring, not Ruth's. Abe returned to the parlor and handed Mona the glass, which she accepted with a simple nod. Into her mouth she dropped two caplets, washing them down with the room-temperature liquid.

"Allergies?" Abe prompted.

"No."

"You, uh, ever encounter any other survivors out there in your travels? Any other enclaves like ours?"

"No."

Her monosyllabic response hung in the air like a vague but disquieting smell until it was dispersed by the arrival of Ellen, Alan, and Karl, then Dabney and, shockingly, the *faygeleh.* Conventional condolences were expressed, handshakes exchanged as well as a couple of hugs and a peck on the cheek from Ellen. Considering he knew Ruth wasn't exactly well loved—or even liked—it was an excellent turnout. She'd have been pleased. After pleasantries and so forth they adjourned to the bedroom and Abe fished out the little prayer pamphlet. Looking a trifle embarrassed, Abe put on his reading glasses and cleared his throat. He'd never liked orating before a group.

"Okay. Thank you all for coming. I know I said that already, but thank you again, anyway. It would have meant a lot to Ruth. Okay." He cleared his throat again. "Okay, so I'm going to read this little prayer, even though I don't go in for all this nonsense. Okay. I should skip the editorializing. Sorry. And to Ruthie I say sorry, too. I can't do it in Hebrew. I don't remember how." Abe smoothed the codex and again cleared his throat. Sweat was pouring off him, his suit darkening further in the pits and back—like it mattered. "Okay . . .

"May His great name grow exalted and sanctified in the world that He created as He willed. May He give reign to His kingship and cause His salvation to sprout, and bring near His Messiah in your lifetimes and in your days, and in the lifetimes of the entire family of Israel, swiftly and soon. Amen.

"May His great name be blessed forever and ever. Blessed, praised, glorified, exalted, extolled, mighty, upraised, and lauded be the name of the holy one, Blessed is He beyond any blessing and song, praise and consolation that are uttered in the world. Amen."

What a load of horseshit, Abe thought amid a chorus of hushed amens. *So be it.*

"Listen, there's all kinds of nonsense you're supposed to do for Jewish funerals, but let's face it, we're not equipped and I've done what I can. None of that malarkey means anything anymore anyway. I'd rather eulogize Ruth in my head than aloud. It's too tough. You people never got to know Ruthie at her best. Quite the opposite, to be frank. But trust me, Ruthie was a sweet lady, way back when. She was a beauty, too, and a good mother. Maybe a little overbearing, but good. Anyway, there's supposed to be a procession and all that rigmarole, but forget it. I don't even remember which is supposed to come first. The tent of prayer. The rending ritual. Without a cemetery to orient me I'm at a loss."

"So what do you want us to do, Abe?" Dabney asked. Maybe

because he was the second oldest in the room he had some sense of the absurdity, as well as solemnity, of the situation.

"I just want Ruthie's body removed from the premises. I know burial's out. Same for cremation. So, all I ask is dispose of it in as dignified a manner as you can. But I don't want to see. I'd rather lie to myself that she got what she deserved."

"Okay, Abe. You got it."

Abe sat on the upholstered bench before Ruth's vanity and watched as Dabney and Alan lifted the enshrouded corpse of his wife of forty-eight years. Five minutes later, they cast her from the roof of the northernmost building like a perished sailor at sea. That roof dropped to another roof, rather than the street, so her body would remain unmolested, to decompose in peace.

Hunched over Ruth's vanity Abe held his head in his hands, the grief beginning to hit him and take hold. All her powders and liniments, her tinctures and paraphernalia neatly arranged on the low table reminded him of the great pains she'd taken to look attractive for him before it all went south. His nose ran but his eyes remained dry. He sniffled and kneaded his scalp. Wife, children, grandkids—all gone. He snorted back the snot and clenched his eyes shut.

"Allergies?" came a soft, female voice.

Abe started, nearly toppling from the bench. He thought he was alone, but there stood Mona in the doorway, clutching her childish bag.

"What?" Abe said.

"Allergies? Your nose."

"No, not allergies. Just plain old anguish," Abe said, adding with a touch of sarcasm, "You got anything for *that*?"

Rather than look insulted or display any recognizable emotion, Mona opened her bag and rummaged through it. "Valium. Prozac. Paxil. Zoloft. Wellbutrin. Parnate. Nardil. Effexor."

Not five words in a row from this girl in the last month and now this checklist of multisyllabic antidepressants. Abe wiped his nose with a tissue and stared at Mona as she crouched by the door, still foraging in her cartoon backpack. The backpack reminded Abe of the baby snowsuits. The more he looked at her the more she reminded Abe of his granddaughter. Danielle hadn't been as phlegmatic, but she took her job as a teenager seriously and was as sullen and uncommunicative as possible. Abe missed her.

"You take much of that stuff?" Abe asked.

"Not much."

"What constitutes 'not much'?"

"Enough. You want?"

"Yeah, I guess I'll try some of that Zoloft."

"Takes awhile."

"How long?"

"Couple weeks."

"And the others?"

"Couple weeks. Maybe more."

"Never mind, then. I'll just deal with it."

"Valium's quick."

"Okay, I'll go with that."

Two tabs later Abe slipped off into narcotized slumber, his body in the exact spot Ruth's had been. He slept the untroubled sleep of a babe.

19

"You can't be thinking of keeping it," Alan said, trying to sound as reasonable and nonjudgmental as possible.

"And why not?"

"Why not?" Alan had so many reasons at the ready he was at a loss for words. How could she be seriously considering taking this baby to term? He was astonished she'd even been able to conceive. Maybe it wasn't even his. That was possible. But what the hell did that matter? His, Mike's, whoever's. This was no time to be bringing new life into the world. He tapped the home pregnancy tester on his knee. "Why not? I really want to phrase this right. I don't want to be patronizing or insulting or anything like that, because you're an intelligent woman and . . ."

"And you're *already* being patronizing. If you're going to hammer me with a whole laundry list of how shitty it is out there, spare me. I'm not blind, I'm not stupid. I'm fully abreast of the state of the world."

"Then how can you justify such a selfish act? How could you even remotely think having a baby is a good idea? Just explain it to me. I really want to hear your rationalization, because that's all it will be. Fuck it, I'm sorry, but there is no good rationale for it. None. Forget telling me. I don't want to hear it. It would be some irrational female desire to procreate. You need something that will love you unconditionally? That's the apex of selfishness."

"Who said anything about that? Don't go putting words in my mouth!"

"Then explain it. I'm sorry. Maybe I'm totally wrong. Please. *Enlighten me.*"

Ellen smacked Alan across the face, hard. "You're totally patronizing me, you asshole."

"I don't mean to be," Alan said, rubbing his stinging cheek, suppressing the innate urge to retaliate. "This is a very emotional moment. Let's calm down."

Ellen sat and stewed, eyeing Alan with newfound scorn. Sure, she was good enough to fuck, but like most men it was only if the rutting was consequence free that it was desirable. Alan hadn't seemed to object to boning her without the benefit of a condom. What, did he assume *she* was taking precautions? Didn't most men put the burden of responsibility on the woman? Alan had seemed so atypical at first, but now? Since the reintroduction to creature comforts like video he'd been a lot less attentive to her needs. Sex, at times, seemed a chore that she'd cajoled him into performing. He'd rather watch movies and comedy shows.

And Mona. Presently she was posing with her clothes on, but how long would *that* last? First a little "innocent" modeling *fully draped*, as the *artistes* say. Then, when she's gotten used to posing, comes the suggestion of undraped sessions. Then, the artist—and Alan had elaborated his theory on the inborn oversexedness of artists during one of their own postcoital bouts of pillow talk— puts the moves on his quarry, and bango, Alan's boning Mona. What would she be like in the throes of passion? Could she even feel passion? Would she suddenly become a chatterbox? Wouldn't *that* be hilarious? Or would she just lie there like a corpse? Maybe Alan would like that.

"You just don't know what it's like," Ellen said, somewhat cryptically.

"You're right, I don't."

"I lost a child! Do you have any idea what that's like?"

That Alan had been through three abortions probably wouldn't count, so he kept mum.

"No, of course you don't."

Even Mike, her daughter's father, hadn't been as psychically wounded by her death as Ellen had. Men just couldn't feel that connection. With men the whole procreation equation came down to: SPURT! *My work is done.*

"Does the human race just call it quits?" Ellen shouted. "Like Peggy Lee said, *is that all there is*? I can't believe that. Those things out there can't run on empty forever. Someday they'll start dropping and then it will be time for us to rebuild and repopulate. That's the function of every organism, Alan. To perpetuate its kind. Is that so bad?"

"It's not that it's bad, exactly, but what kind of risk are you willing to take? What are you basing this optimism on? You see those things out there as being transitory? Maybe you're right. I hope you're right. But since their advent they've shown no sign of going away. Sure, they're rotting. You can see it. You can *smell* it! But they don't give up the ghost and fall down. Not unless you put them down by force. Maybe I could see what you're doing as a positive thing if they were keeling over out there, but they're not. They're not. Can't you wait? Wouldn't that be a reasonable compromise? I could make peace with being a dad a lot easier if I didn't think that giving birth was the ultimate form of child abuse at this point."

"Who says you're the father? Maybe this is Mike's, in which

case this is also my last piece of my husband. Plus, how can I get rid of it?"

Alan had no answer. It was pointless to argue. He leaned over and gave her knee a tender squeeze, mute capitulation, if not actual encouragement. Ellen sat back on the couch and softly began to sing, "*Is that all there is, is that all there is . . .*"

"They can't last forever," Abe said, his voice chemically softened.

Alan paced Abe's floor, periodically looking out the window at the mob.

"Tell *them* that," the younger man said, agitated by his exchange with Ellen. They don't seem to have gotten that memo."

"Eventually they'll run out of steam. Maybe not in my lifetime, but—"

"I'll repeat myself: tell *them* that. They don't seem to be going anywhere. Who's to say we outlast them? They've been running on empty for months. With the exception of Mike, none of us have gone and fed the flock, so what, they'll just do us a kindness and drop?"

"I've seen some of them do just that," Abe said. "Drop. They can't keep going on and on and on, eternally. And if we can outlast them, that'll mean we can get out of this building and move on."

"To where?"

"Anywhere. That's immaterial at this point. But you've gotta cling to some kind of hope. You have to be optimistic," Abe said.

Alan looked at the old man with befuddlement. Though he wasn't about to spill the beans about Ellen's natal bombshell, Alan had come up here to commiserate with the resident curmudgeon, to buttress his negative worldview. Instead he was having a chat with Pollyanna. Abe sat in his armchair, shirt open and little round belly pooched out over his undone slacks. His face unnaturally be-atific, he resembled a scrawny Jewish Buddha.

"You're going to make me laugh," Alan marveled, "and I'm not sure I'm up for that."

"Why? Why laugh? Hope is the most vital asset we have. It's all we as a species ever really ever had. Hope is the only reason to get up in the morning."

"Who *are* you?"

"You've gotta have hope," replied the old man.

"If you start to sing, I'm gonna scream."

"The stuff I'm taking, I wouldn't care."

"Stuff?"

"Mona's a heckuva pharmacist." Abe closed his eyes, chuckling to himself. "A heckuva pharmacist."

"So I sent her out for more of that rope and some other stuff," Eddie said, his smile devious.

"Why?" Dave asked.

"I got me an idea for some leisure activities, but mainly I wanted her out of the way for a while. I wanna check out her digs, snoop around and see if I can figure out what her secret is."

"You still on about that?" Dave whined, pondering the vague-ness of Eddie's unspecified "leisure activities."

"Fuck yeah, I'm still on about it. *She gets to go out*, Einstein. She gets to leave the compound. She's holding out, bro. I *know* it. I can feel it in my bones."

Dave didn't feel like arguing. Instead he slurped another wedge of syrupy peach out of the can, letting it roll against his tongue and lips, hoping the suggestive visuals would derail whatever scheme Eddie was hatching. Instead, Eddie just snapped at him for eating like a pig and then left the apartment. Dave gulped down the rest of the sweet liquid and followed Eddie into the hall, then downstairs. Two flights down Eddie placed a small flashlight between his lips and, aiming the focused beam on Mona's top cylinder, began to pick the lock with some small, spidery tools.

"Where'd you get those?" Dave asked.

"Had 'em," Eddie said, his hushed voice slightly slurred by the flashlight. "Keep your voice down. I don't want the rest of the jerks in the hizzy to catch me in the act." And with that the top lock opened. "Fuckin' Yale," Eddie smirked, removing the drippy flashlight from his mouth. "Never would've gotten it open if it was a Medeco."

He opened the door and in they slipped. Dave didn't feel like a groovy master criminal. He felt more like Dumber to Eddie's Dumb. Or worse. The apartment was almost unchanged from when Mona had taken occupancy, the only difference being she'd moved Mr. Spiteri's recliner next to the left front window. Also, various CDs littered that area, some in their jewel cases, others loose. Several were arranged haphazardly on the windowsill, some data-side up. Eddie scoffed and said, "Bitches never know how to take care of CDs." He lifted one off the ledge and looked at its playing surface. "Look at this shit. Nicks and fingerprints all over it. Remember Gina Copaseti? She never treated shit right. I lent her my Bee Gees box set and it came back like she'd stuck it up an elephant's asshole. I stuck somethin' else up hers for good measure. Payback with interest."

"So what are we looking for, Eddie?" Dave said, nerves and impatience straining his voice.

"Hey, *you* don't have to be here," Eddie snapped. "I'm perfectly happy to do this investigation on my own. You wanna help, great. But if you're gonna honk like a woman, beat it, a'right? 'Cause I don't need that shit."

After a cursory couple of circuits around the apartment, Eddie began to prospect in earnest, opening drawers and riffling through them, closing them in disgust when nothing extraordinary was unearthed. Though he'd never been here before, he had the sneaking suspicion all was as it had been in Spiteri's time, and he didn't even know from Spiteri because his building had a different super. Drawer after drawer revealed nothing but tools of the custodial trade, Spiteri's family's clothes, and other plebeian junk.

"C'mon, Eddie, Mona will be back soon."

"How the fuck you know that? Sometimes she doesn't come back for hours or till the next day. She left less than an hour ago. One more complaint an' The Comet's kickin' you to the curb, bro. For real. Help or vacate. Your choice."

Eddie opened one of the hall closets and began rummaging, cursing softly as a small avalanche of shoeboxes pummeled his scalp. "Your mother's ass!" he shouted, clapping a hand over his mouth and cursing himself for making noise. He lifted lid after lid, finding nothing. "These shoeboxes got nothin' but shoes in 'em," he griped, filing them back on the upper shelf. Board games for stupid foreigners, a scuffed soccer ball, a beat-to-shit toaster oven, two garbage bags full of ratty clothes—it was all rubbish. And clearly not one bit of it was Mona's.

Eddie stepped into the bedroom and switched on the solar camping lantern within. The bed was immaculately made, with taut hospital corners. Either Mona was quite the skilled domestic—which seemed unlikely—or she didn't sleep in the bed. Who knows, maybe the little freak didn't sleep at all. With diminished enthusiasm Eddie opened dresser drawers and foraged, turning up nothing but the former occupant's unmentionables and workaday clothes. There was a box of condoms well past their fuck-by date, but Eddie palmed them anyway. What a waste of—

"*Hey, Eddie,*" came Dave's voice in a whisper-hiss. "*Check this out.*"

Eddie stepped into the kitchenette and found Dave standing on the kitchen counter holding a bumpy sheet of something shiny—it was a blister pack of pills. "Whuzzat?" Eddie said, snatching it from Dave.

"*It's drugs,*" Dave said, sotto voce. "But check *this* out." He opened the top cabinet. Inside were mounds of similar and identical blister packs, as well as prescription bottles of various sizes, all full. Eddie looked at the assemblage of pharmaceuticals and felt both vindication and annoyance that he hadn't discovered the goods.

"See what I told you?" he said. "You *see*?"

"I see a lot of drugs, Eddie. But what does it tell us about Mona? That she's a drug addict? That would explain her zonked out disposition, but . . ."

"*But, but, but.* You sound like a fuckin' Vespa. Maybe it's her whole *everything*, bro. It could . . ."

Both trespassers froze at the squawk of the home walkie-talkie, which heralded Mona's return.

"That was fast," Eddie seethed, stuffing the blister pack into his pants.

"Shouldn't we put that back?"

"Fuck that shit. I wanna know what this shit is. Like she's gonna miss one sheet of it, whatever it is."

"But . . ."

"But me no buts. We gotta lay low while they help her in. How we gonna get out without being noticed?"

"We can't be in here when she comes back," Dave said, sweating.

"Tell me something I don't know. What'd I just say?"

Dave pressed his ear to the door and when the clangor of footfalls subsided he looked through the peephole. He turned to face Eddie and gave the thumbs up. As he opened the door a crack, Dave felt like a burglar in an old-timey silent comedy. Everyone seemed to be in the neighboring apartment—he could hear Alan calling out to Mona. Dave and Eddie stepped into the hall.

"What're you guys doing in Mona's place?" Karl asked. He was standing on the landing out of the fisheye peephole's range, clutching his Bible. Eddie's first impulse was to snatch the Good Book, give the top of Karl's pointy head a good hard swat and growl, "The fuck is it to you, *midget?*" but he thought the better of it. Instead he stalked over to Karl, allowing the full impact of their disparity in height and brawn to sink in—physical intimidation was often more effective than verbal, Eddie found—then he smirked and thug-purred, "For all intensive purposes *we were never here, capisce?*" Karl nodded. "*Bene,*" Eddie said as he and his compatriot ascended the steps. "*Molto bene.*"

30

Alan didn't share Ellen's optimism, if that's what you could call it.

If anything, Alan took some comfort from the hypothesis that he and the others were the last of their kind. The reign of man—nature's biggest mistake—was nearly at its end. What an honor, to be cognizant of the end of your own species, to be members of The Last Generation. The dinosaurs didn't know that their number was up. Alan didn't mourn mankind much. It was a shame that all of humanity's finer contributions—art, literature, music, architecture, *some* science—would in time completely disintegrate, but the notion that the Earth would be free of man's influence, that the planet could heal itself and be cleansed, was heartening. Certainly more so than giving birth to another stupid, miserable, pointless human being. Still, if he wanted to stay—or more to the point *get back*—in Ellen's good favor—and he did—he'd have to quash that kind of thinking.

Or at least dilute it.

He swirled his brush in some linseed oil and studied his subject. Mona sat on a stool between the front windows, one leg perched on the footrest, the other dangling limply a few inches above the floor. Though fully dressed—Alan didn't wish to invite further scorn from Ellen—Mona was barefoot and once again Alan was attempting to not be aroused by Mona's sumptuous calves and now, of all things, her well-turned feet. Most feet he'd encountered, male or female, were functional but unattractive collections of jutting tendons, knots and joints, often rough and calloused. Mona's were just the opposite, their tops smooth and doll-like, almost like adult baby's feet. How could a girl who did so much walking have such pampered-looking tootsies?

An unbidden boner sprang to life and Alan's posture involuntarily hunched. He wore another oversize shirt to mask any protrusions, but still. If her lowest extremities had this effect on him, what would total nudity do? He'd survived adolescence without ever having come in his pants or having had a wet dream. This was no time to regress. He concentrated on technique and execution, his strokes deft and provocative—but not *too* provocative. What a waste that no one of note would ever see these works. He'd always been modest about his art, having been raised to believe humility a virtue. All diffidence had ever gotten him was a whole lot of nothing. He'd never gotten any public accolades and never would. Not that doing art had anything to do with that, but, well, yeah, *yeah it did*. Art for art's sake was pure, sure, but it was also masturbation with a fancier pedigree. Ellen thought he was a genius, even if that was an audience of one. That counted for something, even if she was sore at him.

His erection hurt.

Alan looked away from the canvas he was working on to the most cluttered wall. Amid the myriad zombie studies hung six sizable portraits of Mona. Unconsciously he'd spread the zombies away from the paintings of Mona, manifesting the old precept of art imitating life. Zombies. Mona. Sure, she was alive, but in spite of her fetching appearance she lacked vitality, her eyes communicating no more than those of the undead outside. Reptile eyes. Insect eyes. And yet still the hard-on persisted. Alan tried to will it away, thinking of disgusting things. But what was more disgusting than his waking life? In the old days if he wanted to suppress a boner he'd think about maggots and rotting cantaloupes and roadkill.

All of which seemed rather quaint now.

"*Why not?*" Eddie said, trying not to sound like a whiny little bitch. Mona stood before him, implacable. More infuriating than her unwillingness to comply with his simple, reasonable request was her refusal—or was it inability?—to elaborate. She'd gotten them every little goddamn thing, but now this sudden veto? It made no sense. Eddie mopped his forehead and stared in disbelief at this petite yet immovable object. He blinked as a stinging trickle of perspiration leaked into his eye.

"No guns," she repeated.

"But come on, it's a good idea. You *know* it."

"It's a bad idea."

"But we could start takin' 'em out. We could cut a path for you ahead of time."

"Don't need one."

"Maybe *we* could even go out. You ever think about that?"

"No guns."

"*Fine*, we'll discuss this later. Maybe hold a vote. You believe in democracy or are you some kind of . . ." He stopped himself. What was he going to call her? A commie? That seemed a little out-of-date. "Maybe the others can convince you."

"Nope."

"*Fine.*"

"Fine." Uninflected. It wasn't even snotty. He hated that. Eddie

256

turned his back on her and stomped upstairs, pausing for a second to pound on Dave's door and bark, "Dave-o, grab your gear, we're goin' fishin'!"

On the roof, Dabney snored as he napped under his rickety lean-to. Eddie couldn't understand why he chose to live outside like an animal. *Fuckin' moolie would probably be happier living up in a co-conut tree.* Eddie scowled as he waited for Dave. Fuckin' Mallon might've gone homo, but at least he still knew how to be a man, have fun like a man, whatever. The whole gun thing had put Eddie in a foul mood. Why that stupid little cunt couldn't see the advantage to scoring some firepower was beyond him. What, she was afraid of guns? Guns could do some serious damage to those rotten skinbags down on the street. That's not a plus? Please. Eddie thought about his little encounter in his old digs. A piece would've been sweet. *Pow!* From ravenous zombie to dark, wet stain.

"What's up?" Dave said as he barged onto the tarpaper.

"*Shhh*, I don't wanna rouse the eggplant," Eddie whispered. "You brought the gear bag?"

"Yeah, but what's it for?"

"The Comet wants to go sport fishing, bro."

"Huh?"

Eddie beckoned Dave to follow him across several rooftops until they reached the one furthest south. Eddie opened the bag and pulled out the two heavy-duty Penn reels. "You can reel in a fuckin' three-hundred-pound marlin with these babies," Eddie grinned.

"So?"

"So, we're going hump angling, Davy. Gonna catch me a zombie, bro."

Dave stood back and watched as Eddie put together the rod-and-reel assembly. For a change it wasn't that hot, but sweat poured off Eddie's brow like a mini-Niagara. His eyes were wild. "This'll be just like angling for marlin or sailfish or shark or any of those big motherfuckers. You remember that fishing trip we took to Costa Rica, bro? Same as that, only better."

"Eddie, dude. I dunno, man, this is a little weird, don'tcha think? I mean, what if you actually catch one? And what are you gonna use for bait?"

"You mean *you* don't wanna get on the hook? I'm just fuckin' with you. Okay. Okay, I don't need to use a lure, okay? I can make a noose. Oh, dude, that is perfect. What an awesome combo: fishin' and lynchin'. Call it *flynchin'*! Oh, dude, that's genius. *Genius!*"

Scary is what it was, Dave thought. Eddie seemed more agitated lately, a little zippy. But not zippy as in *zip-a-dee-doo-dah, zip-a-dee-ay*. Zippy like that time he did three consecutive lines of blow in the men's room during a company holiday party with one of the traders. Tweaked.

"Eddie, have you been taking those pills you filched from Mona?"

"Ix-nay on the ills-pay, bro. Keep your voice down. I don't want the nigger to hear."

"You have been, haven't you? You even know what they are?"

"They're her fuckin' secret," Eddie whispered, teeth clenched. "Why else does she got so many of them, huh? Dude, it's so perfectly clear. *I* figured it out."

Eddie stood up, rod and reel ready for action, and cast the line into the crowd below. Within seconds the line jerked, the tip of the rod dipping. Eddie positioned himself behind a sturdy metal steam pipe, bending at the knees for more leverage. "Grab my waist," he commanded as he laughed in triumph. "This bitch ain't gettin' away!" Dave wrapped his arms around Eddie's midriff and dug his heels in. Eddie dipped forward. The thing on the end of his line was putting up a struggle. His bronze biceps bulging with each crank of the reel, Eddie looked like a well-oiled part of the apparatus. It was about the most absurd image Dave could conjure: two men on a roof, aping the Heimlich maneuver, attempting to reel in a zombie

"Help me reel this cocksucker in!" Eddie roared, no longer caring about Dabney.

Dave added muscle and soon a rotted head appeared at the edge of the roof, monofilament cutting into its wrist, which was caught between the noose and its neck. Eddie yanked the rod vertical, cackling at the sight of the zombie's stricken visage. For something brain-dead it looked plenty scared and more than a little pissed. Thick blackened blood oozed from where the line was scoring the epidermis and it groaned piteously. Eddie jerked the rod again, attempting to haul his quarry over the edge. Instead the line cut straight through the purulent flesh and dismembered the wretched thing. With the zombie's weight no longer balancing them, the sportsmen toppled backward, Eddie's coccyx crunching against Dave's groin, eliciting a doglike yelp. Dave rolled out from under his laughing companion and cradled his injured batch.

"Almost got 'im," Eddie guffawed. "The little fish that got away!"

"Who fuckin' cares?"

"What's your problem?"

"Never mind." Dave lay there moaning, cupping his area.

"Wanna give it another go?"

"Do I look like I wanna?"

"*Pfff.* What a killjoy. S'matter with your nads, bro?"

"Forget it, okay? Just forget it."

Eddie sauntered over to the roof wall and looked down, his prize absorbed by the crowd, no sign of it below.

"That sucks," he said.

"Well, what would you have done with it, anyway? Hung it over the mantelpiece?"

Eddie slipped a hammer out of a loop in his shorts. "I wanted to smash all its teeth out and then basically torture it for a while. Cut on it and take it apart and shit."

"Oh. Sorry that didn't work out for you."

Eddie smiled and said, "Thanks," not catching the unconcealed sarcasm in Dave's voice. Eddie clapped his bud on the shoulder and said, "We can try another time, right, amigo?" Dave nodded. "I'm goin' back down, you coming?" Dave shook his head. "A'right, catch you later, bro."

Eddie trotted across the rooftops, then disappeared into the stairwell. As Dave stepped onto their roof, Dabney sat up and said, "Your homeboy is a goddamn lunatic, you know that, don't you?" Dave nodded again. He was temporarily out of words. Words just didn't seem to cut it right about now. Even "inadequate" seemed inadequate.

From his bed, Karl lobbed the Good Book across the room. What was so good about it? It was riddled with riddles, chockablock with useless parables. No wonder people spent their whole lives reading the same tome over and over and over again. No one could make sense of this, at least not in a practical, how-to-apply-this-to-my-daily-grind kind of way. Karl had always noted people reading the Bible in public, especially on the subway. Mostly black and Hispanic people, predominantly women, their brows always creased in intense concentration, and highlighter pens poised to accentuate key passages for future rumination. Maybe it was racist, but Karl had been then, and was now even more, convinced that though they read the individual words, the sum made no sense to these devout ladies and occasional gent. Karl had gone to college and couldn't fathom half of what he read and reread.

Karl knew there was a God, but His guidebook was the work

of human beings, and humans could seldom be trusted. It was a book created by committee, too, which also didn't bode well. Karl had a rule of thumb: any movie with more than three screenwriters was likely going to suck. The stories in the Bible had been circulated plenty before they were set down in ink. It was like the telephone game.

Big Manfred had an LP called, *Satan is Real*, by these gospelers, the Louvin Brothers. Big Manny had found nothing funny about it, however, especially not its title. Satan *was* real to the old man, and there was nothing even remotely amusing about that. Sure, the record cover displayed a hokey image—the lily-white brothers dressed in snappy white suits in the flaming pits of hell, a ridiculous cardboard-looking red devil on the horizon—but the album's message was clear: don't sin, obey the Bible, be a good Christian. Simple as that. The weirdest part was the brothers looked mighty cheery as they simultaneously preached and roasted.

Karl rolled over onto his stomach to ease the knot there, a combination of hunger and disquietude. He hadn't eaten in three days in protest of the food procured by Mona, but what if he was wrong? Maybe she wasn't in league with Lucifer, in which case this boycott was in vain. Plus, if she were an emissary of the Lord, wouldn't his hunger strike be blasphemous? It wasn't like he could just ask her, either. If she were a hellish minion, surely she would lie and say otherwise. But if she was sent by God, she'd likely lie or evade the question, too. It was not for him, a mere mortal, to question divine intervention. And as sure as he was that God existed, he wasn't as certain about Beelzebub. Karl always figured the devil was the invention of man, kind of a scapegoat for rotten behavior. Why be burdened with personal accountability when you could blame Satan?

"This is unbearable," Karl moaned into his pillow. He dropped off the bed and assumed a posture of supplication, interlacing his fingers and tilting his head heavenward. "Am I being tested? I mean, wasn't I being tested *before* Mona arrived? Isn't this whole stinking mess a test? If I starve myself, isn't that protracted suicide, which is a mortal sin? So, I guess what I'm saying is, I should eat, right? If Mona is here on Satan's behalf, I'll need my strength to outwit her, right? Or if she's one of Yours, I should . . ."

What was the point? He gave up. No answer was forthcoming, ever. Maybe on Judgment Day. Karl wondered if the line into Heaven was like the ones at Six Flags. Each depiction he'd ever seen of the line to the Pearly Gates was evocative of the ones at every theme park he'd ever attended. Did technology in the afterlife move forward as it did in life? Had Saint Peter upgraded from The Book of Life to a computerized database? Maybe he just had a BlackBerry or an iPhone.

This was madness. What the hell was he thinking? Karl punched his thighs and attempted to refocus. He was out of practice in the hunger racket. He'd become accustomed to eating regularly again, and now, three days empty, he was going mental.

He stood up and did some jumping jacks and toe touches; grade school calisthenics. He looked in the mirror. Five-and-a-half-feet of solid dork. He trotted into the kitchenette and tore open a Slim Jim, devouring it in three barely chewed bites. Then another. And another. He attempted to eradicate the pungent aftertaste with two cans of Mountain Dew, then felt buzzy as the double shot of caffeine coursed through his system, accompanied by a volley of violent vurps.

An image of Mona popped into his forebrain, tan and bare bellied, radiant as Botticelli's "The Birth of Venus." Karl snatched the Bible off the floor and contemplated swatting himself in the groin to subdue any impure thoughts. Sinners of yore were often selfflagellants. Did medieval times call for medieval measures of self-purification? The caffeine, the caffeine, the caffeine. And whatever dastardly additives there were in those Slim Jims. *Oh mercy.*

"Jesus H. Christ!" he groaned as he swatted himself in the 'nads.

31

"So what's your story?" Ellen asked as Mona sat across from her. They were seated in Mona's apartment, one by each window, Ellen slowly rocking in the Spiteri's creaking old rocker, Mona motionless in her usual chair, feet propped on the windowsill.

"My story?"

"I don't mean to sound confrontational. Or intrusive. I'm sorry. But yes, your story. Where are you from? Who were your parents, what is your background? Who are you, basically? How do you survive? How come the things don't attack you?"

"I guess they don't like me."

Ellen frowned at Mona's stock response. "No, I mean really. Okay, look, I don't want you to feel like you're on the spot. This isn't an interrogation. Just two girls having a chin-wag, okay? Where are you from?"

"Here."

"Here, where?"

"Around here."

"Yorkville."

"Uh-huh."

"What street?" *It's like pulling teeth.*

"Seventy-seventh. And Second."

"Okay, now we're getting somewhere. I grew up in Melville, Long Island. You know where that is? It's near Huntington. I went to Walt Whitman High School. Where did you go to high school?"

"Didn't finish."

"I see. But before you didn't finish, where did you go?"

"Talent Unlimited."

"Really? That's a performing arts school, isn't it? You went there?"

"Uh-huh."

"Okay," Ellen said, stretching out the second vowel, and when that produced no elaboration, added, "And what did you take? What was your *talent*?" Did that come out sarcastic? This girl was unbelievable. She was the most unforthcoming individual Ellen had ever met and it was really trying her patience. But she'd break her, yes she would. What *was* her talent? Stonewalling?

"Singing."

"Really? And yet you're so quiet." Again, was that sarcastic? Ellen couldn't tell, but apparently neither could Mona, who sat there, unruffled as ever.

"Uh-huh."

"What kind of singing? Jazz? Gospel? Pop?" *Pop?* Ellen felt like an old lady.

"Opera. Mezzo-soprano."

Unbelievable. Ellen took a few to absorb this startling tidbit. Whether Mona had been any good or not—or for that matter was still any good—was immaterial. It was almost unimaginable that this introverted girl sang opera. And what about the din always pummeling her eardrums? That wasn't opera. Had Mona dreamt of segueing from opera to heavy metal? Hadn't Pat Benatar done something along those lines? Who could remember? Was it a lie? Was Mona fucking with her? Why would she?

She wouldn't.

"Isn't this nice? Getting to know each other?" Ellen smiled hopefully, Mona looked back at her noncommittally and then gazed out the window. Ellen wanted to get out of her seat, casually step over to Mona, gently lift Mona's chin so that they were looking into each other's eyes, and then slap the living shit out of her. Ellen had tried, but seriously, enough was enough.

What if the embryo taking form in her uterus turned out to be like Mona? Was it something in the air? Maybe Mona had been a vital, zesty, free spirit before all this—an opera-crooning voluptuary. Maybe the same contaminant that spawned the living dead had stunted her personality. Maybe this was some kind of autism. Certain mold could cause that in developing babies. Maybe she was just displaying the symptoms before the rest of them, a result of her youth. That was a possibility. Maybe she was the first, but in time they'd all follow. Nature was all about adaptation. Mona had forged invisible armor. The zombies didn't attack her, but maybe the cost of survival was death of the self.

It makes sense. To survive one must adapt.

But what kind of life is that?

Though it was way too early for the agglomeration of cells in her uterus to do anything independent, Ellen felt a kick in the guts nonetheless.

"I'm jerking off to paintings of a fully clothed girl's ankles. Wow, I'm so fucking great I can't stand it. I am *the man*. I am the greatest living artist and this is what it comes down to. And I had issues about doing whacking material for Eddie? I'm pathetic. *Path-et-ic.*" Alan tossed the soggy wad of tissue out the window. "Fresh protein, kids!" he shouted to the crowd below. One looked up as the jizz-bomb bounced off his empty eye socket. Alan laughed. "S'matter, Gomez, you don't like daddy milk?"

He stepped away from the window, no pants, just a sweat-sodden T-shirt. Not since junior high school had he masturbated to his own art, and it didn't feel good. This was not how he'd envisioned his thirties. But then again, none of the current climate fit the vision of his future he'd had in his past. By thirty he was supposed to have had at least one solo show in Soho, Paris, and London. By thirty he was supposed to have at least one hardbound monograph of his works. By thirty he was supposed to have found true, everlasting love. By thirty a lot of things were supposed to have happened.

Alan sat down across from his most recent canvas, a half-finished portrait of the enigmatic Ms. Luft. The painting was perched on the easel. Behind it was the wall of Mona portraits surrounded by the halo of zombie studies. Across the room were the Ellen canvases and drawings. He couldn't remember the last time they'd had sex. Had they done it since she'd announced her pregnancy? No. Here he was jerking off to the image of a person who was barely there when he had a real, live, fleshed-out, fully dimensional woman to love. Classic. "Fuck you, Erma Bombeck," Alan sniped. "I gotta eat something. I gotta eat some peaches. I need a sugar fix. That's what I'm gonna do. And I'm gonna announce it first and then do it. I'm going to speak in declarative statements announcing my imminent actions and then do them. I am going to get some canned peaches, open the can, eat the contents and then fling myself out the window. What? No. No I won't."

But why not?

"Mona's right. We shouldn't have guns. Because right about now, a 9 mm lead sandwich sounds very appetizing."

Alan chugged the peaches, sputtering as he choked on the last couple of slices, a small, stinging upsurge of syrup leaking out his left nostril. His mother used to scold him for wolfing his food—another indication of his regression. Alan wiped the syrup off his nose and chin and then licked it off his hand, which he hadn't washed off since he'd masturbated. Wonderful. Washed off. Bathed. There was a quaint custom gone dodo. Mona had at least scored cases of Purell, so Alan traipsed over and pumped a couple of squirts into his palm and cleaned up. He stroked some onto his wilted penis, too, which stung as the alcohol penetrated the sensitive skin. "There, all germ free," he said, as if it mattered. "Cucumber Melon," he mused aloud, looking at the label. "As if. Still, it smells nice."

As Alan took a few whiffs from the bottle it hit him that the stench of the undead didn't bother him any more, even when his sense of smell was rekindled by a pleasant odor. The renewed appreciation for scent made him hungrier, and he ate a can of peas. Then a can of baked beans, including the disgusting wad of pork. Staring at his work in progress, he sat down on his couch and noticed he'd only given Mona four toes on each foot, like some cartoon character.

"That's stupid," he muttered as he slipped into dreamless slumber.

"We should get a generator," Eddie said as he toyed with the fishing reel. "I mean, it's not gonna be summer forever. Nobody took my car-boosting idea serious, but if Mona can drive, she should take a car, you know, find a Hummer and snag us some gennies. I could teach her how to siphon gas. Maybe seeing that would plant some thoughts in her head." He grinned smuttily, arching his eyebrows in case Dave didn't pick up the innuendo. Dave frowned. "Anyway," Eddie continued, "It'd be sweet to get some power going. Maybe some AC, for a change."

Dave nodded. "Yeah, that'd be cool. But you couldn't keep the whole building chilled."

"So we get everyone in one apartment and crank it. A sleepover."

"A sleepover. Because I know how much you *love* hanging with the others in here," Dave scowled. "But, yeah, I see where you're coming from."

"For real, right? The people in this dump, they got no vision. Okay, I admit it; I'm not so book smart, but I got life smarts. These pampered Upper East Side homos would just shrivel up an' die if Mona hadn't come along."

"So would you and me," Dave interjected.

"Yeah, but not without a fight. They'd of gone out like babies, all curled up in a fetal position. If I knew for sure my number was up I'd of gone downstairs, outside, and taken a few of those fuckers out, *mano à mano*. If Mona doesn't drive, I could teach 'er. Maybe she could snag a laptop and one of them driving simulators."

"No such thing."

"For real? But they've got flight simulator games."

"No cars, though."

"That's retarded. Five zillion driving games, but none that teach actual driving?"

"None that I ever heard of."

"Wow, that makes no sense."

"Would you have played one?" Dave asked.

"Fuck no. I only like shooters." Eddie dropped the fishing rig on the floor and got up. "I'm gonna go talk to Ms. Vegetable-matter." On his way to the door he picked up a blister pack and popped a pink pill.

"You really shouldn't do that," Dave said.

"Fuck you, Mom. And anyway, these pills don't do shit."

"Maybe they're placebos."

"Maybe they're female shit and I'm gonna sprout some tits. Time will tell, bro, but in the meantime I plan on testing the waters a bit longer."

"Yeah, well when you start menstruating, drop the regimen."

Eddie laughed as he sailed out the door, letting it slam as he tromped downstairs. When he arrived at Mona's door he affected a more sedate demeanor and then knocked. After a few gentle raps he pounded the side of his fist on the door. Fuckin' bitch was probably listening to her death metal or whatever it was. How could anyone listen to that noise? He tried the doorknob to no avail, rattling it in frustration. *Oh come on*, he thought. After several more thuds the door opened a crack, held that way by the chain, and Mona greeted him with a dull stare, her earbuds draped around her shoulders. *If this chick had tits*, Eddie started thinking, then stifled the notion. He was here on a different kind of business.

"Sup?" he said, flashing her his most winning smile.

"Nothing," she replied.

"Can I talk to you about something?"

"Uh-huh." She undid the chain and opened the door the whole way, ushering Eddie in. As he stepped past her he took in their disparity in size, he standing at least a foot taller than she.

"What are you," he began, "like maybe five one or something?"

"Five two."

"Wow. It's so fuckin' weird that a tiny chick like you—no offense—can just truck around town with all those zombies and a big guy like me can't. I can't figure it out."

"Uh-huh."

I'll "uh-huh" you, you fuckin' . . . *No, no. Stow that shit. Make nice.* "So, okay, what I was thinking was this: you're always going out on these errands, right? And the most you can carry is what you can pile in a shopping cart. So that limits what you can score. So maybe, I dunno if you can drive, but maybe you could make the most of your trips out there in the world, if you drove a truck or Hummer or something. Even a Mini Cooper. *Anything.*"

"Can't."

"I could teach you."

"They have to sense me."

"Huh?"

"In a car they can't sense me so they don't disperse."

Eddie was doubly stunned. Not only had she answered his question but also it was a complete sentence and it made sense. Sense. The senses. Eddie didn't even think about that before. The zombies still had senses, even if they were a bunch of rotting brain-dead skinbags.

"Sense," he repeated. "Like maybe you give off a stink—no offense—that those pusbags can't abide. Wicked. Like because maybe you . . ." Eddie cut himself off before he tipped his hand. He didn't want her to know he'd filched those pills. But this was the lynchpin. This was *it*. He felt sure. The pills. The quantity. She'd been megadosing those pills and it made her immune to attack. *Oh, this sly bitch.* And she didn't want to share. He'd tell the others and they'd flip. All those smarty-pants. Should he tell them? Yeah, because then they could decide what to do. He didn't want to flat out accuse her, but if they were all on the same page, like a committee, then they could move as a unit. That was *strategy*. He felt like he did when he was playing hockey. Strategy was never his strong suit, at least not formulating it, but he had some dope—literally and figuratively—that the others didn't. He'd present his findings and they'd take it from there.

"I tried driving once. They tipped the car over." Her dull face actually betrayed a trace of anxiety. She didn't like the memory. "Never again."

"That's really interesting," Eddie said with unaccustomed sincerity. She was a waste case, all right, but she was human. "Listen, I didn't mean to freak you out. I just thought maybe it was a good idea about the car and all. Sorry. I'll leave you alone, a'right?" She nodded and Eddie let himself out, grinning as he turned his back on her, feeling smarter than everyone else in the joint. It was cool knowing something no one else did. And *he* got it out of her. *He* did.

Suck on that, you faggots.

part three

"It would be a total betrayal," Ellen said, rubbing her abdomen, phantom kicks pummeling her innards. "We shouldn't, and you had no right to do what you did. My God, if she discovered what you did it could mean the end of everything we've got."

"Yeah, maybe," Eddie sulked.

"Or the beginning of a brave new era," Karl added. "Really. If she isn't sharing knowledge of how to walk among the unclean then she's done nothing to engender our loyalty."

"*Unclean? Engender?*" Alan echoed.

"What? I'm not entitled to be articulate?"

"Um, of course you are, it just sounds a little unnatural, you know? You never spoke in such a *grandiloquent* manner before."

"Oh, and so what's 'grandiloquent,' then?" Karl bristled.

"It's mockery." Alan pushed back his chair and crossed his legs with a smirk.

"Shut up, both of you," Ellen snapped. "This is serious. Eddie's proposed betraying Mona's trust, and moreover turned it into a conspiracy of *us* against *her*, which, frankly, is pretty fucked."

"Hey, I didn't put it like that," Eddie said.

"No, but that's the gist. And listen, I wasn't going to share this little tidbit with the rest of you, but I'm pregnant and I'm not about to risk poisoning my baby in some experiment with mystery drugs." Ellen looked at her watch to confirm how long Mona had been away on an errand. She felt tired and irritable, some of which was hormonal, but mostly it was disgust. The others offered no comment on her gravidity. Whether that was in deference or indifference was anyone's guess, though Dabney did look away.

"Well, I'm in," Karl said. "I need to know whether she's divinely imbued or just a druggie with a heckuva side effect."

"I guess I'm in, too," Dave said, winning a clap on the back from Eddie.

"Include me out," Abe said, softly. "That little girl has been good to us and I don't plan on returning the favor with treachery."

"Yeah, me neither," said Alan.

"Same here," said Dabney. " 'Less we keep it honest and talk to her about it, I don't want no part of it."

Outside heavy rain pelted the windows, but no one was rushing upstairs to frolic and strip. The sky was an oppressive, ever-darkening gray and the climate inside wasn't conducive to abrupt shifts in mood. Even though this meeting was taking place in Ellen's dining area, four floors above pavement, a bunker mentality prevailed. Ellen wondered if this was how Hitler's staff felt as it plotted his demise. Was that an apt comparison? She hoped not. How about Kennedy's people plotting his? Ellen believed the conspiracy theories. Not all of them, but some.

She got up from the table and stretched, then stepped over to the front windows. Below, the horde shambled, aimless, ugly as ever, pockets of unrest visible from this elevation. Some pushed and shoved, others stumbled, fell from view, trampled underfoot.

It always looked like the least festive New Year's Eve gathering ever down there; Times Square, apocalypse-style.

Behind her the others continued to dicker about whether or not to raid Mona's pharmaceutical stash. Abe had no interest. Since Ruth's death Mona had gotten him hooked on Valium and now he almost matched his supplier in imperturbability. He was like the pod-people version of his former self. It didn't seem possible that a chemical cocktail was what kept Mona safe out there, though pounding drugs certainly went a long way toward explaining her personality, or lack of one.

"Pregnant, huh?" Dabney sidled up to Ellen and took a spot beside her at the window, rain spatter stippling them both with dark spots. Lightning flashed, followed by booming thunder. Ellen just nodded. Karl looked over at the windows and considered the constant thunder and lightning emanating from God's throne in Revelation.

"Is this a joyous kind of thing or an unexpected problem?" Dabney continued. "I don't mean to pry, but it's a big development."

"Yeah, I know."

As he looked over at Alan, Dabney suppressed his urge to ask who was the father. Mike hadn't been dead that long. Maybe she didn't know. If so, they'd never know, not even when—or if—the baby was born. Mike and Alan fit the same basic description, brunette, pale but with a slightly olive complexion. Did it even matter? Not like junior would be headed for college someday. Or even kindergarten.

Ellen smelled alcohol on Dabney's breath. It wasn't beer breath, either. It was distillery-strong, whiskey breath, complemented by cigarettes. His eyes were red-rimmed and hooded. It seemed to Ellen that almost everyone was in a mad rush to be medicated. Or anesthetized. Dabney gave her bicep a soft, paternal squeeze and left the apartment. From the table, Eddie pounded his fist like a gavel and declared the meeting adjourned. He and his confederates would break into Mona's apartment and steal drugs from the kitty. Ellen took a deep breath, the air wet and redolent of death and ozone. Sheet lightning whitewashed the sky, leeching the remaining pigment from an already colorless vista. If the world weren't already over, she'd find this a whole lot more portentous.

Psychosomatic or not, her insides churned, and she wondered if taking this baby to term was a good idea. The zombies weren't going anywhere. It had been over five months since they'd supplanted mankind. For all Ellen knew, the occupants of 1620 were the only people left, at least in New York. What hope did her baby have? Alan was probably right.

To hell with him and his rationality.

To hell with Mona and her lack of charm.

To hell with 'em all.

As the last of her "guests" left, she slumped against the wall, wanting nothing more than to cry, but no tears came. She just sat there, hunched over and desolate. A baby. New life for a dead planet. Was that hopeful and wise, or just selfish and stupid? Perhaps later, in keeping with the narcotics theme of the day, she'd ask Mona to venture out and fill a prescription of her own: Mifepristone, aka RU 486, aka "the abortion pill."

An ounce of prevention, retroactive-style. Better safe than sorry.

Abe lay on the bed on the spot in which Ruth had succumbed. Alan and Karl had flipped the mattress for Abe, since her seepage had done a number on the other side, even with the mattress pad in place. The air in the bedroom was stale but Abe didn't mind. He was comfortably numb. Where had he heard that phrase before? Maybe he just made it up. The room was dark and Abe stared at the ceiling. After a short while he wasn't sure if his eyes were even open, so he blinked a few times to clear that up. Open, closed. It made no difference. The Valium made Abe aggressively apathetic, which he supposed was oxymoronic, but who cared?

For a man as formerly opinionated as he, indifference was unnatural, and drug induced or not, becalmed or not, he felt the unnaturalness deep in his id. It wasn't Abraham Fogelhut's role in the universe to be its calm center. It conflicted with his essential Abeness. Was this what the hippies and yippies experienced, he wondered? When they were all dosing themselves to the gills back in the sixties, when all that nonstop navel gazing was happening, when everything was *a happening*, when *happening* became a *noun*, was this that? If so, Abe, in soft focus, needed to revise his opinion of the sixties drug subculture; it was even dumber and more self-centered than he'd suspected.

Happening as a noun.

Party as a verb.

Vacation as a verb.

Summer as a verb.

Summer as a *verb*?

Jesus H. Christ.

Between the hippies and the yuppies, English was in its death throes. And forget the coloreds and their hip-hop lingo. Ebonics, was it? If the plague hadn't come along when it did, given the trajectory on which English was headed—at least as spoken by Americans—pretty soon the younger generation would be reduced to tribal clicking languages. Maybe the zombies did everyone a favor.

This wasn't relaxing.

It was too soon to have developed a tolerance for the drug, wasn't it?

When was the last time he took a pill?

Take a pill, take a pill, take a pill. *Ugh*, that was what weaklings did. *Take a pill.* The world is shit. *Take a pill.* Your wife is dead. *Take a pill.* The kids are dead. *Take a pill.* Take two pills. Take a whole bottle of pills and be done with it. Fuggit. Forget it. Man was made to suffer. Didn't some poet say that? Somebody said it. Maybe it was a song. *Okay, I'm making a compact with myself,* he thought. *In the remaining weeks I read. I read everything Mona can get her hands on. The classics. I read some, but not enough. And always it was for school. I need to make a list. Let the others do what they will, chase their tails, fritter it away, but I'm going out enriched in the brains department.*

Abe got off the bed, grabbed a bar of Ivory soap and walked up to the roof, shedding garb as he made the ascent. Modesty? Antiquated notion. The downpour drummed against the pebbled-glass skylight, smearing the soot, its rhythm beckoning Abe forward. Let the others cower in their hidey-holes. Or whatever they were up to. From the sounds of it as he passed the Italian ape's digs, some vigorous buggery. To each his own. Abe dropped the last of his attire as he stepped onto the tar paper, which shimmered with wetness, reflecting each stroke of lightning. His body, even well fed, was lank and achromatic. Had his balls always hung this low? Who could remember? The sky looked like a backdrop from an expressionist German film of the silent era—thick, black clouds set asymmetrically against deposits of leaden gray. With the recurrent lightning the buildings all became, at least in flashes, monoliths of pure black and white.

Absolute.

As a youngster Abe had been instructed in absolutes. There was good and evil, period. Good folks and bad. As an adolescent he saw little to contradict that. The Nazis were unadulterated evil, easy to fight, easy to hate. Their atrocities left no room for debate. He'd joined up and fought for good, and even though the horrors were manifold, the cause was inarguably virtuous—and this was *before* he was aware of the death camps. He'd seen brutality in all its gory glory. But glimmerings of gray began to afflict his psyche. His first German corpse conflicted with the propaganda. This wasn't some massive Hun with sharpened teeth—though even as a naïve teen, Abe hadn't really expected the enemy to look that way. But this was just a kid. Skinny, blond, lightly freckled, soft pink lips, and fading color in the cheeks. This wasn't a Nazi; this was just a foot soldier. Just a dead kid in a muddy ditch.

The world was easier to absorb before that moment. Abe had liked black and white, and he'd missed it when it was taken from him. Down below, the multitude groaned in protest of the weather, their plaint drowned out by the pervasive, ground-shaking thunder. There were no towheaded blond kids with freckles and soft lips down there. Maybe once upon a time, but not now.

They were the enemy.

Us versus them.

Black and white.

But even those things lacked malice. They were just automated instinct.

As Abe lathered up, he missed gray.

At least Ivory was pure.

Mostly.

"*Pretty in pink*," Karl burbled. His skin felt funny. Not funny ha-ha, but funny. Funny-ish. "I don't even like The Psychedelic Furs." He looked at the pill in his palm, filched from Mona's stash. Pink. Though the Bible didn't address drug use, there were very clear principles outlined in it that suggested drug use wasn't acceptable. Christians were supposed to respect the laws of the land. But the land had no laws any more. This wasn't recreational usage, anyway. This was a life-or-death experiment. That made Karl smile.

He'd always found the term "experimenting with drugs" disingen-
uous, but that's what this was. He felt very scientific.

And itchy.

And sweaty.

And cotton mouthed.

"She only has four toes."

"What?"

"She only has four toes."

"I heard you the first time. What are you talking about?"

Ellen pushed back from the dining table and stared at Alan, who sat there stirring powdered nondairy creamer into room-temperature coffee, his spoon tinkling gratingly with each rotation. Finally, patience exhausted, Ellen snatched the utensil from her in-the-doghouse paramour's hand and tossed it across the room, where it clattered into the sink. Ellen smiled with petty satisfaction and thought, *She shoots, she scores. Swish.*

"Mona. She only has four toes on each foot."

"What are you talking about?"

"She was posing for me again today, so I could finish up the canvas I'd started—and don't give me that look. Seriously. There's no extracurricular activity and you're not going to guilt me over an involuntary reaction. I got a boner. Sue me. Move on." Ellen scowled but let her forehead relax, the creases ebbing. Alan continued. "I'd painted her with four toes on her feet and was looking to correct that. Not that I need a model for toes, but you know, it was curious is all. So she's sitting there, in the same position . . ." Again Ellen scowled, the word "position" ever linked with carnality. Alan paused, let it pass, resumed his narrative. "And this time I scrutinized her tootsies. . . ."

"Tootsies. How adorable."

"Please? Could you please? Seriously? It's enough, already. The point is I hadn't goofed. She has only four toes on each foot." Alan restrained himself from saying, "each beautifully turned foot," or "each devastatingly sexy foot." He pinched a testicle to suppress the erection he felt inevitable. Just the thought of those smooth, cartoony peds wreaked havoc on his libido. He'd once seen a porn video where a guy pulled out and came on the woman's foot. At the time he'd thought it was the stupidest thing he could ever imagine. Things change.

"So what am I supposed to make of this little revelation?" Ellen said, unmoved by Alan's news.

"Look, forget I said anything, okay? This is what couples do, right? They sit at the table and make small talk. Only I didn't think this was so small. I thought it was genuinely interesting. It was just another thing to factor into Mona's roster of oddness. Just forget it."

"Consider it forgotten."

Alan excused himself from the table and left the apartment. Better he should spend time alone. Was this some hormonal thing? Some pregnancy thing? The roller coaster ride had been fun—was "fun" even the right word? Fun? Interesting. The sex had been good. Stellar. Desperate, but explosive. But this? Did Mike deal with this or was this all some cumulative build up of hormones, grief, and immeasurable weltschmerz the likes of which the philosophers of yore never in their wildest imaginings grappled with? When he thought of it that way, Alan figured Ellen was entitled to some appreciable bitchiness. But it still was a compound drag.

He shuffled downstairs to his flat and swung open the unlocked door, taking in his miasma of death-world renderings, the gooey center of which were the portraits of his four-toed fantasy babe. Did he even want to fuck her? To be honest, yes, he surely did. The world was over, in spite of Ellen's micro-attempt to repopulate it. New life just meant livestock for the ghouls outside, fresh meat for the grinder. What good were morals now? Maybe a sociopath like Tommasi had the right idea. Maybe so, but you had to be hardwired for that kind of thing. Nature versus nurture. Alan was a nice boy, period. A nice boy with a dirty mind, but really, was there any other kind? A nice boy with a clean mind was illusory.

He stepped into the kitchen and opened a package of Cheez-Its, scooping a handful into his mouth. Gone was the rationing mentality. He ate on automatic, not even tasting what he shoveled in. As a thick glob of orangey half-chewed mush wedged in his windpipe, hard edges scraping soft tissue, and he began to choke, the realization that eating had resumed its status as commonplace tickled his brain. Eating wasn't no thang. He grabbed a bottle of Evian off the counter and took a few swigs, lubricating the doughy wad, swallowing hard, forcing it down. Not so long ago he'd have been nursing each cracker, savoring each bite, picking the crumbs off his shirt and putting them in his mouth, making it last. Now he was back to indifferent fistfuls. Alan walked over to the front windows and admired the crowd on York. The ol' gang.

"Hey, folks!" he shouted, waving as if to oldest, bestest buddies. "Hey! How's it going down there? Same old, same old, huh? Yeah, I know. But look at this!" He palmed another batch of Cheez-Its, Evian at the ready, and rammed them into his mouth. He chewed open mouthed like an ill-mannered child, flecks of fluorescent snack food spattering the sill and windowpane. He spat a gob of the near-glowing processed food onto the bald crown of one of the meatheads below, creating a pulpy yarmulke. No reaction from the target; a reliable disappointment. It was always the same faces down there; having immortalized them in paint, pastel, crayon, charcoal, graphite, and ink, he knew their pusses intimately. It amazed Alan that these brain-dead bastards could be capable of locomotion, yet never go anywhere. They milled around, never straying from their immediate surroundings, like penned animals. It reminded him of families he'd observed in the outer boroughs who never ventured into Manhattan, these urban provincial hicks whose entire lives played out in a square-mile radius. The things below were no different. At least veal had an excuse.

Not that it mattered any more. If anything, the majority of outer-borough zombies were probably indistinguishable from their former selves. *Jesus, even in the apocalypse I'm a snob.* Alan wiped his mouth and watched the same old, wishing he could change the channel. Absently, Alan snatched a newsprint pad off the floor and began to sketch the crowd.

Just to pass the time.

"Four toes. Four fucking toes."

"This is more like it."

Three roofs north of Dabney's, Eddie grinned, testing the tensile strength of the jury-rigged swivel that anchored the butt of his fishing rod. He pushed his feet hard against the wooden footrests he'd nailed straight through the tar paper. Dabney didn't want that craziness happening on his turf.

"Yeah, just like those fishing shows on cable. This is gonna fuckin' *rule!*" Eddie let out a rebel yell and chugged his beer. He'd gotten to like warm beer. Dave sat nearby on a folding lawn chair, not sharing his buddy's enthusiasm.

Eddie planted his ass in his makeshift fighting chair and prepared for a rousing round of "flynchin'." The rod felt good in his hands. Sturdy. He cast the line—the noose weighted with a brass plumb bob—and jiggled the pole to test the swivel's motility. Smooth. Beer in one hand, rod in the other, Eddie could almost imagine being on the high seas, maybe off the coast of Cozumel.

"I'm gonna ask Mona to get me one a them New Age tapes of ocean noise. Play that while I'm up here to help create the mood. That shit would be sweet, bro."

"Yeah, sweet."

"You bet your ass, *sweet*." A few gulps of Corona, a light buzz, fishing with a buddy. Things had sweetened considerably recently. Whatever those pills were, they didn't hurt, either. There was a playful, nerve-tickling quality about them, whatever they were. In concert with the beer? Nice. He felt small, electric surges in his thighs and groin. Even if they weren't Mona's secret weapon against being eaten alive, they were okay by Eddie. He closed his eyes and began to hum tunelessly, rocking his head side to side to simulate the motion of a boat. "Dude, make seagull noises," he suggested.

"What?"

"Make some seagull sounds."

"Dude?"

"Don't harsh my buzz, bro," Eddie said, a slight edge creeping into his voice. "Just make some gull noises, okay? Humor me."

Dave hemmed and hawed for a few, then let out a series of awful high-pitched squawks.

"Perfect," Eddie said, even though the imitation was far from. "More, but vary the loudness. Make some sound far away."

Dave had done some questionable things for Eddie, but this was pushing it. Still, he obliged. He felt childish, but that wasn't so bad. It helped him get into it, and soon he was on his feet, padding around barefoot on the hot tar paper, fluttering his hands and screeching wildly.

Three roofs over, Dabney stood up and watched them, baffled. "The hell are those two fools doing?" He stepped over to the low dividing wall and took a seat, slinging one leg over the side as if mounting on a horse. He had a plastic cupful of Maker's Mark and took a sip. Cocktail hour at Bar 1620. Dabney had witnessed some daffy shit in his day, but this won the blue ribbon.

As Dave caromed around the rooftop like a drunkard's cue ball, Eddie's line dipped violently, then bowed as he yanked it upward into a perfect half circle. "Fuck!" he yelled. Dave was oblivious, lost in his seabird impersonation. Eddie dug his feet hard against the wooden blocks and pushed back into the fighting chair, wishing he had a real one, secured to the deck with straps and all. The thing on the other end of the line was a fighter, or at least heavy. The line jerked and whipped around, but the butt remained fixed to the swivel. Dabney stood up and watched, making no move to help or to flee.

"Fuckin' bitch!" Eddie growled, loving it.

His shoulders gleamed with perspiration and tanning lotion, each muscle flexed taut, biceps bulging, knuckles nearly glowing white. The rod pitched forward, nearly toppling Eddie, but he righted himself and threw his shoulders back. Though he thought what Eddie was doing was deeply, profoundly, unfathomably stupid, Dabney couldn't help but admire the moron's tenacity. With obvious effort, Eddie worked the reel and slowly the line rewound, his catch brought ever closer. "Yo, Dave! Dave! Stop bein' a fuckin' bird an' help me out! *Dave!*"

Dave snapped out of his playacting and once again threw his arms around Eddie's waist, Heimlich-style. The two of them fought the rod and over the lip of the roof came two zombies bound together at the throat—a twofer! "Sweet baby Jesus!" Eddie whooped.

As the two struggling bodies flopped onto the roof, Dave released Eddie's waist and ran to grab a brick or two. Eddie gripped the rod with one hand as his catches clawed at the monofilament dug deep into their necks. With his other hand he retrieved from under the chair a ball-peen hammer and stalked closer to his prey. "You don't look so tough to me."

Dave hung back, the proximity of the zombies a bit harrowing. Dabney watched, now swinging both legs to his side of the roof. "White boys want to get themselves killed, that's their affair," he whispered, ready for a hasty departure.

Eddie advanced on the strung-up twosome, one male, and one barely recognizable as female, any feminine characteristics eroded by living death. Eddie now used the line like a leash, jerking the rod to make them sit up and notice their captor. Distracted from their predicament, the zombies, upon seeing Eddie, began to hiss and slobber, thick ropes of opaque, grayish drool hanging from their slack jaws. Eddie laughed. "You think if I knocked all her teeth out she'd give me a hummer?" he asked, smirking.

"Dude, I don't even . . ." Dave was at a loss.

"Maybe I should bone her till she snaps in two. Maybe I should just bust her up into pieces and see which ones keep twitchin', then fuck 'em."

"*Dude* . . ." Dave's lower lip quivered with dismay and disgust.

"I'm just messing with you, Davis. Chill. Like I'd ever in a million years slip it to a skeezer like this. These are desperate times, but not *that* desperate."

Dave recalled Eddie's encounter with the Wandering Jewess and wasn't so sure. Eddie stepped directly in front of the zombies. The line had cut deep into the male's throat and thick, nearly black grue seeped out. His flaking, sun-baked skin was puckered around the incision, the edge frayed and ratty. His eyes were gray and hazy, but their direction couldn't be clearer. Both zombies were intensely interested in Eddie and to a lesser extent Dave, who'd retreated a few feet. Only if his help were essential would he advance. The zombies dropped their claws away from the line around their necks and recoiled from Eddie. "You see this shit? You thought the drugs was barking up the wrong tree? Look at 'em, Dave. They're backing away. See?"

"Yeah, 'cause they're scared shitless. Doesn't mean you're immune, Eddie."

"Killjoy," he sneered, then swung the hammer in a graceful arc and knocked the jaw clear off the female. "Bull's-eye!" He guffawed as the female's hands jerked up to her ruined face in astonishment. "There goes your modeling career," Eddie scoffed, well pleased. "And so much for that blowjob, too. Although . . ." The zombie's tongue lolled stupidly in the jawless opening between her upper teeth and gullet.

Dave turned away and heaved.

"Fuckin' *killjoy*," Eddie repeated. He stepped over to the female and smashed out her remaining teeth. "Gummy bitch." The male began to fight against the noose again. Brain-dead or not, he could sense what was coming and it wasn't a tasty meal or fresh flowers. Eddie palmed the back of the female's head and jerked it forward, severing the head altogether, giving the male more room to claw at the line. Eddie stepped back and watched as the male struggled to his feet and spat and growled.

"Gotta love this guy," Eddie said. "He's a fighter. A fighter who's gonna lose, but still."

The zombie stumbled back as it managed to free itself.

"Can't have that," Eddie said, and with a roundhouse kick sent the zombie spiraling off the roof back to its fellows.

"*Yoink*," Eddie said, flashing his pearlies.

"Promise me you're never going to do that again," Dave said, straightening up from his puking position.

"Why make an empty promise, dude?" Eddie beamed as he popped open another brew. "I just found my new regular sunny-afternoon thing."

Glancing at his lean-to and considering the vacant apartments below, Dabney contemplated a change of venue, thinking it might be time to move this party indoors.

34

"I want to go out with you," Karl said, standing on the landing by Mona's open door.

"On a date?" Mona stared at Karl, her eyes betraying no hint of derision, surprise, or even much in the way of general interest.

"No, *no*. Not on a date," he stammered. "I want to leave the building with you next time you go out. On an errand."

A passable facsimile of curiosity flashed across Mona's face. "Why?"

"An experiment. I want to see if your zombie repulsion has enough juice to keep them at bay with a companion, if your umbrella of safety extends beyond just you. Remember the childhood game 'Ghost in the Graveyard'?" Mona shook her head. "Okay, it was like a variation on tag, only there was a graveyard—the playground, your living room, wherever—and a base. The base was a safe zone. So, one kid is chosen to be the ghost. He's out in the graveyard. Other kids are positioned around the graveyard and have to get back to base. If the ghost tagged you, you were the ghost. But the way we played it was if kids locked arms, or even tied clothing together, you could use 'electricity' and leave the base so long as you were tethered to it with a lifeline. The lifeline carried electricity. Not real electricity, you know, just the power of the base. So you could venture into the graveyard safely and taunt the ghost. Sometimes you all were on base and you'd mock the ghost mercilessly until he threatened to quit. Anyway, I want to see if your gift has electricity. You understand?"

"Bad idea."

"Maybe so, but I need to know."

"More like you need to die."

Karl decided he didn't like when Mona spoke in full sentences. He felt zoomy and his skin prickled. He actually felt electricity, currents flowing through his epidermis. His hairs stood on end. Maybe it was excitement. Maybe it was the drugs. The drugs. What were those drugs? All those years of living a "Just Say No" lifestyle, and now this. Now a lot of things. If Mona was taking speed she sure didn't show it. Karl knew of a white-trash family near his town that cooked up homemade crystal meth. Hopped-up farm boys would roar out of that house in pickups and blast buckshot into neighbors' mailboxes and anything else that didn't move—and sometimes things that did. Big Manfred had pronounced them "doomed."

"So, what do you say, Mona? Can I come?"

"Bring your Bible."

"To stop the zombies? Like *The Exorcist*? 'The power of Christ compels you,'" Karl said, doing a bad impersonation of Max von Sydow.

"In case you need Last Rites."

Karl definitely didn't like when Mona spoke. Drugs. The Antichrist. Some folks were right, others weren't. Mona fell into the latter category. How were they fixed for staples? To the best of Karl's knowledge, all coffers were brimming. He wanted to put this to the test. Abe had mentioned wanting books. Was that call to leave the nest? Karl felt impatient and Mona's impassivity exacerbated it. He wasn't a violent man but he felt the desire to slap her, if only to see what reaction she'd have, if any. Would she get mad? Would she fight back? It was maddening, her demeanor. He wanted to punch her. Not in the face, though. In the stomach. He wanted her to wince and bend over. He wanted to force her to her knees and make her supplicate.

What?

"Mona, would you join me in prayer?" He offered his hands, which now trembled. He was so full of self-revulsion he thought he'd burst. If one could physically purge self-loathing Karl would be the human geyser, spewing from all available orifices. Was it natural madness? The drugs? Who could tell? Cabin fever? "*Please?*" he implored. Mona shrugged and looked uncomfortable—*a recognizable emotion*. Not the one he'd been hoping for, but human all the same. "It's okay," he sputtered. "I'm sorry. I don't want to impose my thing on you. It's okay."

"Cool," Mona said as she gripped the doorknob, closing the door.

"Yeah. Prayer is a private matter. I'm sorry. I didn't mean—"

Mona shut the door and Karl heard her engage the deadbolt. Those things outside didn't have any effect on her, but he seemed to have. He felt powerful for a moment. *I scared Mona.* He grinned, then winced, then ran upstairs to his apartment and retrieved a belt from his dresser and began flagellating his back. After several savage strokes he realized he was wearing his shirt, paused to yank off the garment, then resumed. *How dare I take pleasure in causing her discomfort? Forgive me, Jesus. Forgive me, God. I don't even know who I'm asking for forgiveness from, so forgive me for that. Is it Bud-dha? Allah? Oh, Christ, what if all those terrorists had been right?* Karl had read one of Alan's Phil Dick books, one called *VALIS*. Was *that* the real truth? Alan had explained that in the seventies Dick had a vision and became convinced he was in contact with a cosmic consciousness, which he dubbed VALIS, for Vast Active Living Intelligence System.

Of course, Dick was a loopy speed freak, but maybe he was right. Had there ever been any stone-cold rational prophet? Did that trait even go with the territory? Rationality? Was faith rational? Ever? What about all that craziness John wrote? Revelation was still a hard pill to swallow, though Karl tried nightly. Pill. Maybe it was time for a pill. Karl dropped the belt and skittered to his kitchenette to poke one from the blister mat. A small pink caplet dropped into his palm and he washed it down with a bottle of Snapple tea. *What am I doing? What am I taking? I need a* Physician's Desk Reference, *that's what I need. Maybe Mona can take me to the Barnes and Noble on Eighty-sixth. But how do I justify me wanting that book? Why would I need it? Unless I was taking unknown drugs. Has she noticed missing pills? Plus, if I went out with her would she take me everywhere she goes? Say her pharmacy jaunts are private? Maybe that's why she's reticent.*

As a boy, Karl had chicken pox, his pale, pasty body festooned with constellations of red bumps that blistered and itched like mad. He felt that way now, although his skin appeared normal. Many a saint had suffered. Even non-saints. Look at Job. Was it to be his fate to suffer like that? God was always tormenting His faithful flock. Just look at the world. Was this not evidence of a malicious God? God made man in His image, and man was noth-ing to boast about, really. Flawed, mean, petty, violent, arrogant. This was a creature to be proud of? Maybe that's why God wiped nearly everyone out. But surely those who remained aren't the best and brightest. Karl knew he wasn't. And Eddie? *God help us if he's one of God's chosen few.*

Karl laughed at the thought of Eddie being divinely spared. Karl laughed at the thought of God helping them. What a joke. What a blasphemous joke. The Bible! Drugs! Madness! Karl wanted to go outside so badly he bit his lip and drew blood. He sucked the metallic liquid deeply, savoring it. In his smallest voice he said, "Fuck you, God."

Then, with renewed vigor, begging clemency, he beat his bare back with the belt until it was slick with blood and sweat. A malicious God was not a God to test. With each stroke of the belt, spatters of blood flecked the beige walls, evoking the chicken-pocked skin of his youth.

"What can I do?" Karl mewled. *"What can I do?"*

"Well don't do *that*," Ellen sputtered. She stared at Karl in utter disbelief, as did Alan. "Have you flipped your wig? Okay, just assuming Eddie's theory about the drugs is right—and for the record, I can't even believe I'm lending credence to anything that ape's ever said—but just to give the devil his due, you've been dosing yourself for what, maybe a couple days? What makes you think you've built up a resistance to the zombies? Because your mind is eroding, what, there must be a positive side to the effects of the drugs? Look at the back of your shirt."

"I can't," Karl said. "It's behind me."

"It's stuck to your skin, and that isn't sweat. What the fuck have you been doing to yourself, as if we don't hear?" Ellen made the whip-crack sound with her mouth, adding a wrist flick for punctuation. Karl plucked at the back of his shirt and sure enough it was a bit stuck to his spine. Ellen widened her eyes at him in challenge. "Pussy whipped for Jesus much?"

"Well, anyway," Karl said, wiping his fingers on his pants, then burying the offending digits in his front pocket, "I'm going. *Someone* has to go. Someone has to put this to the test. To prove either that the drugs work for us, or we have an umbrella of protection from proximity to Mona. That her gift, whatever you want to call it, maybe it spills out and would protect a companion."

"Great. Operation Big Umbrella." Ellen scowled. The little idiot's mind was made up. "Well. I'm not even giving you a shopping list. I told Mona what I want, but you, you I'll say good-bye to. Not farewell or till we meet again, but *good-bye*."

"Thanks for the vote of confidence," Karl pouted.

"I have none to give. You want me to lie? Fine, I'll catch you on the flip-flop, my man. But seriously? It was nice knowing you."

Karl accepted Ellen's remarks and made for the door, accompanied by Alan.

"Have you told the others about your proposed expedition?" Alan asked.

"Yeah. Eddie said he wanted to go first, not a little pussy like me, but when I said I might get killed, my guinea-pig status met his approval. Anything you want from me? Art supplies or something?"

"Just come home safe."

Karl stopped and looked up at Alan, emotion swelling in his chest, which felt corseted. Eddie had been his usual self; Dave gave him a pat on the back, but that was about all; Abe was in a Valium-induced state of apathy; Dabney, drunk as a lord, yelled at him, accusing him of hubris and overweening arrogance. He'd begun to cry and then kicked Karl out of his new apartment, locking the door after Karl had been so summarily dismissed. And now Ellen's dressing down. Alan was the only one to wish him well. What was wrong with this world? That was the million-dollar question in a world where a million dollars meant nothing. Alan and he shook hands and then hugged, Alan clapping Karl's back and then realizing as Karl winced that maybe that wasn't such a good idea. Alan looked at his hand, seeing traces of blood on it, and began to apologize, but Karl appreciated the gesture.

"One thing," Alan said, his tone cautionary. "I don't know if those things have regular senses, but I know sharks are drawn to the scent of blood, so you should really do something about your back. I know it's still hot, but maybe a jacket? Something?"

"I hadn't even thought of that. Oh Jesus."

"Yeah. Just a thought."

Karl ran upstairs and pulled off the shirt, the material stuck to some scabbing spots, making them bleed afresh. He poured some water down his back. He needed something stronger. If the lash wounds were there to appease a cruel God, maybe something to exacerbate the pain would go over well. In lieu of rubbing alcohol, he fetched a bottle of cheap vodka from his cupboard and poured it over the wounds. The stinging pumped tears out of his eyes as if he were rerouting the liquid cascading down his spine through his tear ducts. He stung everywhere and the stench of the liquor overwhelmed the room. It burned his nostrils and singed his injured back. Patting his back dry with a towel, Karl then bound his torso in Saran Wrap to seal in any scent of blood. He popped a couple of pills, pulled on a fresh shirt and his windbreaker, then made his way to Mona's, his body tingling. Hoping it would further mask his potentially delectable aroma, Karl threw a few items into a knapsack, then slung it over his back. Maybe it was the drugs, maybe it was the booze absorbed through the wounds, maybe it was adrenaline, but his back was numb. He felt no pain, physical or emotional.

As he passed the Fogelhuts' door he gave it a hard knock. "Wish me luck, old man!" Karl shouted. Silence. He drummed the door with palms flat. No reply.

Fine. Be that way.

"Let's do this," was Karl's mantra all the way down.

Let's do this.

Let's do this.

35

Mona paused on the roof of Dabney's van to watch Karl struggle down the rope. Abe and Dabney aside, the others had all come to see the twosome off and to witness what would happen next. Karl touched down on the roof, losing his footing for a moment. Mona grabbed him around the waist as he steadied himself. Like an overheated radiator venting steam, the onlookers released a collective sigh of relief. Karl's heart pounded so hard he was afraid the zombies might hear it. Gripped in equal measure by terror and euphoria, Karl surveyed the scene around the van: innumerable undead below, friends and neighbors above, the world everywhere. Karl hadn't seen the exterior of 1620 in half a year. How could something so prosaic seem so beautiful?

"This is a real Kodak moment," Alan said.

"True that," agreed Eddie, as did the others whose hearts labored almost as hard as Karl's.

"Okay," Karl said to himself. "I can do this." He looked up at the sky, which seemed bigger and bluer than it had on their roof, some four stories above. He was eye level with the Phnom Penh Laundromat sign. A pigeon skeleton was nestled between the brick and the sign, a couple of feathers still clinging to the husk. Karl looked away from the tiny carcass to the larger, ambulatory ones at street level. "Oh Jesus," he gasped. Several were looking in the direction of the van, attracted by the activity. "Oh sweet Jesus."

"Lemme spread 'em out," Mona said, hopping down onto the pavement.

With a soft thud, Mona hit the ground. The response from the zombies was almost instantaneous. They began to back away, their sibilant hissing more penetrating at this proximity. It was a sound that traveled up and down Karl's spinal cord. It lingered, for emphasis, in the lower colon and upper throat, seizing and massaging both with dead, constricting fingers. He could feel liquid collecting beneath his Saran Wrap armor, the brine basting his wounds. His mother used to marinade roasts overnight in the fridge, bound in cling wrap. He hoped he wouldn't prove to be as tasty to the uninvited guests below. With an iris opened in the crowd, Mona gestured for Karl to join her on the asphalt. *It's now or never*, Karl thought. He released his grip on the rappelling rope and eased himself off the van, first sitting on the edge, then lowering his legs until they were straight, then dropping to Mona's side. The zombies stayed at bay.

"So far so good," he whispered.

"*Mm.*" Mona proceeded, noncommittal, taking a step north. Her pace was slow, deliberate—with Karl in tow, slower than usual. She gave the zombies plenty of time to soak up her mojo and make way. Without actually holding onto her, Karl kept close to Mona, walking just slightly behind her. He'd never been this near to the zombies before, and up close, they were even fouler. The countless iterations on the theme of decay were staggering. Some, obvious victims of carnivorous attacks, were little more than haphazard collections of stumps and gristle, barely held together and yet still capable of locomotion. Limbs ended midway. Faces half consumed by rot—or just half consumed, period. Exposed bone. Internal organs that weren't internal any longer. Karl never realized gums could recede so far. Their skin reminded Karl of overcooked fowl, matte, striated, thick and leathery yet translucent. Yellowed, browned, and blackened. Most eyes glazed by dull gray cataracts. Some stumbled around, sockets bereft of eyeballs. Cavernous nostrils, just vertical openings, black and rimmed with corrosion.

"They're so horrible," Karl stated. "They're so fucking horrible."

"I s'pose." The response to a comment on the weather. Banal. But then again, zombies *were* the weather. A constant. Less interesting than the weather, actually. Weather changed. Karl's walkie-talkie beeped and he removed it from its holster.

"Just testing," came Alan's voice. "How's it going?"

"Uh, okay, I guess," Karl said. "They're hanging back, but it's, uh, it's kinda freaking me out, to be honest."

"Of course," Alan responded. "How could it not? But you're out, buddy. You're actually out there."

Karl nodded in response, then snapped to and pressed the talk button. "Yeah, I'm out here. I'm out here. Look, I can't walk and talk. I need to concentrate. Over."

"Okay, Karl. Understood. Over and out."

Karl clutched the walkie-talkie to his chest, a talismanic anchor to home. His face burned. They hadn't even reached the corner and already he was hesitating. He looked back at the others, still in the windows. Ellen gave a very maternal wave of encouragement and Karl felt like he was back at his first day of school, Mom dropping him off, he being brave. *Don't cry*, he thought. *Please don't cry.*

As they headed north Karl gasped when a naked, hunched, gnomelike zombie edged into view. Its pigmentation was almost human and it bore no disfigurements other than its stooped posture and deep livor mortis in its lower extremities. It cast its nearly hairless head in Karl's direction and he gasped. *Ruth!* She must have fallen from the roof and come unwrapped. Karl stood motionless, staring at his former neighbor. Of all the people he never wanted to see naked, Ruth might be number one on the list. He thought of the late Norman Mailer, *The Naked and the Dead.*

"What's the delay?" Mona asked, not impatient.

"It's Ruth." He pointed.

"Uh-huh."

Karl suppressed that urge to chastise Mona. It wasn't like he'd just pointed out that the sky was above or that water was wet. This was kind of a traumatic big thing, Ruth ambling around. She wasn't bitten by one of those things. She just came back all on her own. Didn't that portend the same fate for anyone? For everyone? Regardless? How would Abe feel knowing his wife was scuttling around in the raw amidst the unclean? Tidy, persnickety Ruth Fogelhut in her birthday suit—or would that be *deathday* suit—loose amongst the natives. It was an ugly sight made uglier. With not a trace of recognition, Ruth's dead eyes glared in his direction as he felt Mona's hand tug at his arm.

"C'mon," she said.

Opting to not radio back this piece of info, Karl nodded and kept step with Mona, whose pace was deliberate, mechanical. She'd likely have made a fine soldier. Maybe she'd been one. Maybe she was some military experiment gone wrong. Or right. She was immune to the zombies. Maybe she was a supersoldier prototype. Maybe her creators were all dead. Or maybe they were still alive in some bunker, monitoring Mona's progress from a safe distance by means of a tiny tracking chip implanted within her.

How did one go about broaching a topic like that and not seem impertinent? Was "I was just wondering" the correct opening gambit? "So, are you some kind of genetically altered superbeing?" *So, am I totally paranoid or retarded?* Karl brooded as he trudged in Mona's wake, the euphoria of being outdoors tabled for the nonce. The other thought, the one that kept cropping up, was whether or not she was even human. That posed an even trickier question of etiquette. "So, are you an angel of the Lord or a demon from Hell?"

"What?"

Mona stopped and looked at Karl with something approximating interest.

"Huh?" he replied.

"Am I demon from Hell?"

Karl began to sweat even more, his stomach doing flips. *I said that out loud?* rang through his skull. *Idiot!*

"What?" he stammered, attempting to feign innocence.

"You said—"

Karl cut her off with a wave of his hand. "No, no, no. Not *you.* No. Ruth, I was thinking about. Ruth. Over there. But she's no angel, anyone can see that. Just a weird thing I was thinking. Just wanted to see how it sounded out loud." He smiled inanely. "Crazy. Not you." He made the loco gesture pointing at himself and shook his head.

"Uh-huh."

Karl longed for his belt to give himself a few choice strokes. The sun seemed hotter down here than on the roof, like it was turned up or aimed by some giant sadistic kid with a magnifying glass—God as megabrat. The air didn't move. Just the flies. Karl's neck skin crawled and oozed perspiration. Between the mortification and fear, his back felt like it was covered with fire ants, the Saran Wrap bandage loosening as it filled with sweat, but hopefully not blood. It stung like the fucker of all mothers. Shouldn't the weather be cooling down by now? No, it was still summer. *Endless summer.* Global warming plus zombies.

Yeah, humanity had somehow done this to itself.

Stupid humanity, Karl thought. *Stupid me. How could I not real-ize I said that aloud?* He wanted to stop thinking altogether for fear of a repeat bout of honesty Tourette's. He needed to stay in Mona's good books.

The Good Book.

Books.

That's why they were making this expedition.

As they slogged west, Karl was reminded of the annual Puerto Rican Day parade, which commenced here on East Eighty-sixth. The crowd pushed back as Mona and he trekked up the center of the street, ankle deep in rotting limbs and rubbish. Maybe this was a little less festive. Karl surveyed the crowd. His mind was swimming, overstimulated. Their path was serpentine, weaving between forsaken vehicles and countless zombies. Inside one car a zombified child in a car seat thumped its head mindlessly against the window, the glass glazed with coagulated grue. That withered tot had been trapped in that car for nearly half a year and was still animate. Karl shuddered. The seemingly eternal question once again flitted into his head: *How long will it be before these things just run out of steam?*

Books.

Let's do this.

Let's do *this.*

"I need to hit the bookstore."

"Uh-huh."

"Yeah. Abe said he wanted some books to better himself. Yeah. That's something, a man his age. I guess that's kind of admirable. 'Course he could just be bored, but still."

"Uh-huh."

"I need some further scriptural reading, too. To maybe find some answers."

"Uh-huh."

"You really never encountered any other survivors during your travels?"

"Nope."

"That's so weird. You ever try calling out? Seeing if maybe you got any response?"

"Nope."

She might be lying. If she were a demon it would be her duty to lie, to please her unholy master. Karl cleared his throat, then hollered, "Is anyone out there?" as loud as possible. He repeated it a couple of times but the only reply was increased agitation in the zombies that flanked them. Mona punched Karl on the bicep and squinted.

"Don't," Mona said. "Riles 'em."

"It's just, if there was anyone out there I . . ."

"Just don't."

"Okay. Sorry. I was just . . . Sorry."

On they trudged, the zombies hanging back, frustrated. The experiment so far was a success. Karl hadn't been eaten. Big success. Huge. This could change everything. As they neared First Avenue, Karl felt buoyed by their progress. The sun no longer felt amplified, it felt invigorating. His leg muscles felt purposeful. He looked up at the sky, which was clear and blue, and felt glorified. He felt closer to God than he had in ages. Or at least fonder. Midway between First and Second, the shrink-wrap around Karl's midriff burst and pinkish brine splashed the pavement. Mona whipped her head around, startled by the wet sound. She stared at the puddle at Karl's feet.

"Your water just break?"

Mona cracking a joke was almost as alarming as the amplified interest the zombies displayed. The scent of his natural soup was like sounding the dinner gong. Though they hung back, their rancor was heightened. The sounds emanating from their cracked, broken faces threatened to void Karl's colon.

"Oh God. Oh Jesus," he whimpered. He wanted to drop to his knees and pray.

"Keep moving."

With stinging liquid dripping from his back, Karl followed Mona's edict. The trip back to the building now seemed like miles rather than a couple of blocks. Long blocks. Avenue blocks, which were at least double the length of north-south ones. *Abe and his books. Abe.* What had Abe ever done for him? What was he thinking, volunteering for this madness?

Volunteering?

He'd suggested it.

Karl wanted to strangle himself.

Don't blame Abe. You wanted that pill book. You did. Blame yourself.

"Get the fuck offa me!" Alan shrilled, swatting away Abe's palsied hands.

Abe moaned from the pits of his collapsed lungs, pushing up plumes of stale, mucus-scented reek. This wasn't what Alan had expected when he came a-knockin' on Abe's door. Ever since Ruth's demise, Alan felt bad for the old guy, up here all alone. But this was bullshit. At first, once he'd gotten Abe's door open, he'd thought the old man was just disoriented, the way he was bumping up against the windowsill. Maybe too much Valium. But once Abe had turned around Alan knew he'd joined the ranks of the undead. And now here he was, wrestling with a zombified oldster in a fusty apartment that smelled of mothballs and something worse.

Alan managed to knock Abe to the ground, upon which he heard Abe's hip splinter. Abe grasped at Alan, but like the old commercial, he'd fallen and couldn't get up. Alan felt queasy. This wasn't comfortably impersonal like his relationship to the things below. This was Abe. Abraham Fogelhut, bearing out the cliché that when one half of an elderly couple perishes the other usually follows in close order—*only now they came back*. Alan scanned the room, looking for something to put Abe out of his misery, but saw nothing obvious. With Abe scraping brittle nails against the grain of the rug, trying to rise and failing, Alan reached the door, stepped out into the hall and closed the door behind him. He felt pretty certain Abe wouldn't be mastering the doorknob, let alone getting himself up and about any time soon. Alan gulped some deep breaths, smoothed the front of his shirt, and then headed down to let the others know about Abe's condition.

36

"It gets merrier and merrier around here," Ellen said, sourness sliming off her tongue. "So what do we do?"

"We have to get rid of him, obviously."

"It's come to this. Evicting our senior citizens," Ellen said, her wryness not abating.

"Well, yeah," Alan agreed.

"*Ugh*. The peachiness of this whole situation is really beginning to wear on me, you know? You die, you come back as one of those. Delightful. Being alive is just the next step to being undead. You think anyone just stays dead any more? Or is that passé?"

Alan shrugged.

"Some must stay dead," Ellen continued. "They must. I mean it's not like there's eight million zombies out there. The streets are packed, but not *that* packed. But maybe they are. Like I know anything. There are probably apartments all over the city packed with zombies too stupid to let themselves out. Fuck. I thought I knew where we stood on this but we don't know anything. I thought it was rat bites or poison gas or some communicable germ or whatever, but it's just how it is now. We come back. *Awesome.*" Ellen took a sip of tepid herbal tea and repositioned her hair clip. "This tea is supposed to calm the nerves." She let out a derisory laugh. "So whattaya think? Is Karl doing great or does Mona return a solo act?"

"Um."

"Yeah, well, if Mona makes it back—and I see no reason to doubt she will unless Karl's managed to fuck up her good thing—she's bringing me a little something special to take care of our situation. So, maybe I'm a little edgy. Just a little. A tad."

"What situation?"

"Don't be fucking obtuse, Alan. The *baby*."

"Oh."

"Yeah, 'oh.' It's the kind of situation that merits *that* kind of response. And don't worry. I don't hate you. You're right. When you're right you're right and you've been right all along to think having this baby was wrong. It's wrong. So today I make it right and take care of it. It'll be taken care of."

Alan let out a long breath, half relief, half sympathy, half something else. That was one too many halves, but the sigh was full of subdued emotion. He didn't know what to do. Pat her on the back? Give her a hug? He stepped over and extended his arms for the latter, but Ellen made no effort to accept the embrace.

"This isn't a huggy moment," Ellen said, voice flat. "It is what it is, and all without the hassle of pro-lifers to complicate things. That's pretty all right. I call *that* progress. Whattaya think the pro-lifers' stance on aborting a fetus in a dead world would be? Would that still be so bad? Not that it matters, but we're making conversation while we put off Abe's expulsion from the building. I'm ragging on you. Don't give me that look. He has to go. Neighbors who will eat their fellow neighbors are not to be permitted. I think that's in the charter. What? What's that look?"

Alan wasn't aware of what look he wore, but he felt completely flummoxed.

"No look," he said, his voice soft with apprehension. "No look. Just my face."

"If you say so. So, maybe one horror show will take my mind off what's on my mind, if you follow. You wanna go deal with Abe and toss him or what? I'm game if you are. I could use the exercise."

Alan fidgeted for a moment, chewing his lip till he drew blood. The coppery taste was unpleasant. Abe was one of their own. But Ellen was right: *no zombies allowed*. Eddie would probably relish a go, what with some of Abe's previous remarks at his expense, but Abe deserved better. He deserved to be put to final rest with some kindness. Some dignity, if such a thing was now possible.

"Sure. Let's get it over with."

"He's feisty for a dead man with a busted hip," Ellen observed as she forced Abe's head down with a mop, the spongy pad pressed hard against the old man's windpipe. Abe's arms flailed impotently at his attackers.

"Maybe we should get the others," Alan suggested, having second thoughts. "Eddie would . . ."

"No Eddie. We don't need that throwback to help us."

Alan looked at Abe. It wasn't Abe any more, but it was. It still looked like Abe. He wasn't some rotting thing. Not yet, anyway. His eyes weren't glazed over and remote; there was rage in those undead orbs. Rage and confusion. Abe caught Ellen's pants cuff in his spastic fingers and tugged, pulling her low riders a bit lower, exposing the elastic of her thong.

"Uh-uh-uh, you dirty old man," Ellen scolded, but the humor was gone. This wasn't funny, even in the sickest way. She pushed the mop harder into Fogelhut's throat, the pressure precipitating a volley of excruciatingly thick, wet sounds of strangulation and cartilage being demolished. Alan fought the urge to retch or pass out and grabbed a large towel from the bathroom, which he quickly threw over Abe's face, partly to muzzle him, partly to mask him. Alan didn't want to see that mechanical simulation of life. With the towel firmly secured over the old man's face, Ellen released the mop. Alan blinked away tears. This was so not right. Abe had probably slipped away into a peaceful, Valium-smoothed death, yet here he was, snapping at them. Abe rocked back and forth, his legs useless. That broken hip had hobbled him. He wouldn't even be able to shamble around out there.

"Keep the towel over his face," Alan snapped. "And sit on his chest. Something to keep him still."

"What? Aren't we going to toss him?"

"We are. But in a minute. Hold his arms."

On the floor Abe undulated, the towel tied firmly over his whole head. He looked like a hostage, crippled and hooded. Alan looked around the room, then spotted a large burnt-orange alabaster ashtray. As he hefted it, feeling its substantial weight and solidity, he remembered his own mom had one similar back when he was a kid.

Alan stalked over to Abe's wiggling recumbent form, lofted the ashtray in a high arc, then brought it down hard on the old man's skull, pulverizing it. The sound, muffled though it may have been, was sickening, but to make sure, Alan repeated the motion five times until there was only crunchy pulp beneath the soaked terry cloth. Ellen edged back, mouth hanging open, her bout of grim wit quelled by Alan's benevolent savagery.

Without asking for her assistance, Alan lifted the inert body, walked it over to the window and dropped it out. He stared as Abe's body rested for a moment on the surface of the crowd below like a body surfer in a mosh pit, before it was absorbed, the new addition sinking to the pavement, lost, soon to be trampled into paste.

No eulogy.

Nothing.

Ellen let some tears escape, not even sure who or what they were for.

Alan offered no comfort.

They both retreated to their respective apartments and closed the doors.

And Eddie caught a big one on the roof.

Three rooftops away from the hump angling, Dabney stubbed out his umpteenth chain-smoked cigarette. Eyes watery and throat scorched from the combination of butts and booze he'd been consuming since Karl and Mona debarked, Dabney divided his fogged attention between the idiot antics of the meatheads and periodically looking for any sign of their return. He didn't know how long it had been since they left. His watch had died.

Eddie had certainly gotten his recreational sadism down tight. The big greaseball would catch one and reel it in with almost no effort, then go to town on it with his trusty box of tools. Wrenches, hammers, pliers—the works. Did it count as torture if the victims weren't strictly human or strictly *alive*? Dabney could imagine congressional hearings on that subject. The freckly mick, Dave, at one point had been cheerleader, spending time offsides shouting half-hearted variations on "Rah-rah, go team go!" Pathetic. But lately he just sat on the wall, head in his hands, brooding, watching his buddy.

Dabney jiggled the bottle by the neck, listening to the liquid slosh around. The bottle had been mostly full when the two had left. Now it was more than half gone. Either Dabney had gone through it fast or it had been a while. He looked over at the other roof. Three dismembered zombies lay in a heap. Catches of the day. Funny way to gauge the passage of time without a timepiece, Dabney mused, too drunk to take into account the position of the sun or other such time-honored pre-Swiss Quartz movement methods. He should have asked Karl to pick up a fresh battery.

Karl.

Would that naïve cracker make it home in one piece? Karl was a poor substitute for his own dead offspring, but Dabney'd made him his surrogate son and he hated the thought of losing him. He remembered ruffling Karl's oily hair. Such a small thing, but he wanted to do it again. When Karl made it back he'd palm that boy's head and mess that hair up good. And now that he'd been bathed a bit, it might even be like white-boy hair ought to be: dry and strawlike, like he imagined Opie's would be. The thought made him smile until his brain converted "when" to "if."

"God dammit."

He tossed the bottle off the roof and, too loaded to go down-stairs, tottered to his lean-to sleep it off.

Eddie yanked the last tooth from his catch's mouth and flicked it from the pliers' jaws onto the pile he'd made. He wore a necklace of ears around his tanned neck, having copped the idea from some 'Nam movie he'd seen. He reached over and retrieved a hacksaw from the box and commenced removing the forearm of the struggling wretch beneath his knees. Eddie hoped they felt pain. They made sounds like they did. Sweat dripped off his bare shoulders, the bandana stretched across his forehead keeping his eyes perspiration-free.

"Yeah, like buttah," he grinned, as the blade sliced through the skin and muscle straight to the bone, then right on through that. These things were seriously malnourished. Sometimes their flesh fell away like well-cooked ribs, not that he had any appetite to try zombie meat. Certainly not since the Mona gravy train rolled in. But it was uncanny how some of these humps had tough, leathery hides and others fell apart like nothing. A few shredded to bits while they were still on the line. A couple of firm yanks to get them over the roof's edge and they were meaty jigsaw puzzles. Disappointing.

Eddie held the extremity up and looked into the bones, which were hollow. Wasn't there supposed to be marrow in there? Eddie's pop had been a marrow sucker, which was totally gross. As a kid he'd watch his pop dig this nasty brown paste out of the bones of whatever meat dish mama had made, and then suck the bone. When Eddie was hungry he'd feel the acid in his stomach eating away the lining. He remembered hearing something about how when you're starving you begin to digest yourself. That's what these humps must be doing, only there was nothing left to digest.

At this point maybe it was just a waiting game. The Comet knew facts they didn't.

"Smarter than the average bear," Eddie said, beaming.

"What? Who?" Dave asked, his eyes averted from Eddie's actions.

"*The Comet.* I'm conducting some scientific Frankenstein shit all up in this bitch. Who was onto Mona's drug therapy? The Comet. Who knew the humps were falling apart? The Comet." Sweat escaped the bandana and ran right into Eddie's eyes. "Motherfucker," he said with a wince. With one forearm he wiped away the offending liquid, with the other he pulverized the hump's head with a wrench. "That's a solid day's work. Those bitches," he said, gesturing vaguely, "they don't have any appreciation for the work I'm doing up here. I'm breaking scientific ground like that nigger who made peanut butter."

Dave shot a look over at Dabney.

"What?" Eddie beefed. "I'm paying him a compliment. I fuckin'

like peanut butter. Anyway, other than the spooky bitch, who else earns his keep around here? Who else is proactive? Remember that *proactive* and *paradigm* shit they used to throw at us at work?"

Dave nodded.

"Remember that time Staci Kulbertson—Tim McTaggert's assistant—remember when she got *loose* at that company party? That was *ill,* bro. She was shakin' that ass like she was trying to get rid of it. I'd of taken it off her hands, bro."

Dave stared at Eddie, not knowing what to say. Where was this coming from?

"Man, I'm sweatin' like a bitch," Eddie said, grinning. "It's man's work wasting these humps. I wish it would rain again so I could shower, know what I'm sayin'?"

Dave nodded.

"Cat got your tongue, Davis?"

"No, Eddie."

"So what's the what, bro? Why the long fuckin' face?"

"I can't do this any more, Eddie" Dave said, tears beginning to moisten his cheeks. "This isn't normal. This is some fucked-up *Abu Ghraib* shit you're doing up here."

"Technically that shit wasn't torture," Eddie sneered.

"Maybe. I can't take much more, anyway. This is some seriously repugnant shit. It's sickening. And if you weren't so gaga from those pills—"

Eddie rose from his task, bloodied wrench gripped white-knuckle tight in his fist, disgust burning in his wide-open eyes. Dave edged away. Eddie's eyes weren't right. They danced in their sockets, animated by lunacy and carnage.

"Why don't you blow me?" Eddie snarled.

"That's real mature."

"It wasn't a figure of speech. I mean it. *Blow* me."

"That gravy train's over, Eddie," Dave said, now stifling sobs.

"Maybe it took the apocalypse to realize what I am, but it's over. Seriously. We're finished. Done. You've got your porn. You've got your *hobby*. You've got your problems. But me? *Me* you don't get. Not any more," Dave said, voice cracking. Then he spun around and made a break for it, leaping the low hurdles as he'd done countless times before. Eddie pursued, but his athleticism fell more into brute categories than those utilizing speed and agility. Dave got to the stairwell housing and down two flights of steps before his wolfish buddy was even to the middle roof that separated them.

"Fuckin' little bitch cunt faggot!" Eddie screamed as the door slammed shut.

"Huh?" Dabney sputtered, coming to. "Whuzzat?"

"Go back to sleep, old man," Eddie muttered as he slunk into the building, closing the door behind him.

37

"Typical," Karl moaned, clicking the talk button. Nothing. The walkie-talkie was out of range.

The exterior of the bookstore was blackened, a fire having devastated the establishment. Though the doors were locked, the windows had burst and tiny fragments of safety glass littered the frontage.

"It's trashed," Mona said.

Duh, Karl thought. Instead he said, "Why didn't you tell me before we got here? You must've been this way before. Did this just happen?"

"I dunno."

"Well, we're here. Might as well go in. Maybe there's something salvageable."

"I dunno."

"Chicken?"

Karl felt penny ante for having utilized a grade school taunt, but it worked. Mona advanced toward the gaping maw of a former display window, gingerly poked at the jagged edge, flicking away some loose chips of glass, then stepped into the charred cavern of the store's interior. Karl followed straightaway, wondering if he could just walk along unescorted. He wished he could stop sweating. He felt parched.

"So?" Mona shrugged.

"So now I browse. I promised Abe a few books. Plus, I need something, too."

The air inside was heavy with the stench of charred matter; walls were festooned with peeling scablike wallpaper, scored and scorched. The display tables had either collapsed from the conflagration or stood like crude ziggurats, the books atop them stepped masses of blackened ruin. The floor was slathered in a thick charcoal paste of burnt paper and stagnant water, perhaps from the sprinkler system, and each step they took was accompanied by a voracious sucking sound. The downstairs was a washout, but maybe upstairs was better. Two escalators divided the main room, both leading up into pitch darkness.

"Did you bring a flashlight?" Karl peeped, feeling dumb for not having done so. Mona nodded, and while grateful, Karl hated her for being better prepared. She dipped into her Hello Kitty knapsack and fished out two headlamps, the first of which she handed to Karl. She then slipped the other over the crown of her head and flicked it on, resembling a miner sans helmet. The beam cut a ghostly white swath through the murk.

"Jeez, that's bright," Karl marveled.

"Xenon bulb," Mona answered, as if that meant anything to Karl.

"What's something like this cost?" Karl asked, flicking his lamp on as they made their way up the defunct escalator. He regretted the question immediately when Mona looked back, the light from her forehead blinding him, but not before he caught the *what-a-stupid-thing-to-say* expression on her face. When they reached the landing they stood side by side, doping out the lay of the land. The left side of the mezzanine was trashed, but the right didn't look too bad. The nice thing was that it was empty, save for the furnishings and merchandise.

"You have any water?" Karl asked, hoping his lack of preparedness was more forgivable than his previous query.

"Uh-huh." Mona handed him a bottle of water. After a few swigs Karl made to hand it back, but Mona waved it off with a curt, "Got my own." That she'd anticipated his absence of foresight made him flush anew.

The bad news was that the "Medicine and Science" section was toast. At least he wouldn't have to explain his need for a copy of the *Physician's Desk Reference to Prescription Drugs* or the like. With resignation, Karl lumbered over to "Literature" and selected a few slightly singed copies of the classics for which Abe had been pining. Mona stared off into space nearby, chewing something. Karl didn't care to ask. He'd asked enough dumb questions for one day.

"Okay, I guess that'll do me," he said, replacing the full knapsack over his tenderized back with great care. As they made for the escalators he spied on a remainder table a stack of fairly intact copies of the massive hardcover celebrating the fiftieth anniversary of *Playboy* magazine. He'd really wanted that book but at the time couldn't afford it. Pangs of chastity and guilt boomeranged around the inside of his noodle, laced with regrets over having divested himself of his porn and sexual trophies.

Except for Lourdes Ann Kananimanu Estores—Miss June 1982.

She'd be in there. Maybe even her whole set, to keep the lonely centerfold in his drawer company. This was almost worse than having to explain away a copy of the *PDR*. No guy wants to be caught procuring whacking material in the company of a female. Fresh sweat began to leak. *This is ridiculous*, Karl thought. *Why should I care what she thinks of me? It's only* Playboy, *for God's sake. It's not like it's* real *porn. It's pinups. Why am I justifying this to myself? This barely qualifies as a sin. It was a sin to have thrown away the bounty I had. This is just a little compensation for my loss.*

With that, Karl snatched a copy of the cumbersome volume off the table. If Mona cared a jot, it didn't register on her face. Karl's reddened nonetheless as he reconfigured the contents of his knapsack to accommodate the large tome. Almost to spite Mona, he snagged a second copy. A gift. With Ellen expecting, surely Alan would appreciate a treasury of the finest fillies ever to walk the earth. Karl wedged it in, then—with even greater tenderness—reaffixed the laden backpack and stepped into Mona's wake.

Whereupon the charred floor gave way.

And Mona's face, staring at the hole through which Karl had dropped, actually registered surprise.

Karl couldn't feel his legs. He couldn't feel anything, other than remorse, embarrassment, and the near certainty that these were likely his final thoughts. *Typical,* he thought again. He could move his eyes, and aided by the beam of his headlamp could make out that he was upside down. Or at least his head was. The rest of him he couldn't see and apparently moving his head wasn't an option. He opened his mouth and produced a pitiable mewl, drool running into his nostril. Above him he could hear the faint creaks of Mona tiptoeing to the escalator, weighing each step, making herself as buoyant as possible.

Once on more solid ground, she raced down the long flight of metal stairs and deposited herself directly in Karl's line of sight. Even upside down, Karl could see she was upset, and that pressed his panic button. A postfall dreaminess had temporarily quelled his mounting hysteria, but seeing Mona's semivegetative visage register distress was profound and terrifying. She didn't say anything, but as her eyes took in the damage, the unspoken appraisal was clearly bad news. The worst.

"Can you speak?"

Karl wasn't sure if she said it or he did. His thoughts were jumbled. His head was the only body part he could feel, and it felt like a water balloon full to bursting. His eyes felt like the pressure behind them would soon propel them across the room. He was panting.

"Can you speak?"

It was Mona. He wasn't saying anything. She touched his face, drying his drool and sweat with a tissue plucked from her silly cartoon knapsack. Upside down, the bag seemed so cute. Mona's face seemed childlike. She didn't seem cold and remote—just fragile and damaged. She's *fragile and damaged*. Karl smirked—or at least thought he did; it was hard to tell, what with being numb all over.

"Can you speak?"

Karl's vision was dimming or the battery on his headlamp was failing. Maybe a little of both. One from column A, one from column B. No soup with buffet. Karl smiled at Mona. Upside down, it's sometimes hard to read another person's expression. "I can't move you," Mona said, her voice thin.

Upside down or not, she was lovely. He pondered how he could have been so judgmental of this otherworldly waif. Mona was no demon. He was certain, finally.

"You're too . . ." She faltered, searching for the right way to say what there was no right way to say. She sighed and squinted, then looked away from his body, which was twisted at the midriff, his legs pointing east, his torso west. Karl thought about the incinerated medical section. That might have come in useful right about now. *Stay focused*, he thought. *Remain lucid. Remain.* "Broken." She'd finished her thought.

He tried to speak but each attempt choked him, his Adam's apple straining, pressing upwards, crushing the words. The Adam's apple. The *laryngeal prominence*. He remembered that from one of those atlases of the human body with the clear overlaid pages. Cross sections of the various systems. Filet of human. How many parts of his anatomy were broken, as Mona put it? All the important ones? Why was Mona immune? Karl clenched his jaw, then with great effort managed, "Wha moon?"

"Why moon?"

"Wha roo moon?" Mona shook her head, uncomprehending. "Wha roo moon?"

"Something about the moon?"

Pointless. "Ah gobba gub," Karl strained, sputtering up fluid, which she mopped away.

"Huh?"

"Imma bag. Ah gobba gub."

"Your bag?"

"Yuh."

Mona opened his bag and felt around. More surprise registered— it was a banner day. With great reluctance she produced a handgun from Karl's backpack.

"You had this the whole time?" Mona was becoming a regular chatterbox.

"Yuh." Big Manfred wasn't about to let his boy head off to New Sodom unarmed. Karl had left it tucked away in its case since he'd arrived in New York, but today seemed the correct occasion to bring it out. He hadn't anticipated being its target, though.

"And what am I . . ."

"Shoo muh."

"I don't . . ."

"Peez."

"Can you feel anything?"

"Nuh."

"I'll be back."

Karl watched her form as it trotted to the blown-out windows, stepped over the threshold, tossed the gun away, and disappeared from view.

38

Alan heard a sharp whistle from the street followed by the squawk of the walkie-talkie that announced Mona's return. He tore himself away from the touch-ups he'd been doing on an earlier canvas of Mona only to see the real McCoy outside, solo, not looking quite as detached as usual. Solo. Alan tore down the stairs and into 2B, so upset by her arriving stag that he didn't even alert the others. As he dropped the rope for her readmittance Mona was just climbing onto the roof of Dabney's van. Ellen stepped up and looked over his shoulder, giving Alan a start.

"Where's Karl?" she asked.

"Good question."

Mona's explanation, monosyllabic and fragmented, managed to paint an ugly portrait of Karl splayed on the carcass of a display table, his upper story turned this way, his lower that, and leaking fluids like a hooptie. Ellen fought the urge to ask if this accident happened before or after Mona had managed to score her "morning after" pills. Timing.

"We have to get him out of there," Alan said, affecting calm. "He can't just be left there to die, or worse, be eaten alive. Before he fell, that whole umbrella thing was working out pretty well for you?" Mona nodded. "Right." Alan exhaled heavily and pushed back on his chair, the front legs off the floor. He didn't want to go out there, but duty called. He walked over to the front window and looked at the horde. "Ugh," he said. "I don't know if I can do this."

"Do what?" Ellen said. "*Go out there*? No way. You're not even primed at all."

Alan whipped his head back at her, flashing the *say-no-more* look.

"Oh give me a break, Alan," Ellen said, not having it. "Karl's out there snapped like a rotten branch and you want to protect the pact of betrayal? Fuck that. You're not going out there. Let Eddie go. Or Dave. They were so fucking eager to invade Mona's stash, let 'em put it to the test." Ellen paused and looked over at Mona, a slightly patronizing tone creeping into her voice. "Mona, sweetie, those guys—Karl included—have been filching your pills to—"

"I know," Mona said.

"You know?"

"Yeah. I can count."

"You *knew* and you let it happen? But they invaded your space. They violated your trust. I didn't want to keep it secret, but frankly the gorillas in our midst spook me."

"I know."

"She knows." Ellen felt almost as annoyed at Mona for knowing and keeping mum as she felt about the conspirators' theft in the first place. "So why didn't you say something?"

"Like what?"

"Like, '*stop stealing my drugs*,' for starters. What is *wrong* with you? What are they even taking? These clowns have convinced themselves the pills are your secret weapon, you know, against the zombies. And you *knew*? I can't believe it."

"Hard not to."

Alan stepped away from the window, Karl's plight temporarily cast aside. He was probably dead, anyway. "Hard not to what? Notice the theft?"

"Side effects."

"*Ooooh*," the couple said in unison. Eddie and Dave's rooftop activities. Karl's schizo religiosity. Side effects. They seemed like natural progressions. Or regressions. But not unexpected. Still. Ellen and Alan felt pretty stupid.

"Severe contraindications," Mona said, carefully pronouncing the words with a hint of a smile.

"So why do *you* take them?"

"Gotta," Mona said, sounding not the least bit defensive.

"What are they?"

"Brain chemistry."

"I just can't believe you knew and let it happen," Ellen said, shaking her head.

"I can get more."

"So, if we're putting our cards on the table," Alan said, hesitating, "*are* they your secret? Could Karl have just gone out there on his own? Could Eddie?"

"Doubt it."

"Why? If they're taking what you're taking."

"Maybe after a few years."

"Why? Why years? Why maybe?"

"They weren't born addicted."

"*Born* addicted."

"Sort of."

It was like pulling teeth from a toothless baby, but slowly a picture emerged of Mona's mother. Not a harried housewife taking part in a clinical prescription-drug trial—just a plain old, garden-variety addict. Mona was chemically altered in the womb and chemically dependent out of it. Alan smiled as he mused, *four toes on each foot*. He remembered documentaries on PBS about thalidomide and crack babies. Four toes and a blunted persona were a lot better than flippers or no limbs at all. So *this* was the key to Mona's immunity? As birth defects went, this one was as Darwinian as they came. Defect or evolution? *Better living through chemistry*, as the maxim went.

And when the drugs ran out, whither Mona?

Did she even need them any more?

Did she ever?

As Karl lay on the table contemplating his imminent demise, he failed to notice he'd shifted his weight off his hips and crossed his legs. From his upside down perspective he stared vacantly across the verge, to the street choked with undead. He glanced up at the hole through which he'd fallen, hoping to catch a glimpse of Jesus or some angel beckoning him forth, home, but no such luck. He wiped his forehead and started counting off the moments left.

"What a moron!"

Karl sat upright, feeling pins and needles where before he felt nothing.

"What an idiot!"

He looked at his hands, flexing the fingers and rotating the wrists.

"What a stupid ass! Thank you God! Thank you Jesus! Thank . . . Oops."

Not being paralyzed equaled glee equaled lack of judgment

equaled shouting. He turned toward the street and saw zombies staring back. "Oh, balls," Karl peeped. The mob amassed by the window frames hadn't quite figured out how to vault the two-and-a-half-foot wall that separated them from their appetizing quarry, but it was only a matter of time. Even if they didn't have the smarts to lift one leg over, repeat, the shoving from the peanut gallery would deliver the first wave over the hump in a trice. Karl massaged his legs, trying to rid himself of the paraesthesia in his thighs and calves. They prickled under his palms, which did likewise. From no sensation to an overabundance in scant moments. Karl would feel blessed were he not on the verge of soiling himself in terror. He dropped to the floor, feeling wobbly, but *feeling*.

For a nanosecond he felt angry with Mona for leaving him, but she was no medico. She was just a girl. A spooky chick. But she'd gone for help. He couldn't wait for her to return. She'd be pleased that she'd been wrong.

The floor felt solid. Then again, it had felt solid upstairs, too. The zombies' ingress was looming. So much for Mona's miracle drug. Fucking Eddie. How could he have been stupid enough to believe Eddie was right about *anything*? He was about as immune to zombies as an ice cube was to a hot plate. He tried the walkie-talkie again, to let Mona know he was up. Nothing but static. Karl did a little spastic two-step, a sort of silent comedian windup, but he didn't know where to run. The divider between them and him was still doing the trick, but once they got in, it was going to be a big ol' feeding frenzy. The first few zombies plopped over the partition and fell in heaps on the sooty ground, attempting to right themselves as more dropped on top of them. And then more. Karl aimed the beam from his headlamp up the escalator. What would the odds be of falling through the floor twice? Tempt fate by fleeing upwards or fulfill the obvious by sticking around down below? Caught between Scylla and Charybdis. Maybe he could make it to the roof. Then what? Jump? One thing at a time. On spongy legs Karl made for the escalator and gripped the rubbery handrails in a half pull, half run to the landing.

"Idiot!" he barked at the top, realizing he still bore the heavy knapsack.

As it dropped to the roasted floor Karl fled to the second-floor restrooms in the back. Maybe, like in the movies, there would be some air duct he could climb into that would lead to safety. He slammed into the men's room—noting for a nanosecond how funny it was that even now he consciously chose it as opposed to the ladies' room—and scanned the dark chamber, aiming the beam this way and that. Drop ceiling, but no grating, no duct. *Typical, typical, typical. Don't have faith in Eddie and never believe what you see in the movies. Idiot!*

No lock on the entrance door, of course. He opened it and peeked out. The zombies still hadn't made the mezzanine. *There's got to be a way out of here. Think.* But without a floor plan it was just guesswork. The first wave of zombies had made it to the landing. Karl couldn't see them yet, but he heard them shuffling, moaning, exuding pure need. Did they scent him, like hounds at the hunt? Maybe his odor was masked by the stink of char. His only option was the stall with the bolt lock. If he perched on the toilet and was very quiet, maybe they wouldn't find him. *Cripes.* The moans were hungry. Purposeful. *Oh Jesus.* It sounded like there were a lot of them.

Tons.

Tons.

With a thunderous crash a large portion of the charred floor gave way.

It's raining zombies. Hallelujah.

————

"Hey, Eddie," Alan shouted across the roofs. "Can I tear you away from that for a minute?"

Eddie glared over at Zotz, then refocused on the struggler on his line. "The fuck do you want? Can'tcha see I'm busy?"

Alan approached with caution, staying one full rooftop away.

"Yeah, I can see that you're busy, but this is important."

"It'd better be," Eddie snapped, cutting the line as it dipped. Stripped to the waist and glistening, Eddie strutted over to Alan. "The Comet hates letting little fishies get away, *capisce*?"

"Yeah. Look, Karl's stranded at the Barnes and Noble on Eighty-sixth, between Second and Third. You wanna go, maybe help him out? According to Mona, he's kind of busted up."

"Figures," Eddie sneered. "Send a twerp out to do a man's work, this is what you get."

"You're all heart," Alan said, involuntarily flinching in preparation for retaliation.

"Don't I fuckin' know it," Eddie said, removing his bandana and mopping his forehead. "Karl wasn't eaten or some shit like that, right? How was he busted up?"

"He fell through a hole in the floor."

Eddie laughed. "Fuckin' *testa di merda*. So he wasn't chawed on? Just his own stupidity got his ass broke? Figures. So, was it Mona kept him safe, or the drugs?"

"I dunno. All I know is what she told me, and she's a woman of few words."

"I heard that. This is good. I wanna put my theory to the test, know what I'm saying? Fuck yeah. I'll play hero with Tuesday Addams."

"Tuesday Addams?"

"Yeah, the bitch from *The Munsters*. Christina Ricci played her in the movie, before her titties blew up."

"Oh, *that* Tuesday Addams," Alan said, thinking, *it's* Wednesday, *you fucking moron. From* The Addams Family? *Hello? "Mazel tov.* I'll go tell her."

Fuckin' Jew, Eddie thought as Alan headed back downstairs.

"*The Munsters*," Alan groused. "Christ, I hope they eat that asshole."

39

"You ready?" Alan asked the ever-more Rambo-like Eddie Tommasi.

"I was *born* ready," Eddie said, eliciting smirks from Alan and Ellen. *We know something you don't know* their internal singsong rejoinder.

Still shirtless, but now wearing urban camouflage pants and jump boots, Eddie dropped onto the roof of the DABNEY LOCKSMITH & ALARM van, his posture that of the stalwart hero of every action/adventure movie lensed from the eighties on up: knees bent, arms out and bent at the elbows, large hunting knife in hand. He even wore fingerless gloves.

Dave was too distraught to see Eddie off. Instead, feeling like an emotional coward, he sequestered himself in his apartment where he cried and began to drink heavily. Although Dabney had shared Dave's current mindset when Karl set out, he very much wanted to witness Eddie's departure. If the bastard returned a hero, so much the better, but if he were to get devoured right out of the gate, Dabney didn't want to miss a single ligament-shredding second of it.

"Good luck," he murmured, toasting with a tumbler of bourbon. He mostly meant it, if only to ensure Karl's safe return.

Once again, Mona created a clearing, then gestured for her companion to follow. With a defiant *just-try-to-eat-me* thud, Eddie dropped to the asphalt and glared roundly at the frothing skin-bags. *G'wan*, he motioned, chin jutting. *Wanna piece o' me? C'mon.* Nothing doing. Buoyed by their reluctance to encroach, Eddie stepped forward, following Mona's pert, round behind. How long would he follow? Could he take the lead? He felt pumped. Even more pumped than on the roof. This was a major rush. Major.

Flanked by resentful spectators, the duo soldiered west on the main drag, their progress greeted by hissing and keening. Mona didn't look back, just straight ahead toward their destination. Eddie didn't care. She was nothing to talk to. He'd rather divide his focus between the crowd and the cleft of Mona's ample, perfectly round butt. The seam of her pants emphasized the division between the cheeks. Oh yeah. Betwixt those orbs was pure, sweet honey. How many months had he wasted between Mallon's flat Irish loaves? Mallon. Dave. His pasty potato-eatin' keister, two slabs of lightly pimpled pancake, white as Wonder bread but not nearly as appetizing.

"So, you think Peewee is still alive?" Eddie said, breaking the silence.

"Huh?"

"Karl. You think he's still alive?"

"Dunno."

"He was gettin' kinda weird, there, clutchin' that Bible kinda tight. You'd of thunk maybe he had God on his side. But maybe not."

"Dunno."

Dunno. Pfff. Always a pleasure talking to Mona. "You ever see that *Ten Commandments* movie? '*Mmmyaaah*, where's yuh messiah, *now, see?*' That shit's funny, right? That's what I'm gonna say to Karl when we catch up with him. All *this . . .*" Eddie gestured at the zombies, not that Mona saw, and continued, "I used to go to church, right? I mean, c'mon. Italian from Bensonhurst? Of *course* I'm Catholic to the bone, because of my moms. But this shit?" Another nod to the undead. "Who could believe in God? So I wanna ask Karl, where's *his* messiah now?"

Nothing. No reply.

"What? You into God, too? Sorry to offend."

"I'm not."

"Not sorry or not offended?"

"I don't believe in God."

Even though they were in agreement, for some reason her response annoyed him. She probably never believed. It's one thing to lose faith; it's another never to have had it in the first place. That was kind of arrogant. Eddie didn't believe in God, but atheists were assholes. Just as smug as born-agains, but colder. Like they were better than everyone else. Better not to talk. Better to just scope that pear-shaped ass. With each footfall one buttock would jiggle, then the other. It was hypnotic. As he allowed himself to be transfixed by Mona's tush, Eddie started humming, then quietly singing, "*I see you baby, shakin' that ass, shakin' that ass. . . .*" Eddie used to dance like crazy to that song. He'd hit the clubs, make with the gyrations and then bring a hottie or two home for some pelvic mayhem. The more focused his reminiscences the louder his singing.

"*I see you baby, shakin' that ass, shakin' that ass. . . .*"

"What?" Mona stopped walking and turned to face Eddie.

Woolgathering over, Eddie stared back into Mona's fish eye.

"Nothin'," he said. "Just singin'. Remember that one?" Mona shook her head. "It's a good one. Groove Armada. That's whose song it was. Yeah. I used to get kinda nice to that shit."

Mona turned away and they resumed their trek. The second her back was turned Eddie stuck out his tongue, then embellished the gesture by flicking it back and forth between his splayed middle and index fingers. He'd never been big on cunnilingus, but he wouldn't mind noshing on the delicacies in Mona's undies. Not undies. *Panties.* Maybe she wore a thong. *Oh shit.* Or a G-string. *Daaaamn.* Eddie didn't care. It was all good. And that ass. That fuckin' ass. As they trudged on, slowly, deliberately, he felt the insistent surge of blood into his groin. *Yeah. Like Moses's fuckin' staff.*

"*I see you baby, shakin' that ass, shakin' that ass. . . .*"

Mona sucked her teeth in that gross disapproving way.

Don't fuckin' judge me, bitch, Eddie thought. *I'll fuckin' rape that ass.*

"I would, too," he said. "Just try me."

"Huh?"

"Nothing." He fingered his necklace of zombie ears, ruminating on punishing that ass. But first things first: Karl needed some rescuing—the little wuss—so The Comet was on it. The zombie ears felt like suede. Or did they? Maybe it was his fingertips. His mouth tasted like the inside of his socks, the texture of his inside cheeks rough like terry cloth. And dry. So dry. Unlike Karl, Eddie had packed a canteen, and drank from it. As the water sluiced down his throat he remembered something from junior high.

"The brain's fuckin' weird," Eddie said to the back of Mona's head. He trotted forward and stood by her side as he continued. "You know? Like, I was just thirsty, right? So I guzzle some *agua* and what comes back to me? This fuckin' book from when I was a kid, with this little baby Mexican or Indian. But I remembered his name: Coyotito. 'Cause as I was guzzling I remembered this line from the book, something about Coyotito's little tongue lapping thirstily or greedily or some such gay-ass shit. I can't remember what book, but I fuckin' hated that kid and was glad when he got capped. That book sucked, but I remember some of it. 'Cept its name."

"*The Pearl*."

"Yeah. *Fuck* yeah, *The Pearl*. Holy shit, I can't believe you knew that. That book *sucked*, am I right?"

"Mm-hmm."

Eddie grinned thinking about that little brat taking lead in the *cabeza*. The more he thought about it the more that flooded back to him. In zombie movies head shots took care of everything. He looked at the throng as it held itself back, fighting its hardwired desire to tear the two of them to shreds. Eddie finger-popped an imaginary gun at them, each a rotting Coyotito just begging for a bullet-salad sandwich.

"And you know what else? Wow, it's all coming back. That big Baby Huey retard and his little pal. Or was that a different book? Petting rabbits an' shit. Same guy, though, right? The writer?"

"Steinbeck."

"*Yeeeeaaah*. Him. Dude, he sucked."

"Mm-hmm."

"Steinbeck. Was he a fuckin' Jew? Is that Jewish?"

"Dunno."

"Sounds Jewy. No offense, I mean if you're a Jew. Jews are all right."

"I'm not."

"Not offended or not Jewish?"

"Neither."

"Cool."

Eddie's mouth still felt like felt, dry and scabrous. The water didn't help. He was sweating like a pig. Did pigs sweat? Isn't that why they rolled around in their own filth, because they couldn't sweat to cool off? And dogs. Dogs panted because they couldn't sweat. Did any animal sweat? Sweating was sweet. Eddie wanted something sweet. A bomb pop would be the bomb, but Mister

Softee had stopped making his rounds. Mister Softee, with his friendly waffle-cone face and whippy-do vanilla swirl bouffant.

"*Try as he might he can never get hard / his name is Mister Softeeee!*" Eddie sang to the tune of the old ice cream trucks' clarion. "*Deedle-ee-deedle-ee-dee-dee-dee-de-dum-de-dum-de-dum-dummm.* Remember that?"

Mona shrugged.

"Your loss, honey. Mister Softee was the shit." Eddie polished off the water. Didn't concern him. He'd pick up a bottle or five on the way home. "Yo, I've gotta take a leak. You mind?"

Mona shrugged, looking away. Eddie unzipped, aimed at the zombies nearby, and doused them. As they stood there and took it, Eddie grinned and shouted, "S'matta, your mamas never told you to come in from the rain?" No response. Not even wrath. Between the zombies and Mona . . . He shook off the last few droplets and tucked himself away.

"There's a whole lotta shit we could steal out here in the world. Fuck, it ain't even stealin' no more. It's just *taking*. Scavenging. It's practically our patriotic duty."

Mona shrugged.

The fuckin' cooze was really chafing Eddie's balls with her attitude. Was that all this was? Attitude? A woman shouldn't ever come off attitudinal to a man. Even Eddie's mom had agreed on that point, and when the occasion called for it, she didn't protest a slap across the chops from Pops. Was that what this Mona bitch was begging for? Women liked it rough from time to time. Just a fact of nature. Eddie let himself lag just a little behind her again. He preferred her ass to her face, anyway. Plus, quiet from the ass is a virtue, especially on a woman. No one loves a gassy broad.

The Barnes & Noble loomed on the left.

"About time," Eddie said. "We go in, find the little jerk. If he's crippled I guess I'll have to carry his worthless ass home. That'll be *great*."

A glint of light caught Eddie's eye as they stepped toward the broken window. As Mona stepped over the verge, Eddie stooped over to investigate the shiny object: a new-looking satin-finished stainless Smith & Wesson 9mm. He felt that surge of arousal again. With Mona's back still turned he surreptitiously slipped it into his pants pocket, fighting the urge to empty the clip into several nearby gristle puppets.

With Eddie away on his mercy mission—hard to fathom the word "mercy" in context with Eddie, but there it was—and Dave sequestered for the duration of his beau's absence, Dabney comfortably resumed his station on the roof. With their so-called "flynchin'" activities on hold the roof felt safe again, even with the dismembered corpses of their last haul still lying in a heap three buildings away. Though it was evident they were beyond locomotion, Dabney maintained his distance. *Why tempt fate?* he thought. Even deeply soused he possessed some sense. More than he could say for the happy fishermen. It was quiet the way Dabney liked it. Just the light flutter of a breeze riffling through a torn sheet hung nearby, and the occasional moan from the street below. Not even flies buzzing around.

Dabney lit a cigarette from the tip of the one he'd just finished and felt decadent. In his days as a breadwinner he savored cigarettes and put some time between them. Last he was paying for this particular vice, coffin nails were going for nearly ten bucks a pack over the counter. He'd started buying from the Native Americans via the Internet for roughly half that price, but still, even at five he didn't blow through them like they cost nothing. Now they did, so what the hell. Live a little, even if the living he was doing was sure to accelerate dying. He poured himself two fingers of bourbon and swished them around the glass to aerate the hooch. Fancy. Sophisticated. And again, it was "the good stuff." He felt very James Bond. Or Shaft. Somebody debonair. That's why he wasn't just swigging out of the bottle.

He drank the two fingers and then poured another two.

How long had it been since Karl and Mona had gone out? How long since Mona and Eddie? Eight or ten fingers later—at least two hands' worth—Dabney shakily put down the bottle and straddled the low dividing wall.

"Giddyup," he slurred, wiping some boozy spittle from his stubbly chin. He dug his heels into the puckered tar paper and slapped the curved top of the wall. "Git along little dogies." He thought of Woody Strode and began to tear up. Woody was long gone. Everything he cared about was.

Once upon a time his wife had called him "adorable."

Once upon a time small children had called him "Daddy."

Once upon a time he'd been his own boss.

Clumsily, Dabney hoisted his ass off the divider and loped putty limbed across the rooftop toward the pile of cadavers. He tripped over the second wall and fell, his numbed palms scraped raw on impact. He pulled himself off the ground and continued north, the mutilated corpses drawing him nearer. It was foolish, but pixilated from the booze, his curiosity won out. By the time he reached those dear, dead friends he was dog tired and dropped his leaden keister into Eddie's ersatz fighting chair. It felt good. Better than the wall.

"Damn," he said, assessing the ruined carrion. These were not the fearsome cannibals they'd been down below. This was a sad mess of humanity, retired. In death it was hard to tell male from female, black from white from Asian from whatever. One of the fractured heads looked maybe sort of Negroid. But the skin was so excavated and overcooked it stymied easy identification. It was obvious Eddie was a total racist, so did hauling in a brother bring him extra pleasure or were all zombies created equal? Dabney sniggered as he contemplated those two crazy white boys snaring undead brothers.

So stupid.

He reached out for the bottle but had left it three roofs behind.

So stupid.

He fell asleep, the hot sun baking his marinated brains.

40

"You know we're completely nuts for having let Eddie escort Mona."

"Mona escorted Eddie."

"Whatever, Alan," Ellen snapped. "Don't nitpick. Eddie's on a wild tear all hopped up on Mona's mystery meds. He was trouble before, now he's flat-out dangerous."

Alan couldn't argue that point. He looked out the window. It hadn't even been an hour since they'd left to rescue Karl, but anxiety was peaking. Ellen was right and Alan cursed himself for his cowardice.

"She might be immune to those things," Ellen said, "but she's not immune to a Neanderthal like Tommasi. We're idiots. And now there's nothing we can do about it."

She joined Alan at the window and put an arm around his waist, the first tender contact they'd shared in ages. That touch, that small embrace, rattled Alan even more than Ellen's words. Though he made no sound, she felt something in his manner change. She looked at his face and caressed his cheek. She tilted her head back and he responded with a kiss that lasted for long, restorative minutes. For all their sexual encounters, this was the first time either of them felt real love for the other. When their lips disengaged they both stared down at the crowd below.

Within the sepulchral gloom of the bookstore, Mona slipped on her headlamp and flicked on the beam. She didn't have another to offer Eddie, so she beckoned him to stay close, within the light, within the umbrella.

"If I find any Steinbecks I'm gonna piss on 'em," Eddie said.

"Mm-hmm."

Mona made a beeline for the table Karl had fallen onto, finding nothing but burnt books in his place and a couple of completely kaput zombies, their backs and limbs broken, the last vestiges of unlife gone.

"He was here," she said, pointing.

"He ain't here now."

Mona looked up, aiming the light at the hole Karl had made, which was now many times larger. That explained the wrecked carcasses and the additional timber. Eddie looked up at the opening.

"That's a big fuckin' hole."

"Mm-hmm."

I'll "Mm-hmm" you, you little bucket of fuck.

"So whatta you suggest?" Eddie said, swallowing his annoyance. "It looks like Karl might've got up on his own steam, no? Them zombies clean their plates, but not so's there's nothing left. There'd be blood or something. Bones. Something *moist*. Some residue." He wiped his sweaty brow. If this Barnes & Noble had a café he wanted to check the beverage case and see if there was any bottled water left. "Hey, does bottled water go bad?"

"Dunno."

One of these days, Mona . . . bang, zoom!

"Think he got up and went on home?"

"We'd have seen him."

She had a point. It seemed unlikely that Karl would have taken a divergent path from the one he and little miss talkative just took, especially if he was all busted up. A noise came from the upper landing and Eddie looked up into the gloom at the spot where the hole was. In the murk it looked like a busted mouth, the splintery floorboards like crooked teeth.

"You heard that." Lacking any clear inflection, it wasn't so much a question as a statement. Eddie made a face as he considered Mona's way of speaking might be contagious. He said it again, this time as an obvious query.

"Mm-hmm."

Suck it up, Eddie, he cautioned himself. *Just suck it up.*

Without waiting for Mona he dashed up the down escalator and ran onto the mezzanine, taking care to avoid the gaping hole. The gun felt good against his thigh, heavy and reassuring. Screw Mona and her "no guns" policy. Finders, keepers. As his eyes adjusted to the darkness he saw nothing unusual: some chairs, the upholstery cooked away, the springs and foundations jutting out, bookcases, books, books, and more books.

"Yo!" he shouted, caution to the wind. "Karl, you in here?"

A soft moan from the back of the landing.

Mona softly touched his bare shoulder and he felt a tingle from head to toe. It was the first time a woman had voluntarily made contact with him since everything went kablooey. What was harder, he wondered, his dick or the barrel of the gun, and which would do more damage if it went off? The light from Mona's headlamp bothered Eddie's dark-adjusted eyes and he fanned it away, frowning deeply as she stepped ahead of him. Those dead eyes of hers. Those pointy little titties. Her nipples weren't hard but they were visible. His dick was very hard. This was fucked up. He was sweating more than the temperature warranted and again his mouth felt horrible; he could taste his breath, which was bad. He wanted some mints. His eyes darted back and forth in their sockets and he could feel his skin, like it was swarming with ants.

The moan sounded again.

"Karl!"

"*Shhh,*" Mona cautioned.

"Why? What's th' fuckin' diff'? We're immune, so it's all good." He gave his erection a firm squeeze through the coarse fabric of his pants. He was freeballing, so no underwear cushioned his jewels and scepter. He moved his hand up and down once or twice. The gun felt good. His hand felt good. His whole body felt like a cell phone on vibrate.

"We're immune?" Mona repeated, eyeing him.

"*You're* immune," Eddie gabbled. "You are. *You.* We got the umbrella going on."

Mona squinted at him in a way that made her sexier and more slappable in equal measure. The moan came again. Mona gestured for Eddie to follow her. He was sick of this follow-the-leader arrangement. *He* was the *man. She* should be following *him.* She should be doing a lot she wasn't doing. Aping a yawn Eddie tossed down a couple of her purloined pharmaceuticals, smacking his lips in a gross, cartoonish manner.

"The Comet needs some water, soon."

"*Shhh.*"

"Cotton mouth."

"*Shhh.*"

They turned the corner and the headlamp illuminated a group of hunched over zombies polishing off Karl's remains, his torso opened like a savaged piñata. Vibrant graffito of arterial spray decorated the bathroom wall, fresh blood pooled in all directions, and Mona had a bona fide reaction: she threw up. Sensing her presence, the zombies recoiled and retreated deeper into the men's room, smearing blood and viscera. Mona wiped her mouth and was about to suggest escape when Eddie opened fire, blasting away huge chunks from the zombies' tatty frames. The grisly collage of hominid stroganoff— some old, some new, some juicy, some juiceless—was an Ed Gein wet dream.

Staid Mona, momentarily wigged out by the gore-and-gun combo platter, hugged the wall behind her and clamped her eyes shut, humming to internally mute the gunfire.

"Yeah!" Eddie bellowed. *"Suck on that, bitch! Suck it! Suuuuuck it!"*

He stood back and pumped off another shot. He didn't know how many were in the clip. He didn't care. He wasn't thinking. He was priapic in his bloodlust, engorged and fully engaged, reveling in the moment. The reports from the gun were deafening. He loved it. This was even better than flynchin'. He *had* to get more ammo. Didn't matter how long it took to find some, this bitch was not going to impede his need for munitions any longer.

"Fuck yeah, baby! Fuckety fuck fuck yeeeeaaaah!"

Unnoticed by her gun-crazed companion, Mona edged away and turned the corner, hunkered down amidst scattered remainders, and clamped her hands over her ears. Eddie pulled the trigger a tenth time, enjoyed the muzzle flash and resultant damage, and found his new toy spent. *Click, click, click.* He looked over in the direction Mona had been to find empty wall. The fuck? Confusion followed by the incomparable sensation of jagged teeth bearing down on bare shoulder meat. His.

Eddie's orbs met those of the zombie whose teeth were dug into his upper arm. Eddie's deep brown and lively, his attacker's gummous and gray. The communication between them crystalline: *I am going to eat you* versus *oh no you aren't.*

Eddie shrugged off his assailant and brought the Smith & Wesson down on the bridge of its former nose, now just crusty cavernous slits. Bone splintered and the thing let out a low groan, but didn't lose interest in its dinner. *So much for immunity.* He scanned frantically for Mona. Another zombie fell on Eddie, teeth bared, bony fingers digging into his waist, not quite breaking the skin, but near enough. Eddie batted away at both, shrieking, "*Mona, help!*" So much for pride.

Mona came around the corner, looking less apathetic than usual, but with her mojo intact. The zombies caught one whiff and, like skeeters from deet, fled. Eddie assayed the damage. A ring of oozing, bloody tooth holes limned his shoulder. His abdomen ached.

"You took your sweet fuckin' time," he growled.

He felt sickened by his girly plaint for assistance.

"I covered my ears," Mona said. "The gunshots."

And yet still he was hard.

"The gunshots," he echoed. "You and guns. What's up with that? You go out and see these fuckers every fuckin' day an' you go all weak at th' knees 'cause of some loud noise? The fuck is that shit?"

Mona shrugged, wiping her nose on the back of her hand. She was gross. Like a little kid, only a little kid with womanly hips and a nice round ass.

"So I don't know how this shit works," Eddie said, staring at his wound. "Do I become one of those things or what? In the movies they always become one of those things. But maybe movies are bullshit."

Mona shrugged.

"God, that pisses me off," Eddie spat. "That little shrug of yours. You're no mute. You can speak. So what's with the little tics and shit? You got something to say, *say it.*"

"I dunno what to say."

Eddie rubbed the damaged spot, smearing blood. He looked at

his palm. It scintillated. He was sweatier than before, his face hot. Burning. Feverish. His mouth felt drier than ever. Maybe it was just adrenaline—his nerves were pretty jangly—or maybe it was the infection.

"This could've been prevented," he said, more to himself than Mona. "But I blame *you*. *You* misled us. Those drugs ain't worth shit." He rubbed his crotch absently, inadvertently wiping blood all over it. The sweat stung his injury. "Fuckin' drugs." He shook his head, face pinched.

"We should go," said Mona, her voice fainter than usual.

"I blame *you*."

"Really, we should."

"Fuckin' drugs."

"You'll be okay."

"I need a pick-me-up."

Eddie yanked her into the bathroom and, amidst the bloody ruins that were Karl and his attackers, palmed Mona's head down toward the sink, ripped down her pants and underwear, then spat into the cleft between her buttocks. It was then that he noticed his dick had gone soft. "Are you fuckin' kidding me?" he shouted at his offending member. Mona pushed back against his arm and Eddie ground her face into the scuffed porcelain, gripping the back of her head with one hand and trying to massage vigor back into his flaccid appendage.

"You're not goin' anywhere," he snarled at her. "And you," he directed at his groin, "you better learn some fuckin' teamwork." He attempted to push his unit in, but it just bent away from its target, spongy as a Twinkie. "This is unreal. Un-*fuckin'*-real." It always bugged Eddie when guys in porn made do with soft-ons, trying to push rope uphill. He never understood how these ingrates couldn't get wood. Now he did and it made him angry.

He released Mona's head from the basin but as she raised it he

ROMAN

cautioned her with his fist. "Nowhere," he whispered, face creased with rage. "*Nowhere.*" Though her back was still to him their eyes locked in the mirror. That was another thing he didn't like about her; she barely ever blinked. She was like a cat. Or a baby. And Eddie had no fondness for either.

He tugged at the uncooperative flesh and with each stroke it seemed more willfully limp. He broke eye contact with Mona and let his focus drift down her face where it alighted on the corner of her mouth, which curled almost imperceptibly into a smirk of ridicule.

"You laughing at me?"

He pulled on his dick harder. That face of hers. That deadpan fucking face. It was almost worse when it showed a glimmer of personality. Personality that mocked him.

"You fuckin' laughing at me?"

Maintaining eye contact she slowly shook her head, pressing herself against the pedestal and washbasin. Her fingers snailed their way along her bare upper thigh toward her underpants until they made contact and lightly curled around the elastic waistband.

"Oh no you fuckin' don't."

Eddie lunged at her and she juked toward the door, unable to run with her pants half-mast. His arm shot out and grabbed her, and as he yanked the small girl toward him, he backhanded her across the face. She stumbled backward, raising her hands in self-defense. With zero mirth, Eddie laughed, the ugly sound echoing in the tile-covered tight quarters.

"That's hilarious. Your mojo don't work on *me*, toots."

Ten minutes later, wiping his hands off on his pants, he stepped off the escalator and made for the sunny street.

The street.

The crowded street.

The street chockablock with zombies.

Oops.

He turned to fetch Mona.

More teeth on flesh.

Not immune.

Not just his shoulder.

Should've worn a shirt.

Bony fingers gripping.

The drugs.

Not immune.

Flesh tearing. More blood. So much blood.

Why didn't she say something?

As he came apart Eddie whispered, *"Ellen would've struggled."*

41

"You can't be serious," Ellen sputtered, following Alan past the barricaded front entrance and down into the musty basement. She was still feeling like they'd had some kind of breakthrough by the window and now here was her inamorato psyching himself up for a quixotic, most likely suicidal undertaking.

"Of *course* I'm serious. You think I *want* to be doing this? I have to. If there's no more Mona there's no more us. She's our lifeline. So, I have to."

"Can't we give it a little more time?" Ellen pled. "It's only been—"

"A day. A whole day. It's like Ten Little Indians, Ellen. We're down two men and Mona. Plus, Abe, Ruth, and who knows what became of Gerri."

Alan placed the camping lamp on a stack of crates and looked around the room. In all the months since the pandemic began he'd been down here only once or twice. There were a couple of cage-style wire mesh lockers for tenants near the boiler, one rented by the Fogelhuts, the other unoccupied. Alan approached the Fogelhuts' locker and gave the combination lock a yank.

"Figures," he muttered. "I'd suggest looking for the combination in their apartment, but that could take forever."

"I'd suggest you abandon this, period."

He wanted to. He really did, but this was all there was to do. He wasn't about to go to Dave or Dabney. Both were borderline basket cases these days, Dave going through cold-turkey withdrawal from both Eddie and the drugs, and Dabney recapturing the days of wine and roses. No, no outsourcing this time. Time to man up, even if he wasn't necessarily the man he wanted to be.

Alan dug around Mr. Spiteri's tools, which lay in a haphazard array on and about a crude wooden worktable by the stairs. There were several toolboxes, which he rummaged through until he produced a thick, heavy-gauge pipe wrench. He took several vicious whacks at the lock, the only result being the bones in his fairly delicate hands being rattled.

"See? Futile," Ellen said, a manic smile splitting her face. "Okay, you gave it your best shot, so—"

"Not that easy," Alan said. He fetched a thick pair of rubberized work gloves off the bench and returned to the locker, smashing not the sturdy lock, but the lightly rusted fitting through which it was looped. That broke away from the locker after ten focused whacks and with a creak, the door swung open. Alan grinned, pleased with his mettle.

"This is the worst idea, ever," Ellen said, panic rising. "*Ever.*"

"You ever read Swift's 'A Modest Proposal'? If we don't get Mona back we're looking at the longest short winter of our lives and a very limited menu."

Ellen rubbed her still-flat belly, absorbing Alan's comment. "That's in very bad taste," she said.

"Maybe so, but this is all I can think of. It worked for Abe. How many times did Abe suggest one of us *young bucks*—" Alan made air-quotes "—do this? Dozens. 'If an old fart like me could do it, what's your excuse?' "

"It worked for Abe because he did it *before* things got so bad out there. There were countless morsels besides him for the ghouls to eat. They didn't *need* to pick a well-insulated geezer."

"I suppose." Alan knew she was right.

"You recall anyone else trying this ploy and succeeding?" she added.

Alan couldn't because no one had. Back in April that Venezuelan from 2B had been shamed enough by Abe to make an attempt and was devoured in plain sight within yards of the building. But he hadn't donned Abe's gear, assuming enough of his own would suffice. It hadn't. Alan pulled the boxes out and ripped them open. Inside were Abe's improvised armor: the *Baby Sof' Suit*® infant winter onesies and the XXXL pair of *Bender's Breathable Sub-zero Shield*® *Sooper-System*™ *Weather Bibs*. Leaving the bib down—as Abe has described in detail many times in the prior months—Alan began stuffing onesies down the pants, padding himself from the ankles up. When he'd reached maximum density he pulled up the bib, heaved on the matching camouflage parka, and stuffed in more onesies. With the hood of the giant parka cinched tight around a scarf and wearing a pair of snow goggles, Alan resembled a camouflaged Michelin Man.

"So," Ellen said, a hint of worried derision in her tone, "how are you going to get upstairs now, Stay Puft?"

Alan cursed under his breath. He should have suited up in the apartment. Already he was self-basting in perspiration. With his gloved hands he gripped the railings and hauled himself up the narrow flights of stairs to 2B. By the time he reached the window with the rappelling line he was soaked with sweat.

"I think we really had a moment, there," Ellen said.

"I know we did."

"I think we really have something, period," Ellen said.

"I think so, too."

"I shouldn't have ever busted your hump about Mona. I know you were loyal. I guess I just needed some drama to pass the time." Alan laughed, not with disdain. With affection.

"I deserve your mocking," Ellen said.

"Don't be such a drama queen," Alan said. Shifting the scarf and balaclava and goggles he smiled at Ellen and she could see the affection, which made this so much worse.

"Can't you wait another day? Maybe they're all okay."

"Ellen," Alan said.

"Just one more day. One."

He touched her face with the thick glove, then removed it to touch *her* skin to skin. Ellen kissed his hand, which was slick with sweat.

"This may be the last I get to taste you," she said, now tearing up.

"No, it won't. In the words of that great statesman, the Governator, '*Ah'll be bock*.'"

Ellen semi-smiled, her face scrunched up, trying to hold back the tsunami of emotion.

"Okay then," Alan said, refitting the scarf, balaclava and goggles, then gloves.

With the grace of Paul Prudhomme, he positioned himself on the windowsill—he was barely able to fit through the opening— swung his legs out, gripped the rope and lowered himself onto Dabney's van. The zombies noticed the motion but didn't seem overly riled. Ellen's heart jackhammered her innards. Her ribs ached. Her eyes felt in danger of escaping their sockets, so focused were they on Alan and the horde below. She couldn't watch. She couldn't *not* watch. With a faint wave, Alan sat on the van's roof, lowered himself to the ground and disappeared from view.

Several excruciating minutes passed and then Ellen spotted Alan's bloated form bobbing up York toward Eighty-sixth Street. Though the zombies didn't make way, they didn't attack, either. When she exhaled, it felt like the first time in her life.

It was more than weird to be out among the undead.

Though he couldn't be certain, Alan felt as though in spite of the temperature and copious garments, he'd stopped sweating altogether. It was unlikely, but he felt a permeating chill. To combat fear he kept his thoughts clinical. He'd absorb the detail he couldn't see from his window for future studies in watercolor and oils. Their skin was matte, but with oily patches, the pigment bleached or discolored. The white zombies were pasty yellow, the black ones gray and ashy. Even the matter underneath their shredded derma, the fasciae, peeled to reveal brown muscle tissue and dry bone. Everything looked desiccated. *What you guys need is a good moisturizer*, Alan thought. *Some Oil of Olay or some Neutrogena. Something with a high SPF rating. I mean, look at you guys.*

He focused on the path ahead. The bookstore was two and a half avenues west. Even at a snail's pace, without realizing it, he'd already made it to First Avenue uneaten. That was good. That was very good. Were he a man of faith he'd think it miraculous.

Since the zombies hadn't made an opening for him he was rubbing elbows with them—even the elbowless. Though there was generous padding between him and them, each contact mainlined straight to his nerve endings. *Focus*, he thought. *Focus*. He recalled self-help gurus like Tony Robbins, with their "can do" attitude and their mind-over-matter mantras. Alan had always taken those guys to be con men, though, so conjuring them didn't help. And really, didn't their shticks always boil down to creating wealth? *Not helping. Not fucking helping.*

Condensation accrued on his glasses and interior of the goggles, the top portion of his view becoming erased by fog. *Great. Soon I'll be blind. Mr. Magoo on a rescue mission. That's genius.* Something shoved Alan from behind, propelling him forward a few paces too quickly. His face contorted under its wrappings, his lips compressed between his jaws, half swallowed to stifle the shriek lodged in his throat, eyes shut, preparing for the worst. He collided with several zombies, but they responded only by growling and lightly shoving back. *Am I immune?* Alan wondered. *All this time, maybe I could've gone out. Maybe I don't even need all this gear. Yeah? Don't get cocky,* his brain chided. *Good idea, brain.*

The slog west was interminable. What struck Alan as odd was that down among them they didn't smell bad at all. Maybe it was all the wadding around his nose and mouth, but they seemed virtually odorless. Did the stink rise? Were they losing their scent or was he merely desensitized? They were ghastly to behold, though, and being in their midst hammered home the improbability of their existence. How did they persist? Some were barely more than skin tarpaulins encasing collapsed innards and strings of sinew. Movement would brush his undercarriage and he'd look down only to see some half-, third- or quarter-zombie inching along the pavement like a semipulverized worm. The most natural bit of genetic programming was the survival instinct, but this was so beyond that.

The crowd seemed to swell as Alan pushed onward, the space between him and them closing, closing, closing. The material of the hunting parka, the uncounted layers of baby snowsuits, all of it, felt inadequate. The undead's emaciated frames, their pointy shoulders—some ending there, armless—their angular hipbones, all of it scraped against the plasticized shell of his outerwear, injecting amplified echoes directly into his ear canals. His pulse thudded in his temples and he could hear his heart laboring. He fought the urge to scream. To laugh. To cough. He wanted to choke. Bile rose in his throat several times and he swallowed it back. *How can they not smell me? I must reek of fear. Any second I might shit myself. Does shit sound the dinner gong? Do they still crap?* Though many people did so at the moment of death, defecating seemed likely to be solely the province of the living. But these things ate living human flesh. After it went down did it just sit in their stomachs or did they expel it? Seeing them in the flesh, it was hard for Alan to imagine them digesting. They were so withered, almost mummified. Did the ones missing their gastrointestinal tract still feel the need to feed? Did they absorb nutrients? So many questions.

Alan felt like the zombie equivalent of Dian Fossey, a scientist studying a contrastive species . . . only dumber.

He looked down at the pavement to check for zombie scat.

Am I insane? I must be. What sane person would be out here in the first place? The padding he wore began to feel like a giant sweat diaper, because Alan felt it must be spraying off him. He stood motionless, pondering his predicament and his grip on it. His eyes focused not on what was happening beyond the the twin layer of fogged lenses, but retreated within, his focal depth confined to his own eyeballs. Things moved there: floaters. He watched the transparent blobs swim in the vitreous humor between the lens and retina.

A fly alit on his goggles, its unexpected appearance making Alan flinch. His spasm attracted some unwelcome glances and the odd hiss. *Oh shit. Don't let me get killed by a fucking fly.* The insect remained on the lens, grooming or whatever it was they did when they fussed with their forelegs. Seeing was growing more difficult as the condensation crept further down the lenses. Alan's eyes darted back and forth, making contact with dead eyes in the mob. It struck Alan that he'd portrayed something inaccurately in his zombie portraits: he'd made their eyes symmetrical, forward facing, their vision binocular. Up close he could see that in almost all of them—the ones who still *had* eyes—their peepers pointed in different directions, one aimed straight out, the other rolled to the side or pointed inward at the nose. Some rolled back into the socket. All glazed with death, grayed and fogged and yellowed. Flies and larvae crawled in and out of the zombies' various orifices, their hosts organic mobile homes.

Alan's head ached.

Maybe there was a word for what his stomach was experiencing, but probably not one in English. Maybe German. And thirty letters long.

Something gripped Alan's ankle and panic bypassed his leg and deposited itself directly in his colon. He looked down and through the miasma saw a legless zombie with only one arm hitching a ride, its clawlike, almost fleshless hand digging splintered nails into the thick fabric of Alan's hunting overalls. *Oh fuck. Oh Jesus.* Alan didn't dare attempt to shake it off for fear betraying his humanity—his edibility. *Maybe if I start moving again it'll go away.* Step after mired step the freeloader was dragged until Alan found himself stuck, unable to impel that leg forward. He looked down again, straining his eyes to fathom the hindrance. Another zombie had trodden on Alan's passenger. Alan tried to disengage his leg from the bony hand. Nothing doing. In death—or would that be *unlife*—was rigor mortis the status quo? Until his hitchhiker's hitchhiker stepped off, Alan was anchored to this spot.

Alan wished he wasn't an atheist.

The other zombie stumbled off the back of Alan's passenger and he moved forward, wondering how long the calf-gripping parasite would hold on.

Situated in a large apartment building, the Barnes & Noble was midway between Second and Third. It struck Alan, as he waded through the crowd, that zombies didn't really walk. The ones that could stood upright, sort of, but they just kind of shuffled around aimlessly, their movement dictated by the group rather than the individual. They were like plants impelled to move by a breeze. The only time he saw them propel themselves with purpose was when it was feeding time. *But I'm moving with purpose. Maybe because I'm moving so slowly.* It had to be scent. Were there scientists anywhere working on answers? Some underground bunker somewhere? If so, was that even a comforting thought?

As he cleared the southwest corner of Second Avenue, Alan felt his passenger again snag on something; this time the sensation was accompanied by the sound of fabric tearing. Alan looked down and saw the culprit, scarcely visible through the haze: not his zombie hanger-on, but a rusty detached bumper. His guest's detached hand, however, was still hooked onto Alan's pants leg, the rest of the zombie lost in the profusion of spindly legs. Then Alan noticed a splotch of something pale and pinkish. *Paint? Chalk?* His own pale skin exposed in the perforation. *Fuck.* The bumper had torn it, too. He transfixed on a small blossom of red dripping down his calf.

The adjacent zombies' postures stiffened a fraction, as did Alan's.

Inches away, one zombie canted its head at an angle that telegraphed its intent: to begin the beguine. *Fuck that.* Faster than Alan would have thought possible the zombie lunged and snapped at him, burying its teeth in the outer layer of the parka, near the shoulder. The padding was thinnest there and Alan felt a pinch. Not skin breaking, but piss inducing. Alan punched his attacker hard and it fell away, leaving behind a couple of teeth.

Nonetheless, the word was out: *dinner is served.*

Scent.

Violent motion.

The zombie's associates heaved toward Alan, their need raw, guileless. Alan swatted at them, punching and shouldering. They were weak but plentiful. He was practically blind, but his goal was within yards. More teeth and limbs bit, pawed, and clawed at Alan. He heard more material tearing. One arm penetrated the outer parka shell and he felt it groping at the bib of his overall. If he started hemorrhaging *Baby Sof' Suit®* infant winter onesies he'd soon graduate to plain old hemorrhaging. The image of his own entrails boiling out filled his forebrain. *No, no, no!* He twisted side to side and the perpetrator's arm snapped off with a sickening pop, still twitching within Alan's coat, its bony digits grazing his right nipple, which stiffened inappropriately. *Oh god, oh god, I'm being felt up by a severed arm!*

Alan drew his arms in, making himself as compact and missile-like as possible, then, bulky as he was, tore ass toward the bookstore. Skeletal hands snatched at him, as did stumps. His hood got yanked down, snapping his head back, material cinching around his throat. He gagged, but kept on. The goggles pulled sideways across his face exposing one eye, blocking the other, his glasses straining between them and his face. Terrified as he was, the sudden rush of air on his wet face felt refreshing. *Don't readjust. Keep moving. Keep moving, you fucker! Do it! No blitz, no fucking blitz! Please.* He rammed forward. Another pair of rotting arms attempted to detain him. *I'm not a huggy person! Get off of me!* He wrenched to one side and broke away. Half blind he saw his objective loom ahead. *Make way for Stay Puft!*

Even if Mona's not in there, even if they're all perished, I'll— Alan couldn't think of anything encouraging. *I'll be stranded here and die. So be it. Maybe I can find some duct tape and mend the rips, provided they don't eat me alive in there.* Alan vaulted over the broken window, palmed the scarf off his muzzle and with his teeth yanked off a glove. Dexterity restored, he readjusted his now defogged glasses, fished a flashlight out and clicked it on. The zombies were right on his ass, stumbling into the confines of the store, the first wave making a nice carpet for the others to tumble over. Alan whipped the light left and right, up and down.

"Mona!" he shouted. "Mona!"

No reply.

With no other options, he bounded up the escalator and cast the beam of light in every direction, deciding on heading deep into the store. He was a goner, but why make it easy for them? Stumbling over piles of burnt books and ruined standee displays he tripped and cracked his goggles on a bookshelf. He peeled off the other glove and removed them. "Okay," he wheezed, breathless. "Okay. Okay." He crawled behind the bookcase and, staying on his knees, ventured deeper into the store's second floor. He could hear the graceless footfalls and ravenous moans of his pursuers. When properly motivated, those fuckers could move.

Edging out of the aisle, his palm made contact with something moist and sticky. He aimed the beam of light at the floor, which was shellacked with a well-trodden layer of semifresh blood that led to the men's room door.

"Oh Jesus."

Rising, Alan looked over his shoulder and caught an eyeful of the mob. They'd reach him in moments. *Ellen was right. This was a stupid idea. Foolhardy. Dumb.* Not concerned with what killed cats, curiosity compelled Alan toward the john, his footsteps punctuated by the audible tackiness of the coagulating blood. Pushing open the door he saw Mona, curled in a fetal position under the sink, her pants pulled down and blood smeared across her thighs and bare ass.

"Mona! Oh my God, what happened? Mona! Mona!"

No response.

He knelt beside her and touched her throat. His pulse was racing so fast he couldn't tell if she had one. He pressed his face to hers. It was warm. He felt gentle breath escaping her pursed lips. A huge sigh of relief escaped his own. "Mona?" he repeated a few times. Nothing. But she was alive. The sound of the mob approaching cleared his head. He stooped over and lifted her up, swallowed some deep lungfuls of air and kicked open the door to be greeted by the faces of several dozen zombies, whose greed melted to disdain as they got dosed with Mona mojo.

And with unfettered joy, Alan laughed.

Back on Eighty-sixth, with the retreating crowd creating a concentrically widening berth, Alan gently lowered Mona to the ground and removed his now—*thank goodness*—superfluous damaged outerwear. As the giant parka disgorged a torrent of sopping-wet baby winter onesies the zombies hung back, snarling, some rocking their heads back and forth so violently they looked in danger of snapping off.

"Wouldn't *that* be a *tragedy*?" Alan scoffed.

Alan made his way homeward, Mona cradled in his arms. In the light of day he saw her face, neck, and shoulders were badly bruised, her cheek bore a long gash and both her lips were split. One eyelid looked puffy and discolored. After the zombies had withdrawn in the bookstore Alan noticed what was left of Karl on the bathroom floor—not even enough to reanimate. Alan didn't bother looking for Eddie, not even for the pleasure of gloating over his corpse. Mona's contusions and disheveled wardrobe told the story. Eddie could rot. Alan's injuries were limited to scrapes and bruises. He sighed with relief.

At the intersection of Second Avenue and Eighty-sixth Mona's eyes opened and, seeing Alan and the clear blue sky above, she actually smiled. It was the single most beautiful thing Alan had ever seen.

"Hey, you," he said, trying not to mist up.

"Hey," she replied. "You can put me down."

"You sure? I don't mind carrying you."

"Who are you, Jesus?"

Though uninflected, Alan gaped at her remark.

"Was that a *joke*?"

"Just put me down."

Stunned, Alan gently angled her till her feet touched the ground. She took a few moments to stretch and get her land legs, readjust her clothes, then fished a folded piece of paper out of her pocket and, with a light limp, started walking with purpose.

"What's that?" Alan asked, keeping pace.

"The list."

Alan was gobsmacked.

"Are you kidding?" he stammered. "After what you've been through? Jeez, Mona, take the day off."

"Can't."

At the nearest pharmacy Mona procured mifepristone for Ellen and herself. After she passed out she had no idea how far Eddie'd gone. Though her privates were the only part of her that didn't hurt, she wasn't taking chances. Ellen might change her mind, but Mona didn't want even the remotest possibility of bearing Eddie's offspring. Alan, noting Mona's pharmaceutical choice, kept mum. They stepped back into the daylight and walked home in silence.

With the sky whitening under the season's first snowfall, Alan turned away from the window. Though the horde was still plentiful, their numbers were perceptibly thinning. Ellen might be right after all. Maybe it was only a matter of time. Alan sat back down at the table and contemplated his next move. Buying hotels was always risky.

"Dude," Mona said, agitating the tiny top hat.

Alan looked at her. She, too, had changed a bit in the months since "The Karl and Eddie Incident." She'd likely never be Miss Personality, but she'd come a long way since her debut. She managed a smile now and again and her sentences, though short, were mostly actual sentences. Ellen absently rubbed her distended belly, feeling movement within—little Alan or Michael junior. Alan hoped the latter, but only time would tell. Maybe it would be a girl. With Dave gone from a grief-inspired suicide—his evicted husk still lingered outside staring up at the building—it was down to Alan, Dabney, and the two women. Cozy. Dabney, who'd abandoned his rooftop shack in favor of more conventional digs, had lightened up on the boozing, though he still enjoyed a dram on occasion. He entered the living room opening a jar of salsa. The chips were already on the table.

He took his seat and dipped a chip.